About the author

Martin Morton lives mostly in the Adriatic on a boat.

Visit Martin Morton at www.martinmorton.co.uk

BLUE ORCHID

Blue Orchid: The Claudia Series Book 8

Other titles in the series:
The Water's Edge
The Water's Depth
Careless Hours
The Mist in the Valleys
Catch Me
Lion and Giant
Trust Only

Martin Morton

BLUE ORCHID

Chimera

CHIMERA PAPERBACK

© Copyright 2021
Martin Morton

The right of Martin Morton to be identified as author of
this work has been asserted by him in accordance with the
Copyright, Designs and Patents Act 1988.

All Rights Reserved

No reproduction, copy or transmission of this publication
may be made without written permission.
No paragraph of this publication may be reproduced,
copied or transmitted save with the written permission of the publisher, or in accordance with the provisions
of the Copyright Act 1956 (as amended).

Any person who commits any unauthorised act in relation to
this publication may be liable to criminal
prosecution and civil claims for damages.

A CIP catalogue record for this title is
available from the British Library.

ISBN 978-1-90313-678-2

*Chimera is an imprint of
Pegasus Elliot MacKenzie Publishers Ltd.*
www.pegasuspublishers.com

First Published in 2021

**Chimera
Sheraton House Castle Park
Cambridge England**

Printed & Bound in Great Britain

Introduction

Hi, and welcome.

I very much hope you will enjoy the unfolding story.

Isobel, our principal narrator, having successfully established her Asian design business with Chou Daiyu and Harry Li in Hong Kong, is now spending more time in London, principally because of her relationship with Conrad Kitter, but also because she feels that Merle McKenzie, running her UK-based business, is losing focus.

Part of Isobel's London time has been spent renovating Conrad's large Kensington house, which is to become their home.

Merle remains married to Michael McKenzie, the disgraced financier, but is ever more distant from him. He is still employed by Gerry Calvert, managing his obscure finances, much of which have Russian tie-ins.

Peter Dickinson, who helped Isobel set up her Asian business, has been spending time in China helping Zhao Meitang take control of her late father's Senlin business empire.

Alphonse Newman, having acquired the Lang Hong Kong-based property business for the Dickinson Group, now has an able deputy for the region in Lang Wanglei, the owner's son. This frees Alphonse to travel more in spite of feeling settled in Hong Kong with Daiyu.

Claudia is being drawn more to the US, where Tania is very successful as group head, but is under increasing pressure from the pace of group expansion, the draw of the family logistics business as her father ages, and the failure to resolve the unacknowledged tensions in her love life.

Claudia and Peter have settled into a comfortable relationship, but still struggle to find enough time together, or real intimacy when they do.

Please enjoy,

Martin.

Blue Orchid
The Claudia Series book 8

1

I plan my time in London so that I get a few days on my own when Conrad's away. I do love being with him, but I get much less done.

I've been surprised by how sweet he's been about wanting time with me. OK, he was the one who made the original suggestion that we become a couple. I was shocked at the time. I'd tried to conceal that, but he'd guessed I might be. He'd expected it, is what he now tells me, but he's more comfortable with fibs than I am. Tact, is what he calls them. I may have told you about the withering scorn Daiyu reserves for that particular sin — that's how she sees it. 'It's very Christian,' she says. 'You just rename sins as virtues.'

I'm actually happier with her approach. So, when Conrad says sometimes, 'You seem to be avoiding me,' he gets a 'Too fucking right, I have a business to run.'

But then I spoil it by saying, 'I like your company too much when you're here. I get distracted.' That's not actually a fib, although he thinks it is.

I've found him surprisingly needy. I've just put it down to how it works with a top and a bottom. I'm used to bottoms trying to manipulate me. In real life, of course, away from playtimes, they can be very assertive and decisive, and I think that's how Conrad is mostly, although the process of agreeing the renovation with him caught him between two worlds. It's his house, he's had it for fifteen years, at least, but he will insist now that it's 'ours,' so I'm both part of 'the couple,' i.e., the client, and I'm the designer. So, he panders to me, his other half, on what 'we' want, but can be very firm (and usually wrong) when we're discussing project specifics.

I'm keeping my own place in Chelsea. Even if we were to marry, I'd still do that. I'd tell you if I understood the reasons why we don't. I'll let you form your own view.

I have a view on the Dickinsons. I call them that if I want to tease her, but their situation's different. He asks her, and has done several times. Not too many, that wouldn't be Peter's way, but she's always said no.

I think she's always reserved her position. I don't think it has anything to do with Alphonse anymore, he seems quite settled anyway, and Jack Stephens, I'm fairly sure, is distant past. I think it's just that Peter's marital history is one of repeated failure, although his earlier wives, according to Alphonse, were very different creatures from Claudia, at least the ones he knew were. Not that I can get a sensible objective view on Claudia from Alphonse.

Conrad's been married, but we never talk about that.

I've never had a proposal that I felt excited about accepting. To be quite clear, I've never got near accepting one, and yes, there have been some!

And I've certainly never felt like asking anyone.

But a 'couple,' with Conrad? I've let it become a maybe. A maybe? It's how we've been for two years. I shouldn't continue in a state of denial. We've been more monogamous than we intended to be, or expected to be, probably. Obviously, I can speak with authority only about myself. He can truly believe all that I've told him. That's not a courtesy I would extend to him. I suspect he's felt he's had to be 'tactful' sometimes.

I don't think he believes my nights with Alphonse are sexless, but they are — and rare, too.

Alphonse's nights with Mei are, however, still animated. It's once a month and he's her only male outlet. It doesn't make Daiyu happy, but she has the stoicism that's a necessary accompaniment to her tactless honesty.

My nights with Mei? They're as rare as my nights with Alphonse but, of course, Conrad, the natural voyeur, is keen to know more — yes, they are more active, but I don't like talking to him too much about them. He sometimes gets just a little too curious, and I've had to spank him a few times for that! Yes, it's one of the games we still play.

At least the man still has a healthy interest in the byways and detours of our friends' sex lives. I won't say I was worried when we made the 'couple' commitment, but I recognised it might have implications. For instance, I could have lived with the cellar staying as it was; after all, I have quite a few happy memories of times spent in there. It was where Will and I first...

I'll probably say more about Will later. We have contact, inevitably. Actually, inevitably is overstating it. Yes, Peter Dickinson is part-owner of Allen Chou Li in Hong Kong, so my accounts get processed in Will's division, but if anything arises, it's someone in the bowels of his team who gets in touch — and they always talk with Daiyu, not me, and certainly not to Harry — he's a salesman, for heaven's sake! But I've even had to meet that woman now. Yes, Martha. I suspect Will had been getting nudges from each of us, but it didn't happen, of course, until he decided it would benefit him — I don't mind a man being...I was going to say selfish, but that wouldn't be right — he is just very focused, and he'd probably worked out that it was something we all needed. Right again, Will!

I even thought of taking Conrad with me for dinner that night. He had what he called a 'subsequent engagement.' I think he'd have been intrigued enough. I did believe, however, that he was doing it for me; he knew there were demons I had to confront, and that was, truly, best done alone. I don't like crediting him with sensitivity, but here I think I must.

Anyway, you can see the problem: I was telling you about the project, specifically the cellar of Conrad's (OK, our!) house, and it was quite central to our old lifestyle, but I let thoughts of Will intrude and I'm off at a tangent.

Much like Merle still is.

I thought the old party cellar was going to be a big issue for Conrad, especially as I could hardly complain about the use it had for him. He himself was almost never active down there, he got only a voyeuristic buzz from all that went on during his party nights — and he made it available to his Arabs; well, for those with wilder tastes. His own active fun he enjoyed upstairs, increasingly exclusively with me, is what he'd said — then he came up with the creative proposal: 'We should convert the basement for Boris, then they can have their own separate entrance.'

Observe the syntax closely! Convert it for Boris; Boris is his Man Friday, the Serbian he rescued and found very useful for all manner of work, some of it unpleasant — and necessarily discreet (I'm probably saying illegal, but that's an area where I don't object to Conrad staying tactful). But 'they' have a separate entrance. So, Sandra was half included in the plan, but not named.

I could accuse Conrad of being ignoble here; he'd made use of Sandra's extreme enthusiasms on many occasions in the past with some of his kinkier associations. I knew he was uncomfortable, however, when she moved in with Boris about the time of the drama and I never knew whether that was because this was 'his' home, and he wouldn't tolerate more people than Boris in it — or whether he was just worried about Boris. He doesn't know how far Boris would go to defend him, but suspects, correctly I think, that there are no practical limits, and he feels a reciprocal duty of care. The drama? Well, nobody's been charged over anything to do with Ellen Calvert's death — just another unfortunate kinky rich lady caught up in an excessive orgy.

The basement conversion was a brilliant idea, though, and my little quid pro quo for him was changing the top floor (Boris's original flat, much smaller than the basement) to a couple of little play rooms for us — and selected guests was to be the idea, but that's been rare. Sometimes he likes an extra lady, but he always gets me to choose which one.

I'm going to trust that you'd already guessed that the 'basement for Boris and Sandra' was my idea. I'd just seeded it very carefully a couple of weeks before his dramatic and innovative solution was triumphantly presented.

Sandra, bless her, is making a real effort to be useful in my business, although she finds Merle, as ever, hard to deal with. But that's not my biggest Merle problem these days.

2

The commitment to spend more time with each other wasn't growing weaker, Claudia didn't think, but she and Peter were managing it ever less effectively, in spite of paying meticulous attention to travel schedules.

With him in Asia for two weeks, there was no need to rush back from New York for the middle weekend and it was a chance to catch up with Will and Martha. It was Will who'd planned the dinner — and then suggested that Alphonse should join them.

Claudia knew it was a US week for Alphonse, just as he would have known about her whereabouts, but they avoided being in each other's company now unless Peter was also there. Will must be aware of all the implications, she thought, and Will told Peter everything anyway. That wasn't wrong, she didn't think, it was just something to be aware of.

It had been, as usual, an intense week with Tania but at least they'd stayed in New York. The business heads had to travel to meet them, nowadays. Even Andy expected to have to make the trip down from Boston for their review of his business. Dinner with him was over before nine that evening and Claudia had headed for an early night. She found it easier not to enquire these days about Tania's lovelife but she was aware that Andy was still some strange part of it.

On the next night, the Thursday, when she had Tania to herself, they'd come close to a discussion on life outside work, but she'd let herself be content with Tania's 'I'm OK, really I am. I surprise myself, but I'm OK. You know I'll talk to you when things change, which is more than you'd do for me, I might add. Alphonse is joining you tomorrow night, isn't he?'

That Tania and Will were office neighbours, was excellent for the corporation's business intelligence but it also meant that the two were well-informed about the softer side of relationships and Will, for all his cool technocrat demeanour, was as interested as anyone in how things were between people.

"Not that I have to respond to that…"

"See! See! That's exactly my point." Tania was gleefully animated. "You're allowed to look knowingly and disapprovingly at Andy and me as you head off to your room, but I ask a perfectly innocent question about Alphonse…"

"Innocent? You said night. You should have said evening."

Tania smiled broadly at her. "I guessed you wouldn't fall for that. You haven't lost your edge, have you?"

They laughed. "I could be offended if you thought I was showing signs of that."

They weren't being serious now; they'd had that all week. It was finally kid sister time for Tania, when the façade of the dynamic chief executive could be displaced for an hour. Even Tania's times at home in Atlanta brought her less relief these days. Her father was slowing, she'd told Claudia, and there was tension about succession. It was a serious issue that would confront them soon, they'd agreed. Claudia had made a mental note that they should talk formally about it on her next visit. Tania still brought her intense focus to everything in the Dickinson Group and the businesses she managed, collectively, were already bigger than Giddings Logistics, and growing much faster. It would be a difficult choice. *But why see things as choices?* Claudia thought. What was best for Giddings and Dickinson was the issue. Tania would see it that way too, however big a part of either, or both, she was destined to be.

"You have seemed more contented lately, though." Tania had touched her hand gently then.

She was, Claudia thought, and she wasn't unhappy about saying so. It was only Tania and Isobel she could have these conversations with, but Isobel was far closer to Alphonse and that put that particular topic off limits. "It's been lovely, but Peter and I need more time together. It's been worse since Wengwei died; his commitment to the ghost, or his own promises, seems absolute."

"I know what you mean. I never have the impression, when he's talking to me about my group, that he's any less aware and attentive than he was before but he just seems, well, less relaxed, I suppose."

"That may be your damned business, madam. I find it hard to keep up with what you're doing and I don't have Funds or Properties to worry about."

"Does he worry about them? I guess I expect his scrutiny in my area, and yours especially — don't get me wrong, I need these conversations, and I've never felt blocked by either of you…"

"I should think not. Tell me when we've ever said no to you," Claudia said, but they were both smiling.

"You know what I mean. I just always imagine Alphonse and the boys have more autonomy than I do."

Claudia laughed. "You're lucky Will adores you."

Tania looked puzzled.

"It's true, they sort of do have more, but that's only part of it. I think Will trusts me to keep a close eye on you, and you're only fifty yards away from him in the office, not that you're here that much. But you chat with him quite often and you make him feel comfortable; he knows he gets the unvarnished truth from you. The others, well, they're harder for him and Peter to pin down and some of their operations are more shadowy. It's who they have to do business with. I think that's what Will wants to talk to me about tomorrow."

"Am I off the hook?"

"Heading home?"

"I don't think of it that way anymore, especially since Debs moved out and I have the place here to myself, but yes. Daddy's too proud to invite me for more than board meetings, but mother's relentless."

"Tell me about it."

Tania looked puzzled again.

"I get the odd charming phone call," Claudia continued, "and I do mean that, they are always charming — but there's always a gentle reminder that they don't see you enough."

"Or you. You're her hero. She wants me to be like you and find some elegant and charming billionaire to latch on to. I keep having to remind her that you haven't latched on to Peter, it's more the other way around. She just doesn't have that perspective. But you are saying you don't need me tomorrow, right?"

"It's Will's show. I won't say he was mysterious about it. I know I could ask, but I was here anyway."

"As, of course, was Alphonse." She was grinning.

"Stop it!"

"Same hotel, too." She was grinning more.

Claudia decided it was best to give up. Tania, nowadays, recognised too that the point had been reached.

The hotel would only be for tomorrow night. Alphonse would fly in tomorrow morning, arriving at lunchtime.

That would give her time on her own with Will.

***

Will had probably been in the office for an hour before she arrived. She'd managed to almost eliminate the 'who worked hardest' component that had been fixed in her since childhood. It was unhealthy, and it was impossible in this group of people. For some, like Peter and, in a different way, for Tony King, one third, now, of the GKS Fund group, what looked like affable socialising was merely a different way of working, and she'd learned that it was even more intense than what she thought of as work. Both were always immensely well-prepared for any conversation, no matter how spurious it seemed in any setting, Tony even managing to sustain his focus very late at night when apparently half-drunk. Peter assured her that Tony was never as drunk as the person he was talking to.

Claudia never stayed late enough to test that — and she and Tony were seldom in each other's company anyway away from the quarterly board meetings.

It was the board room that Claudia occupied, her back to Fifth Avenue. Will arrived looking relaxed for a man whose entrance was timed at exactly 9:00 am ET. They exchanged gentle smiles — hugs and kisses were for evenings — as he sat down opposite her across the large table — it would seat a dozen in spacious comfort, but she had seldom experienced it with more than the six of them and the occasional guest.

Shen Liuwei, Lou, the S of GKS Funds, was not a member of the Dickinson board, but had now been belatedly integrated into his sister's organisation in Shanghai, alongside his brother, Shen Liqiang, Lee, the older brother, and Peter himself. Claudia and Will were expected, at least as much by Meitang as by Peter, to keep abreast of Senlin operations and were formally invited to board meetings in Shanghai twice a year.

This morning would not be about Shanghai, Claudia didn't think.

"I've normally had a briefing paper from you by now. I feel ill-prepared and ignorant about this morning's purpose. Am I wrong to show so much trust?" Her smile wasn't concealing her unease, she didn't think. She'd had a strange reluctance to question Will on his agenda, and she had more than enough to catch up on if their meeting were to be short.

"I've normally had a memo from you asking for just that. Who's losing their touch?" It was said with a warm smile. "Seriously, when I looked at the diaries, it just seemed like a golden opportunity for a... d'you know, I don't really know what to call it." He looked, unusually, almost as if he was looking for help.

"Are you worried? The numbers say you shouldn't be."

He shook his head almost imperceptibly. "You know the scene where the sentry on the battlements says, 'it's too quiet out there'?"

Claudia almost guffawed. "I've had four days with Tania. That was anything but quiet, and Alphonse's fifth new resort opens next month. I'm surprised he's here." She narrowed her eyes as she looked at him.

She got a sly smile in return. "Fortuitous timing, I assure you. He had a week's business here in Florida. We're on his route to Shanghai."

Now he got a sly smile from her. "What are we here for, Will?"

"Do you mind if I say long-term planning?"

"Why would I mind?"

"Because it's principally about people, about us, and one of us in particular."

He obviously meant Peter. "Does he know we're having this conversation?"

"He knows I plan to talk to you. He knows I want the five-to-ten-year perspective on how we organise ourselves." He paused, looking into her eyes. "He said it would be best to start the conversation with you."

"Because I'd been trying to talk to him about the same thing?"

He nodded slowly. "Exactly."

"Well, I've got nowhere, but it's not something I can push."

"He knows that."

For all the easy informality of her relationship with Will, it was still surprising to be handed that insight. "What's he said to you?"

Will was hesitating. "Two facets to that. In the past, when he and I talked about the five-year shape of the business, he was quite happy talking about businesses and geographies, but he'd always pooh-poohed the idea of planning organisations. 'Good people is the answer, my boy, good people'."

She smiled at Will's mimicry of Peter's slightly plummier baritone. "Do you practice that accent?"

He snorted and smiled. "Well, I have to listen to 'my boy' often enough." Then he looked more serious. "It seems to me though, that two things are on the agenda now, that are different, although they arise from the same event." He paused. "I don't like seeming melodramatic…"

She smiled. "I can't actually imagine you being that. But I assume we're talking about Wengwei's death?"

"I knew that wouldn't surprise you. But he talks more to me about you three…"

"We three?"

"Yes, Abbi and Jonah and you."

"He talks to you about them?" She was more than surprised.

"You don't talk about them much."

"Not with him, no." She tried to think when Peter had even tried to broach the subject. The young one's futures were in their own hands, was her view, and that was certainly already Abbi's opinion, although Jonah was displaying the blithe indifference to the future that was common to all his eighteen-year-old friends. The major change over the last six years was in her own circumstances and her relative financial security.

"Look, it's certainly not my place to discuss that with you. I'm just saying that it's one of the major factors in him wanting to be sure this whole thing survives in a form he'd be proud of, and that it provides security to people that matter to him."

"He's sixty-two, and very fit."

"Wengwei was sixty-six." Will was trying to look sympathetic, but she understood why it was necessary to talk. "Do you know what happens if he falls out of the sky tomorrow?"

"No, I don't," she said quickly. It was the great unthinkable.

"He's never discussed it with you?"

"Of course not!"

"Claudia!" Will spoke unusually sharply. "It's a legitimate concern for all of the board but he removes it from the agenda every time I put it on there."

"Yet he's authorised you to talk to me about it?"

Now he smiled again. "I wouldn't want to mislead you. I've simply told him I planned to talk to you about it."

She raised an eyebrow at him, "And?"

"You know that funny harrumphing noise he makes when he has to accept something unpleasant?"

Now she giggled. "Probably even better than you do. But why isn't this on the board's agenda?"

"Because even you won't let him tell you that everything comes to you if he dies."

Will let the point linger, while Claudia had to let a huge hole open inside her — why not feel joy? was the first thought — but she couldn't feel anything; the hole was too large to even find a footing or an edge to clamber up.

Will's voice seemed to come from a long way off. "I'm guessing that it's something you've deliberately avoided thinking about."

It felt like coming round after an anaesthetic. She was wondering where she was.

"You're answering my question, I think." He was smiling. "I'm glad I've cleared the morning for this. I'm going to let the point sink in for ten minutes and then we're going to talk about the future of Dickinson Enterprises."

"Wait, I think I need to understand your point a little better. What do you mean, everything comes to me?"

"He hasn't talked to you about his will?"

"No. Well, he's told me he has one, but it wasn't something I wanted to even think about, let alone discuss."

"That's sweet but, forgive me, it's not very Claudia-like, is it?"

"No, I suppose it isn't. I'm the arch-planner, normally."

"I know. You're the only one I can get to take planning seriously. At least the others aren't as bad as Tony: 'How the fuck do I know, mate? It's in the future,' isn't the input I'm looking for and he's now acquired a Chinese partner who's just as cavalier. Lou seems very happy to adopt Tony's habits. I wish he'd spend more time with Henry." Will smiled and shrugged. "Let's walk to the coffee corner."

They would normally have coffee brought in, but she realised Will was giving her time to reflect. She knew where her reluctance arose from. Brodie Associates had started with Peter's help, but that was commercial support and Dickinson was part owner still of Brodie Gunter Jeavons. That business's value was her creation. The salary and bonuses that came from her group work were the appropriate rewards for her role. So, everything she had, unimaginable as it would have been to the Claudia of ten years ago, had been earned by herself. She knew that was one of the factors that made her discourage Peter from broaching the marriage subject. Now, even without that resolved, he was apparently planning a future where she would be responsible for his wealth and his legacy. She was feeling numb, having to force herself to acknowledge people in the office, and then standing quite still while Will poured two mugs of coffee. Black, no sugar, he didn't have to ask. She didn't know how long he'd been holding it in front of her.

He wasn't rushing the conversation, and with the odd 'good morning' coming in, it wouldn't have been appropriate. "Do you want more time to yourself?"

She shook herself into the present. "No. No, it's OK." She wanted to say that the world's axis had tilted for her slightly but that wasn't a remark she could afford to have overheard. That thought at least reassured her that her brain was beginning to function normally again. "Let's get back," she said. It obviously had to be confronted. She could worry later about why it was affecting her so strangely.

"So, what don't I know? Or, what else don't I know, should I say?" She was trying to be as cool as she could.

At least Will seemed to understand how great the impact on her had been.

He smiled. "I obviously don't know what you don't know but I did guess that would be a bombshell for you. I know there's a lot of unacknowledged pride for you in what you've created with your own business." He paused to let her nod slowly. Then he smiled more broadly. "I'm going to be cheeky now and tell you that you seriously underestimate how much you do for the total business." He paused again to let her shake her head, as if he knew she was going to. "We could debate that all morning and I still wouldn't convince you — and I do know our master tells you and you don't believe him either, but I think I can get you to accept that you have a role and it has a package of rewards that relates to what you do. You'd probably tell me it was excessive — and I could show you other businesses where the chief executives earn vastly more than you do for achieving much less, but that's not the big issue, is it?"

He was right, of course, and she nodded. "But why is it you and I who are having this conversation. What's this truly about?" She wanted to say that she and Peter had no secrets but even she had to admit that she was the one who steered away from some topics. Yes, they didn't talk about Alphonse, or about Jack, and she never wanted to talk to him about Abbi and Jonah, they should remain her worries, she thought, but neither caused her excessive concern — not yet anyway, she thought, but she knew that what Dickinson should become was a big topic. All she was getting from Will now was a look, and he'd become the master interrogator. He could wait. She would have to say what she was thinking. She smiled. "You know you're right as usual, you bastard." He chuckled. "Of course, it's partly about not wanting to think about him not being there, but yes, it's also my little Calvinist way of not wanting to take ownership of something I haven't earned. But I shouldn't see it that way, should I?"

He sighed, and looked relieved. "No, and I knew you'd get there quickly. Now, rather than let this be like pulling teeth — and, believe me, he's even harder than you are to engage on this topic — I'm going to make a few points and see if I can get you to my starting line, but I will say that I'm expressing my own views. If I can get you comfortable, we'll have a chance of getting him to commit."

She was surprised by his approach, but Will, of all people, could be believed.

"May I go on?"

She smiled at him. "Can I stop you?" She knew he knew her well enough to know she was now engaged.

"I think he wants three things: he wants to be certain that you, Abbi and Jonah are amply provided for, and he has a view of amply that vastly exceeds yours, but that's not the difficult issue." He was looking to her to confirm.

"He's been lovely with them, and they've stopped being quite so in awe of him, but I'm touched that you think he cares that much."

"Look, I'm avoiding getting into the issue of your matrimonial or family status. It's an issue between you but I don't think it affects this, so I'm doing no more than mentioning it in passing. OK?"

"OK, and point one accepted. Next?"

"He's proud of how Dickinson operates. He thinks it's still dynamically entrepreneurial and that's fundamentally about having the right people." He waited for her to nod. "I think he's trying to replicate that in Senlin but the jury's still out."

"I don't think Wengwei ceded autonomy to his business parts like Peter does, so the culture's not there yet, but I think your implicit question is whether the Dickinson way of business is critically dependent on the man himself."

They let a silence fall, each waiting for the other to say the next word. She found it impossible to think about — but she didn't have to in this moment. Will had called the meeting.

"Come on, my boy, I'm looking for your views." She couldn't mimic Peter's voice at all well, but it got Will laughing — and looking more relaxed.

"I think he's more fundamentally committed to that than he wants to be but I think, deep down, he wants some reassurance from us, that's you and me, that the spirit can live on. I believe it should and it could, but I also believe that won't be easy."

She nodded slowly, not convinced yet, but recognising it needed to be thought about. "And three?"

He took a deep breath. "I'm going to admit here that I'm anticipating his thoughts and, to a lesser extent, yours, but we clearly have the capacity to pull a very large amount of cash out of the business, so if he, or you, wanted to create a foundation that might be a more obviously beneficial legacy."

"He's talked about that?"

"He puzzles about what he's leaving, and he's started to speculate on what you might want to do — and what the next generation might want to give some shape to."

"The next generation?" He couldn't be thinking of Abbi and Jonah, surely. Will's fixed stare told her that he was. "Abbi and Jonah?"

Will exhaled. "I really am going to have to spell it out for you, aren't I? He thinks about them a lot more than you think he does and he's a little frustrated you won't engage on the topic."

"But they're mine," she hesitated. "Well, they're also Dave's and they haven't given up on each other entirely. They see their gran most days, too."

"But they're his only future. Well, he thinks a lot of Henry's two, but they're ten years younger. He's closer to yours than you think or allow, emotionally anyway. That's for you all to sort out, I'm just concerned that we identify whether Dickinson eats its own cash funding its expansion, or whether it changes itself into two halves, one half of which is a foundation."

"William, my boy," and she waited for the inevitable smile as she again aped Peter's style of address, "as usual, you've pulled a swirl of difficult issues into some clear and manageable topics. You amaze me."

He looked modest, almost shy. "All I'm doing at the moment is getting two of the people I admire most in the world to talk about a few unmentionables. I am banging your heads together, OK?"

She smiled back. "His too!"

"His too, of course, but I'm going to be blunt and tell you for the first time ever, Ms Brodie, that you're, in this instance, a bigger fucking problem than he is! That's why I'm starting with you."

She gasped theatrically, but smiled at him. "Guess we'd better get going, then."

3

Alphonse studied Claudia's sleeping face. On the few occasions they'd shared a bed, it was what he loved to do in the morning's first light — 'softly round your dreaming head' always came into his mind at those moments, as it had done with Éric, all those years ago.

This was different. It was soft three a.m. lamplight on her, and their entwining bodies had merely cuddled their way into sleep. She'd drifted off with a 'I still like knowing he cares, you know,' and he'd abandoned the attempt to keep his half-erection away from her, allowing the shaft to enjoy the still delightful mounds of her arse, barely concealed by the vestigial underwear. 'My bum likes your cock rubbing against me. The knickers just help me feel a little innocent.' She'd been asleep soon after, as had he.

But he'd woken at three. He wondered still what had unsettled him about the day. There were easier ways of travelling to Hong Kong than via New York, but Will had been insistent — and he'd never felt that Will wasted his time. He also understood that planning for a post-Peter world was essential and he'd admitted — to himself, as much as to Will — that he'd given it too little thought.

That he personally would remain comfortable had been obvious to him for years; Peter was generous with salaries and bonuses. The empire of property and resorts, however, belonged to Peter and, in part, to the Shen family.

Martha had laughed when Will gave a brief summary at dinner — nobody did summaries like Will — 'I know that's your viewpoint, husband dear, but you won't mind me reminding you that my bank has a few billion in there.'

'Three point seven, my darling, as if I could possibly forget.' No one caught Will out on numbers, even a banker. But it was a fairly relaxed evening. The couple were still splendid with each other — and with their favourite guests. Not that Alphonse had been with Martha often, but he'd been given enough information about her from Claudia and Peter. He knew that Martha had played a role in Claudia and Jack's problems. He could rightly have called it an innocent role — except that Martha's tastes were unusual and seldom described as innocent. That Will was equally enthusiastic, and therefore well-matched, was learning he'd gathered from Isobel.

But having to contemplate an organisation, even five years in the future, without Peter and he acting in tandem had left him…how was it? Uncomfortable at least.

Even Claudia, the principal beneficiary of the changes they were preparing to discuss with Peter, was unsettled. She'd looked that way when he'd arrived that afternoon and had grown more disconcerted as Will talked through the full implications. That was why Alphonse had asked her, at the end of the meeting as they walked to the hotel, 'Should we make time for ourselves after dinner?'

He knew she would want to talk; he'd guessed she might want to lie in his arms for the discussion — her eyes told him that.

These would be big changes for her, he thought, running his forefinger lightly across the perfect arc of her eyebrow, but it was probably important to plan for it, and to execute it, while Peter was still able and energetic, rather than to wait for the effects of age to impair his thinking. It was typically visionary of Peter, Alphonse had thought, but he was realising now, holding Claudia's body next to his, that this had been Will's agenda. Peter was engaging in it reluctantly, only as an unfortunate necessity.

Was Peter even engaging in it? He didn't let that doubt linger long. He knew Peter had begun to have thoughts about the more distant future: 'I know I'll live forever, Alphonse, but at some point, I need to look beyond that.' That was Peter's way: just a hint that they should look further — 'even beyond your beloved resorts.'

He remembered that discussion last year. 'My beloved fucking resorts, you mean.'

They'd laughed and Peter had said, in his fatherly way, 'I've never actually called them that, you know.'

'I know, but I'd be rich on the proceeds of how many times you've thought it.'

Peter had gone quiet then and said, 'I'm very proud of what you've done, you do realise, don't you?'

That was a memory now that caught him a little. The man's beloved was asleep in his arms. He thought Peter assumed they slept together occasionally, he still almost seemed to push them towards it, but he assumed that Claudia struggled as much as he did with that. He also assumed that her feelings for him hadn't changed. His hadn't for her.

She shifted slowly in her sleep at that moment. Her hand moved to his cock — more awake than it should have been. She didn't open her eyes but murmured, "Not rushing off in the morning, are you?"

He kissed her forehead. "Not rushing off, no."

4

Will tried to restrict weekend business conversations with Martha to Saturday breakfasts, which became accordingly large and lengthy. It worked for them both and they would take turns with each other to plan the rest of their weekends.

Breakfast this morning had been unusually long. "So Claudia is out there, beyond the dreams of avarice, but she has to focus on good works and train her children to be philanthropists. Obviously, I've no direct experience, but that generation has a commitment that's more philosophical than practical. Still, if anyone can do it, she can.

"And Alphonse is given five percent of the Dickinson property portfolio in as tax efficient a way as you can devise. You're not talking about Henry and Tony yet or, bless him, Shen Lou, because you're smart enough to see that's where the real difficulties lie. But what's in it for my beloved? I wanted to ask the question all evening, but I'm a good girl. I couldn't ask with them there. What's he promised you?"

"Nothing."

"Nothing? What's he hinted at? Or is this just you thinking beyond everyone else? I still can't get out of you what we're doing tonight. You're starting to intrigue me, dearest one, you're not normally so mysterious."

He grinned. He would have to tell her, and not spring it on her, but he liked the way she was becoming apprehensive. She was far too focused to be distracted, however. "Breakfast is business. What we do tonight is this afternoon's discussion."

"It needs a discussion?"

"Yes, but you have to wait."

"I don't like that, as you know. I'm not as patient as you are. but you're also being mysterious about your role in the business. What do you see yourself doing? You can usually talk him around to what you want." Peter had been unusually vague, so it had been right to say that he'd promised nothing. "Something's on your mind, isn't it? Never mind promises then, what's he even said?"

Will drew a deep breath. She poured more coffee for both of them. He'd been unable to digest Peter's last words before he left for China, having agreed to let Will start the discussions with everyone. "He just said, 'I won't agree to anything unless you'll agree to run it all'."

"Run what all? The whole thing?"

"He just said, 'Cheerio, see you in two weeks,' and put the phone down." He looked at her. She was expressionless. That was her thinking look. "Are you just thinking, or waiting for me to say something?"

"I can do both, sweet man. But I want you to speak before I offer a view. What do you think he wants?"

"I think he wants someone to develop it further, so it can continue to grow while it's funding his foundation. He's decently proud of what he's set up. He wants to prove, in the face of a lot of professional scepticism," he was grinning at her, and got a poked tongue in response, "that the Dickinson model works. So, I don't think he wants to exit any of the three areas, he sees that as being sensibly diversified. You know, what you always call a lack of focus." He smiled at her. This was a frequent tease between them, but this was not the morning to make the point that her bank thought it was competent to invest everywhere, regardless of business sector or geography.

She smiled slyly. "Well, you've just had my considered professional view, but you'll manage, if anyone can."

He was usually confident of how he could read Peter, but this was different. Peter had been passive in the process. Will was convinced it needed thinking about, but this provoked a memory of moving from sitting on Father's lap and steering the car on the old airfield, and then being told to do everything as soon as his feet could reach the pedals.

"You think he wants me to run everything?"

"It sounds to me like he wants you to show him that you can, and that you want to. Are you surprised?"

"Aren't you?"

"Not in the slightest. But it's an interesting mix of personalities."

They talked at length about each of the people most directly impacted. Martha even knew a lot about Shen Liuwei. 'No, I've met him once, maybe twice, I think, but I've read our bank briefings since a significant client of ours got even more diversified and involved itself with the Senlin business.' He'd been amused; their Chinese whispers and Chinese walls were genuinely Chinese, 'but I'm not breaching anything, just taking a closer interest than I might otherwise do. It was a clever move to put Lou in Peter's organisation for a while and get him away from his sister, but I'm not sure that Tony King is the best mentor.' They'd already spent some time discussing their concerns about Tony. 'And I wouldn't be quite so blasé about your old pal Henry Gideon' she'd said. 'If you're to become the sorcerer and not the apprentice, you'll find attitudes change.' He'd nodded then, and she'd seemed reassured by that. He knew she thought he saw too much good in people, but he was seldom, if ever, caught out, even when disappointed.

She poured the dregs of the coffee into her cup, sipped it, and grimaced. "Stone cold! Mr Coffee's telling us we've overrun our business time — and we haven't even talked about Tania."

"Or your bank. That's more interesting."

"Than your business, or Tania?"

"I meant the business, but I suppose she's approaching a crossroads. I really wouldn't want to lose her."

"You just may need to be creative."

She'd obviously been thinking about it. She'd stopped teasing him about Tania very early on, and the two women were close and spoke often. He knew Martha rated Tania very highly, but he was still nervous about the evening plan, which had arisen out of a contact of Tania's. "Well, we've overrun our business time, but we still need to talk about Tania."

She looked, as he'd hoped, puzzled, then intrigued. She waited, nevertheless, for him to say more. She was the only person he knew who played that better than he did. He guessed he'd learned it from her — or refined it, at least.

"It's a party we've been invited to, by a friend of Tania's. She thought we might be intrigued. It's on the East side." Now he really would try to sit her out.

She looked calmly back. "Would that be at Noah Reid's?"

Now he felt a trick had been played on him. His next question didn't come out as smoothly as usual. "You've been before?"

"To the Red Room, you think?" Now he was confronted by an image of a younger Martha being tied down and spanked. He managed those images as part of a fantasy past, but having to fit it into reality would be difficult. What had been planned as a guilty pleasure was now looking like an ugly confrontation with a shadowy history. But she was smiling. "Oh, the innocence of men. You think Tania and I never speak?" Now he got her mezzo laugh. "My lovely man, she's intrigued enough about us, especially since she'd guessed where my interests lie from the Jack Stephens association…" Her eyebrows rose to check he understood. He nodded and smiled — maybe this wouldn't be hard, she was just enjoying outsmarting him.

"She asked me if I knew about Noah Reid. Thought I might have been to parties in the old days, as she put it." She looked away and sniffed theatrically. "Unkind, I thought…" then she laughed again. "I hadn't. I hadn't even heard of them, the parties, I mean, but I'd heard of Noah Reid — twilight wealth and an art collection. Oh, and a gallery called Noah on the West side that a friend of Tania's runs for him. That's by the by, but I'm going to admit that I was intrigued by the Red Room." Her brow furrowed now. "You weren't expecting…"

"You to be active?" He was in control again. It was a fantasy that peppered their lovemaking, him talking about watching her being caned by strange men. "I wasn't ruling it out." In truth, he was, but he thought the theoretical threat would spice up the evening — and make their own activities back home later even more thrilling than usual. "But Tania will doubtless have told you that the majority of people are spectators, voyeurs — and some never make it past drinks in the reception hall."

She stood up and began to clear away. It was obviously a good plan, but he'd peered into a dark corner of the past — but who could be interesting without those, he thought.

5

You do develop feelings for your bottoms — beyond the mutual play contempt that you both, to some extent, get off on.

I know this is a difficult topic for some of you, but I won't be expanding on it here beyond saying that it's part of the thrill for each of you, but it doesn't spill out over the limits of playtime. I used to play with Michael and feel savage about him for the hour or two we were active but then, with him showered and dressed, we'd be laughing like the best of old friends before he left.

If they can't laugh about the process and, by implication, themselves — bottoms, I mean — I'm less keen on repeating playtimes.

But Michael's requests had become less frequent anyway, and our times together less satisfactory. You get used to bottoms being self-absorbed — selfish, even — but he had become increasingly morose and more demanding. I never like to feel I've reached a physical limit when I'm playing, I always liked to feel there was a further boundary I could have reached. If someone gasps 'harder' to me, I always want to feel that I could respond, if I wanted to, but then hold back, or even stop.

With Michael, however, I'd reached my own physical and emotional limitations — you just don't want to inflict that much pain — while he would become more demanding, and less happy afterwards.

I'm sure he's tried one or two other ladies while I've been away so much — he may even have tried a man, but I doubt that — but he did seem particularly desperate to see me again when he called. I tried to dissuade him: 'It's not really been fun for you, Michael and, to be honest, it's not really been fun for me either.'

This is a point, by the way, that bottoms don't readily grasp. They assume that a top is just a top and will get a thrill from any sadistic exertion. There may be a number like that, but they're neither giving the best experience for anyone, nor receiving it.

So, I end up just agreeing to meet him 'for a chat.' Of course, he hopes I'll relent; he's just being typically bottom-manipulative, hoping I'll find a reason to punish him. Which probably means there is good reason to punish him, and a good playtime would be therapy for him, but that's not the role I can play for him nowadays.

Just to be clear, it's bad etiquette to 'punish' anyone for an actual misdemeanour. They may bring a mountain of real guilt to your door, along with their great need for a cathartic resolution, but the punishment will be administered for a wholly different, and often quite trivial, purpose. He may have murdered his mother, but he'll want to be spanked for borrowing her underwear.

No, he hasn't murdered his mother, but Michael has done a few bad things and his need to talk seems quite desperate. I don't like agreeing, because it feels like it's an opportunity to spy on Merle and I feel I should gather my information there by open and legitimate means; that's just the sort of person I am.

That's not an idea that would occur to Michael or Merle; honesty is a neglected attribute hiding way back in the dark netherworld of a bottom's values. They're even dishonest with themselves.

He knows Merle works for my business, of course, it's how they met. I'm hiding nothing from him, and he's been a good client and a good bottom over the years, so we agree on supper at my place. Supper? Yes, it's not dinner, it's one course, and only wine with it, and we'll keep this business-like: just talk, and he probably knows I'll be having a long conversation with Merle at the weekend. That's seriously overdue.

When he arrives, I realise it's a long time since I've been with him.

I've seen him not wearing a suit before, although it's unusual, but here he is in a red sweater and pale chinos. He's not a bad-looking man: tall, dark — now grey-flecked — florid, but gaunt. He'd been growing a little puffy the last few times I'd seen him. I turn away quickly and hope my surprise hasn't registered. "Come on through," I say, as breezily as I can. It's not unusual not to hug on meeting. My first playtime step is usually to establish the discipline scenario, but this evening isn't play: it's a chat with an old friend that he'd asked for and, for that, my hello was too curt, improper, almost. So, he's uneasy when he sits down, fidgety. I have to make this easier for him.

(Why? Because we tops control everything, in our way; it's all for the bottom's benefit.)

"I'm just going to pour you a glass," I'm at the kitchen worktop now, *"and then I'm going to sit down with you. Tell me you're not hungry yet."*

"I'm not hungry at all, Sades."

This is a Michael I've not seen. The public figure is quite commanding, or was — I've not seen him in company for years, it occurs to me, but he had that confident, ebullient manner that a lot of those privileged, not-very-clever men seem to be able to present. I put the glass in front of him and kiss his forehead lightly before I sit in the chair next to his sofa. He dwarfs it. These little places are fine if you're petite yourself, but they're not meant for big men.

"I don't think you would have wanted to play anyway, would you?"

It takes him a long time to respond, but after a minute staring into the wineglass, he turns to me with a wan smile. *"No, I just wanted to see you."*

Now I move to the sofa and take his hand, *"You could have said, you silly man. I'd always be there."*

That's actually, as you have probably already appreciated, a silly thing to say, but at least it provokes an odd grin from him. *"And you've been how many weeks in England this past year?"*

"Enough to have been available." That's true, in a way. I've managed quite a lot of Conrad time and business time, but no social time. *"Anyway,"* I squeeze his hand, *"no recriminations."*

Now he leans back and, finally, looks a little relaxed. He still has my hand. *"Certainly no recriminations. But I know you're busy. It sounds like Asia's going well, and losing Gerry's business here was no more than a hiccup, was it?"*

You see why you have to be careful with bottoms. I don't know where he's coming from with that point, but it gives me an opening. I squeeze his hand again, but then let it go and sit back myself. The sofa is just big enough to give us a little space between us. "That was getting difficult anyway. I wanted to pull out. It didn't cause too much disruption."

"Well, you've acquired another wealthy patron, I hear."

This is snide. In different circumstances that would help me spank him hard. Well, cane, actually. But the top is always the master of emotions. I'm staying calm, but it's a fucking cheek, trying that dig about Conrad. The strength of my business has my work as its foundation, not my interesting client base. Look, I'm not doing parenthesis on interesting, you should know how it's meant by now. Gerry had his wife murdered, for heaven's sake, isn't that interesting enough for you?

I apologise. You can tell this is getting to me. I don't know why he's here, or why he's looking so troubled. Or why he's being an arse. Although he's always that, to an extent. Time to come to the point. I'm not a chatterer with Michael anyway. "Is it money, or Merle, Michael?"

He exhales audibly and sinks back now. The wan smile returns. "Always both." *He shakes his head — expecting me to guess which, I think.*

OK, so we'll start with the point of more direct interest to me. "I'm seeing Merle tomorrow, you know? I expect I'll get a lot of information then."

Now his head goes back. "Then you'll get more information than I do."

"She's worrying me lately. Do you still worry about her?"

"Of course I still worry about her. I still love her."

That came out a little querulous, and I think he knows it, but at least we're getting near the issue. "Yes, of course you do, poppet, but you know it's the word with the largest number of definitions, don't you?"

He looks taken by that thought. "Seriously?"

"Oh, Michael, don't be an ass! Well, it may be, I suppose. Look, I wouldn't describe your relationship with your wife as normal, but I admit love's in it somewhere."

He seems to be thinking about that, but when he comes out with, "My soon-to-be-ex, you mean?" *It's plain he wasn't thinking about love, his mind was elsewhere — and I'm completely stunned. I have to take a drink. So does he.*

So that's what this is about.

It's well over five years since they lived together. Well over. It was the Will thing that broke them up. That was love for a time, even for her — but that's another story.

Michael and Merle split up soon after she came back from Spain, which is where he'd sent her when the scandal blew up and he had to go and work for Gerry Calvert. They seemed to come to terms with their arrangement; it suited them both. She'd assumed they would divorce, but he didn't want to. She kept the house and a sizeable income, financed, indirectly, by Gerry, who's always been besotted by her; it's her beauty, of course, but also that particular kink of hers that Gerry is addicted to. He seems to keep it under control when he's with her, but she and I don't talk about it now.

I'm swigging wine again before I ask my next question. Well, it's not a question. "But I thought you'd found a happy arrangement."

"We had. That's what I thought, too. We'd even have dinner once a month or so."

"And that's stopped?"

"Yes. She'd rather have dinner with Gerry now, apparently."

Now he drinks. I'm thinking. This isn't simple. It certainly isn't advisable, and I don't know the right way into the topic. Just dive in, Isobel. "Do they still play?"

He is taking his time responding, even finishing the glass, meaning I can distract myself fetching the bottle. I need to stop myself opening another line of enquiry. He needs to speak. Gerry is a very dangerous man.

"I assume they do. I never ask, and I'm never asked to join them these days," *he shrugs — he would always be there for her party piece — and says,* "thank you," *when I put down his refilled glass. Yes, I've topped mine up, too. This is a bit of a shock: Merle and Gerry.*

"Are you worried?"

"Worried?" *He looks almost indignant.* "I'm just unhappy. Why would I be worried?"

I can't believe this. "Ellen's dead. She was..." *I can't finish that sentence. There are some funny thoughts going through my head.*

"Unlucky in an orgy," *he says quickly.* "It was widely covered. Come on, you knew her. She was into all sorts.

She used to get those black men to visit her. She liked it rough."

This is incredible. I have no idea how wilfully blind he's being. I have to stay calm. "You're right, I'd seen her into all sorts, although she'd stopped inviting me a while before." *Now's the time to be careful.* "But I'd never seen her into asphyxiation."

"Oh, it looks like she'd just picked the wrong guy."

I cannot believe this. Michael had arranged a payment for Zivko, Gerry's Serbian heavy, just before the death. Is he really trying to make me believe the two events weren't connected? He was the one who alerted us at the time. He thought we might be the targets. Has he actually now disconnected that in his mind? Wow, maybe he has. Maybe that's how he can keep going with Gerry. He just plays with numbers and bank accounts for him and makes no connections with the associated activities. Maybe it's the only way to survive.

So, he's not worrying about Merle. He's just missing her. My God!

***

Merle and I meet in the office. In theory we're having dinner later. I can't get that far ahead of myself. There's too much to talk about before then, and I'll be surprised if we will still want each other's company afterwards. There are project delays and cost overruns to discuss — control of those used to be strengths of hers — and the contract pipeline is smaller than I'm comfortable with. I'm used to turning commissions away. We're doing that a lot in Hong

Kong — *'Maybe I take holiday,' says Harry. 'Then I'll stop spanking you' is my response — nothing gets Daiyu's eyebrows rising like that does, even though I've not played with Harry since we took him on.*

It's troubling that Merle doesn't seem bothered enough by these problems. I'm already thinking that I need somebody else in London. She doesn't help by blaming Sandra's admin for some of the problems. No dear, I think, you're the boss, you make sure things work. That thought stays unexpressed — because I think I've already decided that I have to act, and that Merle is irredeemable — unless I can find the cause and it can be corrected. We nevertheless create a programme to resolve the issues and I try to remain constructive, and only mildly critical. It's something we tops do a lot; we expect to control, ergo, we take the blame. But I remain objective enough to realise that I have to do something about Merle, even before she tells me that she does have one big commission in the pipeline — and it's for Gerry.

This is a bigger shock than Michael's appearance yesterday evening, but this afternoon I'm ready. I'm on tiptoes in this conversation, I'm the boxer alert for the next punch; well, I suppose boxers are alert for the next twitch. Just as well, I wouldn't have seen this one coming. At least I'm braced and it doesn't knock me out.

She has that look of aggressive defiance that tells me she knows she's done wrong. Well, she knows she's shocked me. I don't suppose she knows the full background. How could she? I think. Michael is in denial. I've said nothing about it, obviously. And Gerry's going to tell her? Of course not, he still lusts after her: takes her to dinner; offers her commissions with the company he broke off with.

"Is that a private commission, or is it Isobel Allen?"

"It's Isobel Allen, of course." *Oh, Merle, how sweetly indignant you look.* "Did you want me to manage it privately? I thought you'd be pleased. You've just been hammering me for not having a pipeline."

"I wasn't hammering you."

"Saying it's twenty-five percent of where it should be felt like a hammering." *Oh, bottoms, how they do love playing victim!*

"He cancelled everything two years ago. I'm surprised you've got him back. But you're closer now, socially, aren't you?"

"A little." *Now she's defensive. Well, indignant and hostile and defensive.*

It means we're getting to the core of the issue, the reason Michael came to see me. "Does this have anything to do with you finally wanting a divorce?"

"I've always wanted a divorce."

"So, what's changed? Anything to do with Gerry?"

Now she's agitated, and taking a long time to answer. "Only indirectly," *she says eventually.* "He's always been behind our financial arrangement. You knew that, didn't you?"

I nod. I did, vaguely. "So, you're cutting out the middleman?"

Now I get another indignant flounce. "You can be vile, Sadie, you really can." *I've now earned the sealed lip petulance that works with weaker men. I'm not rushing this. It's too important, and, yes, I do mean for her. I can do without Gerry Calvert as a fucking client but, current appearances to the contrary, Merle's a friend, and now I'm really worried. I will need to find out more.*

"He's not happy about it, is he?"

"Who?" *I don't know where she'd switched to in that magpie mind of hers.* "Oh, Michael, no he's not. Is that why he came to see you?" *I nod.* "Oh, the poor lamb," *she says derisively.*

Now who's being vile? I think, but, of course, I say nothing. Just the cold stare will do. She knows she's gone too far.

"No, he's not happy. But we weren't going anywhere."

"You've never been going anywhere. It hadn't bothered you before. Something's changed."

Now she's wondering what to say, knowing that she's never in her life kept a secret from me. Not once I'd decided I needed to know something, and that's how I feel about this now. For her sake.

"Gerry does like us to be together more. He's been lonely since Ellen died."

I think you know how absurd that is, but I'm staying calm and not reacting. "What does he say about her?"

"Well, he thought she was fun, and they didn't, as he puts it, get in each other's way. Well, you know that as well as anyone. You did their two apartments." *I'm just nodding. I need to get her talking. She will.*

"And the police got nowhere with it?"

"That was pretty unpleasant for poor Gerry, of course." *(Oh, please!)* "They were round him a lot and had a great time asking him about all her activities, and wanted to know about him and his, of course."

"Of course," I say. "Did your name come up?" She looks puzzled and shakes her head. She can be astonishingly naïve. "No, I suppose not," I say, "it was quite a wide circle anyway."

"Ellen had become quite independent by then. It's more likely they'd have come round to Conrad, after all, she'd been there not long before. Didn't he get interrogated?"

"Had she been there, really?" I don't like playing these games — of course she'd been there, I'd seen her, it was the last big party — but I have to know how much trouble Merle's in.

"Well, Gerry said she had been. He thought the police should have followed that up."

Oh, don't worry, I hated him anyway, even without that little snippet!

"But I think they went off looking for those West Indians she used to pay to visit her. You knew about that, didn't you?" I nod. It was that sad. "They got nowhere with that and then gave up. I think it was a tough time for Gerry and he wanted a little company now and again. Proper company. I think I've helped him."

"So, who suggested you should change your arrangement with Michael?"

"I did!" I make that the third indignant flounce, and it has at least as small a justification as the others. There's no point in pursuing this, she doesn't have enough self-awareness.

I think we'll have to go to dinner.
I'm realising that I do care.
But I also have a business to run.

6

Alphonse was glad he'd booked to go straight to Shanghai. He felt he could deal more easily with facing Peter than facing Daiyu — who'd made no fuss about him not calling in to Hong Kong on his way.

She made a fuss about very little, but she would have been interested in what he discussed with Claudia, and even more in the circumstances of the discussion.

Less with what he'd discussed with Will, however big that looked.

If he talked to Peter about Claudia, Peter would just have smiled, but he wasn't planning to do that. These meetings would be about the property and resort businesses they shared with Senlin after Peter had spent his quarterly three days with Meitang — and Lee and Lou.

Peter's Asian fortnights would have stressed out a much younger man. He spent a few days each time with apparently random itineraries, but always pursuing ideas that had interested him, meeting people who intrigued him, usually from universities or cultural areas, and often from government, making sure he was fully in the time zone before he met with Meitang and her people. Thinking now about Mei, Alphonse smiled as the plane descended. She never became less demanding, or less challenging. But she was doing, people grudgingly admitted, surprisingly well.

It hadn't surprised him. He'd seen, right in their first meeting in Hong Kong over four years before, that she was remarkably astute, well-informed and inventive. She'd come up with the idea to wed the businesses and still meet Peter's principles of control. The doubts would have been about her manner, always brusque, seldom kind, but, having taken over on her father's death, she'd very quickly made people respectful — although he thought fearful might be a better word. It hadn't taken many senior dismissals to establish the right atmosphere.

She'd even made her official father retire. Alphonse had thought that unnecessary and wondered if she was merely being vindictive; there had been some reported slight about her appointment that had been credible enough to make her react. He'd spoken to her about it on one of their four-weekly Fridays.

She'd teased him. "Alphonse, he's my father, imagine the indignity for him of working for his daughter! No, an honourable retirement was the best thing."

"Did you at least tell him yourself?"

"And hugged him warmly, like he used to do for me?"

He thought back to the first Wengwei conversation about Mei's future role: 'Is she ruthless?' he'd asked. There never had been any real doubt.

So Baba, Wengwei, was dead; Fuquin, father, was banished; and Mei was alone — except she had Peter, part-time, and Alphonse, by command, every fourth Friday.

He hadn't expected that arrangement to last. Neither had Daiyu, but he was aware of the tripartite planning that went into his travel schedule to ensure that it did: Hayley, in London, held the master copy, Daiyu's office in Hong

Kong organised all the Asian legs, and Shanghai was kept informed of everything. He'd had a phone call from Hayley a year ago when travel looked a little unresolved — a big US deal clashing with a resort opening — and Hayley had said, 'I've had a message from Shanghai that you're expected in Hong Kong on the Friday.' It was the first time he'd been aware that he was being tracked by Mei's PA, obviously acting under strict instructions.

'Have they contacted you before?'

'Every month, Alphonse, you're a popular man.' He could feel her smiling down the phone line. She'd probably guessed at his strange relationship with Mei.

Daiyu remained philosophical about his commitment to that. Mei was not unambiguously gay, but had clearer preferences than Alphonse. But Daiyu would have worried about his night with Claudia.

More than Peter had done, it seemed. The solicitous greeting was as warm as ever in the Senlin boardroom. "You're looking surprisingly fresh for the schedule you've had. Are you up for a heavy day?"

"If you can declare a long lunchtime, and let me get an hour in my hotel room."

Peter looked hard at him. "Whatever it takes to help you get through. Then I'll have no conscience about insisting on dinner."

"Are we going to talk about Will's ideas?"

Peter smiled slyly. "Some of them are mine. None of them are Claudia's though. Was she very disturbed?"

"Peter!" he said sharply. Too sharply, he realised. "I'm sure you've spoken to her since then."

"And I'm sure you've spoken to her as well. She may be less guarded with you."

But there was no malice or suspicion in the observation. He could respond freely. "Of course I have, we spent time on it afterwards and she was getting used to the ideas by then. I think she'll see big positives in the end, but she'd been very uncomfortable when Will first told her. How was she when you spoke?"

He smiled. "Very cautious, but I'm hopeful."

"Well, I do want to talk about it. All of it. There's a lot to think about — and I'm the smallest part of it all."

Peter shook his head, but he was smiling. "You're by no means the smallest part," Peter reached out, stroked his arm, and looked directly into his eyes, "but I am hoping you'll be the simplest."

Now they were nodding to each other, smiling no longer. There would be some difficulties in these developments: inevitable contests of money and egos and power, a volatile, toxic and unstable mix. Alphonse knew he would somehow be drawn in; even his own reactions had not been simple — or pure.

It was time to focus on the day, the Asian property and resort review. Alphonse had briefing papers from Lang Wanglei, who was now working well as Asian property head, and from Raymond — always on top of resorts — and felt well prepared. Mei's entourage preceded her. They'd hovered outside while Peter and Alphonse had been talking, until Peter finally waved them in. Alphonse always strove to emulate Peter's cheery welcomes, but the master set unattainable standards, remembering every name with apparent ease, in spite of the apparent uniforms of charcoal suits and slim, dark ties. Even Mei's senior PA, who at least was a woman, wore a similar suit, but was spared the tie.

The Senlin head of resorts and the head of properties had each brought assistants, one also female, a woman who'd impressed him before, but the twenty-four-seat table was still only lightly populated, even with the closely clustered trio from Senlin finance. Alphonse, as usual, placed himself on the long side with his back to the window. He found city skylines, especially Shanghai's, too entrancing, and his mind would easily wander if a meeting became boring.

Mei strode in — yes, strode was right, he thought, even for a petite woman — nodded to Peter and Alphonse, it was not quite a bow, not really, then gestured to her team to be seated. It was a well-choreographed entrance. It was hard not to smile, but it was also important not to smile and he managed to sustain the necessary deference to support Mei's position, not that he had ever detected the merest hint that it was, in any way, threatened.

He wouldn't have had both groups together all day. Wanglei, on property, and Raymond, for resorts, met only at dinners he organised. There was little crossover, as he saw it, between their areas, but Mei was building a different sort of organisation, and he respected that. It made the long lunchtime gap look odd, but Peter's 'Alphonse has some European business that needs attention, may we reconvene at two thirty?' was met with boundless politeness — a hint, perhaps, that the Chinese team found the sessions a strain, and a recognition, of course, that the voice of God had spoken.

Mei smiled at him for the first time that morning.

He was glad of the hour's sleep. Resorts, in the morning, had been straightforward: the programme was staying on schedule and the occupancy levels were above planned projections. He'd focused his remarks on the future phases, just occasionally disturbed by the thought that Peter's perspective must now be changing, but it remained, for all the Chinese team, an exciting prospect, particularly when he spoke of his ideas on the Australian expansion. Mei had been, by her standards, restrained and polite, even through her own team's presentations, but she allowed herself a 'The Australia plan needs a lot more discussion, I think,' when he completed his review of that, staring deadpan at him while he had to stifle the smile — and certainly avoid any mention of it having been discussed on their previous Friday evening together while her naked body had been recovering between bouts of passion.

The afternoon was much harder. Zhao Fuquin's first replacement had already been fired and it wasn't obvious that her second choice would last much longer. The man's slides were in English but he found it necessary to speak Chinese. Often, Mei would not wait for the translator before asking a question. *Well*, thought Alphonse, *if I knew the language better, I might think she wasn't even waiting for the man's sentences to end.* It took Peter's skills to rescue the poor man, picking out some of the better points from the slides and asking the man to expand on them. The role was slowly taken over by his female assistant, whose English was fluent, but who nevertheless had to endure an onslaught from Mei, culminating in 'Why are we expanding slower than the Hong Kong unit?'

They were poorly led, and had poor people, were the real answers, Alphonse knew, but he had to offer a 'We're lucky to have a Hong Kong bias on our side. Wanglei would tell you, it's his home. We find the northern markets harder. This city is particularly difficult.'

Mei's next remarks were addressed to her team, not to Alphonse and Peter. In the silence that fell on the crestfallen duo, the translator, sat between Peter and Alphonse, murmured, "Zhao Meitang says the English gentleman is very diplomatic."

"Will you have time tomorrow morning to go through the team's plans in more detail, Mr Newman?" Mei asked. "I think they need more of your help."

Alphonse smiled at the team, trying to revive them. "I have the whole day for property tomorrow if they have time for me." The woman nodded eagerly, the man followed, less enthusiastically, when she explained to him.

"You are too busy, Wang Zhang? Perhaps Yang Li should host him?"

"Host?" stuttered the man, floundering, but trying to recover. "No, make time, yes, yes."

Alphonse had observed Wang Zhang's transformation in the year he had known him from an overconfident bully to a feeble ditherer. He was, nonetheless, very knowledgeable about property, but a poor judge of when to move, and, it seemed, a poor negotiator. He'd quickly lost Mei's confidence. 'He doesn't stand up to me' and the even more derisory, 'And he won't learn fucking English!'

He wondered if she was slowly realising that Yang Li would be a good option. They could discuss that in the time before dinner. He assumed Mei wouldn't intrude on the meal. Peter had a way of making those arrangements very clear.

It was his first topic when they settled in Mei's office after the meeting, "Are you hoping for third time lucky on Zhao Fuquin's replacement, my dear?"

She sat, looking almost demure, behind the vast desk. Peter had insisted she occupy it, even for his visits. 'You must know that the façade is potentially brittle. It will do her no harm if the Great White Giant shows a little obeisance.' Alphonse had smiled at that, he'd not really detected brittle — the nearest had been when he'd had to tell her about her real father's cancer, at the same time as telling her who her true father was; anyone would have seemed brittle then, and she'd recovered remarkably quickly from that. She was good at managing herself. She used him to help that, he knew, just as she used Isobel. Not that he felt exploited, merely a little more controlled than was comfortable. Isobel accepted no such disciplines, but it was a useful way for him of circumscribing his relationship with Daiyu.

Maybe it was useful for Daiyu, too. But that was probably an evasion, he admitted to himself. She seemed quite comfortable with just him.

"That's no reason to keep the wrong man in place." She sighed. "I just don't have your skill at reading people, Peter."

"Nonsense!" he said. Although it wasn't, thought Alphonse. "Your resort people are excellent."

"They're Alphonse's!" was delivered with a pout.

"Is this going to be Madam Chairman's little girl minute?" Peter asked with his best cajoling smile.

"Fuck you!" she said, laughing. "Yes, it is."

"Well, you may have the answer, if you can get over your aversion to having females in senior positions."

She gasped, "Fuck you again!" But after another laugh, she said, "Do you think I do?"

"Well, considering how many brilliant women you work with: Daiyu, Isobel, Claudia, it's striking that your own organisation has none. I know your PA's very good, especially at controlling Alphonse," and Peter's grin there was a little knowing, "but running departments in your organisation, I don't see any. Let Alphonse get to know Yang Li better tomorrow. Do you think she has potential?" Peter obviously did.

Mei seemed to think for a moment. "Hmm, maybe," she said. "You think?"

"I just think Alphonse should get to know her for you. I was impressed."

Mei reached for her phone. "I'll tell the PA to disinvite Wang Zhang for tomorrow."

"No!" cried Peter and Alphonse simultaneously.

She smiled, and spoke Chinese into the phone. "It's done. You boys are too Christian," and Peter and Alphonse were left to look helplessly at each other, and chuckle.

***

It was easier to talk in Peter's suite. He'd assured Alphonse that room service was 'adequate,' then followed with, 'It's actually very good, but I know what your standards are,' and he poured two waters for them,

"You have to earn your g and t. What did you think of Friday? Surprised?"

"I can say surprised, yes, but you're not trapping me like that. What am I supposed to be surprised by?"

"You could say you're surprised and delighted at the prospect of acquiring five percent of the property portfolio."

Alphonse smiled. "I was very surprised, and I am both delighted and very grateful, but the joy for me is working on it with you."

"Even resorts?"

"Especially resorts. Your opposition made it feel more my own."

"Just challenging."

Alphonse guffawed. "It felt like violent opposition."

"There, how proud do you feel now?" He smiled.

Alphonse felt he was right to remain sceptical, Peter was still uncomfortable, to a degree, about the Australian adventure. "How serious are you about pulling back?"

It took Peter a long time to say, "Very. Will's found the right time to ask the question. How much has he spoken about his role?"

"Not at all. What's it going to be? I'll admit I've been puzzling, waiting for this conversation."

"I thought he might be reluctant to say too much. He'll have wanted Martha time to think it through. I've asked him to think about running everything."

"Replacing you?" Alphonse had prepared himself for this, but needed to hear Peter confirm it.

Peter just smiled. "You think I'm irreplaceable?" Alphonse shook his head. The man was not without vanity; it was part of his charm. "I've asked him to think about how it should be run. I think there's a strength in keeping the three areas. It's the best way of feeding cash into the foundation, and that's what I'd like Claudia to develop and own and bring her kids into. But the businesses were, well, are, a reflection of me and that would need to change. If you look at the industry group now, it's different, he and Tania changed it; rightly, I'm forced to admit. You've changed properties, getting us into resorts and tied in with these Chinese monsters." He laughed loudly, "She's worse than her father, I'm delighted to say, a terrifying woman." The laugh subsided to a smile. "But you must see something else in her. Anyway, you've changed the whole area, but I think you'll agree Will's given you a lot of support."

Now it was Alphonse's turn to smile. "Yes, especially on resorts."

"Oh, give over, man, I've recanted, but I might not have done without Will, you're right. Anyway, I'm hoping you'll feel comfortable if you're working with him."

"No question."

"He will be the boss, though. He'll have final say. It's the only way I've seen any organisation function successfully." Peter was offering that tentatively.

Alphonse could now give another slow smile. "I've always found him more reasonable than you are."

Peter guffawed. "I deserved that, I suppose. Anyway, good, that's why I'm hoping you'll be the simplest area." He paused and leaned back in the armchair. "I expect there are a number of complexities for you. I'm just hoping you'll be able to work through them with Will."

"Will you be around?"

It took Peter a while to respond. "I will be, of course, but I'll be focused on getting Claudia set up. I'd rather you lot told me what you wanted from me — and it would be better if it came through Will." He gave Alphonse a long look. "We'll just be friends, after this, you and I." Then, having stayed serious for an unusually long time, he suddenly guffawed again. "Well, I hope we will be."

That made Alphonse smile, and the message was clear. He should work through things for himself, with Will.

"I will look forward to that very much. You know that, don't you?" Peter was planning to give him five percent of something huge, but he knew that this bond was somehow more important. The drop in the corner of Peter's right eye told him he was right. It was time to move on.

"The group, do we keep Tania?"

"We, kemo sabe? That's for Will, maybe with some help from Martha and you. She has her family pulling her back to Atlanta. I think she'd be bored; and I think she knows she'd be bored, but I expect Martha will be coming up with some interesting constructions — any of which will make money for the bank." He laughed again.

"Have we left the hardest till last?"

"Yes, that's a g and t and dinner conversation. Shall we order?"

***

They'd drunk only one bottle of wine. The conversation had been too serious. With less money in the funds, Peter, and thus Will, would have less influence over them but Peter had concerns about 'even Henry.' Peter loved the family, 'although the kids terrify me, but Rachel's wonderful,' but he saw Henry potentially having problems taking direction from Will — 'Henry's brilliant, but Will just has a better business brain, he sees the whole picture' — and he could see a lack of discipline creeping into fund activities; 'the other two are cowboys' and he'd talked about a number of situations that had been expensive, or embarrassing, or both, 'and the fact that Tony and Shen Lou seem to get on with each other worries me even more'. He'd wanted to know how Alphonse saw them all — and become slightly agitated by Alphonse's diplomatic reserve. 'If you're telling me you're not worried, I shall start to doubt your sensitivity', and Alphonse had confided his 'impressions,' as he called them.

He declined the cognac, 'long day tomorrow,' and Peter had looked relieved. He got the blue-eyed stare and the hand on the bicep farewell. "It's been a very good day, thank you so much."

"I need to be thanking you."

"For five percent? I get ninety-five and you've built it all!" They laughed and parted, smiling.

They hadn't spoken about Claudia.

Or about Mei, who was naked in his bed when he got to his suite.

It wasn't a welcome sight, and he couldn't hide the chink in his carapace of charm. "To what do I owe this unscheduled pleasure?"

"It's three weeks for me. You want I should look elsewhere for my pleasures?"

She threw the duvet back. It was a pleasing little body, but he felt little desire, and certainly had no wish to be commanded.

She wasn't insensitive. "These are hard times, my beautiful man, for you too, I know. I thought a few hours in each other's arms would be good for us both."

That, at least, he could understand, and their tightly defined arrangement had caused him few issues — and stopped Daiyu getting too possessive, or too ambitious about how fixed their relationship was to become. He sat on the bed and pulled the duvet up to cover her. "I'll have a quick shower, I think, then I'll wrap your sweet body in my arms." He kissed her lips gently.

She was unresponsive. "Don't worry about the charm. Just bring your body back quickly."

He dawdled in the shower, thoughts of his Saturday morning with Claudia too vibrant to push aside. It had made the day with Peter even more poignant — how much did the man know, or guess? He let the warm water stream past his well-soaped and unresponsive cock, hoping to find a sleeping body when he got back to bed — Mei slept and woke as though controlled by a switch.

He was relieved to find her asleep when he got back to the bed.

His own near-exhaustion from a weekend's travel, difficult meetings and overwrought emotions meant that he would soon join her. Worries seldom stopped him sleeping; they tended to wake him early.

But not so early as she did. It was the middle of the night, the light was slanting in from the sitting room of the suite onto the body bent over his cock, busily sucking him into life. Mei had developed from a reluctant performer to a joyous and skilled exponent. She brought her fierce focus to the technique and an apparent fascination with his cock's responses.

Had he been more than half awake he might have been less amused, but he found her commitment to these episodes of straight sex engaging in these middle-of-the-night encounters, and he would often chuckle later when she'd comment on his oral skills. 'You're wasted as a man, Alphonse, you do that so well.'

They hadn't quite developed habits, their couplings were too infrequent for that, and she was too curious about 'how it could be with a man.' Her early, reluctant experiences, she'd told him, were not happy ones, the men being too rough, insensitive, or just plain selfish. 'I always come first with you,' she'd said quite often. 'And third,' he would remind her. They laughed more than most couples, in his experience. Maybe it was the strangeness of it, but although he knew nothing of her times with Lily, or Isobel, or whoever she was seeing — he suspected it was few, or none, currently — he thought she probably had as much joy with him as with most. And it was a different Mei who shared his bed from the burgeoning autocrat who now commanded a major corporation.

But command she still could, even in these moments. She unwound herself from his cock, holding him stiff while she stretched up alongside him, kissing his lips tenderly before telling him, "Not in my mouth tonight, please, I want you to come in my cunt."

"My condoms..."

"Are staying in your bag." She was straddling him now. "I want to feel your spunk inside me." That made them both laugh even as he felt her sliding down on him, his reluctance finding, as it usually did, somewhere to hide for the duration.

"Do you like my cunt?"

He chuckled again and sent rumbles through them. "You have a lovely cunt. It's very sweet and pretty, but I didn't think it was a word you liked."

"I don't! I only like it for you." She was smiling, and he couldn't help joining her.

"And spunk? That's new, isn't it?"

"First time I ever said it. Horrible word, but I like to be dirty with you, and I only want your spunk. I like to swallow your spunk, but tonight I want you to fill my cunt with it." Even in the dim light he could see her eyes narrowing, but her smile broadening; her hands were on his shoulders, her arms straight. He loved face to face, just as they were; his prick was stiff and deep; her hips and thighs were moving to squeeze him and take him deeper, but it was her joyous smile that was making him follows his cock's inevitable intention — and he was probably releasing even before she began screaming, "I love it when you come, I love it when you come, I love it when you come."

When they slowly disentangled, he manoeuvred her to be spooned by him and both bodies slumped easily into their usual night-time pose, falling quickly asleep again.

When the alarm went, there was a space beside him, and a lipstick note by the bedside.

Friday too with a heart beside it.

Yes, very sweet, he thought, *and I'm supposed to say what to Daiyu?*

He felt a little used, but recognised he had no right. He'd participated fully in their little arrangement. But Daiyu understood these things.

That didn't mean she accepted them, of course. He'd be back in Hong Kong tonight. There would be a lot to catch up on.

And she would know that the coming Friday was a fourth Friday. She usually had something of her own organised to prevent Mei's visits becoming an issue.

But when he told her about tonight, she might be less understanding.

If he told her about tonight.

7

"Private jet again! What a life you lead, no wonder we're too humble these days." Arthur Gunter was driving his daughter to the airport, having had, Tania assumed, a frustrating weekend trying to get her to commit to her future. He claimed to have an open mind about whether she stayed in New York or returned to run Giddings, but Tania knew that was a fiction. She hadn't needed her mother's late-night conversation to confirm how desperate he was. "He just doesn't see the talent here, my dear, and every time you come here and talk to him, I get 'She makes them all look so small' out of him. That'll be my fate when he's dropped you off at the airport."

"He's not listening, Mother. I will look at it, but just taking over what he does, I'm sorry, I should be massively grateful — I know I'm very lucky — but that just ain't gonna be me." Her mother had looked patient, but sorrowful. "You're worried it's getting urgent, aren't you?"

"He forgets little things. That's going to have an impact, isn't it?"

Tania had nodded. That was her own reluctant conclusion. They could sell the business, but that would feel like a betrayal. She'd laughed suddenly. Her mother looked puzzled. "I was just imagining the midnight visitations of Great Grannie Gunter putting her whiskery face close to mine and telling me 'boys and music never made anyone happy. Hard work, wee 'un, that makes for a contented life.' I think she was already half-demented by then, but the point's stuck and I couldn't let her down without fearing the nightmares."

The first part of the airport drive was silent before her father asked, "How's my Claudia doing?"

"She's fine. I saw her last week."

"In New York?"

"Yes, she makes everyone come to see us these days."

"What does she think?"

Arthur Gunter could still catch people with the open question — but not his eldest daughter any more. "What does she think about what, Daddy?"

"Huh," he snorted, but smiled. "I guess I'm just lucky to still get called Daddy occasionally. I wasn't trying to trap you, chicken, what does she think you should do with your life? Run her business, I suppose."

"It's Peter's business, Daddy, and that's how she sees it. Her business, the one she built herself, is the consultancy. Her job is helping him run the whole thing and they let me run the group." She turned sideways to look at her father driving, just as she had done ever since she was big enough to commandeer the front seat. He caught her looking at him out of the corner of his eye.

"You're smiling, daughter of mine, what is it?"

She laughed. "And Mom thinks you're starting to miss things."

"I don't think I miss what matters, but what was funny?"

"The group I run is as big as Giddings, but you call its chief executive 'chicken'."

They both laughed, but when he looked serious again, he said, "It's a lot bigger than Giddings, chicken, we both know that, but it ain't yours, that's the point."

"I know, I know, but if you push me today on your job, in Atlanta, or my job, in New York, I'm only making one choice, but we shouldn't just keep picking at each other like this. It may not be just a simple choice."

"What do you mean?" he asked sharply.

"I don't want to close the door on Giddings."

Now he laughed. "Because you fear the ghost of Grannie Gunter, ha!"

"Please give me time to think about it. Let me talk to Will and Claudia a bit more. I don't know what we're doing at Dickinson. It sounds like even Peter's hearing the dreaded hoofbeats of mortality echoing down the corridor of his life."

"Is he?" Arthur sounded surprised. "I suppose I'm not the only one getting old."

"Ha, mother reminds me that I'm doing that, at thirty-two, for God's sake, but let me do some official work thinking. We're not pursuing a linear path to oblivion, are we?"

He shook his head, smiling. "You have a remarkable way of putting things, child, but you're right. I have to have somebody here who can imagine a different future. I'd just like it to be you and I can't see anyone else. But you'll give it some serious thought now?"

"I will." She'd probably missed an opportunity with Claudia, but Will would be a good place to start, and he was around most of next week, she thought.

They were soon at the airport and, as he hauled her bag from the trunk, it occurred to her that she would have found that manoeuvre easier than he did. God! How he would have hated that! She gave him a big hug, and felt a little more teary than usual. "I'll see you next month."

He leaned back, still hugging her. "Ha, it's only early June now, don't make it July thirty-one."

"I won't, but I'm not promising new thinking by then, either. Let's say year-end as a deadline to agree something."

He mocked a gasp. "You're talking to the chairman and chief executive of a major business."

She grinned at him. "I'm talking to a proud father."

"Always!" And now there was a tear in his eye.

***

She normally got to the office at nine. She preferred to run in the mornings and be available for the West Coast in the early evening, but Will, she knew, was always in by seven. She hoped he had no early appointments.

He was on the phone when she stood in his doorway, but he motioned to her to come and sit down. He was obviously talking to Henry. "I'm just saying face to face is better." He was listening to a lengthy response, and mouthing 'sorry' to her. "You can talk to him, of course, I just think he'd like us to come up with proposals for him." There was a shorter pause, and he was smiling. "Yes, I did mean us, not me. I had you down as a sceptic, not a cynic, and I'd love to see Archie and Miranda. God, it's over a year." They'd reached pleasantries now. "OK, Tuesday afternoon and evening then, wonderful, thanks."

"Am I reading too much into that?" she asked when he put the phone down.

"Probably not, but I wanted to talk to you anyway."

"Not about Saturday, though?" She was smiling slyly.

"No!" he said emphatically, but also smiling. "That's a drink after work topic, if you're free."

"Mos' def! But what's happening? At least you sounded cheery with Henry."

Now he looked serious. "That's deceptive. You know when there's a meta-conversation going on?"

"Completely, but at least my father and I are talking more openly by now. I've promised him some plans by year-end."

He looked thoughtful. "I don't want to get ahead of myself, but Martha and I touched on that in our business breakfast — it's how we spend our Saturday mornings. Sad, isn't it?"

"I'm sure it's very informative and helpful. I think I'd enjoy conversations like that, but we're skirting around something. Come on, what's going on?"

No one summarised like Will. In not many minutes she had a clear picture of how things might change — and she guessed she'd had a more balanced and open version of how he'd initiated the process than most would receive — Will was straightforward, but very clever; he wouldn't push anyone to a decision without giving them all the facts. He was simply careful in presenting those facts. She'd been surprised by a lot of what he'd said — the foundation idea was completely new to her — but it all seemed clear and sensible and, she quickly appreciated, obvious. Even with the potential problems, he hadn't gone through the tiresome trick of asking her to guess; he'd said straight away that Tony and Lou were obvious issues, and when he expressed caution about Henry and Alphonse, she understood that, too — also the point that he wasn't sure why he was cautious, but he was comfortable with uncertainty.

She didn't leap to facile clichés about power and envy. It would be more complex and subtle than that. She'd seen it too often in the men and women who ran the businesses she managed.

"And you'll run it all?"

He'd concluded his summary and that was the only point where he'd seemed tentative.

"Well, that's what I took Peter to mean."

"Oh, Will, come on, if he's going to keep it together, it's the only choice!" And this normally so placid man looked almost touched.

"I do appreciate you saying that."

"If I haven't made it fucking obvious that I think you're brilliant, then I apologise. You never give the impression that you need that. God! I'm sounding like a man. That's terrible." He was laughing now. "We'll have to float my group, won't we? I'm sorry if that sounds self-obsessed, but if he wants to take money out for his foundation, we'll have to let shareholders in."

"That's why I needed to talk to you anyway — and why your discussions with your father are timely. I don't want to leap to the obvious solution, though."

"There's an obvious solution? Enlighten me, maestro."

He was thinking, probably not about the idea itself, she didn't think, but about what to say to her, but she knew she'd get his straightforward thoughts. It was how they worked together.

"Look, this is one scenario — and we'll need to look at several — but we keep all of the group. I think you've pulled it together remarkably well, the businesses are more mutually supportive now. It's a coherent unit. I think it would be an easy sell — well, relatively."

"Thank you for the compliment, but that was us, including Claudia, not just me."

He chuckled. "You thought I was so modest I would ignore my own contribution?"

"Nah! You're the man! So, the plan is?"

"Well, he owns between forty and fifty percent of the businesses in the group, and he won't want to own much less than fifteen, of the total. Well, I don't want us owning less than fifteen, for that matter, or we won't have the control we need."

"Dad has control of twenty-five at Giddings and he doesn't feel he has enough."

"I'm coming to that."

She guessed where this was heading but, unusually, was concerned about seeming foolish — only Will made her feel vulnerable that way, even though he had never actually done so.

"You think any owners might want to buy Peter's stakes?"

"If we're going IPO, I think most of them will want money." He seemed slightly startled, but she couldn't suppress a smile, "In fact, I'm pretty certain that all of them will. If they stay in the fold, with us still running it, they still have all the autonomy they have now, but they all get to take heaps of cash out."

"What if we merge it into a bigger unit? Take on Giddings. The Dickinson Giddings Group, with you as chairman? I'd offer you chairperson but, as Martha would say, how fucked up is that?"

She laughed, and that little joke had taken the focus away from, for her and her father, something momentous. She had to calm herself down. "Lot of ifs in that, aren't there? And that's only one option."

"Completely, but, you know, sometimes an idea just feels right."

"Dangerously seductive, William Uprichard, that's what it is. Who else is in on this?"

"Martha's going to tell me it was her idea — and it did come up at breakfast."

"I'm too excited now. Peter? Claudia?"

"I think they'll want to know what other options we've looked at. I'm seeing them next week. Can you find half a day? Friday?"

"I'll make time. You've kinda disrupted this week's timetable anyway. Do we want Lavinia?"

"Oh, I think so, don't you? She was superb when we set the group up. Hey, has she been to Noah Reid's?"

"William," she said sharply, "what sort of a lady do you think she is?"

"I think she's a Jack Stephens sort of lady, but I withdraw the question. It would be for the Blue Orchid bar tonight anyway. Aim for seven?"

"Aim for seven."

She left his office quickly. She felt extraordinarily excited but didn't want to show too much of that to Will. If it didn't come off, it would be a big disappointment for him, too. She knew herself well enough to use the hour she'd now gained to calm down and think rationally about other viable options.

She would talk to Claudia before Friday, but not until she had a more considered range of ideas. At least she now knew what Claudia's Friday had been about. And Alphonse's too. He would also be impacted. Perhaps Will would say more in the bar that evening.

Perhaps there was no old romance thing.

Nah, she was sure there was still something.

***

Will's office was already empty when she left, but it was barely seven. It was typical, though, that he'd get to the bar first to welcome her in. Still, he could have waited and gone with her — but it was only a block away. The bigger surprise was to find Martha with him when she got there. The waiter was taking orders.

"Here she is!" said Martha eagerly. "Hug me, you bad woman, but don't make me get down off this stool. You tall people are tyrants. Tell the man what you want quickly, or he'll bring you a beluga martini."

She smiled to the waiter and nodded, hugged Martha, and slid up on to an empty stool.

"I'm here to thank you for setting up Saturday night for us. We were quiet little wallflowers, but I was very intrigued."

Tania narrowed her eyes. It can't have been that unusual an experience for Martha. Tania had heard enough about Smarts clubs, and Noah wasn't unique in New York.

"I know what you're thinking, madam, and I've no secrets from Will." She laughed loudly. "And he has none from me, now he's let me meet Sadie."

"Who's Sadie?" Tania was puzzled.

"Have you heard of a lady called Isobel Allen?"

"Isn't she the designer who works on Alphonse's projects?"

"Exactly, but she's also a broad-minded and widely experienced lady who's responsible for a lot of my young man's education, I'm delighted to say, and she's also tremendous fun. Now, I don't know if you'd guessed…well, you must have, I suppose, but I have a little kink and it was nice to see other people enjoying it again. I've been rather nervous about the New York scene, I'm a bit of a public person here, but we had a quiet chat with Noah first. I know you'd vouched for him, but anyone who knows Henderson — well, I don't need to tell you about that."

"No, but he has a very distant relationship with him, I think, and Rod doesn't get invited any more. Mind you, I don't think he ever did, really, he sort of inveigles his way into things, it's the old intel stuff. Anyway, what did you think of Noah?"

"Intriguing, and very discreet, I think. I couldn't get too close to him, though. I know enough to know that he strays into some areas I couldn't afford to be associated with. My official line is that my bank is completely respectable. It's true that sometimes we have to help clients out when they get into trouble. Anyway, I'm babbling."

And she was; that was unusual for Martha. Tania wondered why this most self-possessed of women was agitated.

"I don't know if we'll go again, but it was fun to watch."

"That's all Noah does, watches. It's his kink. He's organised a couple of private sessions for me, but the price is that he watches — and if we're being frank and honest — I've even enjoyed that bit. I never thought I would."

Martha looked intrigued, as Tania guessed she might. Will remained alert, no more — always indecipherable.

"Well, maybe after two martinis we might get you to say more," Martha had switched, as she could do so quickly, into business mode, "but apart from thank you, I wanted to stay involved with the organisation discussion, mainly for my man here and his future, but an IPO would be a nice piece of business for the bank. Although it's only one possibility."

This was classic Martha, always considering the options. She would be very helpful in sharpening up their thinking. "I'd certainly be glad of some help in thinking through my area. It's quite complex."

"Potentially, yes, but it's only complexity, and you two have more than enough brains and judgement to work that through. It's the other areas where the problems are bigger, I think. Anyway, I know you've got Friday planned together, but he and I are committed to working through some of the stuff on Wednesday over a non-alcoholic dinner. It's my only free time this week. Could you join us?"

"That would be excellent, thank you, and if we move on to whisky when we've worked, I think I'd feel more comfortable telling you more about Noah than doing it here in a bar."

"That sounds smart. We work until ten p.m. then and move on to whisky. How's that?"

Tania smiled slyly at each of them. "Yes, but I get to hear all about Isobel."

"Deal!" said Martha quickly, leaving Will looking uncomfortable.

"And Smarts. Wasn't that the name of the club in Tokyo?"

Now Will had a big smile and it was Martha who seemed hesitant. "Deal," said Will, and they all laughed.

"But since you obviously behaved sensibly on Saturday, you can tell me the non-scandalous bits about how you found Noah and his party."

Will was more reticent, but Martha felt quite comfortable, albeit only skirting over the activities they'd observed. "But we spent most time in the drawing room. I spent Sunday morning trying to price the artwork. I was well over a hundred, is that right? Don't you have a friend who does the buying?"

"Yes, Robert. He also runs Noah's gallery on the West side, and my compliments, over one hundred is what I was told two years ago, and I've not read of prices going down since then."

Will and Martha both shook their heads.

8

That was Claudia. We always say we'll talk once a month, but we never quite manage it. I try not to keep track of whose turn it is, but I honestly think I'm more spontaneous, and therefore more frequent. She calls when she's worried. I don't think she does that deliberately, and it wouldn't be wrong if she did.

At least she doesn't hide stuff. She has this big thing about being open with people. It's probably very deep, but it's also partly to do with her Jack Stephens legacy. It means we're fundamentally compatible anyway, we both like being open.

There's a lot about to change in her life now, and she knows I have enough insight to know that it's not all positive, however much it must look like a dream to some people. I'm flattered she feels we can talk.

She doesn't even hide that she saw Alphonse on Friday in New York. I obviously don't ask if she slept with him. Come on! I'm just assuming she did.

But the big news is that Peter is reorganising. I sort of understand it, I think, but I also understand why it's surprised her. He'd normally talk everything through with her, but they have this one area they can't talk about. He wants to marry her — and she won't. I hadn't realised, but she's actually been married twice before. The children are from her second — 'my second mistake,' she called it.

Obviously, you can't really regret if you have children, even I can see that. I don't know if she sees this as a gambit of Peter's to move himself deeper into the children's lives; she's more all over the place on this than I've heard her on anything. She's normally so clear and calm and wise about everything, and she knows she's being handed a chance to do something special, but it's unnerved her.

She says Will's behind it. I would think he's just reading Peter's mind. He's very empathetic like that, our William, the best tops are; even Claudia can see that Peter would like someone else to show him what a different future could look like — and Will's the only person who would or could do that.

Well, that's the way she sees it. She's probably right, but I don't know everybody in the picture. I don't know Henry at all, and I've met Tony King only a couple of times. That was funny. You know how it is when you meet someone you've heard a lot about and you're expected to like them? Yes, I could understand why people would have thought that. But I also understand why Claudia's worried. He would worry me.

I think Alphonse had something with his wife, some little fling. I must get him to tell me more about that.

No, I'm not being gratuitously nosey. This might affect my William. I'll have to keep a watching brief.

Martha asked how I was, apparently. Now, she's a person I was expecting not to like. I'm saying this through gritted teeth, but I know I'll end up liking her. I already admire her; she's impressive, and I could just catch a little whiff of that kink that must keep her and William so close. I wouldn't quite react the same way, but I could imagine her manner bringing out something in male tops — as it presumably did with William — that would make them thoroughly enjoy him spanking her. I would think the top would have to be male. We did have a fun evening together, although I was on edge, but it never got as far as discussing that. It's not even a topic I discuss with Claudia, although she has demurely assured me that the chaise I so cleverly and discreetly designed for their bedroom still gets occasional use.

The word 'occasional' sounded a little wistful. She loves Peter, I don't doubt. She adores Alphonse, of course. But it always sounds to me that the one that got away was the perfect mix. I don't hear about him these days; she's said very little to me about Jack Stephens at all, really.

Peter had been meeting Mei, she told me. I think Mei amuses him slightly but I'm sure he's too smooth and charming ever to let that show — and he does speak very highly of her work and how she's taken charge of things, she says. I'll probably see her in a couple of weeks. I get sent dates from her PA. I send replies directly to Mei telling her when I'm in Hong Kong and available. Although I do have a business opportunity in Shanghai I need to take a look at. It's business, it's what we do, but I still get a little thrill when I come out with it like that: Isobel Allen, doing business in Shanghai! I'll do the trip with Daiyu, but they do like to meet the showman as well. I'm flamboyant, apparently. Of course I am, a little bit.

She did ask about me, but you're fairly up-to-date on that. I told her how surprised I was that both Michael and Merle are in denial about what happened to Ellen. 'It's funny how people deal with things,' she said, 'but I'm glad you said.' It's something she and Peter talk about only rarely, but he's said they need to be wary about Gerry Calvert. In the end I did no more than provide him with an alibi on that fateful afternoon but, as Peter says — and Conrad agrees — Gerry Calvert won't forget that someone was out to get him.

9

That he could remain calm in all circumstances was something Will was aware of in himself — principally because it was more of a struggle for him than people realised.

He'd grown used to his ability to retain and process more information than almost anyone he knew. Data just seemed to sit in his mind and make itself available when required. Even people he esteemed, like Peter and Henry — and Martha, seemed struck by how easily he could summon all points to make a case.

It was a cheap party trick with most to answer any quiz question, best just accepted without comment. He'd even stopped doing it, it was so easy, but when anyone accused him of imperturbability, he tended to lower his estimation of them. Martha knew he sometimes struggled; Peter, he thought, guessed at it; but Henry? That was interesting. Because of their history, he suspected that Henry both admired and underestimated him. That might, under the new circumstances, be either helpful, or damaging.

The Friday, 'Gosh, that's an interesting development for you,' had that edge of condescension that he'd sometimes detected in Henry, who'd obviously been shocked into deliberating carefully about how he should respond.

He would have called Henry a friend — until last Friday. But that he could call that assessment so quickly into question meant that he had to think harder about what their relationship truly was. Henry's friendship clearly came with conditions, with expectations, with constraints and limitations, but, when he'd put the phone down, he realised that his own attitude was equally circumscribed. Then he felt annoyed with himself for assessing friendship in those terms.

He needed no such qualifications with Tony, who was as near to a genius as anyone Will had ever met — the formidable modelling that was the foundation of the Funds group's success had been based on Tony's doctoral work — but he would never call Tony a friend. Nor Lou, for that matter, who played less of a role in Peter's, or his own, deliberations, but who would probably find ways of being troublesome.

It was a relief to all of them that Lou had shown some talent, both for the way the funds worked — the maths was complex — and for the ability to sustain relationships in Asia, even while enjoying London, New York, and, yes, Brisbane. He wondered how wise it had been to let him spend so much time there in Tony's company, but there did seem to have been benefits in the acceleration of the Pacific business. A lot more Chinese money was now coming into the funds.

Peter had challenged Will on his reluctance to celebrate so much success, but had looked troubled when Will had refused to be convinced. 'You know I'm worried you're right, don't you?' he'd asked gloomily, not expecting an answer.

They seldom needed to explain their positions to each other.

Peter was the most extraordinary man he'd ever met, even from the first dinner — at Henry and Rachel's home in Fulham eight years ago — and he'd tried to remain cautious ever since.

He couldn't help but be seduced, though, which happened, he could see, wherever he went, to almost everyone. Even Martha, probably the worldliest person he knew, freely admitted to being 'just a little bit in love' with him. The subsequent, 'Of course, I know where I am in that semi-infinite queue' had been followed by, 'fortunately, I have an even better alternative,' which would have saved her from a spanking, but for the 'If you leave me, though, I'm making a play. If she won't marry him, she couldn't blame me for muscling in.'

He loved her laugh. It was indecently below mezzo when she was feeling horny, which she obviously had been that night. The new situation, however, was engaging her at several levels. "Obviously the mix is unique, honeybun, but it's not unusual for these fabulously successful men to wonder about their legacy and, bless him, he has no children of his own to squander his on. But I do think he's lucky to have her, and to have you to take it on for him."

"You really think I'm part of that?"

She just looked at him, then smiled and shook her head. "Fuck you, William Uprichard, you're much too good to need to squeeze pathetic compliments out of your adoring spouse."

He'd shrugged. "I know, but I do value your opinion above all others."

"Fuck you again, you condescending bastard! Don't make me think it's you who needs a spanking. That doesn't do it for me, sweetheart. I'd have to call Isobel."

"Tania's here soon. I think this is a topic we'll need to come back to."

She'd laughed. "Promises, promises."

Tania arrived soon after seven and the discussion began immediately in the kitchen. The tortellini from the deli below needed only to be basted with truffle butter, so the food preparation was no distraction. Not for the women anyway, who'd each given more thought to the topic than he'd managed in two days. Martha put out a tomato salad in side bowls without appearing to pay any attention to what she was doing, while he applied some focus to what was, he recognised, the simplest of cooking tasks. He handed a plate to each of them when he'd dished up and they seemed to ignore him completely, pursuing their discussion as they took their dishes to the table.

He was at the head while the ladies batted their ideas back and forth, Tania prompting herself occasionally from her phone, Martha from a tablet she'd put by her place before the meal was served. Initially, he'd persuaded himself he was a referee, but began to feel increasingly like a spectator and it seemed entirely natural that he should remove the empty plates and glasses, take them to the dishwasher, and prepare coffee.

The rally seemed to have continued uninterrupted when he returned a few minutes later with the cafetière and mugs on a tray but, as soon as he sat down again, Martha turned to him and said, "Tania's arguing against the link with Giddings because she knows both her emotions and her own needs are playing too big a role in her thinking."

"What have you said?" he asked Martha.

She opened her mouth to speak, hesitated, and smiled. "Oh, no, you don't, I asked you first."

He laughed. "I have two arguments in favour and one against," and for the first time that evening he suddenly found himself the centre of their attention.

He looked to Tania first as Martha began to pour coffee. "I don't have to hedge around this one. You're a superb business leader, and whatever we put together won't become half of what it could be if you're not running it."

Tania looked slightly surprised and looked to Martha, who stopped attending to the cups for a moment. "See, I told you," she said as if that simple fact should have been accepted earlier.

"The second plus for me is that, although the footprint of technologies and activities becomes broader, the way you've set up the group, particularly with the Radius business in San Francisco, means that the links are already quite strong and there are similar operating principles."

"And the one against?" asked Tania.

"Well, there may be two."

"Boo," said Martha. "Spoilsport!" She smiled, but quickly looked serious again. "You know, my darling, how you would have disappointed me if you have abandoned your Solomon-like balance too easily. So, two against, good!" She rested her chin on her hands at the apex of her forearms' triangle.

"That the logic is obvious to us won't be so clear to the market, and anybody buying in would question whether we're allowing convenience and personal needs to dictate strategy — and we'd get a lower price."

"Fortunately, you have a good bank to put the prospectus together," said Martha, looking to Tania and getting a smile out of her.

"You might dupe investors more easily than I can sell this to Peter and Claudia," said Will patiently.

Martha nodded. "Objection two?"

"Well, it relates to the first plus point." He looked to Tania again, "You'd be very stretched, not so much from putting the businesses together, but I'd need some support running the whole thing. If Peter and Claudia pull back, and they should and must, I think, I'd need your voice here to keep Dickinson coherent."

"That's a fair point," said Martha evenly. "Who do you have who can step up and help you?"

Tania seemed to consider it for a moment. "I can see how I'd organise at Giddings, but I'd need to think about the group." She turned to Will. "I'm flattered, thank you, but you're making me feel that my comfort zone has limits."

"Ah," Martha waved an arm dismissively, "we're all just playing at being grown-ups. The danger comes when we start to take ourselves seriously. Anyway, at least we've stopped you ruling that one out."

She was looking with narrowed eyes at Tania, who shook her head from side to side briefly, but then said, "OK, it stays on the list."

"The list?" said Will. "I'm embarrassed to say that you've both spent more time on this than I have since Monday."

"That's because your adoring angels are so desperate to impress you, my sweet," said Martha, smiling broadly, but he realised she was serious.

"Can I hear about your other deliberations?" And he was in control again.

The discussion continued intensely, although they'd moved themselves at some point to the sofas, the ladies still working with electronic devices and Will — 'the dinosaur,' that was from Martha — putting their ideas down on paper.

Martha stood up suddenly. "Can you summarise where we've got to? I need to get the whisky organised."

He was only mildly disconcerted. "Nothing concluded yet, but I'm feeling much better about our meeting on Friday now. I think there are three, possibly four schemes we should work on in more detail." Now he called a little louder, Martha was fetching glasses and water, "That'll just be us and Lavinia, my sweet, you didn't want to be there, did you?"

"Ha." She stopped what she was doing and looked to them. "I do have a day job, and your precious Mr D probably thinks I've been involved too early anyway. Nah, I'm very interested, of course, but you three are better at imagining how these schemes would really work. You'll talk more Peter's language than I will." She busied herself again, returning from the cabinet with two bottles. Tania looked alarmed. Martha laughed. "Don't worry, my dear, it's about choice, not volume. Smooth or smoky?"

"I'll stay with smooth, thank you." Will saw her eyebrows rise as an inch of Glenmorangie went into her tumbler.

He nodded when Martha lifted the Laphroaig bottle and she put large measures into the other two glasses. "I'll get you ice if you want," she said to Tania, "but fifty-fifty water is the house recommendation."

"I'll go with that."

"Good." Martha put water in all three glasses before settling down beside Will. "Now can we get on to the more interesting part of the evening? Noah Reid, how come?"

Tania sipped the whisky, nodded appreciatively, then leaned back on the sofa, coddling her glass as if for comfort. "I'll give you the Noah background, but I'll want some of your history before I embarrass myself with what I've got up to there. Deal?"

Martha looked up to him. "Deal?"

He assumed he'd heard all the stories, of Jack Stephens, and of Smarts, and of a few other encounters from her more distant past, but he couldn't exclude there being another odd surprise. He'd been open with her about his Isobel times; less so about Merle. He'd been too deeply in love, he could still remember, to want to say everything about that, but he was sure he had enough to entertain them.

At some point, in the middle of Tania talking about discussing Henderson with Noah, Martha had moved sofas and sat beside Tania and held her hand, as if preparing to begin before Tania had to reveal anything of her personal activities and, as Tania's narrative was becoming more hesitant, Martha started in with, "Obviously you'd guessed that I was intrigued by the Red Room, and I'm going to guess, if you've taken her there, without in any way expecting a response from you, that it would have interested Lavinia too."

Tania smiled. "No comment," she said, but looked relieved that Martha was now determined to speak.

His wife, as she frequently did, surprised him. He'd heard the stories before, but not paraded so frankly for someone else to hear. Tania looked increasingly rapt, but was suddenly surprised by Martha's, "Not your thing, though, is it?"

She was almost jolted by the question, but held on tightly to the now half-empty whisky tumbler. "No, no," she stuttered, "no, I like…do you mind if I hear about Will first, before I talk about me, and the mysterious Isobel."

"Ha!" exploded Martha. "I don't think Isobel is so mysterious. Even allowing for the awkward situation we were in, we still understood each other very well by the end of our evening. I'm sure you'd like her, but that's not a prediction you should ever make about anyone, is it? Anyway, I have a lot to be grateful for, but I'd better let him tell that story."

***

Martha snuggled into him when she got into bed, her hand moving straight to his cock. "I felt a bit sorry for the poor young woman going home to an empty apartment, when I get this." She shook his half-awake member gently.

"Getting her to join us would be the last thing I need."
"Would you? With her?"
"It sounds like I'd be in a queue."

"Oh dear, not being censorious, are we?"

"No, not at all. I think it helps that we have different tastes. Would her thing turn you on?"

"A few chunky men taking turns?" She was smiling more broadly as her grip strengthened. "I can see the idea appeals to you and him."

He smiled back at her. "You'd have to be very severely spanked afterwards."

"Oh, I'd want to earn the cane. How many would I have to take on for that?"

"At least three, and two at the same time as part of that."

"With you and Noah watching?"

"I suppose it could be arranged."

"Stick your cock in me right now, Mr Uprichard, and fuck my brains out!"

10

Alphonse felt a little unworthy as the plane took off.

He'd had an excellent day with Yang Li. She would certainly be a better property head than either of Zhao Fuqin's successors to date. He'd convinced himself that his assessment wasn't based simply on her ability to speak English. She understood the market well and, if some of her ideas surprised him, they were at least worth considering. He'd felt that way about Mei in the early days and found that she was right, more often than not.

Daiyu would have a view, and that would be a useful conversation.

If she were there tonight.

But she might ask about Mei.

She might even ask about Claudia.

She might not even be there.

It's Tuesday, he thought. *She'll know that Friday is booked.*

They'd fallen only slowly into the pattern of spending most Hong Kong nights together, usually at his place, in spite of agreeing, almost two years ago, to become closer to each other.

His apartment was fatally convenient if she'd wished to exploit it, in the neighbouring tower to the office, and larger than her own. It was always impeccable, he was a fastidious man, but it never quite matched the show apartment gleam of Daiyu's place, in which he always felt too big. But sometimes, if they'd eaten in Kowloon, it was easier to stay there — and it suited him anyway to prevent any drift towards a single home.

He reassured himself that it would have suited neither of them but avoided ever checking that assumption with her.

She had never even hinted that it would be desirable, and she was always careful to leave very little in his apartment. All toiletries were kept in a bag, which could be easily stowed in the spare room, along with only a few items of clothing. Anyone else he entertained would have to deliberately seek evidence of her frequent visits.

He left nothing at hers but, if he stayed the night, there was always a blue toothbrush, a razor, deodorant and cologne waiting in the bathroom for him in the morning — and a clean shirt and underwear were kept in a bedroom drawer for him.

She moved in and out of his life with an unnerving sensitivity. The guilt that sat inside him like an undigested meal was from a recipe of his own.

She'd once said to him, maybe a year ago, 'You're a bonus for me, Alphonse, a sort of a present. I don't want presents every day.' He'd forgotten how it had arisen, perfectly naturally, in the conversation but, while happy to accept the remark, he'd been sceptical about whether it reflected her true feelings.

But he'd had nearly two years of being able to appreciate that almost everything she said was a straightforward description of both facts and attitudes. She was unusual. Only Isobel was similar, in his experience.

Certainly, none of the men he'd been close to had ever been so open. Not Lee, although he had tried — probably more than Alphonse had.

Why only almost everything? he asked himself about Daiyu. He'd never caught her not being open, but he was reluctant to credit anyone with an absolute level of honesty. She seemed, at times, simply naïve — but nobody fooled Daiyu. So, if she wanted to ask about Claudia, or Mei, he would have to say something, even if he never offered her the level of apparent frankness, she gave him.

It struck him again, as it did frequently, that his guilt was his own problem, much of it arising out of what he chose to call tact — and she always laughingly called concealment. That was why it was easy to spend weekends with her; once he'd unburdened himself by exposing the source of any guilt, there was never more from her than some quiet contemplation before they settled into their usual pattern.

Not that how they lived ever allowed a real pattern.

Which suited him.

He thought.

Tonight, would be unusual though, if she were there. His own feelings about the encounters with Claudia and Mei were unresolved enough for his discomfort to be noticeable and, although she never tried anything as crude as 'What's troubling you?' he would always find himself talking about events and feelings with her in ways that surprised him. Claudia always called him enigmatic and, generally, he preferred being that way.

So, he was ambivalent about the text he picked up in the car on his way back from the airport:

Long trip, I know. Thought you'd like to relax on your own, but I can be there if you want me. D xxx

The guilt would remain undigested for twenty-four more hours. But he had twenty-four more hours to work out why the events had troubled him more than usual.

Oddly, once he got over his reluctance to speak, he knew Daiyu would probably help him clear his thoughts. But he wouldn't ask her over. He would send a goodnight text later.

They snacked together in the office at lunchtime the next day. He talked a little about Florida, but spent more time asking her about Yang Li.

"Are you thinking she should replace her boss?"

He laughed and shook his head. "Always right, Chou Daiyu, my compliments." She smiled at him. "Would that be wrong?" he asked.

"It wouldn't be wrong to replace him. But getting rid of three in under two years, hmm…" she was shaking her head.

"Three?"

"You don't count Zhao Fuquin? I know they called it retiring, but, really?"

"You're right, I hadn't counted that one. It seemed different somehow."

"It was different; it was her father."

"Most people still saw him as that, didn't they? Still do, in fact. Was it bad, what she did?"

"No, not for anyone prepared to look past her crime of being a woman." She smiled, she made the comment as a joke, not as a polemic. "Most people accept the party line, that he couldn't report to his daughter, some even thought it was a condition of her promotion, to prevent the Zhao family having too much power," she chuckled at the irony of that, "but most knew that he'd done no real work for years." She smiled at her own comment. "But Yang Li, I just don't know her well enough. Maybe she could do it, though. I've been impressed enough on the couple of times I've had to work with her. But you need to be a special person to work for Mei."

"Why do you say that?"

"You don't think it's true?"

"Oh, I agree completely. I was just interested in how you arrived at that view."

"I think we talk about that this evening." Her look lingered.

"Yes, I think we do."

"I'll be staying." He was getting one of her more intense looks.

***

'I'm staying' was something she said rarely. Staying normally seemed to happen either naturally or spontaneously; seldom was it flagged as she had done in the office earlier. It meant she knew there were things on his mind, and she was signalling that she would still be there after he'd spoken about them, however difficult they might be. He'd never seen her agitated, barely even annoyed, by anything he'd had to say.

It was nearly seven, she would be here soon, and he would have food brought up. That was a signal to himself that he was ready to talk.

She came in with a warm smile and wrapped her arms around his neck. She'd showered and changed at the office.

"You look delightful, but I was thinking of ordering from downstairs. Would you rather go out?"

"No, but I did want to give you the option." She kissed his lips gently. "I'm happier staying in. You can take me out tomorrow. I know you're busy Friday." It was said so matter-of-factly. "Shall I order? You are too conservative with food, you know." Only in China could anyone make that accusation, he thought.

"I know, but please keep it simple."

"I will, you should get us drinks."

"Champagne?"

"Champagne?" She sounded surprised, but it wasn't rare.

"I think you're dining with a wealthy man."

"Is that the big story?"

"Probably. Well, it is a big story but I wouldn't say it was the only one."

She'd retrieved the menu from a kitchen drawer, but looked up to say, "No, we already had Mei on the agenda. Are we covering any other ground?"

"Do you have anything we need to talk about?"

"Ha, are you joking, or hoping? If you want me to invent something to stimulate you, I can try, but apart from two dinners with the Langs, senior and junior, I've nothing to report."

"Both of them? Separately or together?"

"Separately, of course. They're both trying to seduce me. It's not yet becoming irritating."

"Which would you prefer?"

"Oh, senior, no question, but shhh, I'm ordering." She busied herself with her phone.

He'd poured two glasses by the time she was finished. He was charmed by her protracted ordering process; it was always a conversation. It was nearly always worth the wait. She sat down when she was finished, "So, champagne, expliquez, monsieur!"

He talked her through Peter's plans. She was unusually quiet when he'd finished. "Questions?"

She was thoughtful. "There's lots I want to ask about, but I am pleased for them both, well, and for you. I hope they can enjoy each other more. How much do you interfere with that?"

"Not at all, intentionally." He got her scowl. "Truth is, I don't know. I suppose we'll meet less if they're not on the board together."

"Who will you miss more?" He felt puzzled. She went on, "Her or him? I assume, if he's pulling back, you won't be stitching property or resort deals together, so you'll be less in touch with him directly. Do you get five percent of the total, or do you get to carve out five percent to own independently?"

It was a good question. He felt silly for not having asked it, but he was receiving a gift. "I think that will form part of Will's proposals."

"But what would you prefer?"

He thought for a while. It was quite simple. "Probably something for me to own. Yes, I'd like that, a block in London, a block in Miami. Yes, that would feel like wealth. Wealth I'd never imagined. And independence."

"But Will is going to offer you five percent of the total."

"Why do you say that?" He was curious, rather than suspicious, but the answer, as she'd spotted so quickly, was obvious.

"You've just made the relevant point. Because he'll want to keep hold of you to manage the whole area; he won't want you to be independent. He's closer to a genuine gentleman than anybody I've ever met, but he's also smart. Besides, he and Peter will come under pressure from Mei. She won't want you taken away from her property division either, particularly if she's going to make another change of head — and she's given you the opportunity to evaluate the new candidate." She paused, then smiled wickedly. "She's offering you the choice of an assistant. One thing I will say in Yang Li's favour, however: she's not the prettiest, is she?"

He laughed. "You can't say that! Where's the sisterhood? Where's the 'looks shouldn't matter'? She's not the youngest, either, but she does dress very well."

"She does, but that doesn't make her one for Mei, and it doesn't make her competition, either. And sisterhood, ha, I don't think so. Anyway, have you skilfully dodged a question?"

He didn't need to be reminded. "Not deliberately. Missing Claudia or Peter more do you mean?" She nodded. "Both the same, but in different ways." That was probably honest.

"It's not just sex with Claudia, is it?"

"It's not just sex with anybody."

"Even Mei?"

That made him stop — but he wasn't trapped by guilt any longer. "I think it might be for her."

"Oh, no you don't!" she said sharply, turning to face him from their usual sofa position. But then the bell rang. "And that hasn't saved you. You do realise it's a lot more complex than that, don't you?"

"Probably," he said, but he was heading to the door to get the food.

The interrogation didn't restart when they were eating. He knew she would bide her time, and he got her talking more about the Langs and her dinner dates: 'the young one is married; the older one at least is widowed'; 'Is that the reason for the preference?'; 'Please!' and she went into an accurate appraisal of Lang Wenglei's attributes. He was a dynamic and imaginative head of the business in the area for Alphonse, but arrogant and self-centred — not unlike Lou, she added.

They were back on the sofa, all the food and dishes cleared away, before she got back to Mei, and she was sat at the far end. It was not to be a cuddle-conversation, and he knew that was not what he needed.

"What else do you think it is with Mei?"

"Thank you," she said.

"Thank you?"

"For coming back to the topic yourself. I'm seeing signs of hope." He got her cheeky smile. "Anyway, she was always in awe of you, you knew that, didn't you?"

"Well, it took Isobel pointing that out in London the first time Mei came there to make me see it that way, but, yes, and it meant we had an uncomplicated eighteen months travelling everywhere together and working intensely hard without anything intervening. It changed when her life changed, when she found out who real daddy was. You must remember that night." She nodded. He thought for a while. "It wasn't sex she wanted, not then, it was just the reassurance of holding on to someone she could trust, I thought. With so much changing for her, I think she wanted one or two things she could rely on." He hesitated. "Do you see it differently?"

"I'm not that close to her, but I can see that makes sense for then."

"And now?"

"I'm asking you. I don't really give a fuck about her; she can look after herself. You're the one who ends up schlepping guilt around because you have to fuck her and Claudia sometimes."

"I don't have to fuck Claudia."

"Darling man, I'm not sure you actually have to fuck Mei."

"It felt like it on Monday." He rather blurted that out. He was normally more circumspect, and she'd now turned away and was looking at the harbour lights.

"And she still wants to see you on Friday?" The question was asked thoughtfully, not accusingly.

"Apparently. I have had a message confirming it. Sorry."

"Oh, good heavens, don't apologise." She moved towards him and snuggled in. "You don't wear condoms with her, do you?"

He didn't. He assumed Mei's other affairs were pure lesbian. He'd given it less thought than he should have done. "Are you worried?" he asked.

"Not about what you're thinking." Now she sat up and tucked her knees beneath her, but stayed beside him, holding his hands. "Did you come inside her vagina?"

The question hit him like a punch. It was disorientating. "Why?" he stuttered. "How?"

"Is that what you normally do with her?" She was calm, like asking what he'd had for breakfast, but he could feel a big wave building, out in the ocean, a long way off. "Or do you come in her mouth, or how I like it?" Her smile seemed inappropriate, as well as oddly reassuring. She made it easy to talk openly.

"It's a lot of oral with Mei, both ways. I'm quite good, she says."

"No question." Daiyu smiled and squeezed his hands. "But Monday, think about it, anything unusual, apart from it being a Monday and she's seeing you Friday?"

"Well, she sat on me, said she wanted me to come in her cunt. She never uses that word normally."

"Was she trying hard to make you come?"

He felt the wave rolling in closer. "You don't think?"

"How do you feel about fatherhood?"

"No!"

"Have you asked her what precautions she takes? No, don't tell me, this is an 'I just assumed' situation, isn't it?" She treated silence as a reply. "I'm surmising because you've come back a little different. I may be reading too much into it. You're going through a lot of changes in your big relationships, with Peter, with your beloved Claudia, maybe with a very self-centred Mei."

"Claudia's not my beloved."

"Darling man, the two of you probably call it friendship but, whatever it is, it isn't just that. Anyway, that's not the urgent issue. You have to think about how you deal with Mei on Friday."

He felt troubled and threatened. She saw that.

"I may be being too imaginative. You'll find a way of finding out, and you have a couple of days to work out your own position on it. Did you come inside Claudia's vagina, by the way?"

It didn't seem the right way to discuss the dreamy hour he'd had before rushing to the airport on Saturday morning.

But he had.

Daiyu was still holding his hands, as if she were offering the safety of a boat to be merely tossed in when the storm hit, rather than leaving him on a shore to be drowned.

"People react in different ways to pangs of jealousy. I've made you tell me about two recent sexual encounters you've had with other women, and now I want you to fuck me. Come on! Pleasure me and reassure me!" She stood up and pulled at his hands.

***

"Was I very greedy?" she asked, when their breathing had slowed. "I know I was a bit desperate. More than you anyway," she said, but she chuckled. It was a tease. "I am absolutely not complaining, by the way. I didn't have to worry about you coming too soon."

"And I didn't have to worry about you getting pregnant." She did have, they agreed, a peachy bum, and she'd learned to enjoy that way enormously with him.

"I hope I haven't worried you about Mei. I just think she's very self-centred and she'll do what she wants. It's up to you to decide what you'll go along with. I'm more worried about you and Claudia."

He was puzzled. "Why?"

"Well, I agree with Isobel. You both care so much about each other, and about Peter, that you almost cripple yourselves. Well, I can't speak for her, obviously, but it seems to do that to you. I suspect Peter might be more genuinely broad-minded than either of you will admit to. Didn't he used to let anyone fuck his wives?"

"Yes, but those were different relationships from the one he has with Claudia."

She looked a little serious now. "Do you get a little jealous when she's with him?"

"A bit, it's true."

11

Gerry wants to have dinner!

I'm amazed, of course, and he wants the four of us to meet: Merle and Gerry, and Conrad and me. My excuse, 'Not sure where Conrad is next week,' is at least plausible, if not accurate.

Well, it's not even true, of course; he's back tomorrow and here until I leave on Wednesday. I don't mind warping my commitment to honesty for Merle.

No, this isn't tact. You know I'm worried. I need time to think. I even have to consult. Conrad will call soon. He's in Jeddah. Don't ask!

I get a long pause on the phone when I tell him. I do see the value in considering things, which is what he always does, but I'm more mercurial, more trusting of my instincts.

'Are your first impressions so unerring?' is a question he's asked more than once — always with a smile, he finds me enchanting (it's his word, I don't mind it) — and I'm honest enough to admit they're not.

"You don't want to, do you?" is the surprise question I get.

"Do you?"

"No. But that's exactly why we should. This is Gerry keeping his enemies closer. We should do the same. Is anything different happening in your world?"

"Well, Merle and Gerry together is different, and that's my world now apparently, especially since she has him as a client again, but that's not enough to make up for the business she should be getting and isn't."

"She's distracted?"

"Yes, and Michael's depressed and morose."

"Ha! I was asking for news of something different."

He can be quite cutting, my Conrad. He always seems so mild, but...I'm thinking. *"There's a shake-up at Dickinson. You like him, don't you?"*

"Like and admire, yes, although I hardly know him. But what's he doing, and would Gerry know?"

What the fuck did I say to Merle at dinner last week? Nothing! Claudia didn't call until Tuesday. *"Well, not from me. I only heard two days ago, and I've not spoken to Merle since."*

"Gerry?"

"I've not spoken to Gerry since Ellen..." I hesitate. My sentence isn't complete.

"Exactly. You'd better say yes. It can only be Monday or Tuesday, can't it?"

"Er, yes." I'm feeling flummoxed. I don't know what this is about. I can still remember vividly how nervous I was, giving our message to Gerry, and how nervous he seemed, at the start of that conversation, until he realised what a wonderful opportunity, I was giving him. He was sat there, assuring me that none of my friends were in danger, while his wife was being strangled. And Conrad says we should have dinner with him.

"Couldn't you stay a little longer?"

This is a sweet little game he plays: if I did stay, he'd be busy. I'm not tired of it, and I have to get back out there anyway. "I'm behind as it is. I'm only staying until Tuesday for you. It wasn't for dinner with Gerry fucking Calvert."

"You can say no."

"You're saying we should go."

"What are your instincts telling you?"

"That you're fucking well right, again." *See, we're quite good together.*

"I'll talk to Henderson."

"Henderson?" *I need a word that's halfway between surprised and shocked.* "Have you kept in touch with him? Claudia doesn't like him, says he's not to be trusted."

"I can't think of anyone worthwhile who should be, maybe that says something about the company I keep — except you, my darling, of course. But yes, I've kept in touch. He's on a retainer now."

He's just a mite too cynical, is Conrad, but maybe that's the right position to take. Especially if we're going to have dinner.

12

Tania was in his doorway at one on Friday afternoon. "I'd assumed we'd be in here. You just seem to be able to access information better than I can. Well, especially if we're going to look at the other parts of the Dickinson business."

Will looked up and smiled. "See, I've got you halfway there already. Come in."

She sat down in front of his desk. He gestured to the sofas. "No," she said, "we might want to look at screens. It's easier for us if I sit here." That was true, and he'd put his notes into an easy format for them to consider on his centre screen. He already had them there.

"Lavinia?" he asked.

"I've briefed her, she's just waiting for my call, but I've been speaking to Claudia, we need a few minutes on that. Have you spoken to Peter?"

"Not about this, no." She looked puzzled by that. "He'll wait until I have something, or some things, worked out. He always like the illusion of choosing between two well-prepared options."

"Illusion?"

"He's never rejected any of my prime recommendations, even when he's given me a hard time about my choice. Anyway, Claudia, what gives? Is she still unsettled?"

"Less so now, I think. She's getting quite excited about some of it. Now she's worrying more about us."

"All of us?"

"Mainly about you and me, I think, and Peter, if you can't pull it off. She's satisfied herself that Alphonse will probably be OK, and will be a help in you managing the whole corporation."

"That's probably true, but I can't take anything for granted. I think he's fairly open with me."

She looked mildly troubled. "You know I'm open with you, don't you?"

"After Wednesday night, how could I ever doubt that? But I apologise, your question's a serious one, I know, so I'm going to tell you I trust you always to tell me what you're thinking, but I'm not treating your thoughts as commitments until we agree they are. OK?"

"That works for me. How open are you with me?"

He smiled. "Ha, I tell you everything you want to know, but there are some areas where I'm glad you don't ask questions. You've never asked about Peter's Trust, for example."

She was clearly nonplussed. "I've no idea what that is."

"Your father has one. It preserves family money separate from everything else. You know about his?"

"My father's?" Will nodded. "He's said there's something like that we should talk about some time, and that Mother and the law firm know about it. It didn't seem urgent."

"It isn't. But it's a good size, although it's much smaller than Peter's."

"How do you know about my father's?"

"Is that something you would want me to tell you?" He hoped she wouldn't.

"Distraction, isn't it?"

"It is, yes, but if you're coming on board you need to know something about Peter's because it will impact how the main foundation will be set up. He wants to roll it into that, leaving only enough to look after Claudia, Abbi and Jonah in case anything bad happens. Looking after is a term and an amount that would have been unimaginable to me a few years ago, and maybe to Claudia as well. Now, don't take this the wrong way, but your father's would support you and your sisters for a few sensible lifetimes and it's probably never even come up around the dinner table, has it?"

She laughed. "I only ever think of us as comfortable. We've all grown up expecting to work; and we do, as you've seen."

He smiled. "Unquestionably, but Claudia?"

"She was just asking me what I wanted. She didn't want me to feel I was under any obligation to do anything that didn't suit me — or my family. She's even offered to come to Atlanta and talk to Dad. I'd like that anyway, as would my parents, but it might be a useful deal-clincher if we're genuinely interested in pushing these things together." She raised her eyebrows at him.

"It's number four on my list," he nodded to the screen, "at the bottom, there."

She looked. She'd turned her chair sideways. "Which means it's your first choice." She smiled.

"I'm glad we'll be having arguments this afternoon, or we might be thinking too alike. Anything else from her?"

"Yes," she said slowly, "I won't say it was strange, but she made exactly the same two points as you did on Wednesday. If they do this, it has to be with them both pulling back — she won't let him even be chairman, because she knows he'll get dragged back in."

He nodded, and laughed. "Or push himself back in. Isn't she worried he'll want to be busier than that?"

"She would do, but they think Mei will want him around in China, for the medium term at least, she said. That sounds like one formidable lady."

He looked at her, shaking his head then smiling. She frowned at him. "Not unlike you. But you're taller, and blonde."

She gasped in mock horror.

"And you have a little more charm."

She narrowed her eyes. "I'd like to meet this lady, but anyway...." She was obviously relaxed.

"Second point?"

"Yes, she said that she hoped we'd find a solution that meant me staying and working, but with me on the board as well. That was what you meant, wasn't it? I didn't want to jump to a conclusion about that."

"That's exactly what I meant. I knew I'd have their support for the idea, but it's nice they're actively pushing for it." He paused. "There might be some pushback from the men in our circle, but it's early days. I'm seeing Henry next week. As you heard when I phoned him, even that won't be straightforward, but it's Tony I'm not looking forward to."

"Why?"

"Ha, because I find him completely unpredictable. I've no idea how he'll react. Henry will have told him something's up and he hasn't rung me or Peter. Not good signs." But he shrugged. "We'll see. It will be, as they say, an interesting challenge. Lavinia now?"

"Just one more thing. Claudia thought you should give Isobel a call."

He was puzzled. "Is that connected?"

"It must be in her mind, or she'd have waited and spoken to you herself, but Isobel's worrying about Michael and Merle. She said you'd know who she meant."

He sighed and nodded slowly.

"It sounds like an interesting story, but I'll leave it with you. Can you get Ruth to call Lavinia, now?"

He was still nodding as he called their PA.

***

It was an intense afternoon, but by six they'd fleshed out all four options and two still looked very attractive. "I'm not seeing Peter until Wednesday," he told the ladies, "but unless I have a horror moment when I work through them tomorrow…"

"Breakfast meeting?" Tania smiled at him and turned to Lavinia. "Their Saturday breakfasts are their weekend worktime."

Lavinia smiled but merely nodded.

"Well," he said, "if the ideas can't withstand Martha's scrutiny, they'll have no chance against Peter's."

"Oh, I don't know," said Tania, "We've seen them go head-to-head in Tokyo and there wasn't a clear winner, I didn't think. She made it look like he'd won, of course, he's the client, but I think he'd tell you he had to bend a lot to accommodate her. Anyway, I think you have two good alternatives, but I prefer our original. Lavinia?"

"Well," she drawled slowly, "I think number two would be most attractive if he wanted to maximise the initial injection into the fund. Then you'd get more independence from him, but more supervision from other shareholders, and less control over the three sectors. Would you struggle with that?"

It was an astute point. "I guess I'll know more when I've spoken to Henry, and Alphonse hasn't come back yet about what constitutes his five percent. When he works out it's a share in either of our two scenarios, he may persuade Peter and Claudia that my scheme doesn't meet the spirit of their commitment."

"And you haven't talked it through with Ned Kelly?"

"Ned Kelly?" asked Tania.

Will laughed. "Our Australian outlaw. You're right, and I have to get some input before I talk to Peter. I'll call him at the weekend. If you two have any second thoughts I do want to hear them, but we'll go with two and four, OK?" They both nodded. "Can I buy the drinks? Or are you headed back, Lavinia?"

"Jack's in Asia. I'm here for the weekend, so yes, I'd love a drink. You two should be celebrating anyway."

Tania looked thoughtful. "Several steps before that, aren't there? But I'd still love a drink, thank you. Martha?"

"I'll text her."

***

They were in the Blue Orchid, ordering their second drinks, before Martha joined them. She nudged Will after the hellos. "I would like to be next to Lavinia, my darling, please. Could you move round one?" He shuffled the drinks and switched seats. Tania looked intrigued. "I've been desperately eager for the chance to get to know you, Lavinia, but terrified."

Will hadn't been expecting her to tackle their pasts quite so directly, but it was often Martha's way, he admitted.

Lavinia seemed relaxed about being spoken to like that. "Because of the interest we share, or the man we both know?"

Martha laughed. "I'm also worried about what you know about me, but at least you've saved me some embarrassment by admitting it's an interest we share. I'm going to ask you about Noah Reid's later on, but not until I've had at least two of these." She raised the martini that Will had waiting for her.

"Oh, I think I'll need three before I could talk about that. And I hope you're not going to ask about Jack."

"No, I always knew it was a fling for a while." She looked to Tania. "Not everyone comes through unscathed, do they?"

"Claudia, you mean?"

"Yes, but we're not going to feel sorry for someone who has two of the most desirable men I've ever met doting on her." She turned to Will. "You're always my number one, my darling, you know that." She kissed his cheek, but turned to Lavinia. "How close do you stay to Networks now?" The two of them began an intense conversation in lowered voices while Tania talked to Will about her intention to talk to her father as soon as Will had some indication of Peter's agreement to the plan.

The bar filled up and was noisy enough to allow the two separate conversations to continue quite privately until Martha was nudging Will and pointing to the nearly empty glasses. He drew the waiter quickly to him. "Four more, Raul, please?"

"We want to drink to the dragon slayer." She raised her glass to Tania. "I've not met Henderson, but I know a lot about what he does, and beating him deserves a toast but, more than that," she turned to Will, "I hope you won't mind me saying this, my darling, but I was a little bit in love with Jack Stephens, and he was always good to me, truly, in that special way that Lavinia and I like men to be good to us." Lavinia looked mildly embarrassed, but was smiling and nodding. "But he did so deserve someone to call him a cunt. Here's to you!" She lifted her glass to Tania before finishing the martini.

"Here's to you also," said Lavinia, raising the glass with her.

"Now I've made what may be an inappropriate assumption, Lavinia, about where your interests lie."

"Oh, embarrassingly accurate, I'm afraid." Lavinia clearly felt among friends with Martha there.

"But I must stress that Ms Goody-goody wouldn't tell us any more than that you'd been to Noah's, nothing about what you may, or may not have done there."

"I met a perfect gentleman, Geoffrey was his name, I'm very pleased to say. But at the time I didn't have my imperfect gentleman waiting at home. I've never worked out whether it was Tania's, what shall we call it, her intervention?"

"Calling him a cunt, you mean?" asked Tania, smiling and enjoying the conversation.

"Yes, that," and Lavinia nodded, "or if it was me enjoying my independence. Anyway, we're fairly settled now, I think, but you can never really know, can you? I choose not to think about Asia when he's out there. It's not like he wouldn't know where to go, and I can't access the Network files these days, not that I'd actually want to."

"Yes, this one's off next week," said Martha, nudging Will, "and he has his own old network in London."

"I'm afraid both members of your audience are very well aware of not just my devotion to you, but also of my boring respectability," said Will, convinced that they were.

Tania and Lavinia both made mock sympathetic faces, seeming to console Martha. "But boring must be quite nice," volunteered Tania, but her laugh said more.

"How is Robert?" asked Lavinia, with a wicked smile.

"Bitch!" said Tania, laughing. She turned to Martha. "You probably saw him at Noah's."

"You didn't take him to Atlanta, chile, to meet yo' Mommy and Papa!"

He'd heard Martha do southern before. He didn't know how good it was, but it impressed him.

"Oh, I declare, he could meet Mommy and Papa — he's a chahmin' young man — but he ain't goin' neah mah sistuhs!"

"She was, like I said, very discreet about you, Lavinia, but she was pretty open about herself." Martha looked to be somewhat in awe of Tania. The stories had clearly impressed her.

"Well," said Will, "Noah looked like he'd be very happy to organise entertainment for you, my darling. And he might be interested in your input if he wants to set up a commercial enterprise."

"I think I'd rather just go as an interested amateur and meet Lavinia's gentleman."

Will felt fairly sure she was joking, but the other ladies seemed less convinced. Was there a serious desire lurking in the shadows? It had begun to feature in their night-time stories.

The conversation moved on, but the thought stayed with him. After the third round of martinis, there seemed to be some tacit agreement that the pairs would separate for dinner.

The Amarone they almost always had with the pasta at Marcello's meant that they both fell asleep quickly when they got home to bed.

He was awake by five, which was unusual, but not rare, and he needed to put his thoughts about the Dickinson future from yesterday's meeting in order to have something to present to Peter — or with Henry before that, for that matter. He didn't know how long he'd been at his desk, which opposed hers in the office they'd created in the second bedroom, when he felt her naked arms encircling his head. He turned to find her breasts in his face.

"I offer to have myself violently maltreated in Noah's Red Room, and instead of spanking me for my disgracefully naughty thoughts, you come in here and work. Are my charms failing so rapidly that even blunt provocation can't stir you?"

He loved her smiling hazel eyes and the voluptuousness of her naked body. It was a time to break off from what he was doing. He pushed his chair back and pulled her on to his knee. "We can talk about a proper punishment this evening. As you say, you deserve it, but right now, you're coming to bed to sit on my cock and you'll just be content with the paddle on your ass while I'm coming." His cock was already stiff against her hip as she kissed him deeply.

"Yes, master." She freed herself and stood up, pulling him by the hand. "Come on! Cock and paddle will have to do for now."

13

Peter always claimed to enjoy the journey home from China, to sleep well on the daytime flight and be back in the home time zone very quickly.

To Claudia, he never seemed anywhere near his normal self until the next day but, she had to admit, he normally got through the first evening without becoming too drowsy. He'd showered, and looked so fresh she could almost believe he'd had a normal easy day, and not got on a plane at four a.m., her time, that morning. Hannes had put out a simple cold spread for them. It was a lovely, early summer evening, the garden room still full of sunlight. "I haven't said anything to the guys," she said. "I didn't know if I was supposed to."

He took her hand across the corner of the table. "I don't know if you were supposed to."

"Peter!" She felt unusually exasperated.

He laughed. "Honestly I don't. I'm rather dependent on Master William coming up with a workable plan, but I'm desperately serious about making big changes. I've not been so bothered about what I'll be leaving until I've thought more about them."

She guessed what he meant, but she had to admit, she'd always been cautious when talking about Abbi and Jo with him. They liked him, and understood enough to admire him, were even happy that she was happy, although

Abbi saw a little more deeply into the complexities of that. "You do know they'll have their own ideas about what to do with their futures, don't you?"

He guffawed — she loved that booming laugh — "They have two examples in front of them of people who made their own minds up and went their own ways. Yes, of course I know that. We control no one other than ourselves, ultimately, and neither of them gives me any impression that they'll be different. But I also think you've done well enough with them that they wouldn't reject any opportunity out of youthful perversity."

She shook her head and smiled. "I've done well enough, have I? That's your towering endorsement of my performance in the only role I have that really matters." He fish-mouthed mutely until she laughed at him.

He recovered. "You know you always reject any compliment out of hand. I was trying to squeeze one in with an understatement."

"Oh, don't worry. It's also the role about which I compliment myself the least, but you have made a valid point…"

"Ah!" He leaned back in his chair after pouring more wine.

"I do see some of their friends rejecting opportunities that their parents proudly and expensively engineer for them."

"I don't want to do any more than let opportunities open if they're interested. They're provided for anyway."

She shook her head slowly. The trust was a subject that made her uncomfortable. It was unearned, as she saw it.

"I won't put you through more of that. I admire how much you hate the idea…"

"I don't hate it!"

"Ah, if I've nudged you towards mere discomfort, I'm making progress. But please see it as me doing it for myself. I know they're yours and Dave's" — he referred seldom to a man he'd never met, it sounded strange when he did — "but I didn't expect to have anyone like that I could care about. I almost wish I'd never said anything about it."

"You didn't. Will did, and he got into trouble." She was smiling, remembering what had been an awkward conversation.

Peter chuckled. "Ha, yes, from both of us. But now I'm happy that you know and disapprove. It's the excuse I make to myself for you not wanting to marry me."

"Peter, darling, five failures between us…"

"That's not the reason, though, is it?"

"No. It's that other thing. It's me wanting to have earned what's mine."

He squeezed her hand. "I know, I'm sorry, I'd promised not to mention it again, hadn't I?"

"Yes," now she squeezed his hand, "but I still want to know that you want to."

He stood up, leaned towards her, and kissed her lips. "Thank you."

"You are very welcome, now sit down, I've been thinking."

"Oh, dear!"

"There we have the honest indication of how much you truly value my input."

"Unfair, unfair! Do you want Will to tell you how much value you've added to that part of Dickinson since you've been running it? And don't blame Tania for all of that; that's your usual means of escape."

"No, I don't want him to tell me."

"Good, because I don't know yet, I'd like him to surprise me too, but I'm fairly sure we can put at least ten billion together to kick the foundation off."

"That's what I've been thinking about."

He leaned forward, elbows on the table. "You do have my undivided."

"Well, my hesitation initially was, again, about being given something." He wasn't reacting, he'd switched to Peter the Serious, as she called him at times like this. It was what she was expecting. "But it's just another job, isn't it?" Still no reaction, although she'd left a pause. "It's just a different way of acting directly on something more obviously worthwhile."

He was nodding. "That's my hope, but I'm told there are major difficulties in assessing what's truly, effectively worthwhile. I've been talking to a few people about working in the area, without giving away what I'm thinking of. I've just talked about the odd big donation, and everyone stresses how hard it is to make your efforts, and your money, really count. Some of these guys have given away big money and been disappointed at how little gets effectively achieved. So, you're right to see it as a job, and I couldn't think of anyone better to run it. I'm talking too much."

"Oh, no, you're not. I'm finally seeing it as something I could do now. Thank you."

Now he looked sceptical. "Really?"

"Yes, really." She frowned. "You're surprised?"

"You're not just saying that just to please me?"

She shook her head. "Why, oh, why does the most insightful man on the planet doubt his ability to assess the thoughts of the person he knows best?"

The blue eyes narrowed and looked directly at her. "Because the person I know best remains, I'm delighted to say, still a mystery to me." He relaxed and smiled. "But I am relieved now. I can only hope that Will's come up with some ideas by Wednesday. Has he booked that with you?"

"All afternoon at Sandy's. Is it just the three of us?"

"Yes, we're the only three involved in the Foundation, and he's only there because, if he's understood what I want, he'll be the guarantor of future income streams."

"Are you worrying about the others?"

He drank some wine and leaned back. "A bit. I'm not sure Alphonse has looked that particular gift horse in the mouth. We'll see what Will comes up with. But the funds boys usually have their own take on things. It's wrong to try and assess the views of people you hired for being radically different thinkers. I don't know what they'll make of it."

"Shouldn't you be talking to them?"

"I don't have anything concrete to discuss. It's important to me that Will comes up with a plan I can sell to them. They've got wind of something. Tony's called twice about nothing, that's unusual for him, and I've just stalled him, you know, always keeping the future in mind sort of stuff. He knows I'm bullshitting him, but he can't call me out on it."

No, she thought, Peter doesn't get trapped like that. "What about Mei and Senlin? Will you be pulling back from that?"

"Ah, you've spotted my security blanket. That's my way of staying involved in something so I don't interfere too much with your area."

"So, the plan to spend more time with me?"

"Is still in place. You might find it harder to commit to that than I will, once you get into things."

"We'll see, but you had a five-year plan for your role in Senlin…"

"Of which three years remain. It's funny, she talked about that last week, before Alphonse arrived. We'd talked before on the last trip. I don't know what's on her mind. It may be personal. She has an odd way of managing relationships. I think she's quite clever, she gets her emotional nourishment from people outside the business and outside the family — and she recognises that she needs things like that."

"Does she get emotional nourishment from you?"

He pondered, which was strange, the question wouldn't have surprised him. "Well, she does, of course, but it's almost like she's looking for a deeper emotional bond. I'm a poor father substitute, but that's not it, anyway — and I wouldn't say she's outgrown her own father, but he'd be very proud of how she's running his business. I don't know how he'd feel about how she treats her brothers," he chuckled, "but he was pretty shocking with them anyway."

"Is Lee doing OK? It never looked to me like the right fit, to put him back into the main business."

"Ah, interesting," he said slowly.

"What are you up to?"

"I want to hear what you'd do."

"But I'm outside it. I've studied the business, yes, but I'm not very aware of the markets…"

"Blah, blah, blah. Come on, you've had a thought, and it is a topic we've been discussing."

"It seems to me that what they think of as the core has been used too much as a cash cow. OK, funds and properties, resort interests included, are now bigger, but they shouldn't ignore the opportunities to expand out from the industrial group. Lee would be good at adding to that, he'd understand what they could move into, making use of what they're good at. I assume there's less pressure now to get money offshore. I understand why the old man was so keen, I think. He must have worried about how quickly things could be taken away. You're nodding."

"You're brilliant. Mei and I had been picking at that one for weeks."

"You hadn't." She smiled at him. "It just took you that long to get her to have the idea."

He laughed. "Guilty as charged."

"Why was it so hard? She's very bright."

"She doesn't value her brothers, and I think she's wrong. Anyway, we'd set Lee up to think about it, and he came back last week with some good ideas. I think she was quite won over, and he was immensely bucked — and they have a guy who'd do a better job than Lee of running the old business. He's a bit old school, but that's probably what it needs."

"And Lou?"

Peter looked pensive. "That's what Tony diverts to when I won't discuss the Dickinson future with him. He's quite bright and seems engaged."

"But?"

"Ha, yes, he's a little like Tony. Tony always tells you he goes where the maths tells him to, but he never seems more than one step away from the casino to me. Mei also thinks her brother's reckless. Well, she also thinks he's an arsehole, but she has the power and the money, so she's got some control. I have told her, by the way, that I may be reshaping what Dickinson does."

"Was that wise, when you don't know yourself what you're going to do?"

"Probably not, but she was, well, I'm not going to call it worrying, but she was keen to guarantee that she'd have my support for the whole five years I agreed with her father. Then she asked if I might get pulled into my own business more. I just said I was planning to do less, but I didn't know how I was going to organise that yet but, whatever I did, it would mean I'd fulfil my Senlin commitment. She seemed reassured."

"The man of his word. When was that?"

"The previous visit, why do you ask?"

"Oh, I just wondered how long it had been in your mind. I don't think we'd guessed, and there you were gossiping with your little Asian sweetheart."

"I don't think that's the role I'm in. If I ever felt paternal, it's there, but I enjoy working with her," he guffawed again, "more than most other people, I think, but she does get a lot of respect. I think it's genuine." He went on talking about the meetings and the people, leaving the little thought buzzing in Claudia's mind that there had been speculation about the Dickinson future, and the leak may have been in China.

14

I shouldn't have been surprised that Will called. I'd been pretty open with Claudia about Merle and Michael the other day.

I shouldn't have been delighted that he called, but I was. It reminded me, once again, of how those old feelings have merely been suppressed, and not extinguished. That's all you can do with old loves, isn't it? Well, there are a few where you think 'How could I ever have?' but those memories are just best avoided.

He'd given me notice. That may have been thoughtful — he'd texted yesterday to ask if I would be happy to talk on a Sunday — but it probably had more to do with him managing his own time, and, once he'd told me more about the Dickinson changes, and he needed to know of any relevant background urgently, it all fitted together. He wasn't just looking for a reason to call me. Damn!

I hadn't made any particular connections, but I realised that anything involving Gerry Calvert would, at the very least, be interesting to Dickinson, and Merle had made an impact on Claudia when she'd worked on their Barnes house — and Claudia had wanted the full story.

But Will? I need to give you more background, because Michael was once Will's boss. I'm only piecing it together now. Conrad and I have been discussing it over lunch. It wasn't an easy topic, because Boris was cooking and serving. Sandra stayed downstairs. It would have been impossible to discuss Gerry Calvert at all with her there.

Conrad, having given them the basement, likes to keep our mealtimes separate from them. It seems a little snobby to me, but I'm glad we have the arrangement.

I even think twice about having the Gerry discussion in front of Boris; he's had to deal with the man's heavies so I shouldn't expect him to be impervious or indifferent, but I have to accept that he mostly belongs in that parallel netherworld in which things get done differently. It's as if most of us live our lives floating on the water, playing in the sunshine, while all manner of dangers lurk in the aquatic world beneath. We're unaware of it until suddenly a shark or a sharp rock claims us.

Conrad's an amphibian, I suppose. Gerry may be, too, but most of his business, I suspect, is conducted under water, swimming with the sharks.

Will had called at noon. That was convenient for me, but I worry about him. I know it's seven in New York. "Don't you have anything better to do with a Sunday morning?" was my first gambit.

"I'll be going back to bed after this." I deserved that.

Nevertheless, 'that's my boy!' is what I think. I'm getting used to the idea of him with Martha, but she's very different from Merle. More suited to him? I think so. He and Merle? Well, he was young at the time, mid-twenties, and I think it was his first big love. I think Merle realised, after she'd run away and it had finished, that he'd been hers, too. Probably still is her only real big one — dangerous, that, and crippling. I hope you're all sophisticated enough to realise that 'the one that should have worked' is only ever an illusion. All great loves finish for a reason, usually before they reach boredom; by then you've forgotten it was a great love.

Could it have worked? He'd have made it work, but she would always have been selfish. It wouldn't really have been happy, I don't think. They'd ultimately have got bored. Him first, I expect.

I'm dotting around here. I should put this story together simply for you; remembering it all has helped me realise why Will is being so curious, but I can't work out where his thoughts are taking him.

He used to work in an investment company for Michael McKenzie. Michael ran the London office of a global outfit. Will was his star, and his numbers made the whole office performance look, well, acceptable, but barely. Michael concocted a scheme to make a killing out of some work Will was doing — for a Dickinson business, that's how that connection was established in the first place. Michael's scheme went seriously wrong. He even came to me one evening as the crisis hit, desperately worried. In all that wreckage, he'd managed to work out that Merle, his beautiful wife, had been having an affair with Will. I'd been there at the start of that. She'd invited me to their first lunch together. I think she'd foreseen the dangers and wanted me to...to do what? Protect, or facilitate? I honestly think she felt she could get into an enjoyable arrangement with him, but I could tell, right from the start, that they were hopeless with each other in that stupid, besotted way you can get in the early days. That precarious idiocy never deserts you, in my observation, at any age; so, good luck to you, my helpless romantics, it could still happen again.

But Michael managed to bully Merle into going away; he argued, entirely plausibly, that he could destroy Will's career for ever by pinning the blame for the debacle on him. Merle may have been acting to save Will's life and career, or she may have been acting to preserve her own highly affluent lifestyle. Her subsequent memories told her it was the former, memory can serve us like that, but she came to understand that the lifestyle's attendant miseries were a poisonous substitute for lost love.

Will, of course, had the consolation of my occasional ministry to help him through the next couple of years while his astonishing career with Dickinson was building.

Is he a lost love for me? No, don't be silly! I've said before, we're too alike — well, we're both too toppy in an area of major importance; we'd have had to have involved too many other people, and I always saw him as a candidate for monogamy — with the right person. Which that bitch obviously is! I jest, I jest...

But I do adore him still, and I'm thrilled when I hear his voice. I have to concentrate. This is a complex series of changes, potentially, and I'm slightly flabbergasted at what it might mean for him.

"So, you'd be running it all?" I ask, a little breathlessly.

"I'm trying to interpret Peter. I think he's keen to hand over."

"Claudia says you do that better than anyone. Interpret him, I mean."

"In the limited area of business dealings, I normally find us thinking alike, but you can help me understand a little embarrassment that might become threatening, it goes beyond business. Do you mind talking about the Ellen Calvert affair?"

"Why should I mind?"

"The little I've picked up suggests that it was very irregular and dangerous. We have a way of managing funding for exercises like that. I insist on seeing every Henderson invoice, for example, and he knows he'll get a call from me if anything looks too interesting. You know who I'm talking about, don't you?" I mumble a noise of agreement. *"Well, by his normal standards, the costs were small, but I did ask him — and he said your Conrad was involved and spent more on the exercise than he did. Is that true? Involved, I mean, I'm pretty sure you don't know what these things cost. The other point Henderson mentioned was that Calvert funds some interesting operations, and they'd have to go through Michael. I see him as a lost soul, but I still have an emotional link."*

"To both of them?"

"It's only Michael that's of interest. He'd be handling funny money."

"Are you sure? That it's only him you're interested in, I mean."

It's too long a pause before he answers, "Yes, it's only Michael. You're looking after her anyway, aren't you?"

"I rather think Gerry Calvert is taking over that role."

Now there's an even longer pause. He's thinking and considering, like Conrad does, but this is much more than that. Eventually, I get, *"No, that's not something that would worry me. But there's something smelling bad about this. I can't put my finger on it yet."*

"And it's nothing to do with Merle and Gerry Calvert."

"No, not that," he says, much too quickly. "I'm probably worrying about nothing but, the way Henderson described it, it looked like it might be an open issue for a not very nice person, and I've no idea what consequences it could have."

"Maybe I'll know more next week, we're having dinner with them on Tuesday."

"What! Who? Who with whom?" That was more of a reaction than I'd expected. "Who's set that up?"

"Well, Merle asked me, but it's obviously Gerry who's prompted it."

"Did it strike you as odd?"

"Very. After all the fallout then, and it's much too complicated and sordid to go through everything with you."

"Did that start with Sandra's mistreatment?"

You see, I hadn't forgotten that she'd helped me educate him, and neither has he. I had told him about the incidents, and he had wanted to help, but I reassured him long ago that, with Conrad and Boris helping in their different ways, she was better off forgetting her infatuation with 'that lovely Will,' as she refers to him still — not infrequently, either.

"That was the critical time, but I'd stopped having anything to do with Gerry socially long before then, and it was a relief to lose him as a client — except that I don't lose clients, and he tried to damage my reputation, but this isn't helping you, is it?"

"Oh, a lot, actually, but none of it's making me feel any easier. So, what's prompted dinner?"

"We don't know. We both think it's odd. Conrad's only agreed because he thinks Gerry is 'keeping enemies closer,' he says and, according to Conrad, we're now doing the same."

"Your Conrad sounds like a smart man."

"Because he has me, you mean?" *This is getting too serious; I need to lighten it.*

"Of course. Why else?"

Oh, Will, you charming fucker. "What do you know about him?"

"More than you probably think I should." He hesitates. "I hope you're not going to mind me admitting that I made it my business to make sure you were all right."

"Oh, you perfect fucking sweetie, of course I'm not. And you'd have told me everything about anything suspicious, of course." *I'm teasing a little, but it's quite important to me.*

"Yes, if I'd thought you needed to know, but I expect you're already aware that he has some interesting associates among his business connections."

"Oh, Will, it's possible I've even played with one or two. No, probably not, when I think about it. I'm aware that he knows some nasty people, yes, but he keeps me away from them."

"Well, I'd just concluded that you were safe with him — and that he keeps his own operations clean enough, by the way. I'd like to meet him."

"My darling William, he has absolutely zero interest in meeting you." *That's shocked him a little, but I'm still teasing, mostly. "You are younger, taller, unquestionably more handsome, and you're charming." I can't really tell if it's a stunned silence, but it's working, I think. "He just has a better sense of humour!" We're both laughing a lot before I follow up with, "No, not even that, really, but we needn't go into the areas where he and I are better suited, just like you and Martha are. No, I would set something up, my love, the only reason he didn't come to the dinner we had with Martha was that he wanted me to get through that on my own. I think he'd like to meet, but I'm off on Wednesday. If you're serious, I can ask him if he'd like to meet you on his own. I have no idea what all this nonsense is about, but it's bugged you, it's bugging Conrad, and I think it's triggered alarm bells with Claudia. Shall I see what he thinks?"*

"I'd be grateful, but I'm sorry I'll be missing you."

"That certainly goes for me. Now get back to bed and deal with that woman."

"Oh, it's tea and tenderness this morning."

"Interesting night last night?" I can picture him smiling, but he will say no more.

"Again, I'm very sorry I'll be missing you, but you will be careful, won't you?"

"Of course, and I'll talk to Conrad. 'Bye, my sweet."
And the conversation's finished too soon.
Ah, love! You have to have it to lose it.

15

The place in Fulham looked, from the outside at least, modest, and Henry could afford something much more lavish, thought Will, but the conversion, already established before his first visit there all those years ago, had made it a sizeable family home. The glass structure at the rear occupied almost all of what had been the garden and gave a very large space for all family activities, leaving Henry a small room to serve as an office at the front.

His official business residence, in the Sandy Nicholls office off Berkeley Square, he seldom used, and he'd had no trouble persuading Will to come to Fulham for the meeting and the subsequent dinner.

Will had first met Henry when he'd been asked to work on a project for him eight years before. Henry had made contact via Michael McKenzie, Will's then-boss and alumnus of Henry's school — 'don't remember him' had been Michael's comment when setting up the conversation, 'but their GKD Fund is a rising star, you'd better see what they want.'

Henry hadn't been surprised to be remembered so dismissively — 'He was head boy when I started, but it was a contact point for me, and I knew you were doing good work in that place,' had been Henry's phlegmatic response. His own views on McKenzie himself were more damning: 'He runs an old-fashioned business, it's a doomed model, that old school connections crap, ironic that I'm using it myself, but I'm only interested in you, I can see what you've been doing.'

The project had been very lucrative for Henry's fund, but Michael's attempt to circumvent the arrangement had been disastrous. He'd tried to make profits for his own business out of the activities, and his subsequent attempts to pin responsibility on Will had proved only briefly successful. Will lost a job and a lover in the wake, but was rescued by the Dickinson connection, and by the support of Isobel — and of Henry and Rachel, who had the only home he could retreat to for warmth and sympathy, and for the distractions provided by the then three-year-old Archie.

He'd visited often enough for Archie, now eleven, to remember why he was happy to see Uncle William, but not often enough for Will to be less than startled by how quickly the children were growing. Miranda had been only 'on the way,' when all the drama had unfolded.

The welcome from Rachel was as warm as ever; the smile followed by the long hug and 'We don't see enough of you. When are you going to bring Martha again?' Rachel, having seen into his Merle feelings at the time, had taken a solicitous interest in his love-life ever since, but only ever from the perspective of wanting to see him 'settled and happy.' Henry's brusque 'we've obviously put you off having children' may have been a more accurate reflection of the couple's true attitude when Will had first told them that he'd fallen for an older woman. He doubted whether either had guessed at the particular bond he and Martha shared. Henry had never been an attendee at

Peter's old parties, he didn't think — neither had Will, but his curiosity, and Martha's history, had made him research the topic. Henry, however, was dry and cerebral and seemed peculiarly well-defined: a husband and father whose commitment to family was undoubted, if not effusively obvious, but whose obsession with work was very clear — Rachel rolled her eyes, still smiling, when Henry ushered him into the office with a 'best get started, the monsters will be here before four — and we'll lose you to them for a while, but don't worry, they'll get bored with you quickly enough.' 'Then you're mine for an hour, Will,' said Rachel. She'd always been easy to talk to — even when they strayed into work as a topic. Peter always described her as 'the greatest loss to my business — and all I get is Archie as a pseudo-nephew.'

Rachel managed their private investments and, even Henry admitted, was more successful than their GKD Fund, 'but she isn't rung a dozen times a day by clients wanting to know why we're still in this or haven't left that — I'm looking for an AI program for the algorithms to explain what they do directly to the clients — if they call us, they get a robot.'

If Henry was going to be edgy about the Dickinson changes, there was at least a chance of a more sympathetic hearing over dinner when Rachel would be present, and the discussions would inevitably continue.

But now she was holding his arm and kissing his cheek. "I'll let you two get on, but thank you for the flowers, they arrived this morning."

"You're very welcome," said Will. The email to the local florist had become a habit over the years — one he'd never forgotten on key dates.

Once he was alone with Henry, however, the warmth had evaporated, and the tension of the call ten days ago returned. "You'd better walk me through the story again." Will was sensing hostility, but Henry was always cool and rational in his approach to everything.

"This kicked off when Peter finally agreed that he should take a long-term view of the business evolution that recognised what he personally would want to do. It was easy to accept the five-year projections of each of the three areas, even allowing for your sand-bagging." That would have served as a good-natured tease in different circumstances, but Will was using the jibe to provoke Henry into revealing more of his current attitude.

"You make the typical planner's mistake of banking possible upsides while ignoring risks, just like your old friend McKenzie."

The three thoughts that were provoked — I don't bank upsides, I never ignore risks, and McKenzie was certainly not a friend — were registered and quickly stored without comment; Henry was marking territory. This was feeling like a confrontation.

"It's not long since we put that plan together and I don't think we want to revisit it." That got only a steady stare from Henry, not even the barest nod. Henry had agreed to the projections at the time, as had Alphonse, as had Claudia and Tania, who'd even offered 'more growth with more investment' — as she did every year. Only Tony had contributed his perennial 'How the fuck do I know?'

"I'm not even going to say that I was seeing Peter as disengaged from the planning. I think he's taken the Senlin connection very seriously and he seems to me to be trying to make the collaboration as productive as possible." He looked to Henry for a comment but, in the atmosphere that had taken hold, he expected none and the pause became one only of politeness. "But in five years he'll be sixty-seven and I've been trying to get him to think about what he really wants to be doing then, or at least to think about the business functioning beyond his working lifetime. Plus, we've had a few years of both he and Claudia saying they want more time with each other."

"And is that serious or relevant?"

Will's view was that it was probably both, but it wasn't a topic that should distract them. "I think it's serious and relevant that he should think about what he personally wants to do and how that relates to how the whole corporation should be run."

"And are you the man to tell him what he wants?"

"You know how he likes to work. He likes to seed ideas, but then choose which to follow once someone's worked out how they could develop."

"And you're developing the ideas?"

"That's generally my role. It's what we did together when we worked out how we'd reshape the place when we sold off half of the Group, and when we organised the tie-in with Senlin."

"But all the alternatives then had Peter running everything, including, effectively, Senlin. Do the new alternatives have you running it all?"

"The alternatives have as a common element only that Peter is the major shareholder or investor, but has no direct involvement in running the organisation."

"Do they all have a chairman CEO running everything?"

"No." Although both the two preferred, of the four he'd worked through with Tania and Lavinia, did. The other alternatives had the three sections of Dickinson Enterprises running independently. Those options could remain alive for the purposes of the discussion with Henry. They might, ultimately, be preferred by Peter, but Will's view, supported by Martha — who always discussed issues and problems on their merits — was that Peter would be less distracted by having one head above all businesses, rather than risk being pulled into any one of three, particularly if the Dickinson businesses were to fulfil their role of sustainably providing further investment for the Foundation. Martha had said nothing about who that should be beyond 'there's only you who could do it,' echoing Tania's — and his own — view.

"And all this, whichever route you go, is designed to feed the maw of a charitable foundation?"

"I think that's what Peter's most comfortable with, and Claudia's gradually getting comfortable with that. As you know, she has a reluctance to be the recipient of charity." He stopped there. He knew something of the struggle Peter had in trying to settle more on Claudia and her children, but that was irrelevant to today's discussion, he thought.

Not so irrelevant for Henry, though, apparently. "Do you think that's genuine, or a clever pose?"

He at least, as was his usual habit, put the question neutrally.

"I'm personally convinced it's genuine, but it's Peter's conviction that matters."

Henry seemed to spend a long time reflecting on that. "The idea of him starting a foundation, how long's that been kicking around?"

"I only got him to agree to look at it a couple of weeks ago."

"So, his chats with Meitang a month ago covered none of that stuff?"

"I don't know what he discussed with Meitang last month. The first serious discussions I had were two weeks ago." Will trusted Henry, he thought, but that didn't mean he thought Henry was above using tactics to establish facts or assess opinions. "I had the impression I was walking through an open door, maybe she'd been pushing to know how long he would commit to help her. I think it was a surprise to Claudia." Will was being, as ever, relatively open. Relatively was not naïvely, he told himself, but it also meant never being deliberately misleading. If people leapt to false conclusions, he would correct those, but only if he was able to establish them.

If Michael McKenzie had been open with him all those years ago, he could have spared himself a disaster. Working for Gerry Calvert became the only option open to him.

"Have you heard anything about his Meitang conversations?" Will asked. It sounded to him that Henry had picked up something.

"Not directly. When we speak, it's about funds and new clients," he chuckled mirthlessly, "or about when Rachel will come back to work."

"I always get the impression she has more fun acting independently."

"I think that's a pretty accurate assessment. Controlling hundreds of times more money doesn't appeal as much as controlling ours. Do you know what she returns?"

Will did. She let him see her data as the price of being able to ask his advice on odd, rare occasions. He assumed Henry knew. But perhaps he didn't. "She averages seventeen percent, with a low of nine, but she didn't start until after the financial crisis when you and Tony made your biggest killings."

Henry shrugged, but still looked glum. "You seem to be better informed than I am."

"I doubt that. We just chat occasionally. I expect we'll talk about it later. She uses her own models, she says."

Henry shook his head. "I don't think that's decisive, they're all algorithm based, but she reads a lot about the businesses, she's not just number driven, and she tries to put herself in the minds of the key players, and uses what she calls insight."

"A bit like Peter does."

"Yes, but we can't run a business like that. We're not thanked if we guess right, and we're pilloried if we make a wrong call." He paused, but was going to say more, Will thought. "Only half-pilloried if we show our calls were data driven and others make the same mistake. Anyway, yes, she does better than we do — she's probably a better psychologist."

"What does she think of Peter's plans?"

"I haven't discussed anything with her, but you were telling me he doesn't have a plan until you give him one."

"Starting with an open mind is always his first step, and maybe he's been playing with some thoughts with Meitang." Will didn't really think that, but something was on Henry's mind. "You said you'd heard nothing from him directly. Have you picked anything up indirectly?"

Henry shrugged, but seemed reluctant to speak.

"Has Tony said anything?"

"About this, you mean?"

'Of course', would have been the obvious response, but Henry was being unwilling — or provocative.

"Well, I was hoping the two of you might have touched on what you and I spoke to you about ten days ago. I've tried to get Tony. He hasn't responded to my calls. But anyway, I wondered what you'd picked up out of Shanghai."

"Only that he'd been chatting to Meitang." Henry wasn't going to say more. The friendliness, so welcoming during their initial project, and continuing until Will was established in Brussels, had been cooling since the time of the divorce restructuring, when the new shape of Dickinson had been largely engineered by Will, and his influence on Peter had become so much more evident.

"That Peter had been chatting to Meitang, or that Tony had?"

"Well, they both have, as it happens. You know she won't talk to her brother, or he won't talk to her. They really should sort that out. If Peter pulls back, that's not going to be productive. Tony listens to her — he says they're both bright — but he doesn't have the nursemaid talents of our illustrious leader. I think little brother Lou is aware of where the power lies, but that doesn't make him any more diplomatic." Henry at least seemed to be finally engaging with the topic.

"He's making a good contribution to your business, though, is the impression I always get."

"We've been pleasantly surprised. He understands the models, doesn't fuck about with any spurious intuitions, and he's been pulling in business. As you know, we've had two very good growth years in terms of the client base. He just doesn't like her asking questions."

"You none of you seem to like that. Doesn't it go with the territory? Would he want a robot to talk to her, too?"

There was a time when Henry might have smiled, but not today, "You alluded to it before: explaining is wasted time, but giving confidence is a necessary part of pulling more funds in, that's part of the role. Peter's money and his charm are two more elements."

"Neither would be disappearing," he said but Will felt awkward that his comment was inaccurate enough to be almost untruthful.

"So, you're leaving all his money in the Funds. That makes sense, he adds more value directly for us than he does in Property and Group."

Will assumed that was a ploy. Henry would never be able to fake enthusiasm, but here he'd used sarcasm anyway, probably seeing through Will's misrepresentation. That needed to be corrected. "He would need to take significant amounts out of all three to create a meaningful foundation."

"Would you IPO the Group?"

"That's in all the alternatives. Tania's quite relaxed about that. She thinks the unit heads will go for it: they can capitalise their shares but keep their jobs."

"Smart woman, Tania." Again, Henry was expressionless. He probably wasn't being sarcastic this time, Will decided. "What's the timing on all this?"

That seemed like a genuine question, "I'll know more when I talk to Peter and Claudia tomorrow. I was hoping to get yours and Tony's views before then."

"Well," finally Henry seemed ready to engage, "we'll miss his money, if he pulls a lot out, and we'll miss his connections when we're trying to pull more in. From what you're saying, it sounds like we should treat him as no longer available…" That was put as a question.

"Oh, there'd be something, but that's probably a fair assumption in assessing any alternative," Will said.

"If you can IPO early, next year, say, and get started with the injection of funds from that, then only slowly deplete from the funds, we'd have the best chance of adapting. You'll take a while to get the foundation moving anyway, won't you?"

"Well, it would be Claudia and Peter getting it moving, not me, but what you're saying makes sense." It was also the first constructive comment of the day, Will thought.

"What about property and resorts? What's Alphonse doing? Has he just been told?"

There's an ambiguity about 'just' thought Will — only just heard, or merely been informed — one it was best to ignore. "He was in New York with me the day I rang you."

"And he's happy?"

"He's open-minded."

"More complicated for him, isn't it?"

Will would have preferred not to react. "Why do you say that?"

"We're not going to get far today, master William, if we play silly buggers with each other. I really expect you to understand the point."

"You could be talking about Peter's offer to Alphonse, or about Alphonse's relationship with Claudia."

Henry looked slightly startled. He probably hadn't expected Will to be quite so frank. He went on nevertheless "What's his deal with Peter?"

"At the moment, he gets five percent of Peter's property."

Henry was thinking. "As buildings, or as a share?"

"Not yet specified, but I'll be proposing a share. We need to keep him on board, tie him in."

Henry was nodding slowly, and smirking slightly in apparently grudging admiration, "Well done, young William, that would keep you in Claudia's good books," he paused, "and Meitang's, I hear."

"So, you have been talking to Tony." That was the gossip that Tony would feed off; Henry would see it merely as useful intelligence. Will knew Alphonse and Mei were close, but also knew that their relationship would not be one he could easily understand.

Henry was looking more relaxed. "Well, what's going to be our equivalent of the Alphonse sweetener? What are you proposing there?"

"I'm not proposing anything. That was Peter's idea anyway." Will didn't want to get trapped into that conversation. His own view was that Peter had contributed mostly just money to properties — although he knew Alphonse always liked to use Peter as a sounding board on big decisions, but Peter had personally brought lots of business to funds and made GKD much bigger than Tony and Henry could have achieved on their own. He would offer them nothing, thought Will, but Peter might take a different view. "I take your point, though, about managing the transition slowly to give you the least disruption."

"Minimising disruption isn't being given five percent."

"You're comparing apples with blankets. Those are two completely different situations." Will didn't want them starting a conversation with Peter in that way.

Henry was drawing his breath in with a hiss. "Not revealing something of your own attitude there, are you, William? Is that telling me something about what you're recommending?"

"I'm only planning, following this conversation, to build a slow transition into the alternatives. Everything else is between you and Peter. He's said nothing to me about any special arrangements."

"I can't imagine my old friend Tony is going to be happy."

"But what does Mr Spenlow think?"

Finally, Henry laughed. "Because Mr Jorkins won't answer your calls, you mean?"

Will smiled and nodded.

"Well, young master Copperfield, Mr Spenlow here rather thinks that we're powerless to prevent these changes. The great Mr Dickinson has been good to us, we'll have to see what he proposes. So, what are these alternatives you're working on?"

And one simple allusion had triggered the real Henry, the cool thinker who could now look dispassionately at Will's four options while keeping his own thoughts and feelings securely locked away. By the time the tentative knock on the office door came about five minutes after the front door had crashed open, Will had a more robust set of options and had built stronger cases for the two he'd originally planned to let wither — but these were the two which would give Funds more independence, of course.

"Come in," called Henry. Miranda came in first and threw herself at William almost before he'd had a chance to stand.

"Uncle Will, Uncle Will, I didn't know you'd be here." He picked her up and hugged her but kept to her 'no kisses' rule. He set her down to greet Archie, hanging back tentatively.
"I know I shouldn't say, Archie, but, my goodness, you have grown again. Can I still have a hug?" He opened his arms to let the boy shuffle shyly towards him.

***

Miranda commandeered Will for most of the next hour but he managed to squeeze away for a while to be heavily defeated on Archie's car race games. Henry offered Will the office for the hour over teatime to let him catch up with other business. Rachel came to collect him when the hour had passed, and Henry slid furtively in. Rachel smiled and shook her head at him. "It's his hour for the children…"

"They don't want me," he waved an arm dismissively.

"This is, of course, true," she said, closing the door on him.

Miranda rushed up and grabbed Will's hand. "Come with me, Will…"

"What did we say? He'll say goodnight after your bath?"

"With a story?"

"With a story," said Will, fairly sure she'd be engrossed on her iPad by then — much as Archie probably already was. Miranda went upstairs, leaving Rachel and Will in the kitchen.

"A quick précis, please, he's agitated but isn't saying why."

"That doesn't sound like him…" and they both laughed loudly.

16

It's going to be Mosimanns, apparently. I've not been there for a while. "A lot of my Arabs like it," says Conrad on our way there in the car.

It's discreet, it's the private dining rooms that appeal to them, and to Gerry, of course — and I'm quite relieved I shan't have Conrad shushing me, as he tends to do when I'm drinking and we're in open restaurants. But I actually plan to be careful tonight.

They're there before us — Gerry's the host — but the first surprise is not how fabulous she looks, but how decent he does. He's always looked after himself, or had himself looked after, perhaps I should say, but there was always a ridiculous flamboyance about how he dressed, but tonight he could almost be Conrad. Neither is tall enough to be elegant — no Alphonse here — but smart, certainly, and wearing well-chosen ties with their beautiful suits!

In her heels, Merle's the tallest of us all. She looks radiantly imperious and Gerry, normally the peacock, is merely the proud consort. "You look absolutely wonderful," says my Conrad to her — I'll stab him later — but Gerry's not doing too badly: 'more enchanting than ever' will do for starters. But the biggest shock, for me, is the two of them together. There does seem to be something!

Who's kidding whom? I have to push their playtimes to the back of my mind. I don't think they were that frequent, and they were certainly disrupted when she fell in love with Will, but tonight it's holding hands to guide her to her seat and those too long glances of new love — or of subterfuge. That would be him; she can't fool me.

"I want to rebuild bridges," says Gerry as soon as we've sat, and our champagne has been refreshed. Well, there had to be an ostensible reason.

"You must mean with Isobel," says Conrad calmly.

Gerry manages a sly smile. "Of course. I'm pleased that your interest in my Belgrade connection didn't do any harm to our relationship."

Conrad waves that away nonchalantly, "Just doing research. We can't be too careful, can we?"

I don't know what they're thinking but Gerry seems keen to move on.

"There have been times when I haven't been careful enough," he says, and sips some champagne — the pause to make sure he has our attention — "I managed the Sandra situation badly, and I did some silly things in consequence, one of which was losing London's best designer, so I'm here asking, if not for forgiveness yet, but at least to be given another chance." He's on my left and I'm getting an intense stare.

I need to be careful. "I understood you've already re-established a business relationship. Don't we have a contract?" I look to Merle, mainly to escape the stare. She nods.

"We had a lot more, and could have again. I still have a number of properties I want looked at, but I would like to feel it all has your blessing, and the work has your imprimatur."

"It will always have that if Merle is on it." That's true insofar as I check everything — there's a weekly parcel of fabrics comes to the Hong Kong office when I'm there and furniture gets approved only when I've seen real samples — or know the supplier well and like the photos. "I know we're busy here, but if it's planned thoroughly, we'll manage."

Now the pair of them touch hands and smile at each other. I get a very brief, sceptical glance from Conrad, but then we get into a discussion of Gerry's properties. "But I am doing less here. Asia seems a much more active area. You must find that, Isobel. I hear your Hong Kong office is very busy." I do an autopilot thing on life in Asia. It is exciting, and I'm a natural enthusiast, but I'm wondering what the point is, especially when he moves on and asks Conrad about whether he is looking at the area. Then we get a little tour de force from Conrad which is, as far as I can tell, just the purest bullshit. I have no idea what game he's playing, let alone Gerry.

It's in the ladies, after the main course, when I get the 'Gerry admires Conrad immensely.' There may be an element of truth in that, but it's not a line worth pursuing — she wouldn't know what he really thought. "He seems to be admiring you immensely. When did that all start?"

"We've always had a bit of a thing for each other."

That's not quite a lie; in these circumstances, I'm just going to call it flagrant self-deception. "Well, you used to enjoy your playtimes."

There's a flash. "Don't..." *and she stops herself,* "he organised things well for me..."

I can risk a little scowl; she can't expect me to forget or ignore everything — and she had told him to 'fuck off' on the Sandra night and lost us the business.

"Mostly, anyway. That was one bad night, aren't you going to forgive him for that?"

"Of course. He's apologised. We need business." *I don't need to remind her of other bad episodes when Gerry's sadist has edged out his top. I need to find out what this is about.* "But I hadn't seen you as more than play partners."

Now she's relaxing a little. "We weren't really but then we started the dinner thing and it just seemed to develop. I think he was a little lonely — and you know I was." *Probably true, on her part.*

For him? I look at her, finishing the lippie, and she is a very beautiful woman. Why not, I think.
Because it's Gerry, I think.

***

"What was that shit about your Asian plans?" *I ask Conrad as soon as the car's turned the corner on them waving goodbye to us. I don't ask the question aggressively, and I'm getting one of his slow smiles anyway.*

"Well, it's a vibrant region; you're very enthusiastic about it; I really should be looking at it more closely. I need to move away from the Middle East; it's getting too hard to make money. And Gerry's looking to do more outside Russia. Well, away from his Russian contacts, I should say. I didn't prod too deeply, but a lot of the London *properties are Russian money. I can understand his Asian interest."*

"Can you? Really?"

"No, not yet, but I had to sound interested to keep him talking. I assumed that was why you were so long in the ladies."

"It was, but I was researching too."

"And?"

"No, not and! You haven't finished, what are you doing about Asia?"

"I'll have a look. Peter D seems to be doing well out there, as does your boyfriend."

"Alphonse is not my boyfriend. You and I are a couple. I, at least, am taking that seriously." He's teasing, I think, but he's not getting away with that so lightly. "If I were going to have a boyfriend, I'd want it to be the man you're having dinner with on Thursday."

"Ah, the mysterious Will. The one who did all the research on me."

I'm a little shocked; shocked that he knows. "How…" I don't know what I want to ask.

"He didn't hide it, particularly, and I only had to ask Henderson anyway. William was obviously worrying about the company you were keeping. I thought it was sweet, and he couldn't have found anything too bad, you're still here."

"Probably only because I haven't done my own research!" But he's holding my hand now and kissing my fingers.

17

Claudia loved the Sandy Nicholls office and had a twinge of disappointment when Brodie Gunter Jeavons had outgrown its space there. But they were only a walk away and she knew she would court trouble if she didn't arrive early and spend her ten minutes with Sandy, whose boyish, bald-headed ebullience she always found stimulating. She always looked back on the two hours of their first meeting, when she outlined her plans — hopes? — for her consultancy, as being the most influential and affirmative of her life. She was effectively his boss now, but she always felt the junior in the relationship — not that he was ever anything less than respectful, even deferential, when they were together. She had to remind herself sometimes that he was instrumental in helping Peter make her Group head five years ago. It was always the warmest hug when he closed his office door behind her.

"Am I allowed to say I'm thrilled about this?" he asked as soon as she sat down.

He got her narrow-eyed look. "As long as you tell me exactly when you first heard about 'this', as you're calling it." But she smiled at him, knowing he'd be honest.

"Peter talked to me last week from Shanghai, and Will was here yesterday."

"And you're thrilled about what, exactly?" She got a raised eyebrow from Sandy. She knew why, and she didn't enjoy the caginess she felt she had to employ with everyone. Sandy at least always seemed to understand its necessity and extended a grudging tolerance to it.

"I want the two of you enjoying each other's company more — and I do think it's an excellent move, for him especially. Everyone should be able to see beyond their own lifetime, and it's wrong to use children as your excuse for not doing that."

"You don't think he's doing that a bit with this move? He's hoping he'll open something up for my two."

"That's my point; they're not even your two."

Sandy liked to provoke — 'the most productive discussions, my dear' — but this went too far, she thought. "Explain!" came out rather tartly, but she got only a smile as a response.

"They're their own two already. Well, certainly Abbi is, I greatly enjoyed meeting her last summer. Jo is, of course, only a boy. I've never met a male under twenty-three who had a clue what he should be doing; not one with a brain, anyway. I think they'll be proud of what you open up, but it'll be longer than Peter thinks before they'll even think of joining you." He paused thoughtfully. "Probably longer than you think, too."

She felt more relaxed now. "Oh, I think you're almost certainly right, about Abbi. Well, about Jonah, too, and what you say goes for all of his mates — except in one area, of course, where they all seem a little too focussed." They chuckled with each other. "But you'd be good with it all? For your business, I mean."

Now it was his turn to look cagey. "Are you asking about my personal options?"

She hesitated. "I hadn't got that far, really, it's all very new to me. This afternoon will be the first fleshed-out plans from Will. Did he talk about that yesterday?"

Sandy seemed to accept that and relaxed a little. "As I understand it, he's working on four options, any of which I could live with. I think his favoured two are the better ones…"

"Is that how he's described them?" That would surprise her.

"No, of course not," said Sandy, with a big smile, "but those are the sort of things I'm supposed to work out. I get a little money, or a lot of money, and I get a bigger organisation to run, or a much bigger organisation, but I deal with Will, and Tania, maybe, rather than you and Peter, which…" and he shrugged.

"Would you be OK with us just being friends?" She liked him so much, she couldn't imagine not meeting, but he surprised her. He stood up. There were tears in his eyes, his arms were open. "Claudia Brodie, my darling woman, you'd better give me just one huge fucking hug!"

She laughed, stood up, and wrapped her arms around him.

After a while he pulled away suddenly and retreated to his seat, scrabbling for his hankie to blow his nose heavily. She felt nonplussed but a huge smile accompanied his "Please sit down, Mrs Brodie, that's quite enough emotion for one day." He chuckled. "Well, that was a month's worth for me. But the point is, I could make anything work, and I trust the three of you to make a sensible decision. I personally think," and he smiled again as her brow furrowed, "don't look at me like that, you know you're getting my opinion anyway," — that was true, she'd never managed to stop him — "I think it would be best all round, if Will becomes sole head."

She nodded slowly, still fighting to keep an open mind. "Well, I'd better get on and see what he's got to say. But I'll have one more cuddle before I go." She was feeling emotional too and knew a cuddle would help.

***

"You normally just give me two choices, my boy."

"Peter!" Claudia said sharply, making both the men laugh. He was supposed to have dropped that term. Maybe he had something on his mind by it.

"He's just pretending to give me four, aren't you, Will?"

"Giving you four, or pretending?"

Peter could scowl and smile at the same time. "You've done a manful job of trying to hide your preferences, but I have absolutely no problem accepting something even if it's also the best for you personally. The dimensions are: one business unit or three, and a fast transition or slow one. Isn't that what it comes down to, in essence?"

Will nodded slowly. That description clarified the issues for Claudia, who could still be surprised by how the two men saw connections so quickly and tuned in to each other.

Peter turned to her. "How do you see the problems, my love?"

He would have his own views already but needed her perspective to get his own thoughts clear; it was how they worked. "I'm only just beginning to get my mind around what we'll be doing, but I can't imagine wanting all the funding available immediately, unless you're keen to make the point to everyone that it's going ahead…"

"You think that would be wise?" he interrupted her.

"I think we're all worrying about the attitude of the funds boys, but, if we free up money from an IPO next year, we'd look silly if we didn't ask them to manage business as usual until we're really ready to deploy their contribution. That's also the case with Alphonse, to a degree, although we wouldn't park investment there. We should target what we want out of the areas in three years and ask them to manage towards that. I just wish you'd been able to pin Tony down."

"I haven't had anything to pin him down with yet," said Peter with a shrug.

"Are you any nearer now?" asked Will.

Peter smiled slowly. "I am now, my boy, and I thank you for that. So, it's Group IPO next year?" Will joined Claudia in nodding. "We bring half of my holding out of funds over the next three years?" They nodded again. "And find buyers for sixty percent of my property and resort holdings?"

"After the Alphonse allocation?" Claudia was glad Will had asked the question. "And we need to be clear about exactly what you're giving him."

Peter looked slightly puzzled. "It's five percent of my holdings. What's the issue?"

"Two issues, and you've just solved one; it's five percent of what you have now. But is that a share of the whole portfolio, the one he would have to continue managing, or are you carving out something he can actually own?"

Peter looked taken aback. "You think he'd want that? I'd assumed a share. We want to keep him, don't we? He couldn't shrink to manage something small. I thought he enjoyed his global life."

Claudia had no idea what was in Peter's mind at that point. She doubted whether any of Alphonse's relationships would be a surprise to Peter, not even, she had to reluctantly admit, her own. "What do you think he'd want, my darling? You know him best." It was said so matter-of-factly that she felt almost shaken but tried to hide her reactions in a thought pause.

"I don't know what he'd want. He seemed delighted with the idea in New York when he heard," — it would be silly to pretend they hadn't spoken — "but I've no idea what he understood by five percent of what. I do know, though, that if we want to keep generating funds from property, we're much better off with him running it." That was, usefully, true, but she also helped establish that her priority was Dickinson and not the personal benefits for Alphonse Newman. Of course, it would keep him just that little bit nearer to her — but no one was thinking of that, she hoped, only Claudia herself.

Peter still looked thoughtful, but suddenly turned to Will. "I think I'd better talk to him when we're finished here, Will, if you don't mind."

"Yes, I'd rather you did. I don't think he has a problem staying in an unruly conglomerate, as you've often called it, and I'm not detecting any personal animosity to me if we go that route."

He paused. It was several seconds before Claudia realised the men were expecting her to speak, "Oh, no, I think he values you highly. He won't be your problem on the conglomerate route. But I'd be struggling if you keep the separation between the three divisions." It was useful to have a topic she could pretend she'd been thinking about. "I could see us being pulled into the other areas more and that would undermine what else we're trying to do, and you'd underexploit Tania and what she could give."

"We're focussing on Two B, aren't we?" Peter framed the statement as a question.

"Two B?" asked Claudia. Peter looked at Will, who smiled.

"He means I've given him only two options, really, numbers two and four, i.e. Two A and Two B." He looked to Peter, who smiled and nodded. "If you want to make the call today, I'm OK with that, but I gave Henry the impression yesterday that the three-leg options were still live."

"The ones he'd prefer?" asked Peter. Will nodded. "Obvious, really, he just doesn't want his erstwhile junior as a boss. Ha, he effectively recruited you." Peter stroked his chin. "I can understand that attitude, but you're big enough to handle it." Another pause. "More to the point, so is he, with Rachel's help, so that's not your big problem. Look, amongst us chickens, I'm sold on Two B, but if it helps you get Tony and Lou comfortable, I'm happy to let you keep discussing four options until the next board meeting. Is that OK?"

"I'd prefer that, thank you. And I'm very happy about Two B, of course."

"Claudia?"

"It makes sense. I'm very happy about Two B. I think it's better for Tania if you split out the consultancies and put them under Sandy. She can focus on the Giddings tie-in then." She turned to Peter, "I've sort of promised we'll do Atlanta and talk to Arthur and Samantha soon, my love."

"Excellent, we'll fly down after the next board meeting. You and Martha should come down too, Will."

"Is that…" but Claudia stuttered, of course it made sense. Will would be head of Dickinson, it would help Arthur accept the changes. "No, forget it. It's an excellent idea. I hope Martha's free."

"I think she'll be delighted. I'll just have to warn her about her stupid southern accent."

"Ha," laughed Peter. "You should hear this one, but no one seemed offended. Anyway, it means you have Sandy reporting to you, Will, OK with that? And he's the one to pull the consultancies together?" Peter was looking at Claudia now.

"Oh, unquestionably. All the heads like him and they know they'll lose no autonomy."

"So, just the difficult job now."

"The difficult job?" Will looked as puzzled as Claudia felt.

"When you talk to Mei, Will, there's only option Two B. The other options are for discussion when she talks to her brother — or, more likely Tony — she'll understand."

"When can I brief her?"

"As soon as you can get there."

"In person?"

"My boy, I'm working hard on her, but her imperious highness will expect no less. Besides you can catch up with Alphonse et al. when you're out there. You've not been for long enough."

Will was as close to looking flummoxed as Claudia had seen him. "I guess I have a trip to organise, better get on with it."

"You don't want to discuss the package for the chairman and CEO of Dickinson Enterprises?"

Claudia knew Peter was keen to spring one of his generous surprises, but Will was smiling slyly, about to pay him back. "I think Sandy is the right person to come up with what's appropriate, and I'm happy waiting for the board meeting for that." The smile grew a little bigger. "I don't think your package is going to disappoint him."

"Him…" stuttered Claudia.

Peter guffawed. "OK, my boy, you've done me there. You're quite right. But you might not accept."

Will slowly shook his head. "I need to be careful, my esteemed Mr Dickinson, or I could almost become emotional. I would, of course, be thrilled."

"Subjunctive noted." But Peter was beaming, as if he'd cleared the way for his own new journey, and Claudia began to catch some of the euphoria.

18

"You have been here before, haven't you?" said Conrad as he shook Will's hand. It wasn't really put as a question, thought Will. His host then gestured to the farther of the large sofas.

"A couple of times. But that was a long time ago," said Will. There were several reasons to feel awkward about this evening. The past was one of them, but Conrad, whom he was meeting for the first time, seemed very relaxed and almost artless, and Will was bringing no more than a usual level of caution. "And our mutual friend had guided me downstairs, which, I understand, is very different now."

"Ha," Conrad laughed gently, pleasantly, "the whole place is very different now, I'm happy to say. She thinks it was a trick of mine to pull her in, but even I knew it needed revamping." He looked around the large drawing room, which had an airiness in the grand old building when it could easily have looked sombre, "I'm delighted with it."

"But your man hasn't changed, has he? The man who let me in."

"Boris? No, no, he's more important to me than the foundations, is Boris."

"Well, at least my visits here were anonymous. He hadn't remembered me."

Conrad sat down opposite Will and smiled. "He knows exactly who you are, Mr Uprichard, and he'll probably take you down to meet his beloved after he's cooked us dinner. Sandra wouldn't forgive either Boris or me if she finds out you've been here. Don't worry, I don't know what Isobel has told you, but downstairs has had the biggest makeover. It might have been hard for Sandra to accept it otherwise." Will assumed he must be referring to the Gerry incident that had left Sandra hospitalised. "We'll come on to Mr Calvert later, no doubt, that's probably one of the points on your agenda." This was refreshingly direct, thought Will, warming to the man's openness, which must be one of the reasons Isobel was with him.

He was also, well, presentable was the first word that occurred to Will, but he could imagine Isobel shrieking at that. He was dapper and very well groomed, steely grey hair showing little sign of thinning, and an easy smile, there was none of the po-faced sternness that lesser men sometimes affected.

"Now, I'm rather touched that you have evidently found out so much about me. I'd always assumed it was from the best of motives," he paused, raising his eyebrows.

"She means a great deal to me, Isobel; she helped me through a tough time once, but I've always found her completely delightful. I was looking out for her; maybe a little clumsily."

Conrad leaned back and laughed gently just as Boris came in with two champagne flutes. He put them down in front of each of the men. "Thank you, Boris. Boris, you remember Mr Richard, don't you?"

Boris straightened up by the coffee table, folded his arms across his considerable chest, smiled at Will and turned to Conrad. "Mr Uprichard, sir, not Mr Richard. Ms

Isobel brought him here three times. It was eight years ago." Conrad laughed, louder this time, and Boris shook his head, smiling more broadly.

"You see, Will, he misses nothing."

"And excuse me, sir, but my Sandra, she not miss much either. She wondered if…" the voice was deep, the presence imposing, but there was a tentative delicacy about the hint. Will wondered if Boris was worrying about Conrad's reaction, but Conrad was looking to Will with questioning eyes.

"Oh, I'd love to say hello, yes please," he said, genuinely eagerly.

Boris nodded, plainly pleased. "I tell her after dinner. You come see us?"

"I'll look forward to that very much," he said, and, peculiarly, he found he was. The basement had been the location of his…his what? Initiation, education? He had some thrilling memories but it would be useful to see the old place now, much transformed, he was sure, and let the memories detach themselves from any physical location into some erotic imagined nirvana; seeing the place again as it had once been could only have disappointed.

Conrad seemed to sense where Will's mind was. He looked up. "Half an hour to dinner, Boris?" The big man nodded and quietly left them. "Cheers," said Conrad, and raised his glass, too far away across the huge coffee table to even think of clinking. "You can leave out those particular little bits of your past, Will, but I am going to expect, if you'll forgive me, a reasonably comprehensive history of Mr William Uprichard to balance out the research you've had done on me." There was still a slight smile on the man's face. "I think you have a pretty comprehensive dossier, don't you?"

Now, Will laughed, as it seemed Conrad had intended him to, "You'll probably be relieved to know that the dossier is very far from comprehensive. Some of your operations are very opaque — although Henderson did tell me that he had a conflict of interest, since you were now a client, but that I shouldn't worry too much, or attempt to get any closer."

Now Conrad laughed loudly. "I think I probably am relieved about that, but I still feel you owe me a more rounded picture than the one I have from Isobel who, as you must be aware, describes you as young, tall, very handsome." He grimaced slyly. "Those things are obvious, but charming, funny and formidably intelligent are less obvious, but harder to live with, from my point of view." Now he chuckled. "I'm afraid she's had to give me some details on why you and she are unsuited, so I probably know more about your basement interests, if I can call them that, than you'd like me to, but at least it means I can spare you that inquisition."

Will smiled now. "I do find her openness…well, I was going to say refreshing…"

"But it's an ice bath sometimes, isn't it? It's one of the things I love about her, too. But, as you can see, it doesn't make my picture of you very rounded, or do I finally have to believe in a Mr Wonderful?"

That was true, thought Will, who smiled. "No, definitely not. But it's quite mundane, I'm afraid, I certainly have nothing to hide…"

"About yourself, maybe not, but I still want the full picture. There are areas, though, in the work you do, where you must see things that are best left opaque, to use your word. Henderson tells me you're very demanding about the details of his invoices."

"I'm protecting my boss. I'll say more about that later, if we get on to Henderson."

"I think we should, don't you?"

"Forgive me, Conrad, but, while I'm very grateful for this meeting, we haven't really established that our interests are mutual yet."

Conrad seemed unfazed, "Of course we haven't, but I think we can assume that they could be."

Will felt relaxed by that, "Well, I should get on with my little story first, shouldn't I?"

***

Dinner was unadventurously agreeable and prepared with surprising finesse. As Boris was clearing away the main course, Will suddenly heard Sandra behind him, "I'm sorry, Conrad, I shouldn't burst in, I know, but I don't want this one sneaking away."

Will had turned and was now standing with his arms open. That was all she needed; she rushed into them. "Oh, William, it's so good to see you, so good to see you." The hug went on and on. Will could see Boris shaking his head and smiling and he felt free to keep his arms around her.

When she relaxed her grip, she merely leaned back. "My God, young William, the bitch is right. You look more handsome than ever." She hugged him even tighter.

"Let me look at you," he said, after what felt like too long a while.

She eased away. "Oh, Will, please don't, I'm old and fat."

"You're not, and you're still amazingly pretty." Now she reached up and he couldn't avoid the lip kiss without seeming ungallant — but she kept it decently brief. She had filled out a little, but it was a lovely face, and now smiley.

She eased away, still holding his hand, looking to Conrad. "I'm sorry…"

He smiled and waved an arm dismissively. "That's fine, but one thing we do know about Master William here, he wouldn't have let you down."

"Oh, I know he wouldn't, but this lump might have stopped him." Boris, holding a large wooden spoon, waved it at her. She laughed. "Promises, promises." She stretched up again and kissed Will's cheek. "I'll see you later, my love, whenever you're finished. Don't worry about how late."

He kissed her forehead. "See you later." And she was gone.

Will settled at the table again. "I haven't spoken that much about myself since…ever."

Conrad's eyes narrowed. "Forgive me, but you've told me quite a lot about Peter Dickinson, about Martha, about Henry Gideon, whom I've met, by the way, and even about Isobel — at least I now understand her finances better — but I still don't have a feel for William Uprichard."

Will smiled. "And I have a thick dossier that tells me similarly little about Conrad Kitter, and I'm not just being modest when I tell you I'm convinced that what I'm missing is much more interesting than what you're missing. I'm fascinated by your businesses — and I'm a little bit fascinated, I'm going to admit, by the man who put all that together."

Conrad gave a little shrug. "I wish I could say there was a strategy, but it's really a haphazard collection of opportunities."

"Peter says that about his."

"Oh, I can see more of a rationale there. I appreciate some people might think he's too diversified, but I can understand him, I was very impressed — and charmed, of course, as everyone is. Except possibly Mr Calvert."

Will wondered if they were coming to the real reason for the evening's discussion. He glanced towards Boris.

"We'll go back to the parlour and talk. Can you bring coffee through, Boris, please? And two cognacs." He looked to Will, who nodded. They'd shared only one bottle of red, albeit an Haut Brion nineteen ninety, and cognac could be sipped slowly. This might be too important to risk any fuzziness.

When they returned to their sofas, Will looked around ostentatiously. "Parlour?"

Conrad chuckled. "Sorry, little private joke. It's what she called it when she said it needed a transformation. I just annoy her a little by letting the name stick. Anyway," he continued when they were settled again, "I'd trust Boris with my life, by the way, as well as any confidences. I just thought we needed more comfort. You raised your eyebrows about our Mr Calvert."

"Well, it struck me, from what Henderson told me about the Belgrade connection, that Calvert had more to resent about your role in that affair."

"You'd have thought so, wouldn't you? That's why I agreed to have dinner with him, to find out if I was exposed, but he seems to have a bigger thing about our Peter. I'm too much like Gerry, I suppose. I'm just a peripheral competitor, not a threat, although I do try to stay this side of a line. We don't need to talk about that, do we?"

Will chuckled. "I try to keep us relentlessly ethical, but even we have blurry edges. I'm just aware that Calvert is in areas where some people could get jailed and," he hesitated, "I don't want to get melodramatic about it, but…"

"Some get dealt with like his wife, you mean?"

"Yes, there are those areas where Henderson and Peter tell me not to ask too many questions."

"Will that have to change, with your new job?"

"If it all goes through, then probably, but aren't we getting off the track?"

"The track is, what's Calvert got against Peter, beyond festering envy, but we don't have to find or define it, we just need to be aware it's there — and it won't go away when you're in place at the head of Dickinson. I don't think Love's New Dream is all it pretends to be. Isobel tells me his Merle has never forgotten you and that's not going to make our Gerry happy. Anyway, the main point for me out of the dinner was that Gerry's taking a closer interest in the Dickinson changes than I thought he should be…"

"And he's ahead of the game. We've only just started discussing the issue."

Conrad was nodding. "That was my impression. Is that why you're here?"

"Is it why I'm here?" Nothing had yet resolved Will's curiosity about the invitation. "I'm very happy to see Isobel so well settled."

"Ha! If that's what she really is. I'm not going to count on that one, but I do love her being here and, fortunately, we both travel a lot. God, she might be overbearing, otherwise — but I love her, and my main personal reason for meeting you was just to reduce this mythical Will character to human dimensions," he was smiling broadly, "I've only partly succeeded, and we've had the little Sandra sideshow to demonstrate what a wonderfully attractive man you are for the ladies, Master William. Boris will also get fearfully jealous."

Will felt momentarily concerned. It must have shown.

"Don't worry. Those two are very good together. She'll still enjoy the paddling he'll no doubt give her for her outrageous intrusion. It looked like pretty genuine emotion to me though, as is Isobel's," he paused, "but what about Merle?" Conrad had settled again and was no longer jesting. "How big was that?"

Will assumed this was still relevant. "It was huge for me. I was devastated, but Isobel helped me ignore the letters when they came."

Conrad was nodding thoughtfully. "Yes, Isobel thinks all of us bottoms are manipulative, but we can fall in love, I keep telling her."

It felt strange to have this eminently successful man describe himself like that, but Will had learned, mostly through Isobel, to be very cautious in making judgements about people on the basis of their particular kinks.

Boris came in with drinks. "Thank you," said Conrad, "we won't keep you too long, I promise, he'll be down soon, tell Sandra."

"Tell her? I spank her, maybe," but he was chuckling, "see you soon, Master Will."

Conrad smiled and shrugged when Boris had closed the door. "I didn't want the arrangement. Two bachelors bouncing around in here was perfect, but it seems to be better when the women are here. Anyway, I've told him you'll be free soon, even though you've probably got even more questions than I have." He raised his eyebrows at Will, who nodded. "I accept we don't have a basis for trust yet, but dinner with Gerry and Merle was a set-up. We had some bullshit story about him rebuilding bridges with Isobel, and he made a decent fist of looking in love with Merle." He paused, and seemed to consider his next comment carefully. "That is a very beautiful woman, Will, I can understand your…"

"Infatuation, yes. But what would he be setting up?" Will didn't want to talk about Merle, but it was a distraction anyway, he thought.

"I couldn't get near that, I'm afraid, that's why I'm hoping you'll excuse me freeing you to go and see Sandra and agree to stay in touch with me if things develop."

Will was puzzled and, eager as he was to see Conrad's position as helpful, it could be the reverse of that. "What do you think might develop?"

Conrad raised his cognac to Will, and sipped. "I think you might get a phone call. I let Gerry know we were meeting, and I told him where you were staying."

"But I don't know Gerry Calvert at all."

"You do know Merle. Be careful. I may be being paranoid."

"You may just be being appropriately careful." Will raised and sipped. He couldn't imagine Conrad as paranoid.

"When do you fly back?"

"It looks like I'm flying on, not back. I'll be in Shanghai and Hong Kong most of next week."

"Ah, and the world is falling into place around you."

"Hardly, I think I'm travelling under Peter's direction and at Meitang's pleasure, and I'm hoping Alphonse and Isobel will make a tactful show of wanting to welcome me to Hong Kong."

Conrad stared a long time before he spoke. "Your life will soon be harder, young man. If you'd keep your mind open to becoming a friend, I should like that very much."

"You'll forgive my caution?"

"Ha!" was Conrad's loudest laugh of the evening. "I'd have been bitterly disappointed if you'd not shown it. I am, it's true, a lot greyer than Dickinson — but never, ever black. Just stay in touch, please, OK?"

"Thank you," said Will, trying not to sound as grateful as he felt, "I will."

"You have the best number to get me."

"I do?"

"It's the text message I sent earlier — and I appreciate you being enough of a gentleman not to check messages at dinner."

It was easy to like him, thought Will. Hopefully not too easy.

***

The door was open to the lower apartment — it seemed wrong now to think of it as a basement — and, as he hesitated by it, he heard Sandra call, "Come on down, Will."

They were both there when he entered into what was a huge living space. It must have been two rooms before, thought Will, and he struggled to get his memories to match what this home now was.

"Sit down," said Sandra, patting the seat on the sofa beside her. "We have a buzzer, I knew you were coming."

"You like more coffee, maybe? Maybe whisky?" Boris was hovering.

"I'll just have water, please, Boris."

"Maybe sparkling?"

"Oh, yes, bubbles, please. I mustn't abandon excitement completely." Sandra giggled. Boris looked puzzled and mooched off.

"What do you think?" She'd swung around and tucked her legs under her, concealed by the dress which was almost certainly not her normal evening wear at home, he thought.

"About the place, or about Boris?"

She laughed. It was a sweet laugh, but with an edge of nervousness in it. "The place, of course. The lump's adorable, but the apartment?"

"I was wondering how much I would remember, but that's almost nothing. I think it's, well, I was going to say charming, but it's much too stylish for that. It suits you both." Although he thought Boris would look a little out of place anywhere, but Isobel had at least provided something he could look almost at home in.

Sandra pretended to pout. "I knew you'd take her side. She pretended to ask me, but I got the 'you're not having the froufrou frilly, my darling; and pink would be kryptonite for Boris'." She giggled at her half-decent attempt to imitate Isobel, then shrugged. "I know you're both right, really." She reached out to touch his hand. "It's so funny, we hardly ever met, you and I, but I always make her tell me all about you. She loves you, you know?"

"I love her, too. I think she's wonderful."

"Oh, so do I, but I really meant what I said." She looked serious for a moment, but Boris saved him by returning with a bottle and two glasses.

"Please not to let her drink whisky, Master Will, she bad girl. I go to bed." He stood, almost to attention, and half bowed — while Sandra poked her tongue at him.

"Spoilsport!"

He turned to leave, waving an arm. "Hopeless. Bad girl." And then, on his retreat, he called, "You very welcome," to Will's expression of thanks. "Car ready outside whenever you want. I tell him midnight latest," he stopped and turned, "or she talk forever," and he laughed as the tongue was poked out at him again.

She did talk — about her job, about Boris, even about Isobel, but she asked a lot about him, and about Martha, and it was she who said, "I'm afraid I've kept you, Cinderella, I'd better let you go. I've had warnings from all three of them about keeping you too late. But you will be coming again sometimes, won't you? It seems like you and Mr Conrad have things to do together."

It was a pretty face, but also an astute one. "I think you're right," he said, "so maybe we'll get another chance to talk soon."

"I hope so very much, now hug me again, please, properly this time." She stood and held her hands out to him, then wrapped her arms tightly around his waist when he joined her. He put his arms around her shoulders. "And I'd like one good, old-fashioned kiss before I let you go."

He felt drawn into it. She had a lovely mouth, and he didn't resist their tongues playing. She pulled away after a while and smiled at him. "I remember how lovely that was." Then he heard her dirty chuckle as she moved her hips to make his bulge grow embarrassingly. Her hand moved to the front of his trousers. Her squeeze made it grow more, but she let her hand drop just as he was about to pull away. "Ha, ha." Then came the chuckle again, more a cackle this time. "I'm not going to embarrass you. It's just lovely to know that everything still works — the chemistry and the biology, I mean. Just talk next time, I promise."

He found himself chuckling as well as he looked into the smiling eyes. He kissed her lips gently again, squeezed her hands and said, "Go see Boris, I'll let myself out. I think I will be seeing you soon."

She hugged him briefly. "I do so hope so."

***

When he got to his suite, the phone by the bedside was flashing that he had a message waiting. He'd checked texts and emails on the short car journey, nothing urgent had come up. He rang front desk. 'There's a letter on the credenza by the door, sir.'

There was, and he recognised the writing instantly. He hadn't the faintest idea of how he should feel — that was shock, he told himself. Whisky would be the wrong thing, but he couldn't face opening the letter without some crutch. Glenmorangie was the hotel's whisky of choice. That was fine, something seriously pleasant, this wasn't the time to ask room service for one of its more challenging peaty cousins.

He made an elaborate ritual of hanging his jacket. He texted Martha. It was late for him; she would expect only a message. She'd been good about the itinerary revision, even the 'You'd promised me Noah's on Saturday, it's the last chance for a month,' was good-natured. He wasn't sure how genuine his 'You should just go' was. It was true to the letter of their bond, but the spirit? He wasn't sure — and he'd provoked apparent contemplation, rather than rejection, and silence.

Sounds like you've had a fascinating evening. Your Conrad interests me. Can I get a breakfast call tomorrow, my dearest love? XXXXX M

That had come back quickly. They were good, he knew that. They wouldn't be disturbed by whatever this letter contained, the letter whose corners he had been rotating between his fingers for several minutes now, in between sips of whisky.

'Why dramatize, Will?' he thought, then opened it as carefully as he could to leave the envelope as intact as possible. That was a bad sign, he admitted to himself.

My Dear William,

I'm emboldened by the fact that you've chosen the Lanesborough, although the memory may mean little to you, but it had enough significance for me to make one more attempt to engage you.

I do understand, believe me, why my September letters went unanswered every year, but I was hoping, with more years passing, we might at least be able to meet.

I don't know how long you're in London for on this trip, but I would very much appreciate the chance to talk.

Please call me if you can at <u>any</u> time, I do mean that, whatever you're thinking. The number is still the same. If you now no longer have it, that tells me as much as any silence.

Take any acceptable endearment — you can choose.
Your Merle XXX

He folded it away after reading it four times. He sipped the whisky. Then pulled it out and read it again. The colour of the ink and paper, the graceful script, and even the perfume was the same. Would a conversation cure an ache? He was wise enough to know that it wouldn't. He was smart enough to know that worries about the Gerry Calvert overture would be merely an excuse for him, surely; that was Gerry's plot, not Merle's. But, how was she? Whatever was she doing?

He pressed 'Merle' on his phone, curiously impulsively.

"How long do I have you for? Are you alone?"

He was shocked, yet comforted by the familiarity of the voice — and its dangerous enchantment, he told himself. "Yes, I'm alone, and I'm off to China after an office day tomorrow."

"I'd better hurry then."

"Merle, no, wait…"

"You can ignore letters, William, but you're too gallant, I hope still, to ignore a woman in the Lanesborough lobby. I'm getting in a taxi now. There are things we really should discuss, not just about me and about what us was, but more about you. Still, if you're not there to meet me, I'll get the message. I hope I'll see you in ten minutes."

If he could have thought of anything to say, it would have been wasted. She'd finished the conversation. It was twelve forty. She was coming to the hotel. The hotel where they'd first made love. This was probably stupid — but there was a murky background he needed to know more about.

He knew that was an excuse. He was about to meet again the woman he'd been dying to see for nearly eight years.

When he got to the lobby, he was too agitated to sit, pacing back and forth, keeping the doorway constantly in his sight, in spite of convincing himself that her ten minutes would be at least thirty, although the cab journey would be only five minutes at this time of night — a quiet time of night, an occasional couple returning, indifferent to him.

Suddenly she was there. He was momentarily paralysed until eight years disappeared in a moment. He'd seen her the instant she came in, but she saw him as soon as he stepped towards her and the beautiful smile dazzled him once again. He halted one step away from her and reached out for her hands. She stepped towards him and kissed his cheek, then stood back again, still holding hands.

He felt stupidly dumb.

"She had warned me you'd grown more handsome."

His mind began to function again. "She hadn't warned me you were more beautiful than ever." She was, he thought, maybe a wrinkle or two, no, that was silly, she was just the most stunningly beautiful woman he had ever known, the chestnut waves still falling to frame the most ethereal of faces.

"Or warned me that you'd become disgracefully charming."

"Then I should stop standing here feeling stupefied. Are you coming up? My suite's entirely respectable and I don't suppose we can talk publicly," he hesitated, "about whatever it is we have to talk about. Come on." He kept hold of her hand and turned towards the elevators, wondering if he should, but now letting go would be awkward — and she was making no effort to release herself. He even pressed three with his left hand when they entered.

"Thank you for writing. I wouldn't have had the courage."

"Is that what it would have taken?"

"That's how I see it now, although I didn't know that when I picked up the envelope."

"And knew it was me?"

Now he was relaxing. "Of course I knew it was you, same blue paper, same wonderful script."

"It never matched your masterpieces."

"I've never handwritten a letter since."

"Not even to Martha?"

He smiled, relieved that she'd broken what was threatening to become a spell. "No, not even to Martha."

The lift stopped. Finally, he let go of her hand. "It's this way."

"I know a disgracefully large amount about you, I'm afraid."

He chuckled. "I'm going to guess that's Isobel's unbidden stories."

"Oh, no you don't, you have to deal with the fact that I'm the curious one. I ask incessantly."

"I've only ever wanted to be sure that you were reasonably content."

"And what did she say about that?"

He stopped at his door. "We're here. That can wait a minute." He let her in, and she walked straight to a sofa and sat down. He was relieved not to have to fight the unbearable desire to take her in his arms.

"I'll just have water, please. To have something to hold while we're talking, as much as anything. My courage has brought me this far, but it's faltering."

He was feeling slowly calmer. "I have the advantage of not having a clue about what this midnight tryst is about. All I know is that the prospect of actually seeing you again was irresistible, and I meant what I said down there. You are incomparably beautiful."

"You could have seen me any time. You know that, don't you?"

"I've always tried not to think about it. I was in survival mode for a long time. Isobel must have told you."

She shook her head, her eyes blinking slowly. "It was a long time before we spoke about you. I was very unhappy about her opportunism, as I saw it. You were never serious with her, though, were you?"

The question seemed to come out of curiosity, not resentment. "No, we always knew we weren't suited for anything more than... She'd probably call it an arrangement, but I'd just say it was friendship."

She smiled slyly. "With benefits?"

It seemed easy to smile back. "Yes, with benefits." But her being here, this visit, had to be tackled. "Merle, I could honestly sit here for an hour and just look at you, but I had the sense that you had a purpose beyond our just seeing each other again."

"I did, I do, but, forgive me, this is affecting me even more than I feared it might. How hard would it be to sit together?"

He leaned back. "Probably too hard, because it feels like there's nothing I want more in the world, at the moment."

She was on him suddenly, her head on his shoulder, leaning into him. "I'll find it easier to talk like this. Put your arm around me, please. I won't demand kisses, I promise."

And years fell away for him. This was the pose from the couch in his little Docklands flat, the one he could have used tonight rather than taking a suite at one of London's most expensive hotels. 'Why the Lanesborough?' went through his head again; where they'd first made love; so near to her home.

"You're thinking."

"Technically, I'm waiting for you to speak, but I am guilty of remembering moments like this. But you'd better start talking. Why, specifically, wonderful as the moment is, are we together now?"

"I don't know."

Here he snorted. "Now that really has triggered a memory, Merle the Obscure."

She turned to look at him. Her eyes were brimming, her mouth moved wordlessly; she settled back down again, snuggling more deeply into him. "I'm just a bit worried, and I don't know why."

"But you thought I should worry too?"

Now she chuckled a little, a sweet noise that woke even more memories, but she was worried. "I need to say something about me, don't I?"

"Well, your situation has changed, and even Isobel's puzzled."

"About why Gerry, do you mean?"

"Yes, that principally."

"Well, we've had ups and downs, but we have..." she seemed hesitant.

"Played, is that what you want to say?"

"Thank you. You knew that. He understood my funny little kink, better than Michael anyway. He'd always effectively guaranteed our livelihood, too, I hadn't realised how much until recently. But he's changed since Ellen died; you knew about that, didn't you? Of course you did."

Probably a lot more than you, he thought.

"Well, he started to ask me out, he even asked Michael if he minded. It was all quite friendly. Anyway, we became a sort of item. He's funny, and quite easy to get on with really. I know some of his businesses are a bit dodgy — Michael won't say any more than that — but all successful businessmen have to deal with stuff like that, he says. That's true, isn't it?" She looked up at him again. It was true, of course, but few went as far as Gerry Calvert did in pushing or exceeding boundaries.

"Yes, that's true." he murmured, thinking he'd better let her come to the point.

"But it's been a little different lately. He's wanted to get back to doing business with Isobel, then he set up a dinner with Conrad Kitter. Do you know him?"

"I know him."

"Of course you do. You know everything, Isobel says. But anyway, he wanted to know more about Peter Dickinson, and got very interested when he heard about you and some changes. Aren't you going to become very important, or something? I suppose this suite should tell me that. But that's true, isn't it?" She swung around suddenly, tucking her legs under her to sit facing him. "Actually, I'd rather you didn't say. I mean, I'd be thrilled for you, but he knows how much you meant to me once and it's made him start asking questions about you."

"He doesn't know you're here, though?"

"Oh, good Lord, no. And I've no intention of telling him. I'm just worried about why he wants to know so much. Now you're looking pensive."

He felt pensive, but he chuckled. "Well, you did want to make me think, didn't you?"

She reached out for his hand. "I shouldn't be worrying, should I? I was thrilled to have an excuse to try to see you, but now I hope I'm making too much of it."

"Well," he said slowly, squeezing her hand, "I really don't think you should be worrying, but I am glad you've told me, it's well worth me knowing. We are making changes, he's obviously caught wind of something, and maybe he sees a way of making money out of it. Did it come up at dinner?"

"Yes, a little bit. Oh, that'll be it then, him seeing another way to make money."

Will doubted whether it would be that simple, but there was no need to burden Merle with that concern — or about the fact that she was too close to a completely unscrupulous individual.

"Cheeky bastard, actually, trying to exploit me. I've a good mind to tell him…" Will was shaking his head silently, "No, that would be stupid, of course. I won't say anything."

"Not about tonight, either?"

She looked a long time at him, stroking his hand, "No, tonight can be just one big secret, can't it?"

He wondered — would he tell Martha? "From Isobel?" That was a useful proxy.

It made her thoughtful. "I'd rather say nothing."

"About you being here?"

"About you making love to me."

And suddenly it was even more passionate than that first time, years ago. Now they knew each other's bodies, they knew each other's moves, knew each other's needs, knew each other's desires. And he knew, even as he was softening inside her, looking up, almost pained by the beauty of her smile, that he would come again inside her later — if she could stay.

"Kiss me," he said, and her lips melted on to his and he found himself stirring again inside her.

She sat up, her hands on his shoulders. "Already again?" She smiled and ground herself on him.

"If you can promise me an hour, I'll let them take a break."

She looked troubled. "I'm not here to complicate your life, you know that, don't you?"

He eased her off to lie beside him, and wrapped his arms around her. "You've been doing that anyway for eight years, but I think you're trying to help me tonight."

"Well, I was," her hand moved to his cock, "but this wasn't in the plan, although you have made me deeply happy. Too happy, I'm sorry, I'll be staying until breakfast if you'll let me." Her mouth sliding down to his cock stilled the words forming in his mouth. He soon found himself painfully stiff again.

"You won't believe me, but I was prepared to let them take a break."

She slid up, smiling, still holding him. "You used to multi-task. I remember conversations with me sitting on you."

He chuckled. "You could chat while I was kissing your pussy."

"Not for long, my William, I'd afraid you were wonderfully skilled at that. And thank you for not calling it a cunt. You were a beast to me sometimes."

"It was what you wanted."

"That's true, of course. Are you beastly with Martha? What's she like? Isobel's very impressed, but she is a bottom, isn't she?"

He chuckled, talking about Martha made this moment strangely easier — acknowledging the real world around them. "She probably is in that very limited sense." He hesitated. "It's not easy to apply labels, she just has a particular kink, and it matches mine."

"Does she like anal, too? You made me an addict for a time."

"Yes, she likes that too. Have you gone off it?"

She squeezed his cock more firmly, looked up at him and kissed him. "I've never tried it since." They kissed again, more tenderly now. "I've done very little at all, really. Have you been a good boy?"

It hit him suddenly. "I've never been unfaithful to Martha before tonight."

She pulled away. "Oh, Will, I'm so sorry."

He laughed. "Would you rather I hadn't been?"

That seemed to relax her, she chuckled too. "I suppose not. But we both know one person who wishes you had been."

"Isobel?"

"Of course."

"Oh, she has her interests, and she has Conrad now. Did you like him?"

She seemed to think for a while. "I thought he was too careful, I couldn't see into him. Gerry seems impressed by him. Do you think he's the one for our Sadie?"

"He's as close as any, I think, but I don't think they impose constraints on each other, so maybe it'll work. She does seem happy."

"Yes, I thought that. But what about you? Do you impose constraints?"

"In theory, no; in practice, yes — until tonight…"

"I'm sorry…"

"Oh, please don't. I expect I'll locate guilt somewhere in my baggage over the weekend but, unless you tell me I'm making your life complicated or unhappy, I'm not going looking for it."

"Does that mean you're going to eat my cunt now?"

"It means exactly that."

19

"Look, I'm not staying if I'm making you two feel awkward," I've been working with Daiyu all day, we had a lot to catch up on, and we've just arrived at Alphonse's for a pre-dinner drink. Well, I've been up to my place for a quick shower and change, she's just come here and got ready.

"No, no, no, it's not you," says Daiyu, and looks to him, as if for approval to speak. I don't detect any sign that he gives it; she just carries on anyway. He loves her for that as much as I do. *"It's the two of us who have the problem and it's not going to be helped by you abandoning us."*

Alphonse just looks unusually helpless but doesn't disagree.

"Am I actually here to help? Your agony aunt?"

Alphonse smiles but the expression flummoxes Daiyu. *"It's someone who advises on the resolution of emotional issues,"* he says, overly formally, yes, but quite helpfully.

"A busybody, is that what you mean?" We both chuckle.

"It's not how I like to see myself," I say, *"but it's unusual to see you two like this."*

"It's Mei," says Daiyu bluntly, *"I live with this once-a-month thing because it suits us."* She hesitates. *"No,*

that's shit, I don't really like it and dinners with Lang Senior don't compensate me."

"Do you fuck him?" I ask — to break the atmosphere, as much as anything.

"Don't be..." there's a flash of anger before she realises that I'm not serious. "No, I don't," she says, calmer now, then looks to Alphonse. "I would if I wanted to."

That's a rather querulous challenge, I think, and not the real issue, "Of course you would, poppet," I say, "but it's not the point, is it? What's changed with Mei?"

"You tell her," she says sullenly to Alphonse.

"Nothing's changed with Mei," he says patiently. Disingenuously, I think, and not like him.

She waits a while, just looking at him. She keeps looking at him while speaking next to me, "She fitted an extra appointment into the calendar in Shanghai and still came here last Friday." There's a silence. Something more is coming. "And she's made him come in her vagina each time!"

I just burst out laughing, but I know from their faces it's more serious than that. Still, we have to ease off on this, it's not the right atmosphere for a discussion, "Well, it's one alternative, I suppose," I say and the two of them look to each other, and both burst out laughing as well — thank God! I don't mind solving problems, but let's do it sensibly.

"Have you actually been raped, Alphonse?"

The smile leaves his face as he shakes his head and looks puzzled.

"Yes, most men struggle with that one," I say. Now it dawns on me, and I feel a little stupid. I look to Daiyu. *"You think she's trying to get pregnant?"*

"Of course she is!" she says vehemently.

"You don't know that," he says. This isn't like him at all.

Now she's talking to me as if he weren't there. *"I told him after the first time. I don't care what they do between themselves, but I warned him. If she sits on him and says, 'fuck my cunt, fuck my cunt' she's up to something,"* she turns to him again now, *"and you let her do it again!"*

I can think of something frivolous, but it's not the time. *"Did you ask her about it?"*

"I did the second time." He looks to Daiyu. *"I'd been alerted."*

"And?"

"She said 'of course not,' she just likes it that way occasionally."

"Huh!" Daiyu flounces. I've seen that seldom.

"I'll try and get more out of her highness next time we're together. I have to do Shanghai in two weeks." I think for a moment. *"Guys, we are all convinced it would be a bad idea, aren't we?"*

Daiyu, I can tell, wants to leap in, but she's smart enough to hold herself back. Suddenly Alphonse realises he's the focus of our attention. *"Of course it's a ridiculous idea."*

I'm not sure that's truly what he thinks.

"It's easy to stop, though, isn't it? Just don't do it that way. It's not like it's your most preferred orifice."

Now at least I've got Daiyu giggling but he looks less than happy. Then a thought strikes her. "It may be too late already." There's a pause. "She'll have to get rid of it." He gasps. *I'm a little shocked: that was surprisingly callous.*

"We know Mei, if she's gone to this much trouble, she's done it with conviction," I say, "and she doesn't have many people who can tell her what to do these days. Alphonse?"

He's become very thoughtful, "I think you're making too much of this. She says not anyway, why disbelieve her?"

Daiyu just groans. *I can understand that. We tell ourselves that gay men understand us better, but they don't have a clue, really.* "Can you just agree to abandon that strange little perversion with her?"

He looks unnerved, a little irritated. *At least I've brought a smile to Daiyu's face again.* "Perversion?" he asks, looking puzzled.

It's very unlike him to be this thick, he deserves this, "Normal intercourse, of course. If you have to have a vagina, my darling man, there are two perfectly serviceable specimens in this room that we can make available — and I can talk far dirtier than Mei." I look to Daiyu, who's smiling and nodding, "I'd want Daiyu's permission, of course, and, frankly, I'd rather you chose hers, as I'm sure she would."

I finally get a wan smile out of him. "I hope you're not right," he says.

He doesn't sound convincing, but that's not a point to pursue right now; we can't do much about what might be happening in a womb a thousand miles away.

"But no more of that nonsense!"

Now there's a glint in his eye. "Oh, I don't know about that, I've just been offered two vaginas."

"Ugh!" says Daiyu, folding her arms across her chest and looking away from him.

"You'll get one, if you're lucky, and it has to be one in this room, and you don't get either before dinner."

"And you're paying!" she says, without turning around, but the atmosphere's improving, he's recovering.

"I would love to buy you dinner. Are we ready, or do we need time to compose ourselves?"

"Fuck you!" she says. "You'd better have booked Shangri-La."

"Of course I have. Isobel's with us."

"You are doing your best to exclude one vagina from your options, aren't you?" But she's smiling now. She's very good. And my offer was only theoretical, she knows that.

***

I'll settle in London with Conrad, is what I'm thinking, but I don't ever want to give up this harbour view. Maybe he should develop some interests out here, share our time, maybe. The two of them are holding hands now, at least, but Daiyu has noticed my preoccupation. I don't get more than a look though; she doesn't pester like that.

"I can't imagine not being here now," I say.

"And Conrad?" she asks.

"That's what I was thinking, whether he'd want to spend some time here. He was giving Gerry Calvert some

bullshit the other day about wanting to get something going."

Suddenly Alphonse is alert. "Can I ask how that came up?"

I go through the whole dinner saga. Daiyu even goes through her ordering ritual surprisingly quickly to stay tuned in to my story. I'm surprised to get such close attention. I mean, I still think it was a weird evening, but I didn't expect my tale to engage these two that much.

I've sort of finished, and we've been eating, when Alphonse looks up and hits me with, "You know Will's here next week."

"I did not know that, dude," I say, trying to hide my shock by quoting one of my favourite movie lines.

"I've just picked up his itinerary from Penelope," — this is the infamous presence who seems to control the entire Dickinson operation from a dungeon near Berkeley Square — "I've been asked to keep Wednesday free. It's all last minute, Peter decided Will should take Mei through everything, he's got Monday and Tuesday in Shanghai. I think he's still trying to pin Tony down. I think the best he'll do is find Lou, not that Lou likes to spend much time near his sister, but she'll probably order him to be there for Will. Anyway, we'd expect our changes to generate some interest, but Peter's worried about how much seems to have got out already, and who's got hold of what, so your Gerry Calvert comment was interesting."

I'm in turmoil, though — how could Will not say! Fortunately, we're distracted by dishes being cleared and I've a chance to sneak a look at my phone. The absurdity of the overwhelming relief that there's a text! I don't need to read it, I just needed to know. I catch Daiyu squinting at me with that little smug smile on her face. Of course I'm being ridiculous, he's married etcetera, we know all that, but I don't like the thought that it's not a special bond we have, but it just takes 'Will' in my inbox and I'm ridiculously happy. Anyway, woman, stop it, there's plainly something big going on around all this. I wouldn't say Alphonse looked worried, but he does look serious. Well, he should do, it affects him in a big way if I'm understanding it correctly.

Not as much as a baby in his life would, I think, but that's popping into my head less often as we three get into our usual business discussions. He has a pet project in Australia that he's finally getting off the ground — and he wants me to get involved. I don't really have time, but I'm not missing out. Daiyu's been down there once and is keen on the site, so it's getting late and Mei's vagina and the Dickinson changes have been left in the dust of the discussion — and those two seem happy enough to be left now. And I want to read my text. If it's only a couple of words, I'll be happy, as long as it's a dinner invitation.

The two of them make a show of inviting me in, but I'd already pressed thirty-two before he pressed twenty-nine and we'd managed hugs and kisses on the way up. I think they'll be all right to do more of that themselves when they get in.

I fling myself on the sofa with my phone as soon as I'm in. It's longer than I dared hope — and he does want to meet, could I do Tuesday or Wednesday? Of course I can, my darling, I don't care what's in the diary — that's not like me normally. He'll be in Shanghai by Sunday, maybe he could call. Wow, this sounds like business. I didn't get much out of Conrad after their meeting. I don't get much out of Conrad anyway. I had, of course, a ridiculously effusive text from Sandra, but I'd expected that. I'll push for Tuesday, then maybe I'll get Wednesday as well, he and Alphonse might need my mediation skills.

I imagine the two downstairs are just beginning to benefit from those now.

20

It had been a long day of conversations for Tania. She liked most of the unit heads but the unremitting self-interest apparent in all conversations she'd begun to find wearing. Yes, they would all become much richer men — only one woman among them, who'd also been determined to establish what would be in the IPO for her. The consolation for Tania was that, with each of them having much smaller shares, they would be easier to replace. It was a theoretical consolation only, she told herself between calls. They were all running pretty good businesses. She was saving Andy until last, with his understanding; she'd called him first, said she needed an important conversation about Dickinson, but could she call him last so they could be more open-ended. He offered to fly down for the evening. 'Doesn't fit tonight' had been hard to say, but they had at least established a way of dealing with each other.

She was just relaxing from the penultimate call when the text came; it was Martha: *Can you call?*

Best done now, thought Tania. "Hey woman, what's up, man detained?"

"Man diverted. PD has sent him to Shanghai to tie up the Asian end of this thing. I understand, of course I do, but I'm a bit pissed."

"Yes, you were planning a fun naughty night tomorrow, weren't you?" The subsequent silence surprised

Tania, until a strange thought hit her. "Are you thinking it might be more fun by yourself anyway?"

The further silence felt like a confirmation. "Well, I admit I was intrigued last time, but we just watched a little." There was more hesitation, unusual for Martha. "What would you do?"

Tania was flabbergasted, but that reaction wouldn't help Martha, and Tania had had her own adventures there. "If that was my relationship basis, I'd go for it."

"Well, it is our basis, but only theoretically."

"You mean you haven't…"

"Neither of us has, so far as I'm aware."

"I certainly don't get the impression he has…" Tania was teasing — and it worked.

"What are you suggesting?" came a little frostily from Martha.

"He, gotcha, you haven't, have you?"

"Certainly not." It sounded almost indignant.

"Nice try, but you're thinking about it, arn'cha? I'm with you woman, but you ain't getting any prissy tact from me. Do you want to talk some more about it?"

"It's why I rang…"

"Look, I'm having dinner with Robert later. I promised I'd get Andy out of the way now. Why don't you have a drink with us before we eat and talk about it; join us if you're free. He could even be your plus one tomorrow, I should think."

"I was more interested in that man Geoffrey that Lavinia talked about."

Tania had guessed that, but it was a difficult topic. "We might need to set that up for you, but it's best discussed with Robert. Shall we do that?"

"You won't be there tomorrow, will you?" Martha sounded unnerved suddenly.

"Good God, no. I'm off to Atlanta tomorrow, I have my Daddy to deal with on this new stuff, then I'm on my way to the West Coast. Will you want Robert to fuck you afterwards? He's quite good."

"I'm not sure whether you're relaxing me or making it much worse."

"Come on, diffidence isn't your style. Either you build this into your lives or you don't. The way I see it, you two could do that almost better than anyone. It's not like you're going to fall for anyone, is it? Even if you get addicted to Geoffrey, the most you'll do is have Will watching the next time."

Martha laughed, relaxing now. "Maybe if we could meet for that drink."

"Look, we'd be delighted. Can you be at Le Bernardin at eight?"

"I'll be there, and thank you."

"Oh, don't thank me. You realise you've just made Will available for me, don't you? Fair's fair."

Martha laughed, as Tania had intended. "Oh, missy, I don't think your sweet little ass would enjoy what he likes givin'. If you've never been tempted by Geoffrey, you ain't gonna want my William."

Tania laughed now. "I think, Mrs Uprichard, I've just had to absorb too much information. See you at eight."

***

Robert had tried to organise a table for three, but Martha was very insistent she wouldn't stay.

"I'd expected her to be charmed by you," said Tania when they sat down. "I didn't realise it would work the other way. She intrigued you, didn't she?"

He grinned. "Of course, and she's prettier than you said."

"I think she'd done some prep once the invitation had been issued, but she is pretty, I grant you, for an older woman."

"Miaow."

Tania laughed at herself. "I'm going to come clean, Master Robert, I've been through a lot with you, but I didn't expect to be made jealous this evening."

"Oh, my precious one. Nobody could replace you, but you want her to relax and enjoy tomorrow evening, don't you?"

"Are you actually going to?"

"Take her? Definitely, you heard the gentleman promise."

"You know what I mean."

"I don't. Do you mean organise Geoffrey? That depends on what Noah says. I imagine he'll know somebody, even if Geoffrey's not coming."

"I don't even mean that. You told her you'd organise that anyway. I'm asking, what happens if she wants afters."

"Well, if that's what the lady wants." He spread his arms, as if the request would have to be met. "What do you think? You know the history. Some of them just like the punishment. I rather hope she wants more, but I won't, personally, if you disapprove. But I'd find someone for her, she deserves that — and there would be many willing, as you can guess."

She thought for a while. "I've never thought of her that way. I've always seen her with Will since they've been together, but I can see what you mean. I suppose you'll have to, if she wants you."

"Are you ready to order?"

She'd been managing her life like this for a few years now and it suited her; mostly Robert; occasionally Andy; sometimes small gangs at parties; and an occasional individual on her travels. Robert would sometimes bring Ray on New York nights — and the two together were probably the most fun; men on their own ran out of steam too quickly, but Ray was always tactful enough to leave Robert with the breakfast duties, as he called them — a touch ungallantly, she thought.

But she'd wondered about Martha and Will. It had been a huge surprise when she first found out — she'd been with them in Tokyo and hadn't put them together at all — but, now she knew them, and was close to them, it seemed a lovely, almost enviable arrangement and she'd begun to question what she might be missing. But now Martha wanted something more, or was it just something different? And what would that do to Will? He was more important to her, certainly at work, but emotionally too. She was looking at the menu without reading.

Robert had just ordered. "You've been miles away," he said. "It's scallop, then monkfish for you."

"Mmm, yes, thank you, sorry, I was thinking about Martha and Will."

"Thinking? Or worrying? They're grown-up people, you know."

"I know, but I thought I sort of envied what they had."

"Maybe you'll envy what they have next even more. I didn't get the impression this is a woman looking for an alternative. I would guess they've probably played games around the idea."

"Do you think so?"

"My love, it's what you've always done, isn't it? Haven't we just been filling in your little fantasies at Noah's playtimes?"

"Yes, I suppose we have. Well, at least we know she won't fall for you, you're much too frivolous."

"You say that, my love, but as you said earlier, she already has done a little."

Robert wasn't a man without a little brittle vanity, she thought. "Not as much as you did for her."

"Ha, that's true, but to come back to your earlier point, that's got nothing to do with fucking."

"I suppose you're right." She raised the champagne flute to him. "Cheers, my darling."

***

She normally flew to Atlanta on a Friday evening. A private jet business had helped her form a small society with a few other people who occasionally needed to make the trip. Sometimes she'd be alone in the six-seater, and sometimes it would be full, but she'd known Friday would be a long day, so she'd booked for herself on the Saturday. It meant there was time for Robert at breakfast and for a run in the park — at least that gave a clear cut-off point for their time together but, when she thought about it, he was always gone by lunchtime — and they'd never spent successive evenings together. That suited her, and it only peripherally struck her as her plane took off that it also probably suited him. They were no Will and Martha, and she found she was thinking more about the couple than seemed sensible or healthy. They were probably two of the most grown-up people she knew. They would work it out. She really shouldn't worry. Claudia would tell her not to. But she couldn't talk to Claudia about it.

Arthur was there to meet her. He picked up the bag plane-side after he'd hugged her hello. "It's a lot for one night."

"I'm flying on west tomorrow."

"Oh, I didn't know." She'd told her mother, who would probably have said. She had a difficult conversation ahead of her with her father and nowadays she worried about how competent he might be to grasp it all. That was today's big topic. She could multi-task well, but she could also focus, and that was what the afternoon needed. She let him struggle putting the bag in the trunk, she took her seat, offering to help with luggage would be even more embarrassing.

"I had a call from Peter Dickinson yesterday. That was a surprise," he said as the car pulled away.

It was a bigger surprise to her. Why hadn't Peter said something? Don't react, Tania, she told herself. Why hadn't Claudia called?

Her father negotiated a turn with exaggerated caution. "It seems he has some big changes planned."

"What did he say?" This was irritating. She tried, as always now, to stay cool.

Arthur chuckled. "Darling child, this is business, isn't it? You're going to tell me your version."

"You think it might be different from his?"

He was still smiling. "I usually find that two versions of the same story differ, sometimes quite significantly. Isn't that your experience? You're a big girl now, chicken. There ain't much I can teach you these days, but this sounds like it could be important. Important enough for him and my lovely Claudia to want to visit next month. Your mother and I have had to clear a weekend in the diary. She's thrilled of course; he is, according to her, just one of the world's most charming men."

She still felt out of sorts. "Not charming or thoughtful enough to have told me about calling you."

"Aw, honey." He chuckled. "I specifically asked him not to — and that obviously went for Claudia, too, and, now that you're looking all grumpy about it, I can see he's a man of his word. As I was sure he would be."

"Daddy, are you playing games with me?"

He guffawed. "Oh, chicken, you are cross, aren't you? You don't often call me Daddy." They were silent for a while. He was smiling. "I still kinda like it."

Tania was still feeling irritated, but only at her father now. If Peter had been sworn to silence, of course he would have respected that.

"I assume you've got your story all prepared."

"We have some options. I wanted to go through them with you." Peter was aware of the four options now, he'd been with Will on Wednesday. At least Will had debriefed her, the last true gentleman, she thought — and then Martha's Noah plan came into her head again. She couldn't get distracted by that and what that might mean for Will. She forced herself to think about Peter, he had bought into option four as a first choice, or Two B, as Will was now calling it, in some strange code they'd developed in the meeting. She should concentrate on that — and on the possible implications for Giddings.

Arthur was impassively concentrating on driving. He was normally more talkative.

"Do we have a clear afternoon for this? Or does Mother have other plans?" She wanted it tied down today, not have a plane deadline in front of her tomorrow.

"Oh, her only plan is to hear what you've got to say." That was a shock, Mother never talked business — only a little about the people. "Ange, too."

"Ange is here?" Now she couldn't hide her surprise. Arthur's continuing impassivity told her that he'd expected her to be shocked. She hadn't seen her little sister since Christmas, and it wasn't as easy a relationship as she had with Debs. Ange was the most aggressive of the three, a belligerence she brought to her legal work, Tania had heard. "Has she come just for this?"

Arthur chuckled. "She likes to see family now and again. It's a good thing."

"And Debs?"

The car stopped at a light. "She was busy," but Arthur turned to her and winked, "and you two are too close."

That made the rest of the journey curiously quiet.

Samantha, having listened for the car pulling up, was opening the front door and was ready with a big smile and a hug. "Well, darling daughter, I hear you might be bringing guests next time."

"I thought that was very far from certain, Mother," said Ange curtly. She'd been lurking in the hall, behind their mother, before giving herself to the perfunctory sisterly hug.

Still, she's in a dress, and a smart one, thought Tania. Ange was obviously taking this seriously, but Tania was still puzzled about how her father was playing it.

"Mother!" tutted Samantha. "Do you hear what she calls me now? That's a bad habit she's picked up from you, child."

Tania smiled. She was used to the dislocation between her life in a job bigger already than her father's and, potentially, much bigger, and the usual parental modes of address at home, where she might still be sixteen.

Ange was more visibly discomfited by being still the baby, in spite of what was becoming a successful legal career in Dallas, so she stuck more rigidly to the new formalities; Samantha was unvaryingly mother now.

Arthur came in. "Wendell's parking the car, he'll put your case up. Are we saying three thirty in the library? I thought you might want to settle in first."

"Three thirty's fine. I could start now, but I'd like a few minutes with Mom first." That would be unavoidable, anyway, she thought. "Oh, and I need to make some copies, now there are three of you." She raised her office bag.

"I'll get those, you all get on."

So, Ange would be joining them, thought Tania, no chance to pick off Mom separately. That was probably a good thing, keep the discussion simple — no family-political complications, but no doubt Ange could inject those, as she already had done about the Dickinson visit — or the possible Dickinson visit.

Samantha detoured via the kitchen — to get the inevitable iced tea organised, thought Tania. That left her sitting opposite Ange amongst the huge plants in the orangery, finding nothing to say in these awkward circumstances. When Samantha sat down, next to Ange, there were no such inhibitions, and the first topic was inevitable. "So, who's it been this week? Robert again?"

"Dinner last night." It was easiest to let mother think of her life in New York being one of relaxed, semi-detached monogamy.

"He's the art dealer who's too scurrilous to be allowed to meet us," Samantha told Ange. Not for the first time, thought Tania, as Ange's eyes rolled.

"You know I don't want him thinking it's serious, and that certainly goes for you and Dad."

"It's two years now. More than, probably, I'm sure it took you a while to mention him. But at least he's not married, not like that one in Boston. I suppose we'll find out later where he pops up in all of this, will we?"

"It's in there somewhere, but not fundamental to any changes. What about you, Ange? How's the Dallas dating scene?"

"I've had to cancel dinner," was said gracelessly. It surprised Tania and Debs that their younger sister appeared to struggle. They agreed she was the prettiest, and her smile could be lovely — but it was seldom used, and that had got worse over the Dallas years. Tania was not close enough to enquire any closer and Samantha rescued the conversation with Atlanta gossip, which was coming to seem more distant to both of them.

It was Ange who finally said, "I'm sure Dad's in there waiting."

Tania was keen to get on, but glad she hadn't had to show impatience. Nor had her father. He could have summoned them: they were ten minutes late.

They sat on four sides of the large table in the place that had served as a study during their at-home time in the student years. That had been serious enough then. But this was real life now.

Tania went through all four options. Neither her father, nor Ange, would have accepted less, and her sister, in particular, would have latched on to any unconsidered or too briefly described alternatives.

"Now, can you tell me why the good Peter calls option four Two B? I got the impression it was his preferred one."

Peter had obviously been frank, which is what she'd expected, but Will's version in their conversation yesterday morning, after she'd sent him the communication packet she'd prepared for her family meeting, was that all four options had to remain in play until the board meeting next month. Will had seemed unusually distracted, and no longer even clear about his travel plans, but she knew he was on his way to Shanghai over the weekend to sell Two B to Zhao Meitang, so Peter was showing a clear preference. From all she'd heard,

Will's task might be even more awkward than her own this afternoon.

"I understand from Will that he'd divided them into the two that keep the three sectors separate, and the two that keep them all together, of which the second he'd called Two B."

"And is the first of those Two A, or Not Two B?" asked Samantha with a knowing grin.

"Mother, that's silly," said Ange sharply, but Tania smiled at her mother and nodded faintly. Ange carried on, "Why would you want to keep three such different businesses together anyway? Surely they should be allowed to focus?"

Arthur was nodding, he wanted to hear the answer.

"It's a good question." Tania tried to avoid sounding condescending.

"None of that B/S here, missie, it was a good question."

"I did say it was a good question, pops."

"And this is a serious meeting. I'm not pops!" He seemed strangely tetchy.

"But you want me to be missie?" The cheeky riposte usually worked.

He looked disgruntled, but slowly smiled. Tania had a sudden sense that he wanted to help, but was staging things for Ange. Somehow, for whatever reason, he wanted her to become convinced as well.

"As I understand it, he'd rather have the group all together under one man he can trust and talk solely to, rather than get drawn into three areas of discussion. It's important to him to have the group prosper so it can continue to fund the Foundation, and that he and Claudia can focus on that."

"Well, that strikes me as a wonderful idea," said Samantha, then hesitated as the others all looked at her with varying degrees of surprise on their faces. "Oh, I just mean the foundation idea, I don't know about how you organise the business best for that, but he does seem to have done a wonderful job on that, but that's his personality, isn't it, his charm?"

"But if that is the strength of the group," said Ange, looking sceptical, "you couldn't replace all that drive and flair with a career finance man, could you? Isn't that what this Will is?"

Tania knew she needed to react calmly and not get defensive, "He's really been the chief organiser at Dickinson for three or more years now. He works all the ideas through to give Peter the choices."

"And he's guided Peter to this Two B?" asked Arthur.

"And not to Not Two B," sniggered Samantha irrepressibly.

"Mother!" snapped Ange.

"I do think it's his preferred option, yes." Tania tried not to be distracted.

Her father looked relaxed and was smiling — but wasn't yet convinced. "It's the option that gives this Will the most power, isn't it? I'm not surprised he's pushing for that." His eyes narrowed. "It also gives you the biggest job, missie, doesn't it?"

She had to let him get away with that, she knew. As did he, he was testing her.

"It does. Can I come back to that?" She didn't wait for agreement. "Peter wants himself and Claudia to be as free as possible to build this foundation. He sees that as being a lot of work, principally hers, but he knows he'll have to support her."

"I can understand that," said Arthur helpfully. "The guys I know who do a lot like that find it real hard to make their efforts count. There are too many charlatans with begging bowls."

"Arthur!" said Samantha sharply. "That's unkind."

"Maybe, but it doesn't make it untrue, though — and tell me how many events you've come home from unconvinced that our money you've so generously bestowed is going to the right people."

Samantha looked unhappy, but the observation had been plainly valid.

"I can sort of understand that it suits him, but Ange made a good point about focus in three areas. He must think an awful lot of this William. Anyway, Two B looks big for Tania Gunter, too."

"I'm not going to deny it's my favourite, but that'll be Peter's decision, obviously, and Claudia's — and, to some extent, yours."

She looked around; they were waiting. "I have two reasons for it being preferred. We found when we put the group together going on for three years ago now, that we built a good bridge to Giddings with the Radius acquisition. It's made us more efficient and responsive here."

"I'm pleased Giddings is still us to you," said Arthur. That was a needless jibe, she thought, but she had to trust his agenda.

"Of course, I'm a director, and the place is performing better."

"And you're family," said Samantha.

Not helpful, mom, thought Tania, or maybe… "That's part of my second point. But the first point is, if we IPO the whole thing, including Giddings as a unit, we have a success story to sell."

"And you'd be running it?" asked Ange acidly.

"That's the idea," said Tania, trying to sound balanced, and not be put off by the attitude.

"You realise, Father, that you'd be working for her, could you live with that?" That was put venomously, Tania thought, but Arthur seemed unconcerned.

"Let's park that. I can see a certain logic in the proposition, but what's your second reason?"

"It's not a good one, Dad, but I'll be torn otherwise. I love this place and the business, and I know you always wanted me to run it. Well, I know it's a big business, and I hate to sound arrogant, but I love the other things I do as well. This way, I could combine them. I honestly believe there's a good business logic, Will and Peter do, too, but I'll admit, it's also right for me."

"See!" said Ange. As if that proved anything, thought Tania.

Arthur was thinking, waiting to speak. "I like the plan, chicken."

"But working for her?"

"Ange, Ange, calm down. I wouldn't do that," said Arthur. Tania was shocked but tried not to let it show, she had to trust him now to have thought this through. "It's one of the things that makes it attractive to us." Samantha was nodding too. He looked to Tania. "I want to retire. Can you manage it without me?"

"If you'll stay as a director." She hadn't thought this far, but it could be ideal, although she'd need to recruit a boss.

"Of course I would." He smiled. "Peter made the same point. Seems you two either think alike, or you fooled me about not talking to him."

"I didn't…"

He was still her father, and if he really thought that she could have tried to trick him, well, that hurt. He waved an arm to calm her down. "I didn't think I'd lost it. I trust both of you completely, and I'm sure I'm right to do that. So, here's what I'd like to go with; my conditions, if you like. Your mother and I went through this yesterday."

Ange was looking a little shocked. Tania was still surprised but ready for anything now.

"It was part of the discussion with Peter, including what I'm going to tell you about Ange."

"Me? This involves me?"

"More than you think. Listen up. There'll be a couple of things you'll have to do. My twenty-five percent of Giddings, well, that's fifteen plus the trusts' interests, gets rolled into this whole unit. Your business, missie, is probably worth twice mine, if we take your William's estimate of the projected market cap — obviously we'll look at that in detail, but my price is that I control at least ten percent of the total when it's put together. OK?" He looked at them. "Well, he's said he'll agree if Will tells him to, that's the way it'll be structured, with us as ten percent of the Dickinson Gunter Group, and Peter as the same."

"He's agreed that already?" Tania was surprised. Will had said nothing.

"He's thinking about it."

"But the Giddings name stays." Ange was being querulous, but was intrigued presumably by what her role was.

"Of course," said Arthur patiently. "It's the brand on the Giddings business, but the group gets known by investors. Now, here's the thing, my ten percent gets controlled by you three, with Tania as the managing representative in the business. You'll together have the same share as Peter Dickinson, chicken, it makes sure you have a powerful voice. I just need you to draw up how we best make that happen. Ange, can you do that? But none of you can sell without the other two's permission, understood." Ange slowly began to nod. The necessity had been immediately obvious to Tania. Arthur went on, "And the sweetener is I gift each of you three million now so you can't plead any short-term needs, OK?"

Even Ange looked surprised, and pleased.

"Now the other thing is, he wants some help with the Foundation. He wants an American perspective, to make it more global, and he wants a legal brain. Can you help him?"

Ange was stuttering. "I'd need to look at what's involved."

"Of course you will, Flossie, but you need to impress them when they're here in four weeks. We don't want a weekend of your Sourdough Sally faces."

Ange looked momentarily huffy. Tania suppressed a laugh. Samantha chided, "Arthur," worried he might put her off.

But Ange was up to it. "Well, I'll be delighted to meet an older man with charm at last, rather than what I've had to grow up with. But thank you. I'm intrigued — and obviously delighted with three million."

"That's only if the deal goes through, though."

"Of course," they said in unison.

He waved his papers at Tania. "This is splendid work, chicken, you always impress, I have to say, but I'm embarrassed by how much that English gent raves about you," he turned to Samantha, "but your mother and I can stand it."

***

It made for an unusually happy evening. Ange seemed to have found a place back in the family. Arthur left them at his usual early bedtime but Samantha, who kept Tania talking normally, also left early to leave the sisters on their own. Ange was happy to talk work, and New York and Dallas for a while, but grew more reticent when relationships were discussed. She was evidently aware that Tania led a more 'adventurous' life, as she called it, but seemed reluctant to divulge much about her own situation. Tania didn't push, the newfound atmosphere had been hard won, and Ange had always been brittle, but at least there was a hint that she would welcome an invitation for a New York weekend. It was enough to let Tania feel that her sister was curious about what 'adventurous' was and might want to try experiments away from Dallas. At least Tania felt warm enough to make the invitation genuine, and confident that Robert would find someone to broaden her sister's education.

But not at Noah's, definitely not Noah's. She woke early with, she admitted, too much curiosity about what might have gone on there, and an inappropriate conscience that any subsequent personal crisis for Martha, but more especially for Will, might be, in some way, her fault. She found herself, soon after six, making coffee in the kitchen. While it was still brewing her mother appeared, as if by some intuition.

"Now, you're not telling me you're leaving early. We have David coming to lunch."

They hugged. "No, I'm not leaving early. Wait!" There was a smile at the corner of her mother's mouth. "I am committed to lunch, Mom, especially if Ange is staying, but what's with the David thing. Are you plotting?"

Now it was a full smile. "Of course. I've had two little thoughts."

"Oh, God. Just reassure me that any thought of a romantic link between David Wilkins and me is long forgotten. I only ever get business messages now."

"Oh, good heavens, yes. He's much to nice a man to waste himself on you." The smile wasn't leaving her mother's face. "Are you making that for me?"

"I wasn't, I didn't expect you. Were you listening for me?"

"Expecting you. You have a lot on your mind. I thought you might want to talk," then Samantha chuckled — it was one of Tania's favourite noises — "but not, obviously, about the things you never want to talk about."

"Ange is coming to New York for a weekend."

Samantha looked briefly surprised. "Are you going to lead her astray?"

"I hope so. A little."

And the chuckle was there again, then a smile. "Good, although that might interfere with my lunch plans."

"You're lining him up for Ange?" Tania was pouring the coffee into mugs.

Samantha took hers. "Would that be so wrong? Come on, let's go through." They went to what had become the conversation sofa in the drawing room.

Tania had been thinking. "Not wrong, but have you ever seen a piece of matchmaking really work?"

Samantha shrugged. "I suppose not. Not for any of you three. But that's not why David's coming, really. Your father wanted him here."

It dawned on Tania suddenly, "Are you thinking…"

"That he might run Giddings for you, yes, well, it's your father's idea, of course. He and I talked about it on Friday after Peter called. He asked if there was anybody you and your father could trust to run it, as CEO, he said, with you as Chairman and President. Your father would like you to think about it"

"And you've been sent as diplomat?"

"Tania Elisabeth, be ashamed of yourself." This was good-natured mockery. "Your father's perfectly capable of that conversation with you, but I wanted to catch you before anyone else stirred. You think quickly, child — well, you've always amazed me — but you do prefer to digest your surprises. And I will admit that I wanted to open your mind to your sister's possibilities. You're OK with that, if anything happens."

223

"Of course I'm OK with that."

Now she got a conspiratorial smile from her mother. "But it shouldn't stop you showing her a little of New York life." And Tania had a feeling that her mother understood more about her New York life than she really wanted her to — but it led quickly into a conversation about Ange and Debs and their lives — and Samantha's glimmer of hope that Debs was finally settling into a relationship that might last longer.

Debs, now in Chicago, hadn't gone that far in her phone calls with Tania, but it was an impression that Tania was getting.

"But you're worrying about something, darling. I'm not going to pry, but it seems like business isn't the only thing on your mind. Men?"

"You're right, of course, but it's not about me. It's a couple I'm close to." Then Tania thought: the Dickinson visit would likely be with Martha and Will. This was certainly not a topic she could discuss with her mother. Fortunately, Arthur wandered in with his own coffee mug.

"Evenings I leave you two in peace, but I figured I had some rights in the morning."

Tania stood up and kissed and hugged him. "I wanted to talk to you anyway."

"Why, has your mother got you on one of those embarrassing topics you need to escape from?" They all laughed easily together.

Samantha stood up. "I'll leave you."

"Are you two orchestrating this?"

"Not a bit of it, child, but I expect you've been told we've been talking about a lot."

"I think you've been very creative. I'm thrilled that you like the plan, well, especially the way you've worked on it."

Samantha, who'd hovered by the door, no doubt worrying that her matchmaking scenario might get discussed, seemed reassured enough to leave.

"Well, as you'd worked out before me, it solves my biggest problem. I had a darned hard time not sounding too enthusiastic with Mr D, but he was there ahead of me. Had you talked to him much?"

"Hardly at all about this. Oh, he knew I was torn about Giddings, I've talked to Claudia a lot about that. But these changes, no. I mean, I've worked hard on them with Will, but he's had all the discussions with Peter."

"He must be a remarkable young man."

"He is, Daddy, probably the man I admire second most in the world."

"Now don't you start that, young woman," but they were laughing with each other. "He's married to the banker, isn't he? Will she have to get involved? She sounds a little fierce; even Peter is a little in awe."

"I think she's wonderful, and we have talked about these plans, but it'll be left to a team at the bank now to manage the IPO. She'll stay out of it, partly because of the Will connection, but she's too senior anyway now. It all gets too messy otherwise," and Tania wondered for a moment about how she'd just meant that, "anyway, you've invited David to lunch."

"Your mother's doing." Arthur held up mock-innocent hands.

"Daddy!" She eyed him sceptically.

Now she got mock-guilt, "Yes, I encouraged her. Would it be so bad an idea?"

"I'd like you to tell me first."

"See! You've got me working for you already. You ask my views, then make your own decision." He was plainly finding this amusing.

"But at least I will actually consider your views."

"Oh, a dagger to the heart is an ingrate child. I thought I'd taught you to listen."

She laughed, she was only teasing, "You did — and now I am. So, David Wilkins, tell me."

He leaned back, becoming serious now, she thought. "You've always been right, of course, he could never have been the number one. But he is very bright, and he can bring people with him. He just wouldn't have the big ideas — well, maybe the ideas, but not the balls to push them through. For me, it really depends on how much time you think you can spend on Giddings. My impression is that Peter sees you as Will's number two, so you have to look at other stuff as well."

"I'm finding it hard to look that far, but, two things: Giddings would be by far the biggest company under the group umbrella, so it would need and deserve attention; and it's where my heart is, so it's always going to be the most important thing."

She loved her father most when he got a little teary, but she was feeling a little that way herself and they fell into a hug.

When they pulled apart, she said, "It's not a bad idea though. You think he'd go for it?"

"Talk to him. That's why he's coming." Then she got one of his knowing, squint-eyed stares, "it's certainly not to be lined up with a second-best Gunter, which is what I think your mother's planning."

Tania grinned broadly. "No comment."

The walk around the lake on her own after breakfast settled her mind about the business plan and she had a clear idea about how to handle the conversation with David. She wanted to talk to Will about the reception Two B had received in the Gunter household. It was material to his discussions, and she should talk to him, rather than Claudia or Peter, but it was nearing eleven pm in Shanghai.

She'd sent a text:

Great discussions here. Ultimately 2B welcomed — for all the right reasons. Happy to talk if you can. T xx

She'd had a reply soon after, as she'd known she would:

Excellent news. Tied up here with Lou. Talk tomorrow. W xx

But that brought her back to Martha. She had a business excuse to call, even if her principal purpose was only to reassure herself. The day was getting warm, but her favourite lakeside bench was shaded by the pines in the morning.

After six rings she was about to think better of the idea but suddenly, "Hi, honey, you checking up on me?"

Well, at least that sounded guiltlessly cheery. "Of course. I could say I wanted to hear you'd had a good time but I'm going to be honest and say I've been worrying about you."

"Oh, it's Sunday morning, the hour for truths and revelations. Why are you worrying about me?"

Normally Tania found conversations like this easy. She could guide them. But sometimes, she thought, you encountered a master. There was no point in playing games around this one. "Martha, I admire you and Will so much, I just wouldn't want anything to happen. That's the core of it."

"It won't, honey. Oh, I had a wonderful time, by the way, in a way that you could probably understand only if you shared my particular little kink. Am I really saying this on a Sunday morning? Hell, who else can I tell? I'll have to tell Will some time, but I want a few days before that. Hah, if the marks don't go, I'll have to tell him next weekend, but that Geoffrey seemed wonderfully competent and I told him my timetable. I'm afraid I found it thrilling. I'm just hoping my beloved will enjoy the scene too."

Tania, by now, was feeling relieved, and intrigued. "You think he would?"

"We've talked about it, but talking and doing are different, aren't they? But anyway, my devoted husband has been unusually elusive this weekend."

"I've just had a text." Maybe that was tactless, rather than reassuring.

"Oh, I've had a few of them, but not when I was expecting them. No doubt he'll tell me tomorrow. I suppose he's allowed his own secrets. You've still got plenty of yours, your Robert was frustratingly discreet — and gentlemanly, I have to say. You sure you're not serious about him?"

"Martha, I've watched him fuck at least two dozen different women. It doesn't make it easy to get serious, but I do like him."

"I'm going to guess he's seen something similar… and your lengthy silence is telling me I'm right. Well, I applaud you, but I thought I'd let you know I'm not two dozen and one. But he did provide me with entertainment. I do need that at the end, I have to come, and this powerfully built dark-haired guy."

"Ray?"

"Yes, that was his name. He was good, and I had fun. Once was enough for me, though. I'm afraid your Ray wasn't as much of a gentleman as your Robert. He had one or two things to say about how he'd enjoyed your company. But I'll confess, I was being nosey, so it seems fair to share this morning. Oh, I even had a long talk to Noah afterwards. I hope he didn't realise quite how nosey I was being with him. He's on our radar for suspicious business dealings. I'm only telling you because you need to be careful, especially now. You're becoming very important, girl. I'm guessing Two B's gone down well."

Tania talked at length about yesterday's meeting, with Martha providing the occasional encouraging comment.

"Well, sounds like my man's going to be very happy — unless something else has waylaid him."

"Are you really worried about that?"

"Not really, but everyone has a past. But we also have futures, I need to see if we're going to build this in. I must go, honey. You've done ever so well, but I have a date with some arnica cream. I'd rather manage how he finds out. Will I see you this week?"

"West Coast."

"OK, have fun, and ring whenever. You know you can, don't you?"

Tania laughed. "Well, I do now, I think, we've just exposed more confidences that I've shared with anyone, except maybe Lavinia."

Now Martha laughed. "Another Jack Stephens victim. You're the only one that's beaten him, my love. I'll see you soon, and thanks for calling — and for getting last night organised. I had a wonderful time."

Tania looked into the lake for a while, only partly reassured. Martha hadn't seemed to want more than a little excitement, maybe they could build that into their lives. But what was with Will?

21

This was an awkward journey when fully planned, thought Will, but missing the Friday evening flight had made it worse, particularly since he had to manage all the rebooking himself.

Penelope would doubtless have done it better, but his revised itinerary would need to remain secret.

'Missing the flight' would be his excuse. It was tenuous. The people who knew him, those that mattered, knew how utterly reliable he was. He needed to fix on a story.

He couldn't invoke bank discussions; it was Martha's bank, that could be easily checked.

He couldn't invoke Henry, his principal London contact, Henry was too involved — with everyone.

He couldn't invoke Merle; the truth behind the delay, or the text message that had made him stay:

Not too much damage, my darling, heart still intact, I think, but longing for more. Must you rush off? One more night, please, before another long silence. It would make it more bearable.

Your loving Merle XXXXXX. Now delete!

He should have texted back later, on his way to the airport, he knew, and not reacted by telling the Lanesborough he needed another night — but he'd done that, and replied to her, even before he'd rebooked flights;

daring himself, after years of relentless commitment and self-discipline, to do something impulsive. Daring himself to risk feeling again what passionate and overwhelming love used to feel like.

But Martha? That was love too, wasn't it? He was certain. But it was different from the feelings he'd had for Merle then, the feelings rekindled last night: the complete abandonment to the voice of the heart. Getting ready to meet her again, he showered and remembered — paying such scrupulous attention to cock, testicles and foreskin — the beast rose to remind him that love's subterranean voices were equally powerful.

Equally?

Were they more? Worth risking so much for? Just to feel again briefly that trembling delight that came with holding her naked body in his arms, listening to her enchanting laughter, feeling her relentless desire for him — aware, too, of his for her.

In the morning there had been no missed taxi, merely a rush to get packed while so reluctant to leave the delectable naked body still lying, tempting, in the bed. The voice had said, 'You mustn't worry, this has been wonderful, but I'll be thinking of it as my Olympic Games. Just tell me it'll be once every four years and I'll train for that.' He'd smiled, but had realised already then that he would want to seek her out the next time he was in the city, to know again those searing feelings he had spent eight years forcing himself to forget.

The guilt that journeyed with him had been for her, not for Martha. For Martha he had merely to cover tracks to ensure his time could be explained. The journey would anyway make it a lost weekend. Lost? Yet he'd found what had been lost. Or he'd found something, and now he had empty hours and miles of travelling by himself to work out what that was.

He was still distracted when Lou met him in the Four Seasons bar. He didn't share Alphonse's and Isobel's bright-eyed fascination with the city — but they were, in slightly different ways, buildings people. Will was about people themselves, albeit understood and explained in the language of numbers — but that wasn't Merle. Stop it! he told himself. Focus on Lou.

He'd been surprised that Lou had accepted the invitation. Will still wanted to reach Tony, Lou was serving as a proxy; that might help him understand some of the underlying feelings in Funds. He still couldn't identify whether Henry's antipathy had been personal — about the junior bypassing him — or professional, wanting independence and more complete autonomy. Lou had seemed motivated principally by the thought that he would get the full picture before his sister — 'You see Meitang Monday, yes?' The 'yes' had sealed tonight's dinner invitation, the dinner that Will's revised travel plan had barely rescued.

"You feel OK? You look like shit," had been Lou's not unfriendly greeting when Will got to the bar.

It was probably fair, thought Will, who'd slept unusually fitfully on the journey's stages and who had the prickly, myxomatosis eyes that long journeys engendered.

Will had smiled, and reassured Lou that he felt better than he looked. Will found himself almost always capable of sustaining his civil demeanour. It was close enough to friendliness to keep most conversations warm and open; even with Lou, it appeared, although he'd reminded himself to be wary of the disappointed princeling. "And I'm delighted you've found the time. It would have felt like a wasted weekend otherwise, just travelling."

"Must be important to come all this way," said Lou with a sly smile.

"Oh, there's always a lot on here anyway. I need to keep in touch with your finance team at Senlin, and the Hong Kong businesses need looking at. It's useful to tie everything together, but it's good to get a head start this evening."

Lou nodded silently. His English hadn't been bad when Will had first met him, but his London and New York time meant that any everyday colloquialisms could be used without fearing the furrowed brow. It wasn't language you had to worry about with Lou, he thought, and he couldn't win Lou over if he tried using standard blandishments to conceal purposes. He could tell that from the frown and the raised eyebrow.

"But you're right that the main purpose is about something bigger. What have you picked up about Peter Dickinson's plans?"

"Not much, I thought you'd tell me."

"Ha, well, I don't know them yet." Now Lou's frown got bigger. "But I am the one putting his options together for him. He's starting to think about the corporation beyond him, and about what he should do with his money. He likes to see a range of clear choices. I'm just trying to work out how each of them could work — and I need help with that. Does that give us a good start for our dinner conversation?"

Lou looked appeased, but Will's meta-mind reminded him to be wary of comfortable assumptions. What he wanted from the evening was to understand Lou's plans. "Sure, let's go through. I figured you wouldn't want to go out to eat. Meitang can spoil you with the birds' claws tomorrow." He put on a wicked but friendly smile; he'd noted before that Will struggled to be enthusiastic about local cuisine, but it gave them a chance for small talk while they read menus.

When the waiter had taken orders, Lou started, "What do you think Peter will do about Senlin?"

He'd tried to put the question casually, but it was inconceivable he didn't know — Peter would have reassured him at some point. "I think he regards his commitment to your father as sacrosanct. That was a five-year programme, with three years to run."

"Three years to make Peter Dickinson even richer."

"And three years to make Senlin bigger, better focused and more efficient, so, also richer, don't you think?"

"Zhao Meitang richer, maybe."

"I understood your father left you and Lee well provided for." Will knew the details of all the arrangements. The men would, in all circumstances, be comfortable, but Mei effectively controlled everything. Their share allocations, which could make them truly independently rich, could not be sold for ten years. Peter had been trying to argue that down to three. He saw the dangers of 'festering resentment,' as he had put it to Will.

"There's a lot of wealth bound up in the corporation for you."

"My English is better these days, Mr Will, I understand 'bound up in.' That means also not easily freed."

Will smiled. He hadn't been trying to fool him, merely push him to take the longer view. "There would be ways of doing a deal if you really wanted out. Someone would fund you on a hidden contract, for a discount, of course." That had been Will's suggestion to Peter when the discussions were stalling — it was more practical than ethical, but didn't go beyond Will's grey zone, or Peter's.

But Lou's, "I know," surprised him. It was as if he'd already decided. Then he quickly added, "But the discount would be too big," with a sly smile. "Why would I abandon future riches?"

Will wondered whether Lou had given more away than he'd intended. For now, it was just useful to note that Lou might lapse in unguarded moments. There was no need to provoke his defences by an interrogation. He'd asked for the evening to 'put Lou in the picture,' and he was glad Lou's desire to listen before Will would talk to Mei had made Lou accept. He went through all four options as even-handedly as he could.

Lou listened patiently, asking few questions, then considered for a moment. "But options two or four would be under one head, one and three would be independent groupings…" Will nodded slowly, Lou smiled, "each with more focus."

Will smiled back. Lou was sharp, and not to be underestimated. "That's the strength of those options, yes."

Lou was nodding slowly. "But harder for Mr D to detach himself. Harder to leave a legacy. Is that what obsesses these old men?" Will tried shrugging non-commitally. That just provoked a harder stare. "In the end the only way my father could ensure that was to put the bastard in charge." It looked like Lou was trying to provoke him. "And where does that legacy end up?" Lou didn't have perfect self-control; he was letting feelings show.

"You might have children yourself, Shen Liuwei." Will didn't think that thought would calm Lou, but it at least stopped him and made him appear to think.

He chuckled mirthlessly and shrugged. "Yes. Who else could?" He paused, but came back to the options. "But if Mr D stands back, Mr Will, you have a big job with options two and four, yes? Anointed successor?"

"It's Peter's corporation, however it's structured, but he'll want someone pulling everything together, whether it's in three parts or one."

"But there's a big job if it's one. It's only a staff role if it's split, isn't it?"

"That's what we've got to work out, that'll be for the board meeting next month. I'm still talking to everyone about how each of the four could work best. I'm seeing Alphonse again on Wednesday and I need to catch up with Tony." He spoke as calmly as he could. There was no point in letting Lou know how irritated he was getting with Tony's elusiveness.

"But they all leave you in the middle, don't they? As top dog or as dogsbody." Lou chuckled at his description. Will laughed with him; it was funny, he thought, and illustrated why he thought Two B was the right way forward.

"I'll have a role in there somewhere, I'm fairly sure."

Lou was nodding, waiting to see if Will would say more, but he didn't. "Oh, Mr D says you're the man. When he started talking long term and the commitment to Senlin, Meitang pushed him hard about who would help in the future. He said you." He paused. "But that's only as long as he stays biggest shareholder, isn't it?" Lou lingered over the point. Will let it register, but only that it was in Lou's mind. With friendly connections, Peter had almost absolute control. It wasn't worth discussing. Although, had it been so, he wouldn't have discussed it with Lou. Will needed to play a few thoughts through there.

"You've discussed this with Meitang?"

"Of course not. We don't speak, you know that. Mr D doesn't like it. He just insists that the three of us sit together with him for the big meetings — like about the future of Senlin. He's a clever man, Mr D, you can't help liking him — and, to be fair, he does listen to Lee and me. The bastard doesn't."

"Lou!" Will said sharply. It felt right to register some displeasure.

Lou raised his hands in acknowledgement. "I know, I know, I apologise. My half-sister, OK?"

"I'd prefer sister."

Now Lou looked obdurate and shook his head.

"I'll call her your sister, or the Chairman," said Will.

"Call her Meitang if you want this discussion to continue," Lou was staring grimly.

Good, thought Will, we've got some emotions and resentment in the mix, that might help uncover problems. "Meitang it is, then." That was an easy compromise. "So, where did that discussion end up?"

"He's your Mr D, he won't let himself be pushed by Meitang, but he did say he'd committed to five years, but he wanted to do no more. I think he was trying to appease Lee and me but, of course, we prefer it with him there — and Lee said so — not very straightforward, you know my brother and his, ha, I like this word, his circumlocutions — I learned that from Henry, it's what Tony calls bullshit," he was smiling, as was Will now, but he was going to say more, "and then he said he would be working on Senlin longer than he would be working on Dickinson. Mei asked him what he meant and he said Claudia was pushing him — and you already had some ideas." Will raised an eyebrow, surprised only that Peter had raised the subject, but it didn't really answer the question about the information leak. "Yes, you, Mr Will. Have you been lining up the big reorganisation to get yourself in the big job?"

"It's true I've been encouraging Peter to look at the business beyond himself but, as you've seen, I'm giving him a range of options."

Will was getting a sceptical stare. "Henry and Tony think some options are better for Mr Will."

Will shrugged. He'd learned long ago not to challenge people who looked at everything, including others' motivations, through a prism of self-interest. "That's a decision that Peter will make with the board."

Now Lou leaned back in his chair, "He's trying to train Meitang about how to get her way subtly — like he always does." He gave a hollow laugh. "But he has talents she doesn't have."

Will smiled. That was incontestably true, but Peter had had to build his corporation. He wasn't handed it by a dying father, a man who'd seen Meitang as far more capable of building... what? A legacy, was that it? It didn't matter, not today. The immediate challenge was to make sure Dickinson and Senlin were on the right paths, and Will had got enough out of Lou now to understand where some obstacles lay. He could leave that and get Lou to talk more about his business, and himself.

Lou, with his questions answered and food and drink in front of him, was engaging, albeit cynical about his fellow man. He seemed to have developed a good relationship with Tony — and Will already knew that casinos and girls figured in that, although Lou did no more than hint at that. 'I like Tony, he's easy to be with, and the clients like him.'

That had prompted a thought, and an opportunity for a little flattery: "You do seem to be on a roll with new client acquisition. Are all these Asian contacts yours?"

"Mostly, but some new money coming out of Europe, wanting a home in Asia."

An alarm had been triggered. Henry was careful in Europe, and even Tony, in New York, had systems for checking sources, but European money coming into Asia might not be so clean.

"You've done the checks on that?"

Lou hesitated. "Oh, sure, we have good systems here too, you know, some of the stuff we turn away."

That happened with Henry, he knew. Was there more Lou might tell him? "I'm not going to pretend that we could say that the original sources were clean. I just have to be sure it comes to us clean. It always finds a home in the end of course."

"Tony sometimes wonders if we're too..." he hesitated and chuckled. "Too fuckin' prissy, is what he says."

Will smiled but said nothing. It was one of the sources of tension in Dickinson: Peter's insistence that Will lay down and audit the standards for client acceptance. "Being caught even once would be bad for our reputation."

"Of course." Lou waved an arm, chopsticks like a baton. "But, like you say, it always finds a home."

Will wondered what he might need to check. Somehow, tomorrow, he would need to ask for a study on the Asian funds market — a study independent of their own business.

Maybe in the morning he would be clearer, with less jet lag, with a mind clear of Merle. Yes, she'd been there all evening lurking and, back in his room later, she'd helped him to fall asleep in the way she had done on lonely evenings years ago — but now the fantasies were enriched with fresher memories.

But he'd got off a text to Martha:

Good dinner with Lou, but it's left me thinking. Feeling groggy now but would love to disturb you Sunday evening. Only business talk, I'm afraid. Missing you badly WXXXXX

He'd wondered if he should mention the Noah event and ask if she'd been, but he couldn't face the thought of having to tackle a topic like that. She might when he called in the morning. That would be one of the dangers, but he couldn't ignore the lurking suspicions that Lou had somehow planted in his mind.

Only business talk? NFI! Well, tell me you love me first, then you can talk about anything. Sleep well, my love MXXXX.

He did.

22

Penelope had tried to put him in the Peninsula again. I had to intervene. 'The Mandarin, darling, please, all the meetings are this side on the island,' I'd had to email. I think I irritate her, but she knows she has to comply. Well, I think she does. I've had no problem changing any arrangements for the past year. I like to think Peter's had a word. Now, that's a man I'd like an evening with!

I said evening, children. I'd like to bask in the charm and compare notes on lots of things.

Now, for an evening followed by a night, I'd choose this evening's companion, happily married though he is.

Come on! Some of my best relationships have been with happily married people — sometimes with both halves of a couple. Yes, and together.

I've been leading a quiet life lately, however. Conrad and I have fun, but we're no longer rabbits. Tonight with Will, will be quiet. I'm just going to be thrilled to have him to talk to for a while.

I'm comfortable waiting in the Mandarin bar on my own. Yes, you get the odd American offering to buy you a drink, but I smile and say my man's just coming. It doesn't always work, sometimes 'Just fuck off!' is necessary, but the ones who are sensitive enough to take the hint, well, I like to encourage with a smile and a kind word.

If I'm on my own? I don't do that anymore. But here he is anyway, exactly on time.

My embrace is unseemly for this culture and place, but I get an equal hug back — and a kiss on the lips! OK, only a light one, but it's how lovers should be.

Oh, I know it's been years, but once a lover, always a lover, is how I prefer it to be.

"Now, young man, I like to think this might be the only relaxing part of your trip so, take a deep breath, order a drink, and don't think you're rushing me with anything."

He squeezes my hand, lets me sit down again, nods to the waiter, and pulls his chair nearer mine. "You're probably right, about it being the only relaxing part, so I've no intention of rushing anything. You look amazing, and I still adore you — and I also like the choice of man you've made. Has Conrad spoken to you about our dinner?"

The waiter takes his order. Will's eyes ask me if I'm ready for another. I shake my head. These evenings are too rare to spoil by getting blurry.

"He thinks it could be the start of a beautiful friendship." I ham up the accent, not expecting him to get the quote, but he does.

"I think I'd have to be Louis, and not the murdering bar owner."

"So, the corrupt policeman, and not the noble hero, eh? That's not the way I see it."

"Don't!" he says and raises his eyes. I obviously look puzzled. He smiles. "Don't worry, we'll come on to that, no noble heroes here. I'm afraid we've lots to talk about."

"Oh, dear," I say, smiling.

He smiles back. "*But none of it affects your business, which is performing splendidly.*"

"*I know, but I still prefer to stay under your radar. Surely I'm insignificant?*"

I get a smirk from him. "*I have a very good woman who keeps an eye on you and of course I get an update before I ever talk to you.*"

"*Of course you do,*" *I'd be kidding myself if I thought that was special attention. Will is the most meticulous person I've ever met,* "*and I'm glad we don't have to talk about that. You also got to see Sandra again. That made her happy. Do we talk about that?*" *I give him a suspicious eye and wonder what he'll admit to.*

"*Are you speculating, or do you know?*"

"*What do you think?*"

"*I think she's probably messaged you.*" *Good boy! I smile and nod.* "*And she may even have said that she demonstrated to her own satisfaction, with my semi-reluctant participation, that she's still pretty enough to stir me.*"

I chuckle and think, 'Well done, Will, we can still talk about the important things,' but now he's a little on edge, and hesitating. No point in me prompting him, he'll tell me if he wants to.

"*Sades, there's something I'd like to get on to later, and you're the only one I can talk to.*"

"*Merle?*"

He looks thunderstruck. "*How... has she?*"

I squeeze his hand. "*It's only intuition, darling, but I've always had oodles of that.*" *I want to hear more straight away, of course, but this really needs careful handling if anything's happened. She keeps dangerous company nowadays. "I've heard nothing, so I don't know how significant your issue is, of course..." I think I do already, he's never normally edgy. "But we can agree to leave that until after the main course. You've lots of other things to tell me." He's nodding, still looking awkward, he's had Mei, and Lou, and he has Alphonse tomorrow — and that's going to be harder than he thinks. "I have a feeling, my love, that something simple on room service is going to feel like a more relaxing arrangement for this evening's discussion."*

He laughs. I was serious. He realises that, of course. "I was on the verge of suggesting that myself, but it was the arrangement word that triggered some memories."

Of course, it's how I used to refer to the relationships I participated in, which weren't relationships in a classic sense. It's what Will and I had when he was recovering from Merle; now I wonder what he's got into again. Just because he's almost perfect, I think, doesn't mean his life is going to be without complications. No life worth living should be. "But we're still leaving Merle until after we've eaten," I say firmly.

He laughs again. "Yes, but it's not the most difficult problem."

But when we get on to it later, I believe it is. That's something I can see more clearly than he can, in spite of his other issues looking middleweight horrendous.

He starts with Lou, having asked if we could regard Conrad and Sandra as dealt with, although he did say he'd be calling Conrad very soon — I think Conrad's expecting that. I asked if he'd be getting in touch with Sandra. He pretended to look disapproving at that little joke, but then lightened up. 'You think I want to deal with Boris?' he'd said. That's it, Will, let's not get too serious about everything. 'But you would risk taking on Conrad, wouldn't you, I mean, if anything happens with us?' It was a wan smile, he was too distracted to respond then — these other problems must be serious, too.

Lou had obviously worked out that Peter was thinking of big changes. That locates the first leak in Asia. It doesn't take it back to Gerry, though. But Will has picked up a hint from Lou that new money is coming into the region and he'd had doubts whether Lou was being truly frank about how close he and Tony were to that. He's already talked to Henderson — who I got on with, I must admit, but he does have his detractors, not least Claudia. But this is a topic he wants to talk to Conrad about. Sure, go ahead, I'm thinking. Conrad already has his own suspicions.

He wants to know what I think of Lou, but I can't add much to what I learned a few years ago. Mei seldom talks about him. She talks more about Lee — I think those two are making that work. Will had seen Lee. 'Seems to be doing OK, or will be; he and Mei are happier with what Peter's suggested. He will look into new areas: they must be linked to the core business, but they have a good man who can run that for him.'

'You think that's a good idea, do you?' I'd teased him. He'd smiled. Of course it was a good idea, it had been one of his. I'd guessed.

This is the point where we stop bothering with the half-eaten club sandwiches and it gives me the chance to snuggle into him on the sofa. He and I stopped playing years ago; he's in love with Martha and they're profoundly well-suited, is how I read it; and he has to tell me something about an incident with his first great love, all right? Got it? This is close friendship, and I do enjoy having his arm around my shoulder.

First, he has to tell me about Mei, but he starts with a question, "Are you picking up any changes in her?"

"About her becoming more imperious, you mean?" I don't want to tell him about the suspicions that Daiyu and I have yet, I want to see what he's picked up.

"Well, she is that, I suppose but, apart from Lou, the people around her seem to show grudging respect — not that they'd divulge anything to me, I suppose, but the finance team seem very aligned with what her aims are and what her programme is, and I pushed them very hard on that this morning — without her in the room. I also had to meet a property woman Peter and Alphonse had both asked me to talk to. Mei was there for that and yes, she was a bit imperious — but it is the part of the business she understands best, isn't it?" He doesn't need my nod, but it is where she was making a career, "Well, it was Mei who put the hard questions, but the woman stood up well to her, much better than the two time-servers she's had running the division since her father..." He hesitates. "I mean the official father, of course."

"Of course you do, poppet, but I think that illustrates why we're better off alone up here, and not in the restaurant."

"Where your fingers wouldn't be inside my shirt, stroking my chest, you mean?"

"Exactly," I say, but now he gets the full hand and not just the fingertips. He doesn't move away. I think we're relaxed. "So, has she fired the other one already?"

He chuckles. "Not officially, no, but he wasn't a party to my meeting, and when Yang Li had been dismissed — and that's not too strong a word — Mei asked what I thought. I said 'I thought you were very hard on her,' and she had been, but Mei just laughed and said 'she has to stand the heat.' I thought she'd done that very well, and I said so — and Mei had given ground where she needed to. So, more imperious, yes, but she's smart enough to have the respect of some good people and, more importantly, show respect for them. I'm not saying the finance team adores her — but they don't make mistakes, because they know they'll get picked up. No, it was something else that seemed different."

"Hmm, you're going to have to help me on that." My hand's a little deeper in his shirt now. I want to distract and let him tell me what he thinks he's finding.

"Well, you know the way Peter's tuning into what happens after him, that's part of this big restructure thing..."

"I thought it was you pushing that,"

"I just try to guess where he wants to go..."

"In the way that suits you best..."

"Don't you start," he says quickly, but he's chuckling, I can feel it in his chest, "I've had quite enough from Lou and Mei — even Lee managed a sly dig about who would be running everything, but at least he's seeing the plusses of the changes we've made for him, so he's a natural supporter. Anyway, we were talking about Mei, and when

we discussed Peter's plans — it was just the two of us at dinner — in her apartment with her own staff, no less — it seemed to make her thoughtful about what Senlin was for."

That led into a long silence, it was making me think, of course. *"And you know something you're not telling me."*

"What? No!" But I had become distracted.

He squeezes my shoulder. *"You've stopped stroking,"* he says, and I had. Restarting doesn't help, of course. As he rightly says, *"You're just kind of confirming it now. What is it? What am I missing? She's got thirty years of running that place ahead of her if she wants it."*

I sat up at that point and turned sideways towards him. *"She's a woman. She might be thinking she's got three years to find someone to do it for."*

He realises immediately, but his mind's a little big for something this simple. *"Yes, but gay couples find all sorts of surrogate systems — or any sort of impregnation of one of them. She could find someone younger..."*

He stops there. The penny, as they say, has dropped. Sorry about the cliché, but the man's an accountant, get over it! I'm quite proud of him. *"She wants a baby herself?"*

"Don't sound so shocked, my William, just because your Martha and I have avoided too much of that desire, doesn't mean it doesn't affect a lot of women."

At this point he looks really shocked, more shocked than he should do. I avoid the temptation to ask 'What's up?'— because it's coming anyway. *"Would you put Merle in that category?"* he asks.

My God! So that's where this discussion was headed. This confirms what they've been doing. But let's take this slowly. I doubt whether he should worry about that. *"So, you did fuck her."* I'm nestling in against him now, he gets my hand on his chest.

"We made love, Sades." He sounds wistful. *"I was late leaving. I stayed Friday as well."*

"God, that's terrible." I can feel him tensing, my head's on his chest and he can't see I'm smiling, *"Something's made William Uprichard change his plans!"* I try to squirm away but can't avoid the slap that hits my arse. I settle in again. I might like more of that later but for now we have a problem. *"Is it going to have consequences?"*

I put that deliberately as an open question; he understands its complexities, *"I've spent the weekend travelling here wondering about that. She says it won't — she says she wants Olympic Games frequency."* I can't see his face, but I'd guess he's smiling at a memory. *"I don't want it to have consequences. I do love Martha."*

I let my hand slide down to his cock. *"But he's not so monogamously devoted, is he?"*

"He has been."

I believe him, but one small touch tells me that he's not dormant — none of them is, in my experience. I tap his heart, or somewhere near it — my face is probably on it, technically. *"So are we worrying about this, or about Merle's pregnancy?"* We have to get his mind clear on this. I sit up, ever the opportunist, but I am being helpful. *"I doubt whether you have to worry about that. Over the years I've known her she's never given any indication it's on her mind, but you don't believe the Olympic Games bullshit, do you?"* Of course he doesn't, he's shaking his head. *"Ah, but you are thinking about future London trips.*

Or he is…" and I slide my hand onto his cock again. "Let's just establish and accept that he has a mind of his own, shall we? Have I taught you nothing about the irrelevance of guilt?"

***

I hadn't exactly forgotten how wonderful it was, but my occasional fantasy with my best vibrator hasn't been doing justice to this experience. I'm reassured by the stiffening lump against my hip that there'll be more later and, bless him, he's smiling as he talks about our memories. Any hint of guilt would be insulting — a denial of all my education — and inhospitable.

"Did we finish the work bits?" I asked — I do love the languorous way his finger still strokes my clitoris; she'll be ready again whenever he wants, but this is the walk along warm, wet sand before we plunge into the waves again.

"I haven't the faintest idea," he says disarmingly. That's probably as close to a fib Will, will ever get.

"But if I ask you now, it'll be summoned instantly from your memory banks."

I get that boyish smile I love. "It's lovely making love with someone who knows you so well."

Careful, Isobel, I think. That's put me a little on my guard, but he laughs! "Have I used the forbidden expression? Oh, punish me!"

He's teasing me! "I would, you know."

"I know, Madame Dominatrix, but the beauty of greater physical strength…"

It's all so unexpected. His hand has moved to behind my knee, he pulls and I'm across his lap. I'm being spanked! I squeal in protest, briefly. He pauses, but only to readjust my position. I'm mollified by the hardening cock against my side. "It's time for you to bottom, my sweet. If I say I was making love to you, I'm not going to tolerate pedantic, tyrannical disputatiousness."

I'm not so much into bottoming, but if the top's good — and I'm prepared... but tonight I'm not prepared, not at all... but I love the strong, lean body... there's a hard slap, wow... and the command in the voice... so I find myself shuffling to present a better target. It's a big, hard hand and I'm beginning to find it thrilling. After ten or so, he pauses; one hand's stroking my back tenderly, the fingers of the other are playing with me, stroking and pushing in. I've come twice earlier, but I already want more. He has a way with fingers, I'm obviously wet enough for them to be everywhere, and a way with the firm grip around my waist, and I love the feel of the hard cock against me. He's good enough for me to give myself to this. I can be a bottom for a while; just do as he says and does, and let myself be pleasured.

"You need a little more," he says.

"I'm nearly there," *I murmur. My arse is a warm glow, and there's a finger in it and others playing with my cunt.* "Just a moment more, just a moment more." *I really do want to come again now but he won't let me, I know he won't, he's been too well taught.*

"No, not yet." *His fingers ease away.* "Kneel. Stick your bum up!"

"You make me wait just so you can enjoy doggy!"

That earns me a really hard slap — which is, of course what I wanted, and I do get some doggy for a while. Oh, it is such a nice cock, I will be eating it again later. But he's left me! He's leapt off the bed — but he's back quickly with one of those lovely long wooden shoehorns. I can imagine they get stolen very frequently, but that irreverent thought is immediately shattered by the flash of pain across my cheeks. The noise comes a split second before — and we tops love a good noise, the wooden shoehorn is very good in this respect but I'm way beyond academic contemplation. This fucking stings! My mind's a bit scrambled. He gives me time to adjust. He strokes my back, and my thighs. And kisses my lower back — then, briefly, strokes my clit again, but I know there's more to come.

After five more I'm beginning to get into it. Real bottoms get there quicker, in my experience, they kind of prime themselves, they bring anticipation, but now even I'm pushing my bum a little higher for him. We have a rhythm now. I think he gets his timing from my breathing. After a dozen or so I suddenly feel a gentle wooden tap on my fingers. They've made it, mysteriously, on to my clit. "Do you really want to come like that?" he asks gently.

"I don't suppose I do," I mutter indistinctly into the pillow — my moving my fingers away has given him the message.

"Six more," he says, "and then we'll see. I want to come inside you anyway. You should wait for me!"

"Yes, sir," I say playfully — and am rewarded with a spectacularly firm slap. I almost scream. I stay on a high for the next six; I guess that sharp one was a bonus. But he's moving now, the cock is mine again, oh, that's so nice

and deep. Oh Will, I hadn't forgotten, I hope I'm not going to regret being reminded. Now we're moving to his rhythm. I can handle that.

"*I love my handiwork,*" *he says, keeping his cock deep but obviously leaning back to look at me.* "*I should make sure you come first, but I can't wait…*"

I love moments like this with him. I can come as soon as I like, I'm already stroking myself gently, but I want… I want… and there he is, and I can release myself. God, that's glorious, so glorious.

After we've slumped, we doze a little. Well, I do. We're entwined when I come round and he's gently stroking me. I look up and he's smiling. I get overwhelmed by a silly feeling of relief. "*You can live with this, can't you?*" *My God, Sadie, I think, he's been topping me, let him have control.*

"*Only if you can accept that there was a little love-making in there.*"

We kiss, long and tenderly. "*Oh, all right,*" *I say, with a mock pout,* "*but only a bit. I saw borderline sadist in there.*" *He chuckles. He's much too confident to see that as more than a joke. This was too lovely though.* "*You realise Merle will have a problem now, don't you? You're quite good, as well as fucking adorable.*"

"*I have one myself.*" *He hesitates.* "*Well, I have two I think.*"

"*Martha as well, you mean?*" *I hug him. I'm not at all precious about him having to think of other women while he's cuddling my little naked body. Well, a bit, I suppose; he's not entirely wrong with this being a bit like lovemaking, with all its attendant complexities.* "*I *personally think you'll be fine. I'm not on a mission here, I'm having too much fun and pleasure, but I do think you two could have fun expanding your horizons a bit. You can still stay deeply in love."*

"Oh, Sades," he says, and hugs me now, "this is quite simple with you. I adore you, and you're an important part of my life." Now he chuckles. I pinch his skin. "Ow, what's that for?"

"You need to explain what's funny!"

He chuckles again. "Well, you're a brilliant top, and that's why we are an arrangement, as you call it, and not much more — if I accept what you say — but you've been such a perfect bottom for half an hour!" He strokes my arse. It's not stinging anymore, but I can still feel the heat — lots of it.

I kiss him again. "I'm not going to deny I enjoyed it, but I do prefer being in control." I pick up the shoehorn and wave it threateningly at him, but I'm smiling. I throw it on the floor. "My control later." I take hold of his cock now, it's just getting crusty as our juices dry. "But I'm going to limit myself to torturing him while I sit on your face." I get that lovely chuckle again, I can enjoy it now I know why it's coming. "But I'm not sure we've finished working, have we?"

The beauty of focus is that men can literally think of one thing at a time. Of course, the one thing they focus on a lot of the time is sex, but Will can move away from that for a while now and I know we'll work through the other issues. I'm not sure how much to say about Alphonse, anyway. I'll trust Will to be careful; I just need to warn him. Oh, and I'll need to say more about Mei and Alphonse. That would be a complication he'd have to factor in.

23

Alphonse had always got on well with Will. There was, he thought, a great deal of mutual respect, and Will had been helpful and supportive when Alphonse had been pushing the resort programme. It was too easy, however, to get lured into assuming an emotional bond existed when a project like that came together; cooler reflection later had made him realise that Will had assessed the programme entirely on its merits, which included an appreciation that the man driving the activities, Alphonse himself, was splendidly competent. Even running the development plan to budget and timetable had not led to less scrutiny by Finance, and Alphonse knew his occupancy numbers and profitability were constantly monitored on each site. So, although his respect was in no way diminished, in fact it was arguably enhanced by Will's mastery of all the facts of his business, he had come to recognise that the relationship they enjoyed was more functional than he'd once believed.

He also asked himself if he felt any jealousy about Will's apparent preferment — but it was a simple observation that only Will had the skills to oversee everything, if that was what Peter wanted — it was not so easy, however, to be so clear about how he felt about what Peter's feelings were. He'd never seen himself as a favourite son — until someone appeared to usurp the position.

He'd set the meeting start for ten. His habit was to keep early morning free for US business, but only two brief conversations had been necessary, and he'd quickly dealt with emails — including the reminder of his next Shanghai appointment. He felt both amused and irritated by Mei's PA observing that his schedule for that week had changed and now included an Australia trip to the Whitsundays; she was doubtless ensuring that he would still be in Shanghai for the Friday evening. His feelings about those meetings had changed since his conversations with Daiyu and, more especially, Isobel. He would need to talk more directly to Mei and challenge her — or simply use a condom and blame 'other opportunities' that had come his way, but his skills as a dissembler would never withstand her scrutiny, especially if the ladies were right. Although a condom would be a good way of provoking the discussion. He was pleased with the idea when he was disturbed by the faint sound of Daiyu's laughter coming from the boardroom next to his office. It was nearing ten. He should prepare to meet Will, then it struck him. When he left his door and looked through the glass wall, he could see the two of them sat next to each other at the large table. Daiyu, immaculate as ever but perhaps glowing a little more and the tall man with the copper hair who turned as soon as Daiyu had spotted Alphonse and waved him to join them. Will stood immediately and gave a warm smile and Alphonse felt a slight pang of guilt about denying the man feelings of friendship. The man was blandly handsome and exuded something that Isobel, at least, seemed to find very attractive and, if he judged her posture and movements correctly, so did Daiyu. He went in, brushed cheeks with Daiyu, and shook hands warmly with Will.

"This must be your favourite office," and Will gestured into the reception area, rather than out to the harbour view, "although your guys did a wonderful job getting mine and Tania's done." He turned to Daiyu. "We're the coolest in the building by far, but nothing I ever see comes close to this."

Daiyu almost seemed to blush as she said, "It is our shop window," but then she smiled teasingly at both of them, "so your people should perhaps complain less about our refurbishment budget."

"Well," said Will slowly, "what you book as refurbishment is twice as high as any equivalent office, but I'm told a significant amount of promotion money goes into it as well." Daiyu looked almost coquettish, rather than offended. "I only get told these things because there are people in my division who think I'm too supportive of the peculiar financial shape of your business," Will added. "They think I'm too soft on the pair of you, but I can understand that any client would be thrilled to see what you can do." He smiled slyly, "But I doubt if any would want to spend quite what would be necessary to produce this. It is marvellous, nevertheless. I am a major fan."

Daiyu wore a triumphant little smirk as she left the room. "You'd be surprised at how many want a lavish entrance. Anyway, I hope your business discussions don't go on too long, gentlemen, Isobel and I are hoping to join you for dinner."

That hadn't been discussed, thought Alphonse, and anyway, a thought occurred; he turned to Will, "I thought you were…"

"Oh, I caught up with Isobel yesterday evening, but she did warn me of this plot." He smiled at Daiyu. "And I very much hope we can make it."

"I hope so too," said Alphonse, hoping that a show of charm would mask his merely tepid sincerity. He felt awkward about the impending discussion. "Are you going to tell me where you are with it all?" he asked as Daiyu closed the door behind her.

No one he'd ever met presented business cases quite like Will. He always felt the presentations were concise and transparent, even on the issues of how the possible organisations would be run. He had, as always, a strange feeling when Claudia's role was discussed; he could never see her as a third party under discussion; he always empathised with how she would be feeling. Here the changes would be major and would, potentially, make her content — and that would make him content too, but about her, not necessarily about himself.

"I assume Tania and Claudia are happy about the Group structure?" he asked when Will had covered all four options.

"Especially so now, I think," said Will. "Tania's got her father on side with us embracing Giddings, so that solves her major headache and gives us real scale when we IPO. I've had only a brief conversation with Claudia. I think she thinks that's the best plan. Has she said anything to you?"

Alphonse felt a prickle of resentment — why should Will assume he knew about Claudia's thoughts — but Will was not an insensitive man. Overreacting would be too revealing. He simply shook his head slowly. "No, she hasn't, but I imagine it's Funds where the biggest problems will arise."

"You're right, I think," then Will gave a sly smile, "but I'm not making any assumptions about the property and resort area being fixed or easy in any option. Would you mind giving me your perspective first, though, on what you think Funds might be concerned about?"

Alphonse shrugged. He had nothing to conceal; he had nothing at all, in fact, yet. "I've not spoken to them about this." That was almost true. His call with Tony was scheduled for later. "I've not spoken to anyone about it apart from Daiyu and Isobel. I'm just assuming you have more difficult characters to deal with. You go back a long way with Henry though, don't you? What does he say?" For Alphonse, Henry was cool and rational, but fairly predictably and openly focused on his own interests; with Tony and Lou it was probably similar, but Tony always seemed to be reading a different script.

"Henry is looking for more autonomy out of the reorganisation. He sees downsides to losing Peter's money and his support — other investors like him being part of it. I think that's true even here, isn't it?"

Alphonse nodded. "Especially since the Senlin connection."

He got a long steady stare from Will. If Will had spent yesterday evening with Isobel, she would have updated him with the ladies' Mei theories, but Will wouldn't follow that avenue, at least until the main discussion was concluded. "Well, I think Henry sees that only Fund autonomy would be a compensating prize. Lou, I had a conversation with, but it's Tony who's being elusive and I can't wait until the board meeting before pinning him down. My working assumption is that he's against it anyway but wants to be as independent as possible."

That would be my working assumption, too, thought Alphonse. Tony was a little wild, but he got on better with him than most men whose wives he had slept with. He felt irritated with himself for letting that little thought creep in. He and Will had bigger problems anyway to deal with: Alphonse's problems. "Can we talk for a while about how overall control's going to be applied in these four options?"

"Of, course," said Will, quite openly. "Well, it's simpler than that." He went to the whiteboard at the head of the room. "In any option there will be Dickinson Holdings, through which money will be fed into the Foundation." He began writing names and drawing arrows in a neater script than almost anyone else could manage on a board. Alphonse could tell that Will had started with a whole picture in his mind. "I'll put one and three to one side, if I may…"

"Because the three areas stay autonomous?"

"Exactly, whereas two and four function a little like Dickinson does now…"

"With one head of the whole organisation?" Will nodded. "Who wouldn't be Peter?"

"That's his intention."

"It would be you." Alphonse put it as a statement, not a question, as much as anything to see Will's reaction.

It was calm and neutral, which was as admirable as it was irritating. "That's one of his thoughts."

"And what happens if he chooses one or three?"

"Then they function as independent entities. Peter becomes effectively a shareholder of each, but they have their own heads, or joint heads in the case of funds, where Peter becomes just another major client. You would obviously head property and resorts, with Peter as your major investor…"

"One of the major investors," said Alphonse. "Your wife's bank is currently another, and if Peter wants to take money out for his foundation, then someone else has to buy in."

Will smiled calmly. "I'm spared too much domestic debate on that. Martha isn't close to property these days, but you're right, of course. Shall we get into that in more detail later, or do you want to handle it now?"

"I'd rather be clear about the overall picture first."

Will paused, evidently considering something, then smiled again. "Lou made a point the other day about someone being either top dog or dogsbody. I think he meant me. It was funny, and accurate to a degree, but the top dog is always Peter."

"What will you do, though, Will?"

"I don't mind coming on to that, but my first job is to offer Peter options that could work and see what he's comfortable with — and what can guarantee him the most secure returns for the Foundation…"

"Without dragging him back into the business." That left them both looking at each other, Alphonse wanting this to work for Peter and Claudia, but also for himself — and the prospect of Will in between them wasn't truly welcome. "Or Claudia," Alphonse added. "How's the Group supposed to work without her? You'd be needed for that, wouldn't you?" Maybe there was a big enough role for Will in that, big enough to keep him away from Funds and Properties — maybe that was what Tony wanted to talk about. He'd called on Monday but had been content to wait 'until after you've spoken to The Boy,' which was Tony's customary way of referring to Will. That had made sense to Alphonse, but it registered with him that Tony had obviously been thinking about the changes already.

Will remained unnervingly calm. "Look, I'll admit there are some obvious people in certain positions. Tania does a brilliant job, we all think, but when you look at the consultancy companies and the addition of Giddings, it does look complex enough to need more support. So, there's an obvious attraction to a consultancy grouping, probably under Sandy Nicholls..." Alphonse had nodded, that made sense, and would please his friend Sandy. "You just have to ask yourself where that plugs in. I don't think Claudia or Tania would deny that they're emotionally very close to those businesses and they probably need to be helped to detach themselves from them, so I think you are looking at a chairman for the Group, particularly in options three and four, where we've added Giddings and separated the consultancies."

It made sense to Alphonse, and left a clear role for Will. "That could be you?"

Will shrugged. Alphonse had the sense that he'd just lowered the debate, he was putting people first, letting a tail wag a dog — but that was usually what Peter preferred anyway, he thought. "I assume I'll be in there somewhere, but that's down to the choices Peter makes."

That could just sound naïve, but to Alphonse it was beginning to sound disingenuous, and he decided to excuse himself his own reproach for not lifting his vision higher. "I'm probably starting to sound cagey, Will, and the more you leave obscurity about what you'll be doing, the more uncomfortable I get about what's really driving these changes."

Did Will look irritated? It was a fairly provocative statement, but Alphonse didn't think he did. He was looking directly at Alphonse now "If I'm asked what's the best way of guaranteeing the best possible long-term funding for the Foundation, while giving Peter and Claudia the maximum freedom to run it, then I have a personal preference for option four, which would need one person running everything and acting as the principal link with Peter and Claudia. I would like to be that person."

"Why?" Alphonse knew his question was tetchy, but these responses were too bland. Will was either too cool, or this had been stitched up already, and neither Peter — nor Claudia — had told him about it. And Will was very slow responding now.

"Because I think someone has to do it, and I'm probably in the best place." Will sat down now, he'd been standing beside the white board, marker in hand, for a long while. "So, there you have it, when we talk about it in New York next month, I'm tending towards a preferred option for Dickinson, which I think best meets Peter's objectives, but yes, it does happen to coincide with what I'd prefer for myself."

"Thank you for that," said Alphonse, and was pleased to see Will relax slightly. At least one layer of the onion had been pulled away — but it had left Alphonse feeling discarded, and needing a break. "Can we take half an hour and check other things?"

"Of course," said Will, apparently at ease with the idea. "Then can we talk properties?"

"Of course," said Alphonse, but he'd struggled to make himself sound willing. It was his business, strangers peering in felt wrong, and Will now felt like a stranger.

The break didn't calm Alphonse; he found his questions intensifying. He spent the last few moments of the break in his office looking out at the harbour, taking deep breaths; there were too many streams of thought eddying together, eddying and muddying.

Will was waiting. "Have you thought about how you bring the property organisations together?"

That caught Alphonse off guard. Had Will planned that? "What do you mean?"

"Well, I've grouped properties and resorts together, but my impression is you run them separately and they have different ownership structures: property is Peter and the bank; resorts is Peter and Senlin, fifty-one, forty-nine; and there's a Senlin portfolio which Yang Li will manage but you have a role in, and Dickinson has a stake in as part of the arrangement he came to with Wengwei. Would you want to roll all that together as one organisation?"

Alphonse felt momentarily stupid for not having considered it — but these were separate companies, and Mei was becoming as protective about the autonomy of Senlin assets as Peter had always been about wanting to ensure control of any enterprise, he part-owned. "I suppose I'd assumed we'd be aiming for a clean separation. Peter's never really been comfortable sharing. What's your proposal?"

"I'm just trying to work it out, but I need to ask a delicate question first. What's your understanding of what Peter's offered you?"

"What's he told you?" This seemed like cat and mouse to Alphonse, and he'd rather play the cat.

"He's told me his wants you to have five percent."

Alphonse nodded. "That's what he's told me, yes."

"But five percent of what? Five percent of properties, or five percent of his share — he's sixty percent owner, or did you understand it to include resorts?"

Alphonse had understood five percent of Peter's share only, but was he negotiating now? It hadn't seemed right to question a gift — and he had no real leverage to bargain with, only that Peter clearly wanted him to continue to run the area. "It is supposed to be a gift, Will, and I'm trying to remain really grateful, but it feels like I'm getting drawn into some sordid negotiation."

"Please," said Will, with some feeling, "I'd be really sorry if I left you feeling that. My understanding was also that it's a simple gift, well, something that recognises that a great deal of his property wealth is there because of you. OK?"

Alphonse was OK with that. Yes, it was generous, but, in round numbers, he knew that Peter's share could be valued at twelve billion now, and that Peter had put in less than three, over the years, to achieve that. Adding nine billion to the value had come principally from Alphonse's efforts, so five percent of twelve billion was magnanimous, but easily justified. It had also provoked an odd sense of his relationship with Peter having been commercial, rather than, as he'd realised that he'd come to see it, emotional. He had an odd and ugly sense of being paid for his love. He knew, or assumed, that the thought was wrong, but nothing made him feel quite comfortable.

Will carried on. "I'm just looking at it from the perspective of what frees up funds consistently over time, what reduces Peter's input — and his opportunity to interfere, that also needs controlling." Will was trying to get a smile out of him with that, but Alphonse wasn't comfortable enough to offer that pleasantry. "I see you as being instrumental in making that happen. You could be running a global property group with almost fifty billion in assets — and owning part of it."

He paused. It wasn't a thought that had occurred to Alphonse, the obstacles seemed immense — and he wasn't at all sure it was what he wanted. "Are you talking about Senlin and Dickinson tying in more formally? Each owning shares in a big unit?"

"That would be the idea. Do you think Meitang would be attracted to that?"

"My impression is that she likes to control everything. Senlin, even with its banks' stakes, would own less than thirty percent. Her father hated having only forty-nine of resorts, he only took that because he trusted Peter."

"Wouldn't Mei trust you? She admires you immensely."

Alphonse, whose world should be opening up with these new horizons, felt curiously hemmed in by them —

as if his life would be even less his own in the future. But Will was looking expectantly at him. This was a significant question. One he would rather avoid.

"How far are you with this thinking? Who's a party to it?"

"You and I. It's only just forming in my mind. The first two questions are: does it make sense; and does it appeal to you?"

"The first question is: would the investors like to see that come together?"

Now Will leaned back and narrowed his eyes. "I've got into the habit of trying to work out what's best for the investors and putting propositions to them. It's what I'm trying to do here. I'm quite excited by this thought, but it stands or falls with your enthusiasm for it."

"Doesn't it stand or fall with the investors' enthusiasm?"

"Yes, but my reading of them is that they'll be enthusiastic if you're enthusiastic — but at the moment you look like a man waiting at the dentist's."

Finally, Alphonse had to smile. "I don't know yet how I feel about it. I'd been attracted by the idea of taking a couple of major properties as my five percent, London and Florida maybe, and just being independent."

Will was nodding slowly. "Are you keen to sever your Asian connections?"

It was a question that was becoming more pressing, "My Asian complications, you mean?" That was a silly lapse, thought Alphonse; it was too revealing, he liked to stay so private normally — enigmatic was Claudia's most common description of him, even when he didn't feel he was being so with her. His complications were no business of Will's, but he seemed to have provoked reflection, rather than curiosity.

"I don't suppose anyone lives a simple life." Will sounded almost wistful — utterly unlike himself.

This was the wrong time to be curious, thought Alphonse. He should just feel relieved that his own indiscretion hadn't pushed Will to ask questions. Sure, there were complications, but these discussions had a profound bearing on what he did and where he lived and he had an uneasy sense that his relationships needed to be fitted in around that, even as they contributed to his disorientation.

"But there's a fundamental point here that we should clear up."

Good, thought Alphonse, this was Will being back to being Will. "Go on."

"I have made the assumption, which I'm also hearing from you, that you get five percent of Peter's property portfolio." Alphonse nodded. "I'm afraid I've assumed, in all four options, that it's a share to bind you in, and not a gift to set you free."

"That would be more logical," said Alphonse, trying to conceal a sense of being coerced. "I suppose we should clarify that with Peter."

"Do you want me to do that? He might feel awkward if he feels you're questioning his gift. I could just say I need it for my clarity in putting these ideas together."

That might even be helpful, thought Alphonse, but I'm the one who put the property empire together, I'm the one who's been close to Peter for fifteen years. I'm the one who was offered a gift, in recognition, I thought, but as an inducement, it now appears — to Will, at any rate. He became conscious that he was no longer sure of Peter — perhaps his relationship with Claudia was making Peter's feelings towards him change. "I think that's a conversation I should have."

Will seemed to consider, then nodded slowly. "I just thought you might find it helpful if I cleared up any misunderstandings." He paused, waiting to see, it seemed, if Alphonse would react, but this had become more elemental, this was about his relationship with Peter — and he didn't want Will interfering. "I will need to get it clear soon. My model assumes you as head of global property in each of the options. I know you need personal clarity, but, can I ask, is that such a bad alternative for you? Or are you looking for a way out?"

Had he been in a different mood, Alphonse might have seen that as a helpful question. He recognised that seeing it as intrusive, even provocative, was a response Will probably didn't deserve. This was a time to stay enigmatic. "Not at all, I'd just like a little more clarity on what my own options are — and it feels like I need a little more information."

"I can understand that," he paused, "but can I call it my working assumption that you would be the property head in all four scenarios?"

"Well, it will have to be somebody, whether it's me or not. So, I don't think the nature of my gift will impact your proposals. Would you have different people running funds, if Henry and Tony aren't happy?"

Will looked to be thinking while he was nodding. "I'll be just trying to present these options as clearly as possible at the board meeting. I'm hoping we'll all make the best decisions on the day."

"For each of us personally?" asked Alphonse — and he knew he was being provocative, even a little childish — but it was an understandable response, he thought, to feeling manipulated.

***

"So, how was the Boy?" was Tony's first question when Alphonse called him. "Got his mega-job all sorted out yet?"

Tony was clearly feeling at least irritated by the process, and, it appeared, by some of its objectives. It was too early for Alphonse to voice his discontent; better to find out first what was on Tony's mind. Tony was no friend; Alphonse was very aware that when they'd worked together to get Asian funding for the resort programme that it helped Tony corral some new wealth in the region and expanded the Funds considerably — and that had accelerated once Lou was fully engaged.

"He's making a decent job of saying he's got four possible options and it's up to the board to pick one — or none." Will hadn't discussed the 'none' option, but Alphonse would be surprised if Peter were to opt for one of the four in the face of united opposition from Funds and Properties.

"But was he honest about his favourite, at least?"

"He was honest about what would be best for him. But you seem to be well-informed, considering he says you're avoiding him. What's that about?"

Tony hesitated. "I've had all the stuff from Henry, without the Boy's 'best for Dickinson' bullshit."

"So, Henry's against it, is that what you're saying?"

"Mate, we lose lots of money and our star attraction, and as compensation we get fuck all, just a chance to contribute nobly to an as yet unnamed charity, presumably of madam's choosing. Nothing against Claudia, I can understand your feelings, but it doesn't feel like we're getting a deal out of it. I understand there's a sweetener for you, and I can see that's deserved. I just don't see why we're being cut adrift."

"Shouldn't you be talking to Will or Peter?"

"It's a higher priority for me to see what my alternatives are. I don't want GKS dropping out of the top ten because Mr D is feeling the hot breath of mortality. So, that's me being frank with you: my priority, new funds in time for when this blows up. What's your priority, anyway, what's your deal?"

"No one seems clear what my deal is."

"Mate!" Tony exploded, "I thought Peter had put a proposition to you. Five percent, wasn't it?"

"Five percent is what he said, but not five percent of what, and in what form."

"Aaaah," drawled Tony, "and you were too polite and charming to ask Daddy about this Christmas present, is that it? And now you're thinking that the box is so tied up with strings that you can't even open it. It's designed to keep you in harness, like Boxer the horse."

The feelings he'd been through with Will flooded back in again. It had been naïve not to ask questions, and it would take a very reassuring conversation with Peter to stop him feeling manipulated. "It could still be a very attractive proposition."

"Freedom, isn't that what we want? Independence? Not working in a conglomerate for a bean-counter?"

"I think that's not the right way to look at Will."

"I don't care, mate, I'm not going to call him 'boss', and neither should you. Look what you've built for Dickinson, it must be over ten."

"We reckon his share's twelve."

"And he's put in how much?"

"Less than three."

"You think the Boy could produce wealth like that?"

"Tony, he works in different ways."

"Well, he won't be working as my boss."

"I don't think I'd see it that way."

"Until your next resort expansion comes up for review and you get a 'your occupancy levels have been a little disappointing, Alphonse, I think we should sit on this one until you can demonstrate blah, blah, blah.' You don't need much imagination to picture that, do you?"

Alphonse didn't, but he wasn't being won over to Tony's cause. "Are you saying you'll go for options one or three?"

"We're looking for autonomy, and our biggest priority is replacing the funds that Dickinson takes out." Tony went suddenly silent.

"Or replace Dickinson?" If Peter were no longer the major investor, his control would lapse.

It took a while for Tony to respond. "We're having a chat here about our mutual interests, OK?"

"That's what I understood, yes."

"Confidential, just between us."

Now Alphonse paused, but there was nothing to be gained for him personally by not listening. "Yes, just between us; and Henry, I presume?"

"Henry, of course."

"What about Lou?" This would be interesting, thought Alphonse; he wondered how well integrated Lou was in Tony's plans, how independent of his sister was he trying to become. If Peter added her stake to his, he would be hard to dislodge as principal investor.

"Lou's with us. Talk to him if you like." Tony paused. "You may find he thinks you're too close to his half-sister to be trusted, so I don't think you'd find him very forthcoming."

"No, he's not a natural partner for me. I might call Henry though, when I've got my ideas clearer. Well, I'll call you back when I've thought about it."

"But where are you now? Planning to work for the Boy?"

"Planning to consider my options."

"Your options, not the options."

Alphonse smiled to himself. Tony often seemed reckless, but that was a front, every small detail mattered. "Exactly right. My options."

"Good on you, give it some thought, let's keep talking."

"Just one thing, though, Tony."

"I know, you're going to tell me that you've got some understanding of what they're trying to do."

"I never said you weren't clever. Should we meet up? I'm down there in two weeks."

"I'm not. I'm either in New York or up with you. But I'll tell Breeana, she'll be thrilled."

"I'd rather you didn't."

There was raucous laughter from Tony. "Ha, yes, your life's already too complicated, isn't it? Shame, that little thing she thinks she's got going with you has kept her quiet for a while. Never mind. Let's just keep phone lines open, we should stay up to date with each other."

"Makes sense. Thanks for the call, lots to think about."

"For you, yeah, but we have to act. Talk soon."

"Yes, talk soon."

Then he called Peter. He got Penelope. "They're in a big meeting with some charity people all day, Alphonse. I can get a message into him. Would lunchtime do, or should I call him out?"

"No, lunchtime's fine, thank you."

"That'll be around eight o'clock for you, right?"

"Right as always, Penelope, and thank you." He smiled to himself, she was always right, and it gave him the chance to avoid dinner.

24

"I can't work out if the meeting made you uncomfortable, or your missing lunch." Claudia patted Peter's stomach. "Although that probably didn't do any harm. What was that?"

They'd travelled, as usual, separately. Taking two cars, and two drivers, irritated her instincts but he wasn't the only one, she conceded, who had 'other things to tie up' when they happened to be working in the same place. This evening she'd arrived back later than he had; there had been a meeting with Sandy and a long call to Tania. She'd changed quickly and come down to find him at the table in the garden room, waiting to start his g and t — a little habit he'd developed 'to control his intake,' as he put it.

"That was Alphonse," he said. She sat down beside him as Hannes emerged with her drink. "We should talk about that." She tensed slightly, always half-expecting a different conversation than the ones that always ensued.

"And did that affect you more than the meeting? You were quite hard on those people, you know."

"Too hard?"

"I'd have been much harder. I will be much harder, in fact, but you're normally so charming, especially when things really upset you."

He squeezed her hand and smiled wanly. "I'd been told to expect some funny numbers, but the actual amounts that get frittered in overheads, in advertising, in fundraising, compared to what ends up doing good, well, I found it shocking, frankly. Of course, it doesn't do any good to attack people. Did I do that?"

She smiled and sipped her drink. "No, not really, I just know you too well, I suppose, but I'm glad you asked the questions. I was getting very edgy. That one woman with her snooty, 'Forty percent admin expense is quite typical in this type of organisation, Mrs Brodie,' I would willingly have slapped. So, was that it, or was it Alphonse?"

"It was probably Alphonse, but I can't really work out why I'm uncomfortable, and he seemed unusually evasive. I rather wish he'd rung you."

These were the little things she was so wary of, sensitive to when a trap might be being sprung, but Peter always seemed so sincerely encouraging — and part of her assumed that he knew how they were. "Is he fretting about what you're giving him?"

He squeezed her hand again. "That's part of it, and I should have been clearer. I'd meant a five percent share but I can see how I could have been misinterpreted, but I want him running everything, of course, I thought it might be exciting, but he seems to be having thoughts about wanting to be a little more independent, more settled maybe," he looked out into the sunlit garden in its resplendent green fullness, "and I can understand that very easily." He looked into her eyes. "Did I tell you I love you, by the way?"

"No," said Hannes, entering with a bottle of wine, "me, you tell you love her, but Madame Claudia you keep completely in the dark, you don't deserve her. Anyway, it's sea bass, so," he raised the wine bottle, "Sancerre?"

"Sancerre is good, Hannes, thank you," Claudia said, chuckling. "But he does tell me sometimes, why, only last March, no, wait, that was last year." She lifted his hand and kissed it as Hannes left, chuckling with her.

That he was unsettled didn't puzzle her. She assumed she was part of that anyway, that it was part of the human condition to be always aware that things could be different, but Alphonse, evasive? That would be new — except in the single area of his relationship with her, where even Alphonse reluctantly assumed that Peter knew more than he was supposed to. "And what is my master of insight and perspicacity reading into this evasiveness?"

"I'm assuming it's to do with the changes. Will's having a hard time pinning Tony down, and he'd warned me that Alphonse was feeling unsteady. I asked Alphonse about Tony, after we'd talked through his five percent thing, and he said he'd spoken to him briefly, but only about possibly meeting up. I asked if Tony had said anything about the changes. That was where I thought he was being evasive, but I didn't want to get into an interrogation."

"Couldn't you ring Tony?" asked Claudia, keen to head off any request that she call Alphonse.

"I could, but it tells me something if Tony won't speak to Will, or if Will can't find a way of finding out. These are the sorts of issues that Will would need to clarify. If he can't do it without the chairman label, he may not be our man."

"Doubts?"

"Not really, I think he'll work it out. He's even calmer with people than I am, and as insightful, in his own way. People underestimate him, I think. Tony certainly does. Still, it might have to be plan B."

"Plan B?" Peter had mentioned nothing about a plan B.

"Tania, of course."

"Of course," Claudia stuttered.

"Ah, Hannes, excellent," said Peter, as Hannes came in with two small plates of smoked salmon.

Actually, thought Claudia, that would be the other alternative — if it were to stay as one enterprise — and she dearly hoped it would, or Peter would be forever drawn back into at least two of the business sectors — and today had shown her that she would need him to bring some sense to what they would be striving for with the Foundation; they were dealing with some very difficult people. "I still hope Will can make it work, though."

Peter waved an arm. "Oh, so do I. I think he will."

They moved back on to the Foundation, with her hoping Alphonse would call soon. New York of two weeks ago seemed so far in the past now.

25

"I'm delighted to find you in," said Will as he hugged her. It was earlier than she would normally be home.

"Well, you've Penelope to thank for that, husband darling. Your communications have been terse, to say the least. As usual, she sent me flight details and told me who was collecting you." She hugged him and kissed his cheek. "I'm guessing the meetings have been tough, and I thought you might want to talk."

He did, and he was glad there was plenty to discuss without risking straying onto the Merle encounter and, as he thought that, he found it strange that he didn't see his time with Isobel as a potential conversational trap. "Are we going out?"

"Is my cooking so bad that you'd put up with all that travel and…"

"Your cooking is wonderful. And I'm thrilled you're offering." He hugged her again and kissed her, happy to feel the familiar body in his arms.

"Well, it's not going to be that special. Pasta or risotto?"

"Pasta!" She raised her eyebrows. "You're stirring all the time with risotto."

"Ah, so you do need to talk."

"Definitely. But you must have news. And did you go to Noah's?"

"I did," she said slowly, but emphatically, "and it was very interesting, but I thought we should let you get business off your chest first."

He wondered about her night at Noah's, it sounded like a bigger story, but one it would be too easy to get distracted by. He changed quickly and then poured drinks. She had started preparing a sauce, onions and peppers being neatly diced. "I'm not really hungry yet, could we sit down first?" He went into the drawing room and opened the wide windows on to the terrace, but street noise — and the fear of being overheard — always limited their business conversations outside. They sat on the big sofa and let the warm summer air and the hum of the city's myriad voices, with their distant car horn and siren punctuation, waft gently in.

Will brought his gifts of succinctness to every conversation, but Martha always wanted more human colour. It both helped and hindered that she knew everyone so well now. He'd foreseen the bump in his narrative that Isobel might represent, and was plotting the story carefully.

"So, you'd missed her in the UK?" He'd nodded then. "I am interested in this dinner she had, the one with your old flame. She wasn't convinced about why they were invited, you said."

"No, she wasn't. and neither was Conrad, he'd told me much the same."

Martha looked thoughtful, but that could be about a number of things. He'd mentioned Merle as naturally as possible as a necessary prelude to meeting Conrad. "And is Conrad finally the thing for Isobel, do you think?"

"She refers to the two of them as a couple. Well, she claims he refers to them that and she goes along with it."

"But does she still play, though?"

"I've no idea."

She gasped theatrically. "William Uprichard! I refuse to believe that you had a dinner with Isobel Allen without getting into personal gossip — and I admire the woman enough to believe that she would be quite happy talking about herself and what she got up to. And," she continued emphatically, "she would have wanted to know something about your exploits. Now, I know we have to get back to the Alphonse issue you were talking about, my bank still has a lot of money in that business and it's largely because we have faith in him. If he pulls out, I think our property people will look at their investments. That won't give Peter the solid base he needs for his Foundation plans."

Will felt rueful. "And like I said, I'm also not sure where Funds are. When Tony won't talk, he's usually up to something, and Henry wasn't euphoric when I spoke to him. I'm still the apprentice for him, I think."

She slid towards him and took his hand. "Do you think Peter's leaving it all with you to sort out as a kind of test?"

"He hasn't said that, but it's what I would do, so you're probably right."

"You think he'll want everyone going along with the chosen path?"

"That would be ideal, but I've no idea how hard he would push if he sees people being difficult for their own ends."

"He wants this for Claudia remember, and for posterity."

"Oh, talking about posterity…"

She snuggled closer. "Is this suddenly getting interesting?"

"The girls have a theory they're teasing Alphonse with."

"The girls? I'll ignore your latent sexism, but who are we talking about, Isobel and…"

"Chou Daiyu…"

"Yes, yes, of course, design partner in Hong Kong and, wait, isn't she close to Alphonse?" He nodded. "I love this. It's so much more interesting than the bank."

"Where boring people lead boring lives?"

She took a large swig from the whisky tumbler. "I've said my story comes later. What are the ladies thinking?"

"Did you know that Mei likes to see Alphonse occasionally?"

She sipped the whisky again. "I didn't, if I'm interpreting you correctly. Am I interpreting you correctly? We're talking about two gay people, aren't we?"

"Well, if Alphonse had a label, I think bi would be better."

"Now you've got me thinking about Claudia's relationship with him, but let's not digress… oh, no, wait a minute…"

"Do you want the third seat around the cauldron?"

"They think Mei's trying to get pregnant?" He nodded. She whistled. "Ooh, what does Alphonse say?"

He chuckled. "Not something I wanted to ask him about directly."

"I don't suppose Isobel was quite so timid with him." Then she lapsed into thought. Now he took a drink. He'd considered it on the flight home. He could understand, he thought, how a thirty-something woman might get drawn to that, if she were gay, and had a desirable male available, and vast resources to manage childcare. He'd found himself wondering at times on the journey if that would be fair on the child, but at least the thing wouldn't be subjected to the pains of being pulled two ways — he could remember those times vividly still from his own past. It was the one topic that was sure to distract him. He found her studying him when he looked at her again, "Were you thinking about fatherhood?" she asked. "I never wanted to raise it with you, I just assumed you'd come to terms with the fact that we wouldn't, or you'd never have started out with this old lady." She looked concerned.

"Oh, no, you're right. I hadn't." He smiled. "I'd hate to seem ungallant, but that was clear to me right away and I didn't give it any thought when I was falling in love with you. No, I was thinking about childhood then."

"Your own?"

"Yes, or Mei's child if she has one. I was just stopping myself getting censorious. There are hundreds of ways you can fuck up a child, nobody means to. But Mei might find a way of not doing that." He chuckled. "I know she'd hate to fail at it."

"But how sure are we?"

"Witches around a cauldron, my love; never known to be wrong, are they? I have no idea. It's one more thing that has Alphonse feeling out of sorts. But I've talked enough about my lot, I think you have the picture." She nodded. "OK, now I want something salacious from you. You've been to Noah's, you must have something. What happened?"

She sat back, a little away from him, and finished her glass. This looked more ominous than gossip. "I had a very good time there," she said, but looked serious.

"Did you take anyone?"

"Tania lent me her friend Robert." She paused again.

"She sees him quite often, doesn't she?"

"Well, that's the word of the day for fucking apparently so, yes, she sees him quite often and you know enough about Tania's enthusiasms to know…"

He smiled. "That there's not always just two of them, yes."

"Good." She seemed to relax a little at that. "Anyway, he was a perfect gentleman. He picked me up from here. I did champagne and a few nibbles, he asked if I wanted anything else and I said I didn't think I did. I assume he had supplies with him, but he talked about the pictures in here. He was sort of condescendingly complimentary. He had suggestions he'd like to make, but only if he knew us better, he said. I felt a little miffed. He was selling the idea to me as an investment. We have pictures because I like them, for fuck's sake, but I was getting nervous then."

"Why? You'd seen Noah's before." Then a thought seemed to step out into the street in front of him. She was going to tell him something unexpected — and he was curious, and somehow excited. "But you wanted to see the Red Room again?"

"Well, it's a fantasy we use a lot at playtime, isn't it?"

"Me watching you being caned?"

She held out her glass. "Can you top me up? I need to show you something."

His hand was shaking slightly, unsure of what to expect. He measured the Glenmorangie and water with careful precision and took it slowly back to her. She sipped, then put it down. She spun round on the sofa, tuning her back to him, hitched her thumbs into her waistband, and pushed everything down quickly to her knees as she bent over in front of him. "I've been a very naughty girl."

He stared at the suddenly proffered arse. "I can see that," he said, as he reached out to stroke her cheeks. There were visible lines, which must have been vivid initially, and he could still feel faint ridges. He didn't know how he felt; empty mostly, he thought, as if horror and excitement were being whisked and were leaving a void in the middle as they were being stirred with him suspended in it. This was something to work through. It had been a fantasy topic, but here was striped reality.

She stayed where she was. Martha had some wonderfully provocative ways of being a bottom. "I'd almost have had time to hide it," she muttered indistinctly into a cushion, "but you're here a day early, and when Penelope told me that, I thought, 'yes,' I want to show the man I love how bad a girl I can be, and then maybe he'll spank me again, but even harder. Will you? I want to be punished. I want to be told never to do it again." She was mumbling into the cushion, but he heard every word distinctly.

He stroked her again, aware of how quickly his cock was responding. He loved her arse — her ass, as she called it — and, striped, it looked even more perfect. "Sit up,

Martha, pull your pants up," he said sternly. Oh, this could be a wonderfully exciting game, he thought, other consequences — emotions, doubts, jealousies, wrecked feelings — would have to wait.

She moved slowly, hesitantly, to cover herself and kneel up, not looking straight at him.

"You will definitely not be told never to do it again."

She picked up her glass, she seemed aware now that he was engaging in her play ritual.

"You will be told to make yourself available whenever I wish to see you caned."

She sipped again and settled into the story.

"I shall enjoy that very much," he said. Now, in that moment, he actually thought he might, but that was irrelevant. The next hour was what he was setting up, their fantasy playtime. "I should have enjoyed it very much last Saturday, had I been there. I hope it was very painful."

"Oh, it was, it was."

"But you didn't tell me. You were 'just going to watch,' you said, yet you went seeking thrills for yourself, didn't you?"

"I did, I did. I'm sorry."

"You're not sorry yet, Martha," she looked puzzled, "but you will be in the next hour." This is what she wanted. It was what he wanted now, he wanted to feel free to cane as hard as he ever wished. She was smiling, but a little nervously. He knew how cold he could look. "You're a woman who likes afters, though, Martha. Did you have yourself fucked after the caning?" It was a hard question to ask but it shouldn't be left floundering in some fetid pool of obfuscation, now was the time to be clear and open.

"I'm sure you did," he said. She seemed reluctant to answer. "I have two simple questions, Martha, don't make this hard for yourself. I am entirely indifferent to any response bar concealment. Was it more than one, and was the penetration anal?" It was a peculiar joy to keep the conversation so stilted, so stylised, so fantastical — but they were real stripes he'd been confronted with.

She looked down into her glass. "No, to both questions." She looked up at him almost defiantly.

"Good, but the next time, of course, when I arrange to have you caned, the answer will not be no to either, and I shall take a particular delight in seeing you take a very large man behind you. I want to watch a huge cock being squeezed into your arse while I'm coming in your throat." She seemed oddly reassured now, as if they had disappeared into their habitual fantasy world, but it wasn't the same now — not for her, he assumed, and definitely not for him.

***

"I'm very glad we're not going out. I couldn't possibly sit down." She was sprawled across his naked body on their bed. "I don't think you've ever caned me that hard." She was looking up at him and smiling.

"I don't think I've ever heard you come that loud, but you were very brave about not screaming."

She kissed his chest, then lay her head on it. "Ah, point of honour," she hesitated, "no, it's probably more that I didn't want any loud noises to inhibit you." She looked up again, "True confession time, but I'm not going to deny that I did last weekend partly for its own thrills." She looked hard at him now. He knew he was looking calm; he had no idea yet whether the wound of her adventure would prove painful, he was still in the glow. "But I really wanted to be naughty enough for you to cane me as hard as that." She settled again.

He stroked her back tenderly. "Can we agree that we've just about reached a limit? I admit your story helped me cane you harder, but I'd reached an emotional barrier. I'm hoping you were at both of your limits, emotional and physical."

"I was," and she kissed his chest again, "but there's a nice little maggot of a thrill in knowing that you're not at a physical limit yet. If I were just a little naughtier, maybe, then there might be more to fear."

"Or enjoy?"

She chuckled — that wonderful warm, dirty rumble that he loved. "Oh, no, mister. I'm going to inspect the damage in a minute, but any more than just now, I can assure you, I would fear."

"But it might happen?"

They were silent for a while. He wondered who should speak — but the top should interpret, he knew that from Isobel, and from his own more limited experiences. "Well, it might happen, I can tell you I still feel excited by the thought of seeing you being caned." It was true, he did. "You're quiet," he said, after a while. "I'm getting the sense of a future experience being organised."

She was stroking his arm. "Will you be just tolerating that? Or really enjoying it?" Now she'd moved to look into his eyes, waiting for his answer.

He knew that tomorrow, or next week, it might be different, but tonight: "I should love to watch you being caned." She closed her eyes and smiled, then settled again. He could be brave now, although this might just be fantasy — no matter, they could work it out later — "I will also want to watch you being fucked."

Now she twisted to free her hand for his cock, which seemed to be recovering as the conversation progressed. "By something bigger than this?" she asked playfully, waving the stiffening shaft.

He chuckled. "Definitely, I want your arse completely stretched."

She laughed with him, "Honey, you're not actually a small man. That felt like another physical limit this evening." Now, she squeezed him, "But, just so we're clear, I utterly loved it." They settled into a long quiet cuddle, with him slowly imagining a new, possibly more thrilling future, with her gently stroking his cock.

The silence went on too long. He wondered, afterwards, whether she'd timed it, or merely sensed it: the right time to ask the question. "That was my provocative indiscretion, Master William, now what do you have to tell me?" she asked sleepily.

"Nothing."

There was silence for a while. He didn't think he felt tense. She obviously felt that he did. "That was a somewhat speedy response, my darling." She was right, it had been. Now her hand gripped his cock more firmly and she wriggled to look at him again. "I'm not going to believe there haven't been at least moments of lust, or lascivious thoughts." She looked harder, "Not one single erotic fantasy in all that time away from me? Or is my loving husband so boring that no one even thinks of coming on to him?" Her hand left his cock and went to his face, she looked troubled suddenly, "Will, there was something, there is something. What is it?"

"Isobel!" he blurted.

There was a moment's silence — then she burst into laughter. "My God, William, that's nothing to be ashamed of, for heaven's sake, stop being so furtive. I'd just assumed you did anyway. I mean, I might prefer it if you'd just paid someone, but Isobel, well, she's practically a friend. And I'm delighted to have it confirmed that you find women of a certain age attractive. Ah, but wait," now he wondered what was coming, but she still, thank God, looked playful, "our lovely Isobel is a top. What did you two get up to? Did she make you... I've always been a little intrigued by that, you know."

Now he really didn't know how much he was being teased, "I think I'm more of a top than she is, or maybe it's that I'm less comfortable as a bottom. Anyway, I spanked her a bit, I'm not sure how it came about..."

"Oh, yes you are, William Uprichard, and you're going to tell me while I'm sucking this lovely cock, but you can go wash him first, I wasn't really ready for everything this evening."

"Come with me?"

"No, you go, and be quick. I want to get some Arnica on my poor sweet ass."

"You just want to look at the damage."

"Sure as hell, I do. I like my badges. Now go wash, it's my turn to hear a story."

She was still rubbing cream when he got back to bed but she quickly arranged herself with her head towards the bed's foot. He would almost be talking to her cunt — he knew what she planned. When his story reached its climax, she would move her clit on to his mouth and take his cock very deep and they would both come together.

But she wanted the story first.

"I'd met Sandra at Conrad's."

She looked up from his cock. "Wasn't she another part of your education?"

"Yes, yes, now get back to my cock."

Her mouth was already there, but she broke off again. "I know you find multi-tasking hard, my beloved, but surely stroking my clit while you tell your story isn't beyond you... don't you dare!" she said sharply as he raised his hand to spank her — but then he moved his fingers to where she was seriously wet. "That's better. So, Sandra, and if the story's good I suck harder."

"Don't make me come until I've told you about spanking Isobel." Her grip tightened, and she took him very deep in her mouth with an eager, guttural, almost animal noise.

"I had to admit to Isobel that Sandra made the most of our goodnight kiss and got a reaction out of me, well, let's be blunt, she gripped my cock — so Isobel proceeded to do the same, making the point that, even if I have a conscience, he certainly doesn't."

"None of them do," she said quickly, but got straight back to his cock. But then broke off again, "Does, none of them does!"

He laughed. "Ah, what they teach you at Vassar."

"You mean grammar, or cock-sucking?" But she was on him again instantly, and he moved on to the battle between the tops "And I just used physical strength, I'm afraid, but once I'd subdued her, I went for the long wooden shoe horn. It was a lot like the first brush I spanked you with..." Now his cock was very deep in her mouth and she was straddling his face, her pelvis moving almost violently on him as he left any barrier behind, moving his tongue between clit and vagina as his cock pumped her mouth full of cum while they both groaned loudly.

She had a lovely way of licking him as he softened, and he loved moving his tongue around her as she relaxed — but he was careful to keep his hands away from the violent red patches on her arse — he wondered for a moment if he should feel any guilt, but they'd both had a thrilling evening.

She turned slowly to lie beside him. He laughed to see flecks of his cum around her mouth, but wiped her frown away by licking them off, showing them to her on his tongue-tip before swallowing, and making her laugh. She snuggled in beside him and slid her hand on to his cock again. "In the spirit of honesty and openness with which this evening has been conducted, my precious, I'm going to say that I'm being very brave about Isobel. I'm very glad you've been naughty too, but especially glad that you've told me..." she paused. "But I am burying some little feelings of jealousy and, while it's not my place to discourage repeats..." she looked up at him. "I think I'd like to know about anything, and I'd like to know that it's not going to be frequent."

"Less frequent than Geoffrey's canings, I assure you."

"Good!" She squeezed his cock and settled. "And it's not like you saw Merle."

***

He wondered, over the following days, what had given it away — some twitch, some gesture, or just some innate intuition of hers.

Anyway, she'd left, and the place was weird without her.

26

Henry Gideon had encountered Michael McKenzie in two phases of his life, and he was ambivalent about the experience in both cases. McKenzie had been head boy at Henry's school and had bestowed no more than a distant, quiet contempt. In the second phase, Henry had sought McKenzie out. By this time, he ran the London office of a global finance business. Henry had assessed that good work was being done in that office by Will Uprichard. Henry had, effectively, hired Will as a part-time consultant in the earlier days of the GKD Fund. Will's input had enabled them to make bigger bets with confidence and the arrangement was very promising. McKenzie, in skirting the rules of the arrangement without any disclosure to Will or Henry, managed a catastrophic blunder which cost his firm lots of money and him, ultimately, his own job; but that happened only after he'd fired the innocent Will in the act both of blaming him and of taking revenge on him for his affair with Merle, McKenzie's wife. The Dickinson Corporation willingly found a home for Will in its Brussels office and that appeared to be the end of the matter.

So why was McKenzie contacting him?

He'd not allowed the call through at first. Henry liked to think about what any business angle might be. A little research was necessary, a little preparation. McKenzie himself had been rescued by a Gerry Calvert, which was a name Henry had heard of, but whose sources of wealth were obscure. Henry took a pragmatic view of that; all he — and Peter and Will, for that matter — required was that the funds at the point of takeover came from a demonstrably legitimate source. This led to occasional aggravation when existing clients tried to bring money in through new channels but, in the main, it served everybody well that the GKD reputation was for probity and prudence in its sourcing, but for innovation and for impressive returns in its delivery ever since its inception.

Peter Dickinson had liked their approach and established them with a sizeable investment. He was followed quickly by a number of his contacts and that gave Henry and Tony a jump start, helped by some very favourable publicity in the financial press. The contract conditions Peter signed them to had seemed almost irrelevant to two young investment managers who were making a huge breakthrough.

Now, leaving GKS, as it had become since the Senlin tie-in, with a contractual inability to take any clients with them, would mean almost starting again. Yes, with stellar reputations, but no clear answers about why they would have left. This wasn't politics, this was real business: the people they would need to impress would not be won over by easy deceits.

But the prospect of working directly for Will, the young man he'd rescued — the accountant, the mathematician, the pleasant-enough chap who remembered to send your wife flowers — did not have the appeal of working for the incomparable Peter Dickinson, charming, insightful, well-known and very justifiably widely respected. So, he might hold his nose about a conversation with Michael McKenzie, but it was important to explore new avenues. He knew that was what Tony was doing — and probably Lou, too.

So: "Michael, it's Henry Gideon. You called last week, I believe, I'm sorry it's taken me so long to get back to you," had started the call, and that had led to today's meeting at the Sandy Nicholls office near Berkeley Square.

The fifteen kilos McKenzie had shed since their last meeting had left him looking gaunt — but he looked better for having lost the flab and high colour. He'd also lost the flamboyant, perfectly knotted ties, apparently, but gained grey streaks in his hair. He'd been an imposing figure, even at school, but that air had left him. There was a watchfulness now, bordering on furtiveness, which at least suggested he was more aware of the world around him than he had been.

He'd not lost the easy conversational manner, but Henry cut straight past the attempt at small talk. "Business is good, thank you, now, tell me, are you working exclusively for Gerry Calvert?"

"McKenzie Calvert is a partnership…"

"In which all the funds are provided by Calvert."

"Not all, no," said McKenzie edgily.

"You plough back in your two percent every year, do you?"

"Most of it, yes."

"And other investors?"

"Work through other companies…"

"But they're all connections of Calvert's?"

"Mostly."

"Or connections of connections, it's hard to get much information."

McKenzie seemed to feel less threatened now. "That's how everyone likes it, discreet."

"But clean?"

Now McKenzie managed a slight smile. "Demonstrably so at the important interfaces." He paused — for effect probably, thought Henry, he couldn't imagine McKenzie being too spontaneous. "I imagine, though, that most money traces back to potentially questionable sources, even yours."

Henry nodded slowly. That was an easy enough assumption. "We make sure we're very well insulated, as I'm sure you do."

"Of course," said McKenzie, with a smirk that conveyed no credibility. For GKS, however, even a suspicion of questionable sourcing would have been damaging. McKenzie Calvert had a much lower profile.

"So, are you looking to put some of your investors with us?" Henry was still unclear what McKenzie wanted — 'co-operation' and 'mutual benefits,' McKenzie's phrases in the phone call, would normally have attracted a 'bullshit!' response — certainly from Tony — but these were unusual times.

"I thought this might be a moment when we could get business moving the other way." That would normally have been an absurd suggestion, but McKenzie looked strangely confident, as if he'd come by some knowledge of the imminent changes in the GKS position. "I thought you might want to look at some new opportunities."

"I'm struggling to understand why opportunities like that might be interesting for GKS."

"They wouldn't be for GKS." He paused. "But they might be for G, and possibly for K."

That was unnervingly accurate. Henry had to follow up, as much as anything to find out how McKenzie was hearing this. But it was an interesting opportunity for him anyway, possibly for Tony too.

"Why are you interested in G and K?"

"Your skills and your technology." He smiled slyly. "You weren't noticeably modest about either when we met a few years ago, and your fund's done even better since. Gerry and I thought you might sell or rent your skills to us."

"As consultants?" That might be a way of insulating themselves from any dark money flowing through the McKenzie Calvert system.

"That would be part of it, yes, on performance-related fees that would go to you and not Dickinson — or his Foundation."

"His Foundation?" Trying to play dumb was awkward.

"Henry," said McKenzie, relaxing and almost teasing him now, "he's holding meetings with charity organisations. Come on, it's leaking." That wouldn't necessarily reveal the Foundation as the plan, thought Henry, but it was mattering less and less where the original story had come from. "So, you lose your stellar investor, well, a lot of his time and a lot of his money. That's going to make new business harder to come by, isn't it? And existing business harder to hold on to, I should think.

Won't some of them look for an exit when PD starts pulling big money out?"

"Our fund performance speaks for itself." But Henry knew it would be unnerving when big players and institutions saw Peter's commitment declining. They might buy the Foundation idea, but more would see it as a sign of withering confidence and problems in the pipeline. "Anyway, we couldn't steer them to you, we have a three-year block on poaching old clients."

"Rachel doesn't. She could have the contract with us. You could work it out between you."

Henry was now deeply unnerved, but wasn't sure why, and reacting too hastily was not his style.

"Look," said McKenzie, "we're interested in you because we know how good you are. Better than us, obviously." He tried a modest smile and a shrug. Not bad, thought Henry, I could almost believe you. "That's why Gerry and I wanted to look at whether we could work a bit closer — and we thought the time might be ripe to talk." He paused. "I think I'm right, aren't I?"

"You're not wrong," said Henry, despising himself for the cliché. Was he really thinking that? No, but he had two reasons for not shutting this down. "So, do I meet Gerry Calvert? Find out what might work?" This was important. Was the money man really behind it?

"That's what I was hoping you'd suggest. Do you have an evening free? Tomorrow or Thursday? Would you bring Rachel?"

"Not Rachel, no," Henry hadn't blocked the possibility of her having a role, but not as a pure piece of subterfuge, "but I can do tomorrow."

"Gerry will probably pick Mosimann's, is that OK?"
"That would be fine," said Henry, disturbingly aware that it had probably already been booked.

***

He may have met Gerry Calvert at a gathering in the city, Gerry seemed to think so — 'four or five years ago, you'd won an award.' Henry could remember an award ceremony, it was the last time he'd been drunk, but he had no recollection of the man who was ushering him to a chair in the small dining room, although Gerry had the strange familiarity of someone whose face you knew from pictures; Henry had been studying all he could of Calvert, and had tried not to get too distracted by the mysterious, or exotic, death of the man's wife two or three years before. He was aware that there was some Dickinson connection. Henry knew he didn't have enough curiosity about scandal. It was an important precaution, particularly if it affected sources of money. He knew he should read more widely.

His curiosity about financial affairs ran deep, but even his knowledge and skills in that area had not enabled him to form a clear picture of Calvert's wealth. That he was involved in many businesses had quickly become clear, but his level of ownership was obscure and, Henry concluded, kept deliberately so. He certainly controlled billions, but how much he actually owned was still an unknown.

He'd smiled to himself during one break in his research, reflecting that, on any given day, Will Uprichard could give him a very accurate number for Peter

Dickinson's total net worth. Ah, Will, he'd thought, you are a very bright man, am I being too hard on you? Too precious about my position in our relationship?

A similar thought occurred as glasses of Krug were brought to the table. Here it looked like a desperate attempt to impress or flatter him. With Peter, it would have been a natural part of the world and the man, and Henry wondered if he wasn't, once again, being too precious about himself. Rachel's occasional 'arrogant snob' jibe was always put good-naturedly, but in quiet moments he knew there was at least as much truth in it as humour.

"Of course, it wasn't the first time I'd become aware of you," said Gerry, as he raised a glass. Henry raised his, nodded, and did his best to look curious.

"When Gerry helped me out after my cock-up," this was McKenzie, and Henry felt relieved that the blame for that was being manfully and rightly shouldered, "I also told him how well you'd done out of it. That was true, wasn't it?"

"Well, it was one of the things that led ultimately to the award, as I remember."

"I've had my eye on you ever since," said Gerry, then he turned to the waiting staff. "We'll take twenty minutes if you don't mind, then you can start us on the short tasting menu with the wine flights." He turned back to Henry, who shrugged and nodded — food wasn't that important to him, which annoyed Rachel.

"Michael's been doing a very good job for me, but he knows I've put out feelers to pull in more expertise. I don't think you'll have noticed our enquiries, we can be pretty discreet…"

"I had noticed that you're discreet," said Henry with a smile. "I've not found it easy to disentangle what you're into."

"Ha!" Gerry laughed, amused and pleased, apparently. "But you won't have made a direct connection to some of the placements we've tried to make with you."

"I hadn't, but we do turn quite a lot away. Are you saying…?"

"Some of the people I do business with wouldn't clear your hurdles. One of Michael's skills, well, his main skill actually, is that he can manoeuvre money into legitimate sources so that we don't have to hold our noses." He paused, then looked at Henry very directly. "Look, I'd like your help, we're getting busier and Michael's becoming overwhelmed, but, as I said, optimising returns is not his skill anyway." He turned. "That's fair, Michael, isn't it?"

"Yes," said McKenzie, unabashed. "I'm better at making sure the streams are clean."

"Or appear clean," said Henry, slightly acidly, wondering what that would provoke.

McKenzie looked taken aback suddenly, but Gerry was unperturbed, "How deep do you look into your sources? I'd insist on at least two levels between our money and drugs or arms traffic, but we stay clear of that anyway. We just sometimes have to help friends of friends out. I would guess you insist on more insulation, and anyway, that's not where the real money is, as you know."

This seemed like an open conversation at least, thought Henry. "We want it all clean and, for anyone new, we get it, so that might inhibit this discussion, but there's no point in me being prissy. Some of our big investors' sources of income change over time. They're the ones we have to watch for, and we sometimes have to have conversations with them. I'm under no illusions; they're as inventive as they are unscrupulous. But we persuade them that their best interests are served by remaining legal." Gerry was nodding, apparently thinking. "But we all observe the clash where pragmatism meets principles, don't we, but we try to come down on the side of the angels, although even there, people could argue that we pay an irresponsibly small amount of tax — but that affects other parts of our group more. So, apart from us three, who's in on this conversation? I should warn you, I don't keep secrets from Tony." He looked at each of them. "I didn't check with Michael, sorry, but that is my understanding of where this conversation can be discussed."

McKenzie looked perturbed, but Gerry waved an arm. "With your partner, of course, and with your wife too; she's brilliant, I gather."

Henry was uncomfortable again. He hadn't shut his mind to the idea, but it was too early to discuss it, "You're very well-informed, I give you that. She embarrasses me sometimes, her returns are better than ours."

"Is that because she doesn't have idiots like me asking lots of stupid questions?"

It was easy for Henry to smile and nod at that. "She has only me as her pet idiot, and she's not always flattering, or even diplomatic, about the questions I ask. But the important point is that we proceed with this topic on the basis that I can discuss anything with Tony, OK?"

"And only Tony." Now he was getting a hard stare from Gerry.

"That's what I meant, yes, only Tony. But I'm still no wiser about what we're discussing."

***

In the cab, on the way home, he was feeling uneasy, but intrigued. Money was money, his job was to maximise it. They had a consultant GKS used who policed the money sources; they took guidance from him and had conversations where necessary. Few clients quibbled. Henry simply assumed they were more worldly than he and would find other places to invest money that GKS found 'potentially embarrassing.' That had been Peter's expression when he set the department up at the very beginning, and Henry and Tony were aware that Arno Dace, the man Peter had insisted they employ, had a direct line to Peter if he ever felt he needed it. Henry had received a few phone calls from Peter in the early years, but things had run smoothly for a long while. He found himself wondering, looking out absently on the still busy streets, if he shouldn't have used Dace a little more as a source of intelligence, but it was too late now. He would risk leaking the Calvert conversation. He doubted whether Calvert McKenzie used a man like Dace.

It had become clear that a lot of Gerry's activities would have been questioned, but the money was in the West now. Gerry had simply been well-connected, through his old logistics business, to many people in Russia and he'd 'found ways of helping them.' OK, the money was here now, 'and they'd like us to find better returns for them

— and you'd be surprised at how respectable they want it to be.'

Henry had remained studiously neutral at that point. 'I guess they reach a point where legitimacy becomes pragmatic,' he'd said.

Gerry had reacted slowly before he smiled. 'I think we're understanding each other.'

Henry wasn't sure they were, but it wasn't distaste he was feeling; it was suspicion, but that wouldn't stop him discussing it with Tony.

***

He'd expected Tony to be more enthusiastic when he called him the following morning, but Tony was surprisingly thoughtful. "What's up, mate?" he'd needed to ask when Tony's response to his account of the evening had been to ask more questions. "You don't sound too keen. Going off the idea of striking out on our own?"

"No, no, it's not that. No, it's Lou."

"Lou? Look, I've told them I'd only discuss this with you."

"Ha, I love how snooty-nosed moral you get about confidentiality, but don't worry, I understand. No, I don't need to talk to Lou about your Mr Calvert. No, the interesting thing is, he's getting similar questions himself out there. Well, he may even have been digging himself. He's certainly been more active since this all came up. He's finding there's a lot more than his father's money looking for a home out there. People talk to him now because they know his nose is out of joint with his sister.

He talks to them because he's keen to put a distance between himself and her."

"They know she's his sister?" Henry was slightly shocked, but then reflected that, if he himself knew, why wouldn't some Chinese with much more interest in the situation make it their business to find out. Tony was chuckling. "What's up? I suppose you're saying that they do?"

"Oh, mate, I love you, but I sometimes wonder what planet you live on."

It wasn't the first time Tony had expressed that thought, and they'd both been aware, right from the beginning, that there was great strength in the differences between them; Tony always much bolder, more unruly, Henry strictly disciplined, deeply analytical. The horrendous arguments of the early years were milder now and their admiration of, and acknowledged reliance on, each other had deepened. "I don't suppose it matters."

"Well, it does in that our boy seems well enough connected to be able to pull in money, but not if we're GKS. These guys he's talking to don't want to be near Senlin. They were enemies of the old man and would hate the idea of doing business with his daughter."

"Would Dace approve of them?" There was a long pause.

"It didn't sound like you'd want him looking at Calvert."

"I know. I want to think about that a bit more."

"But you've still got an open mind about us going it alone?"

Henry sighed. "I wouldn't say it's an open mind anymore. I'll just feel demoted, demotivated and trapped if we stick as GKS."

"OK, let's think about it some more, but here's to KG."

"KG?"

"We can't call it GK, we've been that for years."

"But KG, King Gideon?"

"Yeah, has a ring, doesn't it?"

"Fuck off!" They laughed as they finished the conversation.

27

It had been nearly a week since Martha had left and only one message had been returned:

You've obviously been schlepping unresolved issues around for years. I think I'm entitled to some time to deal with mine. I'm not telling anybody. If you do, that tells me something. M

He supposed he thought that telling anyone else would tell her it was finished. And it wasn't, certainly not for him, and it didn't sound like it was for her.

But just leaving like that?

She was normally so rational, so considered, but he'd reflected many times since Thursday evening that they'd never had a crisis before, never a major argument; any fights had finished with laughter — or sex. But what had been bubbling up, unknown or unacknowledged by either of them? She'd so lightly sought adventure on her own, some easy gratification of her still, he had to admit, enthusiastic kink — what did that indicate for the future? And he'd found it too easy to fall into bed with Isobel. But fun was allowed, that was the theoretical agreement he'd had with Martha, and also what he'd learned with Isobel. He was thinking often these days of last Wednesday and the dinner Alphonse had missed. It had been enjoyable. He'd seen a different Daiyu: she was funny and vivacious, not quite Isobel's equal, but they were lively together, and she was almost beautiful. She probably was beautiful, Will thought, but he always liked to keep his judgements away from extremes. She was also wise; wise enough not to comment on whatever Alphonse was thinking and feeling — or speculate on how important or lengthy his phone call might be — and smart enough to leave Will and Isobel together later. She disappeared before coffee with an: 'Early start for me; be good, you two,' delivered with a suddenly more serious expression.

Isobel had, inevitably, ordered whisky — for both of them — and had put on her serious face by the time it arrived. "Now, about tonight," she'd said as she took his hand.

"Haven't we just been given a warning?" A thought struck him. "You haven't said anything about last night, have you?"

She laughed in that way she had. "Oh, my lamb, don't look so worried. Of course not." But she smiled slyly. "As you've seen, though, she's a smart lady. She'll have guessed. Now, I would love a repeat of last night, but, as you've said, we have just been warned." Then she paused and smiled. "And we'd have to talk role reversal anyway." She laughed again and squeezed his hand. "No, no, poppet, this is too serious. Well, it would be if we allowed ourselves a repeat, but my point is, you've seen the danger of allowing repeats, haven't you?" He'd nodded. "That fishhook gets in too deep. You've been thinking about Merle, haven't you?" He'd nodded again and started to speak but her finger was on his lips. "Shh, now, it's such a dangerous thing. If we two let last night happen again now, it would affect us. Yes, even me. And even though, thrilling as it was, we once again demonstrated why we're not really suited, it's still dangerous. I'm too close to being in love with you, and that's a problem you have, even after all this time, with Merle."

He'd nodded again, and not even tried to speak.

"I happen to think you're with a wonderful woman. I've even stopped hating her."

He was aware that his smile had been half-hearted, "I know you're right."

"I think you two could have even more fun together, but you need to get past this Merle thing, and your own monogamy hang-ups."

But he hadn't got past Merle then, not soon enough in that fatal conversation. There'd been something lingering, lurking in his thoughts last Thursday, and Martha had tuned into it.

Now she'd gone, and he didn't know for how long; it was six days, and the last thing he needed, with so much else to think about and with focus, normally a constant companion, so elusive, was a buzz on his phone and 'Merle' on its face.

It would have been better to ignore it, but he always tried to avoid the coward's way. "Good morning, oh, maybe good afternoon."

"It's afternoon, and I'd promised myself I wouldn't pester. I'm not pestering, am I?"

"I don't think so." He had no idea, he hoped she wasn't. For all the turmoil, for all the dreams and beauty, she wasn't his answer. "You've caught me at a good time."

"Because I'm not meaning to pester, really I'm not. I meant what I said about the Olympic Games."

"Look, I love hearing your voice, but I do have the sense that you want to tell me something."

"Well, I do, but I'm not sure what or why."

He could feel himself getting irritated, but London had been his own fault. He hadn't had to give in, and he had no desire now to hurt her feelings. It wasn't her fault that he was still in love with her, that she'd been his waking fantasy that morning. "I'm now moving from my desk to my favourite chair and you're going to tell me what's on your mind." He smiled, Merle would, he was sure, respond well to being told, as she'd responded well that morning as he'd pulled her naked fantasy body across his lap.

"You're organising something big at Dickinson, aren't you?"

"Ha, well, I'm trying to, but think pear-shaped if you want a description of its current status. Why? What's come up?"

"Well, you've come up twice in my domestic conversations since we…" she hesitated.

"Since we met."

"Yes, since we met. Gerry asked about you last week, apropos of nothing."

"What was he asking?"

"Just what you did at Dickinson now, what you were like. I was worried, first of all, I thought he might have been having me followed; he knows you're big in my past." She hesitated.

"Is that something he would do?" The man was sinister, was Will's default assumption.

"He could do. He's a careful man, he likes to know everything, but he didn't seem to be asking in a suspicious way. He just wanted to know what you were like and how important you were in Dickinson now. I said I didn't know but that Isobel would. Then he asked if I was ever in touch with you. I said I'd given up writing to you years ago. Those are fibs I can manage quite well."

"But you had stopped writing. That wasn't a fib."

"But 'being in touch with' would be a pretty mild description of our Lanesborough nights, wouldn't it? But that's not why I'm ringing," she added hastily.

"Go on."

"Well, Michael had asked about you too. He asked me to dinner last week, that came out of the blue, and he started talking about that time all those years ago. He's never done that, but he was also asking about that chap you were consulting for when everything blew up."

"Why was he doing that?"

"Well, I thought he was just tidying up the memories of his life, you know, the way you find excuses and rationalisations for the mistakes you've made — oh, maybe you don't do that."

"Oh, no," he said ruefully. "I do do that."

"That was said with feeling, my love. Do you need to tell me something?"

"No, I don't," he said quickly.

"I'm hearing that you do, but you're not going to."

"You may be right, but Michael was asking about what? About Henry?"

"That was his name, yes. I couldn't remember at the time, but the funny thing was, when he rang me yesterday to cancel last night's dinner, he'd asked to meet again, and I asked him who his hot date was, I got his supercilious tone and he said Gerry and Henry, and then changed the subject quickly, as if he'd wished he hadn't said it. Isn't that a bit funny? Why would Henry have anything to do with them again? I know you said he made big money at the time, but it can't have been a happy ending, even for him."

"Oh, Henry did well out of it," he said absently, but his brain was spinning. That would be an unholy alliance.

"Do you want me to ask Gerry about it?"

"No!" he said sharply, too sharply. "Look, Merle, sweetheart. I'm going to thank you very much for the information. I don't know what it means, and I'll need to find out more about it, but please don't go pursuing any enquiries, will you?"

There was a pause before she said, "Well, no, not if you say so. But is it serious, then?"

"I've no idea. It could be, I suppose, but the last thing you need is for Gerry or Michael to think you're talking to me."

"The last thing you need, you mean."

This was Merle the Petulant. It was a useful reminder. "I really do mean for you."

"You sound like you care."

"Of course I care, I knew that even without the reminder."

"Reminders. It was two nights, remember."

"I remember very, very well, thank you." He needed to take the seriousness out of this. She was with dangerous people, but he also needed any of his own follow up to be unsuspected, "It's a shame the Olympics is only every four years."

"Well, don't they have other championships in between?"

"They do, I think, every year, isn't it?"

"Deal! And could we do dinner next time as well?"

"We could, and I could bring a special paddle."

"No, I could bring ours. It's been languishing in a drawer for eight years."

"I suppose that counts as a romantic thought." They both chuckled, and he felt relieved.

"You will give me notice, won't you? Or am I pestering now?"

"I'm the one who brought up the paddle, but, back to your original reason…"

"And it was a reason, wasn't it? It's useful for you to know."

"It could be very useful, thank you, but it's only useful if it stays between us. I need it hush-hush."

"I understand."

He doubted whether she did. Gerry would have ways of dealing with a leak. He would need to be careful approaching Henry.

"I am very glad you rang."

"Why?"

Merle the Needy. "It's potentially useful information and it's lovely to hear your voice."

"Does that mean we can talk again sometime."

"I'd like that very much." That was, unfortunately, true.

"Well, you ring me next time, then I'll know you mean it."

"I will."

"Promise?"

"I promise."

"I'll let you get on then. 'Bye, my love."

When he put the phone down, he was missing Martha,

***

It was late afternoon when Tania leaned in through his door, "Busy?"

"Of course, but you're priority. What's up? You're looking too pleased with yourself."

"I've been meeting banks."

"Isn't that my job?"

"Ha!" she said impishly as she sat down. "Yes and no."

"No, seriously, it should be. What have you been up to?" He did feel disconcerted, mistakes could happen like this.

Suddenly he had serious Tania now. "I'm here telling you now, aren't I? Have a bit of faith."

That might be a fair comment, but he would reserve judgement. "So your news is?"

"Well, I'm representing two businesses, remember. We want Giddings in on the IPO, so I needed to talk to our bank... the Giddings bank, I mean. Our bank's Anglo-Asia, of course."

"You said you'd been meeting banks."

"Yeah, I know. Look, it was a bit spontaneous, but Martha had given me a contact."

"Martha?"

"Yes, of course. I know she's above that, but I knew she'd point me at the right person. What's up there, by the way?"

"Nothing!"

She eyed him for a while. "You can say 'fuck off' you know." She smiled. "In fact, I think you just did. So, anyway, she told me I could talk to Al Frederick, she said you'd already briefed him."

That was fair. He had. He nodded — it was still a breach of protocol, but it was Tania's way.

"Anyway, he was keen to meet up and when I said I was meeting the Giddings bank this afternoon, he sort of invited himself along. I said I should talk to you, but he seemed very relaxed and said banks usually worked together, as if it was the most natural thing."

Will was nodding, but feeling uncomfortable. There was too much of this spiralling out of control. "It is, that's true, but usually with the CFO."

"Will, darling, I take your point, but you ain't CFO of Giddings. That was the meeting Al Frederick invited himself to."

"I will be CFO of the joint enterprise."

She frowned and shook her head. "You may well be more than that, but this isn't like you. Do you want I come back later?"

He drew a deep breath. "You're right, no, I'm sorry, I just need to be involved in these things."

"I've come straight from the meeting and I'm asking for forgiveness. I know you'd prefer I'd asked for permission..." She drew a deep breath, then smiled. "But fuck you!" They laughed together.

He suddenly felt more relaxed. "OK, what's the fine mess you've gotten us into now?"

"That's better, and I don't know yet, is the answer to that, but the two guys seemed to get on well."

"It's a big payday for both of them."

"Now who's the cynic?"

"Sceptic, never cynic."

"Getting them all in, aren't you?"

"You brought up forgiveness."

"It was one of yours."

He smiled again. "Fair enough, now get to the point."

"That's my boy! Anyway, they're valuing us at fourteen and Giddings at seven." She looked at him expectantly.

He nodded slowly. "I was looking at twelve and six as minima, so that's good."

"That means I've added nearly five billion to the Group in two and a half years."

He loved the childlike enthusiasm she brought to serious business, but it had to be said: "You have spent over two billion in doing that!" He got a poked tongue for that one, and laughed ridiculously loudly. "And you haven't got fourteen billion for it yet."

"Well, that was interesting. Al asked if we'd want to go with a private placement. They have some people who might want to buy in big. Would we do that? If we could get the price, I mean."

"It's a thought, but they'd probably be trying to buy in cheap, and we wouldn't want anyone with more than twenty percent."

"Because of Peter and Dad, you mean — or for the poor bastard who has to run the thing without tame majority shareholders?"

"Yeah, but we'd be interested in some big lumps. What have you told them?"

"I've told them, Mr CFO and Chairman-elect, that I couldn't possibly comment until I'd discussed it with you."

He raised an eyebrow as he looked at her.

She cracked first, but they were both laughing. "I've told them we'd be interested," then she looked serious again, "but they shouldn't talk to anyone without discussing it with us first."

He smiled at her. "That's my girl, thank you. And well done, forgiveness bestowed!"

"Thank you, master, now am I going to buy you a drink so you can tell me what's up? This hasn't started with the Noah thing, has it?" She looked worried.

He didn't want to talk. "I'm going to admit there's something, but it wasn't Noah's — and I'd rather not talk about it just now. I mean, I thank you, and your appalling sensitivity, but we're having a blip, that's all. I hope, anyway."

Tania looked strangely moved — teary, even, he thought. "You know I think you guys are wonderful, don't you? Come on." She was standing beside him, insisting on a hug. It was a long one, but she closed it with a kiss on his cheek. "I'm pretty certain you'll be fine."

"Yeah, me too."

But he wasn't.

28

It was a bit of a shock at first, Conrad's call and his "Are you busy at the weekend? I'm thinking of coming to see you." I wasn't busy, particularly, but I must have sounded hesitant. "I'll understand if you're doing something, but I'm going to be there next week anyway."

"So, you thought you'd cadge a cheap room for the weekend while you sort your jetlag out, is that it?"

"Oh, I'll take a free fuck into the bargain if you like."

Well, that did stop me in my tracks. It wasn't very like him, I'm the outrageous one. I was spluttering.

"Look, there are some interesting conversations I'm setting up, but my prime purpose is to come and see you. Now, I can wade through a bit of indifference, but hostility will get me changing my flights."

He sounded quite sniffy, I got that, I'd been caught on the hop. "No, no, no, you prat! That will be lovely. Actually…" Oops, this was going to be a true confession moment if I wasn't careful. "I'm excited now. When are you coming?"

"I land on Friday afternoon," he said, but he'd lost his ebullience. Still, I couldn't tell him it was the most romantic gesture I've received in years, could I?

"I am so thrilled, I'll meet you. Send me details."

"You don't have to."

Oh, Conrad, don't be a wimp, I thought. "Fuck off, you're coming around the world to see me. I can make it to the airport for you. I'll be the flamboyantly dazzling little brunette with a nameboard saying 'Mr Kitter'." *I got a little laugh from that, thank goodness.* "What's the business anyhow?"

"That's the funny thing. It's a connection of Gerry Calvert's, but he thought it was more in my area and it sounded promising when I rang the guy. I could have videoed some more but face to face is better and, I'll be honest, I wanted to come and see you anyway."

"Oh, Mr Dazzling Romantic, couldn't you just have come without needing an excuse?" *I got a silence, I was actually quite excited but I wasn't handling it well.* "Well, you get one free fuck anyway!" *Now I got a laugh and I thought, if all's not exactly right with the world, it's certainly a little better now.*

***

We're lying in bed on the Friday afternoon. He's dozed a bit, but he did very well, considering he's had a long flight and he's not what I can call young anymore. I nudge him. I don't want him sleeping too long now. He wakes fairly easily, looks momentarily disorientated, then smiles. "Was that my free one?"

"What would you have paid?"

"A grand, I suppose."

"A grand! I get three in Shanghai. I'm exotic."

"Blow jobs aren't that exotic."

"Mister! I'll be introducing you to my pet hedgehog if you keep this up. And no more freebies."

"So, the next one's three grand, is it? Not sure I'll bother."

"OK, next one's a fiver, then."

"It's a deal." He kisses me very tenderly and begins stroking me.

"That's very lovely, my sweet, but I have booked a table in the Mandarin." I take his cock in my hand. There's not a lot of life in it, to be honest, although the limp little thing does try to respond. *"I think if I feed you first, he'll have more fun later."*

"For five quid, I should hope so!"

I laugh. I do love him, I realise. This is all a bit strange for me.

***

"I don't need a plan for the weekend," he says when we've ordered, *"but do we have one?"*

"After you've spent a fiver on stage one tonight then, you mean?"

"Is it free if I say I love you?"

"Oh, no." I try to look shocked. *"It's three grand if you say you love me. You know how expensive love is."*

He smiles. *"Do I get the hedgehog in that?"* I laugh.

"Nah, hedgehogs are extra. But there is a plan," and I chuckle, *"and it will cost you, so I recommend the fiver deal tonight."*

"No 'I love yous' then? So, what's the deal?"

"I've chartered a boat and skipper. I've always wanted to do a trip round the islands."

"Brilliant. Not too early, though?"

"You up for another fiver in the morning?"

"You think I might be overestimating your allure."

"Listen, buster, you can only be overestimating your own stamina. But the boat's ours for the day. I've said not before ten, though, then we're seeing Daiyu and Alphonse for dinner."

"Wonderful," he says, but suddenly he's looking thoughtful.

"What's up? I thought that was a good idea. You don't want just..."

"No, it's a very good idea. I wanted to talk to him anyway. I almost rang him to book time."

"You could have done. Why didn't you?"

"I had a phone call from your William earlier in the week. I have a few loose ends dangling out there."

"Alphonse, Gerry, Will, who else?"

"Well, I would have rung Peter, but Will specifically asked me not to."

"Is he keeping secrets? That doesn't sound like him."

"No, it's not that, I don't think, but he's got a number of issues with what he's trying to do, and he doesn't want Daddy feeling he has to sort them out for him. I can understand that."

"Does he know you're in touch with Gerry?"

Now Conrad's looking very thoughtful, but then he takes my hand and I get an unusually intense look from him. "No, he doesn't know I'm in touch with Gerry, but let's be clear about that. Gerry was in touch with me, and

*I've yet to find out why. I should know more next week."
He kisses my fingers. "I will tell Will when the time's right,
I promise, but he has enough on his plate at the moment."*

*"I know," I say, and I get attentive Conrad for half an
hour while I update him on everything going on here. No,
not about fucking Will, of course. I mean, it's not going to
be a secret between us, it just wouldn't help the current
discussion.*

*I've given a pretty thorough summary of the issues and
where I see the problems and he says, "Not least with
Alphonse, from what you say — and what Will's said."*

"What's he told you?"

*"Pretty much what you said, although I didn't get
the..."*

"Shh!" I say sharply.

*He looks a little offended with me. "I appreciate you
were talking in code, Ms Allen, and I shall remain
completely in code also when talking about anonymous
possible pregnancies. My God, half of my information in
business comes from overheard conversations. I do know
how to be careful, you know." He's right, of course, and I
feel a little stupid, but he's smiling. I'm quite proud of
myself for staying discreet, 'talking in code' as he said.
"Anyway, I was a bit surprised about Alphonse. Is he
feeling a little deserted or betrayed by Daddy, did you
think?"*

*"He may just have been wanting to escape. He's
getting too many complications and commitments here.
What's your angle?"*

*"Well, he's a very good property man, and I'm moving
more and more that way."*

"You know, I know very little about what you do really."

"We said it was better that way, remember, but that may no longer be true now, with all your emotional and financial commitments to the Dickinson business." He knows Peter helped us set up this Hong Kong business, of course.

"Am I going to find out more now, then?"

"For reasons just discussed, not in an open restaurant. That's one for your sofa and the harbour view later, I think."

"Short of a fiver, are you? Can't afford the fuck?"
My hand gets kissed and he's smiling.

***

He didn't spend the fiver, and he's asleep now, poor lamb, but I like having his naked body next to me. I can wait until the morning for sex, and I wouldn't have missed the last hour for the world.

I've known for years, of course, that Conrad is in league with some very dodgy people, I've met enough of them at his parties in the old days. I thought it was just in the Middle East, but it's broader than that, apparently. He says everything he does is clean, but he probably has a more elastic definition of that than I would. He's had to admit that his business is not unlike Gerry Calvert's. 'But my links are with Arabs, mostly, and his are with Russians.' He was in oil to start with, I was right about that, but then his new friends found his network interesting, and he set up a number of different businesses with them. He keeps minority stakes but makes sure he has control. It's lots of import-export, he said; he looked at me at that point to see if I understood. I didn't. 'It's cleaner now than it used to be.' There had been a long silence at that point, as if he was deciding whether to confess something. He'd picked up businesses that were moving money around, fake invoices, mis-pricing, etc., he said, and he had a logistics company and that had helped. Over time he'd got his friends to clean up their operations to stay ahead of the authorities. 'But not before some of us had made fortunes and put the money into more legitimate channels.' When he said that 'a few I'd set up wanted to stay shady. I understood, I got out with no hard feelings, but no one's been caught yet,' I laughed. 'What's up?' he'd asked. I told him: 'You sound regretful.' he laughed, but didn't really deny it. 'It was fun, Sades, but I sleep better now.'

And there he is, sleeping better, my Conrad, global criminal — or former criminal, I hope — but I smile and cuddle into him.

***

We eat breakfast at the apartment. We keep this simple, it's fruit and coffee and he puts a twenty pound note beside my plate. "Keep the change, darlin', it was worth it." *He's in a sunny mood, and it's catching.* "I hope nothing disturbed you last night."

"Only that you offered a grand to start with — after you'd tried the goods." *A little cloud of seriousness crosses his face.* "No, of course not. I suppose I'd guessed you'd been a naughty boy in the past. Will said he couldn't really pin down where your money came from."

"Good!" Now I look puzzled. "He's a smart man, your William, I'm really impressed. He's not naïve at all so, if he's not found anything, then I'm probably looking OK. I may even have got out too early." He's chuckling now.

"I'd feel awkward if you were still in it."

"I'm near it, Sades, don't paint me white, and I was taking a pragmatic, not a moral view. You probably remember the two Arabs I introduced you to a few years ago."

He's introduced me to a lot of Arabs, but I know exactly who he means. *"One of them disappeared shortly after and you didn't travel so much for a while."*

"Correct." He smiles as if it's a fond memory, but then he seems to shake some sense into himself. *"That's part of what made me get closer to legit, that and the fear of getting caught. I say I'm worried about the authorities catching up, but the truth is, they're miles behind; the problems are these little vendettas. So, I'm glad I'm out of that now."*

"Are you sure?"

He ponders a moment. *"Well, all life has risks. I think I've minimised them now. I'm more likely to die of a hedgehog attack these days."*

He's reassured me, I think, about the legality and the dangers, and the rest of breakfast is just funny.

We've been on the boat a while before we get back to the topic. I live here, but the place still thrills me, and I'd been sitting on the top deck with him still in awe of a skyline I see most days, and we're out into some islands before I get back to chatting. He's not a natural chatter *anyway — and he's plainly thrilled with this boat trip idea — which is just as well, because it's costing him more than a very expensive fuck!*

He likes the boat, and asks me if I'd like one. "That's not why I'm doing this!" I'm a bit miffed if he thinks that, but then it crosses my mind. "I suppose a lot of your friends have them." He nods and I can imagine the gin palaces in the Gulf.

"This is perfect for the day." He looks genuinely happy, especially when we anchor in a wonderful little bay among lush hillsides. "The boats are lavish in the Gulf, but all you can see is sand." The skipper's wife, I assume that's what she is, has put some bites on a table and there's a bottle of champagne — he's not coming all this way for some Pinot fucking Grigio — and we get back to the business discussion. "What's the Gerry connection?"

"I think he thinks I've done better at going legit than he has, and this man here is interested in that, apparently."

"How does he know that? About you being better at legit?"

"I told him. He rang me up after our dinner and wanted to chat. I'd have made him come to the house, but I didn't want him bumping into Boris or Sandra — and I still worry about phones. We went for a walk in the park and fed the ducks."

"You fed the ducks!" Two grown men with questionable histories. It sounded ridiculous.

"Boris always wants to know where I am and when he knew who I was going to be with, he said he'd follow me, and he gave me a bag of bread when I was leaving the house. Feed the ducks, he said." I still looked puzzled. *"It's*

an old trick. It makes people stop a while, gives him a better chance of seeing who else is following."

"Was anyone?"

"No." Conrad laughed. "It's just his old Balkan war habit, but it's quite reassuring. Anyway, Gerry was talking about getting cleaner — putting more distance, as he put it — but his friends are nastier, not so easy to wean off the theft and thuggery, but he's trying to show them how they can make more legitimately now. After all, they've stolen all they can. Ah, maybe not true, they could strip the Hermitage, I suppose, but most of the industrial base has coughed up what it can."

"How much did you tell him?"

"Not a lot. I haven't met him that often but, the thing with Gerry is... well, he can be telling you a completely plausible story..."

"And you think you can't believe a single word."

He smiles. "Exactly, but the man next week is Chinese and not Russian."

"How did Gerry meet him?"

"You think he'd have told me the truth?"

"No, I suppose not."

He laughed. "I had a friend once, Tony Cartwright his name was, and I swear he thought telling the truth would be an insult to his own imagination. He'd far rather tell you a story."

"You think Gerry's like that?"

"Oh, no," he said, "Tony was funny and charming — and mostly harmless."

"Gerry worries you?"

He looked calm. "No more than other people I've dealt with. I'd just be very careful doing business with him, but that doesn't mean there isn't business to be done."

"But look at what happened to Ellen."

"What do you know about Ellen? Before you started meeting her at parties, I mean."

I tried to think back. "Not a lot when you mention it. I think she was wealthy when she met him, divorce I'd always assumed, but they were hard party people, just not quite attuned. She liked rough sex and he was a top. Well, he's a sadist, really, but anyway, they started going their separate ways."

"So, you didn't know she was Peter Dickinson's first wife?"

That completely floored me. I had absolutely no idea. It made for a strange afternoon. It was a wonderful trip, and Conrad seemed very taken with it, but I couldn't think straight. Not for a single moment.

***

I was getting ready for dinner and it was still bugging me. He was looking fresh and shiny as he came up behind me. "It's surprising how little mention that got. I don't know who knows. I wouldn't mention it tonight."

"You think Alphonse doesn't know?"

"So far as I know, only Henderson does, and I'm not supposed to tell you." There's a funny expression on his face in the mirror. I think he's betrayed a trust and might be regretting it. I stand up and turn around. "You're a lovely man, Conrad, thank you for trusting me with that."

He seems relieved, it was troubling him. But he's just told me something about how he sees us, he's telling me much more now. I've learned an awful lot in the past twenty-four hours.

***

For all that Daiyu and I work full time and have no domestic commitments beyond keeping our own places sparkling, there's still a male/female split to the evening. It may just be that Conrad has some specific questions he wants to put to Alphonse, but it seems to me that they fall too easily into their beloved 'focus' while we manage to skate across and over the ruts they allow to dictate their paths. If they hadn't been quite so intense in their property discussions, they might have noticed that Daiyu and I were quieter than usual. We'd had a glance at each other early on that confirmed that we thought the topic was interesting; it's property, for heaven's sake, we have a professional interest. Also, that anything that was engaging the men so intensely needed to be understood, more for what it told us about them than about the subject itself. It's a subject on which Daiyu and I both have valuable knowledge, but does either of our heroes ever think to consult us? Not even Alphonse! Say what you like about gays, but they're still men! Mostly! I'm not getting polemical, it's actually a fascinating evening, chiefly for how the guys are trying to work each other out. It's easy for us, we can carry on talking while we're listening to them; they have their natural 'focus-orientator' of maleness to prevent them listening to anything we say.

Yes, it pisses me off on one level, but it's a huge advantage to be able to tune in to two conversations at once. Most men I know can tune into half a conversation at best: that's the half when they're speaking.

But there's a fascinating dynamic in the discussion we're tuned in to — for both Daiyu and me. Conrad's got Alphonse talking more and more animatedly about property markets around the world, and Alphonse is asking plenty of questions about the Middle East, where he admits to having a relative blind spot, he says.

If I didn't know Conrad better, I'd suspect him of trying to rekindle Alphonse's enthusiasm for a global perspective. He's just left subtle hints that he'd consider anything less to be parochial, small time. I even feel quite proud that I have a two-centre business, but Conrad isn't smarming me directly. But Alphonse isn't so easily duped as I am. When we break up to leave, it's Alphonse who's saying, "So, Wednesday then, you know where our office is, don't you? I'll be there by two, and you won't do anything before you've spoken to me."

Conrad's nodding, like a small boy taking instructions — but I suspect he's been the master of that conversation.

"Were you setting him up?" I ask when we're back at the apartment.

"No!" he says indignantly. "He's a very smart man. I couldn't do that."

Conrad is now getting my sceptical smile.

"Look, I want to do more in property and he's one of the best. I'm just glad he's keeping a wider perspective."

He gets a squint from me — it's not quite a frown — "Conrad Foxtrot Kitter, if I catch you playing me like that..."

"Promises, promises," *he says with a smile.*

29

It had been difficult to get Martha to agree to a drink. Tania didn't feel good about the 'I'm worried it was me setting you up with Robert for Noah's' ploy, especially when Martha saw straight through it: 'You're just trying to make me feel guilty to coerce me,' then she'd sounded particularly spiky, with 'What's he said about it?'

Tania had countered with, 'Nothing like as much as you just have,' and that at least got Martha laughing and suggesting the Blue Orchid at seven.

She had two martinis on the table, confident Martha would be punctual. "Wow!" she said appreciatively when Martha arrived three minutes later.

"Don't!" said Martha, sliding up on to the stool, but the sly smile said she was pleased Tania had noticed. "And thank you for getting the drink already."

"Well, you know what happens if you have just one in front of you."

"Ha, not so much to me anymore."

"I doubt that. You look fabulous." And that wasn't really an exaggeration, thought Tania.

Martha patted her leg. "Kid, the competition's too hot, I have to make such an effort when you're around."

This, at least, was Tania's normal Martha. She'd been helpful, but distant, in the business calls, but almost aggressive, initially, at the drinks suggestion, but here she was. Tania lifted her glass, "These are so dangerous, you can't let them get warm."

Martha hesitated, then barely sipped. "Why have I let you talk me into this?" She seemed slightly frosty again.

"Because you've got nobody else who would."

Martha seemed to reflect a moment, then attacked her martini. "Pathetic, aren't we? Who do you have to talk to?"

"Only Claudia, and she's usually a continent away, but, come on, we're not doing the pity party. I don't think Mr Unmentionable is talking to anybody. It's only that he was so determined to say absolutely nothing that I guessed something was up." She held up a hand to stop Martha launching into a rejoinder. "Stop, I'm saying nothing about that. Christ, you and I, we have a million things to talk about without him."

"You were standing up for him." It was said more as a plea for support than an accusation.

"I absolutely was not." She took Martha's hand. "I admire you two so much." She hesitated a moment. "Well, I love you both, but that's too much on the first martini." She was getting a smile now. "And I absolutely trust you to sort it out, so I'm not bothering about it at all."

"Not even a teensy bit?" asked Martha, with a gesture of closing her fingers together — and that started them giggling, just as two men approached their table — only to turn away when they got within two yards. Tania, who'd been getting ready to rebuff them, turned back to Martha to see a fierce expression set on her face, which turned into her usual smile when she turned back to Tania. "Sorry, you may have wanted company."

"Other than Medusa the Gorgon, you mean, not in a million." They were giggling again. "Anyway, Al Frederick, I wanted to thank you for that."

"Helpful?"

"I'll say! And dynamic."

"Yeah, those guys move quickly."

"Uh huh, and that got me into trouble." Martha looked puzzled. "He invited himself to a meeting I was having with the Giddings bank, and my CFO thoroughly disapproved. He told me off."

"He was right to do so, and Al shouldn't really have invited himself. Anyway, he was impressed." Then she raised her eyes. "He only just stopped himself commenting on how you looked…"

"Were you preparing your emasculation stare?"

Martha laughed. "My Medusa look?"

"Exactly."

"Ha, I'm rather well known at the bank for that. No, he was impressed, of course, by your mastery of everything to do with both businesses — and how you had your Giddings man eating out of your hand. Anyway, Al's a fan already, he'll do a good job for you."

"Well, they're coming up with numbers we like."

"Fourteen and seven?" Tania nodded. "What were…" Then she stopped and looked a little emotional. "I'm sorry, let's get away from a topic where he's on first base, can we?"

"Where's the outfit from?"

Martha sniffed. "Nice try, kid, but I went shopping at the weekend, that doesn't move us far enough away. How do you stay so stylish, apart from having a clothes hanger as a figure?"

"I have a terrible confession." Tania was relieved, this was giving some distance. "I never have time to bother, but my mother has an obsession with how the female power CEO should look, and I'm lucky my size doesn't change, so I have a constant supply of whatever this year's look is."

"Two things I hate about that…" and the conversation meandered off into a pleasant evening.

But by the time they were halfway down the Soave, they'd got on to Robert. Tania supposed that was the price of keeping the conversation away from Will. "Well, I see him more than anyone else, I suppose."

"And what does Andy feel about that? That must be difficult altogether, isn't it?"

"Well, it's easier now. There was a time when we had one of those 'being in love' phases…" Martha laughed. "It wasn't meant to be funny, Martha." But she found herself laughing too. "Let's face it, we're better off with Ray."

A thought seemed to strike Martha, "He's the one we share, isn't he? Let's drink to Ray." They were giggling again.

"Will you see him again?" Tania regretted the question instantly, but Martha seemed to have reached a point of not caring.

She thought for a moment. "Ray? I don't think it matters, it could have been anyone, although I'm glad it wasn't Robert. I'd like to borrow him for non-sexual activities occasionally, would you mind?"

"Of course not. Anyway, it wouldn't matter if I did."

Martha suddenly gripped her hand. "Oh, it would, my love, it would matter a lot to me if it mattered to you." She sat up straight suddenly, as if shocked by her own intensity. "Anyway, it would matter, but he can do dinner, you say, and tell me what pictures I should invest in." Now she leaned forward again. "It's funny, I found the topic of investing in pictures a little sordid; not in principle, you understand, but in terms of actual decisions on particular items in my apartment. Sordid!" She laughed. "And then I expect the poor man to take me to meet Geoffrey. Some people might find that sordid. I do, in some quiet moments, but I've lived with the kink a long time — and Geoffrey was very good." The reverie seemed to stop her. "I'm sorry, that's not your thing, is it?"

"Oh, I have my own thing, as you know. Ray participates sometimes. He's good, but not irreplaceable." And they were laughing again.

"And Robert?"

"Well, his role's a bit more unique." She thought a moment. "But he's definitely available for dinners and art discussion. Sex too, if you want it, we're not precious about that."

"I need to be more like you."

She was obviously back to thinking about Will. Tania felt awkward now. They'd been avoiding it. "Well, I'm not going to be more like you, Geoffrey's not for me." That came out almost disapproving, she thought, too censorious. "I mean, I found it fascinating the first time I watched it in the Red Room, I had to go and be fucked straightaway — and I've used the bench for my own ends, but I've never got into the stripes. Is it a big high?"

Martha seemed distant, but she responded, "Oh, huge when someone gets it right." She snapped back into the present. "Some people just like the thing itself, but some of us need a Ray." She smiled.

"Or a Jack Stephens."

Now Martha laughed. "That was a very enjoyable man. I believe Lavinia still thinks so, doesn't she?"

"Oh, I think so, but she's careful to stay a little detached."

"Was that Claudia's mistake?"

"Do you call it a mistake, or just say it was part of life? She has enough problems anyway. Well, not problems, just complications."

"Well, we all got those, don't we?"

"I know it sounds like BS, but aren't there opportunities out there? This isn't just about Noah's, is it, this you and Will problem?"

"No, it's about thinking there wasn't a problem, and then ghosts re-emerge. Mine, I knew about." She drifted off into thoughts again. "Actually, I suppose I knew about his, too, and some people never get over that first big love thing."

"Did you?"

Martha exploded laughing. "Oh, yes, thank God. We were so unsuited, but he was a dear man. My problem is I like to control things…"

"Amen to that," said Tania, raising her glass, and they both laughed.

"But then I despise men who let me do it."

"And Will has it right?" It seemed the risk could be taken.

"Better than most, I suppose." She drew a deep breath. "Oh, fuck it, better than any. But he has to get over this first big love thing."

Tania wasn't convinced he did.

"This isn't for talking about, young woman." Martha had drunk most of the wine, and it was beginning to show.

"No, of course not," said Tania, who didn't have a problem with necessary lies.

30

Conrad's meetings had been in Shanghai. He'd flown back that morning to meet Alphonse. By the time he got to the apartment he was looking tense. I'd left work early to be sure to be there for him. I can't remember the last time I did a 'little woman' thing like that.

It was nice.

But I won't make a habit of it.

Nevertheless: "Sit down, I'm cooking later, but you look like you could do with a drink first."

He smiled wanly. "I don't like it looking that obvious."

"You could just accept that I'm getting to know you quite well."

"While you, on the other hand, continue to surprise and amaze me. I thought I got the key for the place because you'd be late back."

"No, you got the key because I'm putting a claim on you. This is now your Hong Kong address."

"Are you sure? I thought this couple thing bugged you."

"Oh, fuck off, Conrad, that's not on tonight's agenda. You have Alphonse and Shanghai to tell me about. Which is the one that's making you stressed?" I'm mixing tonic in the gins; he's leaning back, getting ready to talk, I hope.

"I think I get stressed until I understand things, and I don't really understand Shanghai. Alphonse, well, he just worries me."

"Worries you?"

"Well, not me for me personally, but for a few people that matter — and for himself. I like the man, and he does know his market — even the Middle East, which he says he stays clear of, he understands better than I do. We talked a lot about that for reasons I'll come on to." I looked puzzled. *"Shanghai,"* he said, which meant nothing to me, because I was more interested in Alphonse.

"Is he wavering?"

"I think he has a problem with the idea of Will in between him and Peter. I talked a bit about Will and how I saw him. I said I didn't think the man would get in the way and I'd always expect Alphonse to have Peter as a friend. He somehow didn't seem so convinced. Is that the Claudia thing, d'you think?"

I bring the glasses over, put them in front of us and sit beside him. "It probably is, but the two of them have themselves to blame for that. I think Peter would be big about it. I suspect he already knows the status. He's been very tolerant of his wives in the past. I still can't get over Ellen. I can't believe how cool he played it. He was the one who sent us the text the night we found out. Remember that?"

"Do I ever? We were at the Dorchester celebrating, weren't we? I'd wondered why he'd taken so close an interest, but that got overwhelmed by everything else. Oh, I didn't bring up the Mei thing with Alphonse, by the way, and neither did he, but he did talk Shanghai property,

which was funny, because that was what these other people were talking about."

"Other people? I thought it was just one."

"It was initially, but the man I met did say he had friends he might want to introduce me to."

"So, you met more people. What did they want?"

"They have a lot of money. They want to place it wisely, where it can't easily be touched, in jurisdictions where not too many questions get asked, but where it stays safe without them having to..."

"Are you going to say 'intervene?'" He was looking a little uncomfortable by then. "Why don't you just assume you can't shock me. I've met your Arabs, who kill each other. You tell me Gerry's Russian friends don't worry too much about that sort of thing." Then I faltered over Ellen Calvert again. "Sorry, Ellen just brought that a bit closer to home. But as long as you're away from too much danger, I'm not going to worry overmuch. But for heaven's sake, I'm a big girl!"

Although I wasn't actually sure I was quite that big, but anyway, I think I'd relaxed him.

"Well, if they can get the money out to West Asia or the Middle East, it's quite easy to place it in businesses or property and it can be quite secure and hidden. If they just put it in funds, it's easier to see and claw back, and I'm talking about other so-called friends clawing back, rather than the authorities. Well, sometimes it's just corrupt authorities." He paused and considered. "Mostly corrupt authorities, in fact. It's just not worth speculating on it too much, but here's the funny thing..."

He takes a sip. I'm going to get one of his little dramas. I'd rather just have the plot synopsis, but I fear I'm going to get the whole novel.

"Their English wasn't very good, and neither was their translator…"

"But she was pretty."

"How did you…" *I just shrug, and he gets there quickly.* "Anyway, I was asking about what they did locally and one of them talked about high-performing funds and GKS got mentioned. There was some muttering that didn't get translated but I played dumb to try to understand more but the translator was just told to shut up, as far as I could tell. I had my host on his own for dinner and his English was good enough, but I had to be sure he wasn't aware of all my connections. I didn't know what Gerry had told him. Anyway, long story short…"

"Thank God," *I mumble as I snuggle on to his chest.*

"Am I boring you?"

"No!" *I can't conceal my irritation.* "Please just get to the point."

"Well, the two points are, no, three points, actually…"

"Conrad! Get on with it!"

But I can't shake him that easily. "First point is easy: they want me to help set up Middle East connections to get their money into business and property. We'll use two of my businesses to start with and then, if that works and we're all happy, they can build their own, with me having a share, of course."

"I'm going to start gnawing lemon soon."

"It's all right, that was the boring bit. Point two is moving money, and that gets done by Michael McKenzie."

"Thank God!" I almost shout.

I've puzzled him. "I thought it might interest you, but... are you that pleased? I mean..."

"I'm only pleased you've finally got to something interesting."

"Well, your Michael is a star, apparently. I'd always thought he was a bit of a duffer, from all I'd been told, but he's been helping them move money into Europe. Now, although Gerry likes that, his friends aren't so keen. They think it's their patch. That was interesting, I got on to that with Alphonse, when he was talking about London..."

"Conrad!"

I get a smirk. I think the threatened digression was a tease, "So Gerry's not exactly being magnanimous or using my superior skills at legitimising operations, he just needs them off his patch and I've no doubt he'll want a share of whatever we set up," he shrugged, "which is fair enough."

"But he's tried to deceive you!"

"It's up to me to interpret what he says. You think I've told him the truth about everything?"

That was a fair point, now I felt naïve. "What was your third point?"

"Well, my man was a little cagey. His friends were into GKS a little, but didn't like the Shen family connection — especially with the old man's illegitimate daughter running it, but they were being offered good terms by a new fund that's being set up."

"And that's interesting?"

"By Shen Liuwei? Isn't that your Lou? I tried not to seem too curious about who, just said I wanted to spread

some money out here, and that helped him talk more. Something you could learn from that, my darling, I think."

I hate the smug smirk, but maybe he does have a point. "You really think they're trying to split off and go on their own, Lou and that lot?"

"Well, given all else that's happening... can I come on to Alphonse now?"

I groaned. "Go on, you've got me hooked now."

"Nah, I'm hungry. Aren't you cooking, or something?"

He got my fists pummelling his chest, but he just laughed, and we ended up in the kitchen area. I'm a top when we play, but he's definitely a boss in everyday life. Things just seem to have to happen the way he wants them to. He's on a stool at the breakfast bar and I'm busying myself getting a meal ready that's far more complicated than it should be, but I'm enjoying it. I can't just put things on a plate; I have to design what we're eating.

He's a little in disgrace. I've told him it's the naughty stool. He's been looking for nibbles in the kitchen cupboards. "This is the first time I've cooked for you, Mr Kitter, and it'll be the last if you don't bring appetite and appreciation to the table."

He just smiles and, to be fair, he does get back on to Alphonse. "I think he's expecting Peter to take his time pulling money out of property. There'll be a big tranche when they IPO the Group and they can build the Foundation slowly after that, but he's worried about how much autonomy he'll have with the new investors. I told him, if I were buying in, I'd be investing in him; the last thing I'd want to do is interfere with his decisions. I asked him when the last time was that Peter really interfered.

That was interesting. Peter's more involved than I'd assumed."

He looked at me at that point, as if I should know something, and when I thought about it, I said, "Actually, that's a point Claudia's made more than once. He poses as this effortless dilettante, but he works ceaselessly and knows people everywhere."

"You see. I was picking up a little anxiety in Alphonse. He is brilliant, and he always seems so supremely confident and the master of his organisation, but he relies on Peter a lot, and he's actually nervous about how he'll do on his own. He's got something similar here, of course. Her supreme highness Zhao Meitang is running everything now, but her basic competence is in property and he likes to talk things through with her."

31

The plane was gliding down into Hamilton Island and Alphonse found himself chuckling at his own stupidity. He wasn't a stranger to bizarre travel schedules, but the next ten days would be absurd. Somehow, though, the familiar sights of the islands lifted his spirits as always. Luke hadn't had to work too hard to persuade him: 'These are critical decisions, Alphonse. It's big money and delays if we don't get it right now.'

Luke was the architect on his Whitsundays project and, although his confidence was high in what Luke would deliver — the first two resorts he'd completed were excellent — he knew they were at a phase now where looking at pictures and models would be insufficient. Alphonse knew the site, he'd first checked it out three years ago and, of all the resorts he'd built, this was the one with the greatest emotional commitment. He'd loved this place since backpacking through all those years ago. But now he had to walk through and feel the land and check the views, all with the images of the buildings in his head. He wanted to picture the outlook of each of the villas, what the pool surroundings would be, and imagine the guests' walks through the property.

Luke was waiting to meet him. He almost walked past until the big figure called, "Hey, mate!"

He spun round. Luke was a tall man, but he'd been wearing a suit every other time Alphonse had been with him. Here the bright shirt and shorts were undeniably neat, but very different, and the big Aussie hat with the sleek shades underneath lent additional anonymity. But Alphonse got the voice, and the lanky physique.

"Luke, you didn't have to," he said as the man picked up his bag. He pumped his arm, check-weighing it and grimaced, "All this for three days."

"Don't!" said Alphonse, smiling. "That's got to see me through Shanghai and New York."

"Oh, and we couldn't ever let standards slip, could we? But do we really need the full wardrobe?"

It was a cheery tease, thought Alphonse. Luke probably knew him just well enough for it not to be offensive. Luke, for a straight, paid a great deal of attention to his own appearance, that had always been Alphonse's impression — and today's more leisurely ensemble confirmed that: bright, yes, but well-pressed and tasteful — so he could take the remark as an appreciative compliment and not as a homophobic dig. Alphonse could always glide above them but let those observations help build his opinion of any speaker.

He felt surprisingly relaxed with Luke, increasingly so as the projects had come to fruition and all the important details had been attended to. Feeling that the execution would do justice to the vision on these projects was vital, and Luke had succeeded as well as any.

"Qualia would have picked me up."

"Listen, it's hard enough hiding who we are and why we're here. Let me do the talking, and let's try to make you look a bit more like you're on holiday before we get there. Jesus, you'd even look smart in a tee shirt, though; can you lose the jacket, please, and undo another shirt button?"

They could have stayed in the property Alphonse had bought, but there were complications about which staff would be retained and which would be let go, and, as Luke had noted, 'You need to be properly looked after, mate, get a reminder of what you've got to beat.' Yes, and a schedule like this needed hotels with an impeccable laundry service.

Once he'd checked in and they'd met at the bar, it was easy to keep to their code of discretion, no business talk in public areas, but discretion was soon obliterated by a cry of, "Alphonse, you bastard, I knew you'd be here!"

He leapt up. "Sue! What…" and he saw Breeana standing demurely behind her. "Wow, how lovely to see you!" He gave himself to the inevitable hug but kept the presence of mind to make introductions so he could leave Sue with Luke for a moment.

"Luke, this is Sue, a friend of mine, we've done some sailing here." He smiled as he saw Luke wince when his hand was gripped, but he got a sailing question out quickly — and they could be left a minute.

Breeana was hanging back. He stepped towards her for a gentler embrace, which she only slowly relaxed into. "You need an explanation, I expect," she said softly into his neck.

He pulled back, his arms still around her waist. "Can't I just say how lovely it is to see you?"

She looked up with a half-smile, and he was struck, once again, by how pretty her eyes were. "For now, I think you're being too gentlemanly to say the truth."

He kissed her cheek and smiled. "Nonsense! Come and meet Luke. Luke, this is Breeana, she was sailing with us, she's the wife of Tony King, one of our fund guys."

Luke stretched out a hand, looking confident he wouldn't suffer again like he had with Sue. "It's lovely to meet you. I've heard of him; actually, I think I've met him, trying to get me to put money with him a couple of years back. One of those evenings of his in Sydney."

"And did you?" she asked pleasantly.

Luke laughed. "I don't think I'm in that league yet. I could say he was polite about letting me know…" and the other three laughed. "Well, I didn't know him like you do." He chuckled. "I can still remember it vividly: 'six figures is good, mate, but seven is better.' But I will say, about a year later, when we got a lot of publicity about these resort projects, I had a little email from him. I can remember that, too: 'Well done, mate, we could be talking soon.' I thought, 'You arrogant shit!' but it made me smile."

"Did you get back in touch?"

He laughed. "Ha, I'm not there yet."

"Well, we're not buying the drinks," said Sue. "Maybe we've got the wrong guys, Bree."

"Oh, I don't think so," said Luke, smiling, but looking at Alphonse and Bree.

"Well," said Sue, "as long as you're not a poofter like this one here."

"Talking of poofters," said Alphonse, "where's Jerry?"

"Ha!" Sue laughed loudly. "Off to see his girlfriend, I expect," she said, closing her eyes and shaking her head, but not looking unhappy. "Nah, I've just told him it's a girls-only trip to the boat."

"Are we just lucky, then?"

Now Sue rolled her eyes and head around. "Alphonse!" she said in exasperation, "you're the guys who're supposed to be sensitive."

Breeana looked embarrassed — Alphonse got the picture and Luke, wittingly or not, got the conversation quickly back on to the boat and sailing. "Yes, we keep her here in the marina," Sue was saying and Luke, plainly a sailor too, got into the spec of the boat while Alphonse managed to sit closer to Bree, leaving the others in the chairs on the opposite side of the table, talking animatedly, Sue not pausing for breath to correct Alphonse's order of a bottle of prosecco. 'Champagne!' she'd shouted instantly and imperiously, barely interrupting her discussion with Luke.

"I can't say she made me," Bree said, "but when I let her know that Tony said you'd be here, her plan was hatched immediately. Then I thought you weren't here, they said they had no Alphonse Newman booked…"

"I got Luke to book everything." He lowered his voice. "we try to stay discreet."

She nodded, she understood, she knew what his business was. "Anyway, like Sue said, he'll only stay in Qualia, but we can have a drink there anyway." She touched his hand on his chair arm. "Are you OK? Tony says there may be big changes."

"Maybe," he said. "Has he said much about it?" He hoped she didn't know. He'd be torn between trying to get more information, and feeling he was exploiting her.

She shrugged and sighed. "No, he doesn't say much about much."

Alphonse felt relieved. "I think we're talking about it more in New York next week."

"Are you going there from here?"

"Via Shanghai." She looked surprised. "Yes, not one of my cleverer moves but Luke persuaded me this was important and urgent. But it's wonderful you're here."

That was what she needed to put her mind at rest, he thought, but it had the advantage of being sincere. Their communications were infrequent, and invariably sweet, and her underlying level of neediness was never intrusive; he wasn't much more than a regulation gay friend, he didn't think. Well, he occasionally reminded himself, he was a little more than that, but she seemed happy to accept the status. He was a manner of escape for her, a way for her to assert herself to herself. He wasn't unhappy if that was a role he could fulfil. It meant he didn't have to be too discreet about life in Hong Kong and Shanghai, although he was relieved to have that story interrupted.

"Luke's invited us to stay for dinner," said Sue loudly.

"Of course he has," said Alphonse, smirking.

Sue turned back to Luke. "He's such a cheeky bastard, this one," she said. "But your mate's a smooth talker, too, Alphonse…"

Luke joined in. "I was going to suggest we hired a boat anyway, we should…" and he looked around him to make sure no one else was listening. There was no one, but he spoke more quietly anyway. "We want to get all the views from out at sea," Alphonse was nodding, it was a good point. "And we should check out swimming in the bay."

"Can we anchor…"

"Where you're interested in?" Sue was smirking, Alphonse was worried about what she would say next. "We'll be fine," she said quietly. "I don't know if we'll get the rags up, Alphonse. Your mate seems keen, but I don't know how much time you've got. Can you give us a full day?"

"If you don't mind Luke and me talking work a lot of the time."

"You do what you want, give us a chance to get a couple of long reaches in."

"We might be spreading plans out in the saloon."
She waved an arm. "Plenty of space. Good, that's Wednesday sorted, well, we can do tomorrow night on board, if you like." And the waiter was there to take them through to the dining area.

***

He wasn't surprised by the call at eleven, although the ladies had left soon after dinner. "Are you coming back up? I feel I should have asked you."

"You should have. But I'm here now. What's your room number?"

In two minutes, she was in his arms, kissing him. "Won't Sue think this strange? You've just left her?"

Bree leaned back, a knowing look on her face. "Alphonse, sweet man, she left me. Your friend was much freer with his room number than you were with yours." He must have looked surprised. "Oh, come on," she said, "you must have picked it up." He nodded a little, he had. Now her smile grew broader, "You know what she's like, and I didn't want her forming a queue behind me this time." He chuckled. It was still one of his oddest memories, the first night on the boat with both of them visiting him. "Talking of which," she looked into his eyes, "condoms?"

"Shouldn't we talk for a bit?"

She slipped her dress off and stepped out of it. "Later, maybe," she said and kicked her shoes away, stood in front of him and looked up. "Or maybe we talk now." He felt relieved. "But naked, I insist." That wasn't too hard, he thought.

***

She was spooning back into him an hour later. "So, what did you want to talk about?" she asked.

"Well," he said, "we didn't even finish the condom discussion."

"Did you have one, by the way?"

"I always carry one, you know that."

"Is that the one that's seven years old?"

He laughed. "No, but they don't get much use."

"Do I need to worry? I mean, you don't; as you probably gathered, those were my first two orgasms for a very long time — I'm not much into DIY, but I do imagine you down there occasionally. I wasn't trying to avoid talking earlier, honestly, but I was a bit needy." She wriggled around to face him and kissed his lips. "I'd obviously like to make you come later but you're a bit distracted, aren't you?"

"I'm sorry."

She put her hand to his face and kissed him again. "Please don't be silly. I appreciate my demands were a little urgent, as you've just experienced, but I do want to be here for you. I just hope part of that will be sucking your cock again while I'm sat on your face later. But what do you want to talk about?"

"Well, first of all, are you OK?"

She guffawed. "Oh, Alphonse, thank God you're too fucking sweet or I might have to fall in love with you. I'm fine, really, I am. Well, I could happily live with you coming down this way a little more often. After all, you're too well protected in Hong Kong now for me to get away with coming up there again. But what's the Shanghai thing? Is that a romantic connection?"

"That's probably the most complicated part of it all."

He talked about Mei's story. Breeana had visited him in Hong Kong as the original deals were being put together, but it had been Tony talking about 'Wengwei's bastard' that had fixed Mei in her mind. "I don't think her brother likes it very much, does he?"

But he'd told her about Lee first, the other brother, and, for the first time in a very long time, it was easy to talk. Bree was so disconnected from everyone. It was hard to talk even to Isobel these days, she was so close to Daiyu and to Mei; and it had got harder and harder to talk to Claudia — even to contrive an opportunity.

"So, you were in love with Lee?"

"I was for a time."

"And?" He knew she wanted an answer, or at least an insight, but he found it impossible to describe with any ease. "Too possessive? Too monogamous? Too easy?" she asked.

He laughed. "Not that, no. No, he had family disciplines and expectations pulling at him; as the older son, especially."

"While younger son could break all the rules…" and she was talking, quite unbidden, about Tony's new 'partner-in-crime.' "Tony doesn't say much, of course, but he's still leading a wild life, I think, and been spending a lot more time in Asia over the last couple of months. I also think he's found a soul mate. He still thinks Henry's wonderful, he always says, but it's always been obvious they're very different; that's what makes it work, Tony says. I've only met Henry twice. I liked him, but he's a bit dry. She's lovely."

"Rachel?"

"Of course. We're talking Henry. Please don't tell me that's complicated."

He chuckled, and cuddled her. "Not so far as I know."

"Well, let's get back to this Mei, then. Tony says she's gay."

"She is."

Now he got a sly look from her. "Alphonse," she said slowly, "I'm not sure you're giving me the full story, or do I have to go down there again to show you that gay isn't so simple? Have you fucked her?"

And it was put so artlessly, and so swiftly, that he hesitated.

"Gotcha! You have, haven't you?" And it was easy to nod. But she was studying him carefully. "It's not simple, is it? What's making it complicated?"

It was easier to talk to her about the women's theories, and Bree wanted to know how it would affect him. He felt so unsure.

"It's not so crazy, you'd be a lovely dad, if she'd let you be one at all."

"I don't know about that."

"About being a dad, or about letting you be involved."

"I hadn't got as far as being involved."

"Well, it sounds like she's enough of her own woman to let you work that out between you. But you'd certainly be a far better dad than Tony."

He felt curiously comforted as he snuggled into her and, as their arms wrapped around each other, he found his cock was rising to meet her.

***

It was a wonderful three days. He enjoyed working with Luke, they saw the project similarly, even, at the end of the first morning in the hotel room, after the "Alphonse, don't bring the budget up every time I have an idea!" comment.

Alphonse had felt relaxed enough to laugh. "I suppose mine would be even more extravagant?"

"Yes, mate, and they're more numerous." Luke had laughed with him.

"Didn't we put a contingency in the budget?"

"Of course, but that had gone before the coffee break." Alphonse always tried to stay calm, but he must have looked concerned. "Don't worry, we can always snip something off Isobel's"

"That's not something I'd even dream of attempting." They'd laughed louder.

"I know," said Luke, "but it's much harder for John now Daiyu's in cahoots with Izzie." Daiyu had worked in Lijun's architect's business on his first resort project as the number two until joining Isobel to start the design business.

"You don't call her that. Izzie?"

"Not to her face, mate, no, she scares me." He was smiling broadly. "But what is it you call her sometimes?"

"Sadie?"

"That's it. There's a story behind that, but that's for later." They'd got rapidly back to work until lunchtime, when they snacked and then buggied down to their own site. With the plans clear in his head, it was easier for Alphonse to picture how all the buildings would change and how guests would see and feel things.

They worked more on the second morning in the big saloon on the catamaran and were almost oblivious to the boat being anchored off Chalkies Beach. It was a sudden shock to look up and see the vast stretch of Whitehaven Sands running north.

Bree came in. "Skipper says she's stopping for lunch and she's taking no refusals on the white wine." She looked a little tentative.

The men looked at each other. "I think it's been a brilliant day and a half," said Alphonse. "I think we've earned it."

"Woah, I was getting more worried about punishments for mutiny."

Alphonse smiled. "Just obeying orders last night, were you?"

Luke looked oddly bashful. "Were we loud, or something?"

"Didn't hear a thing," said Breeana quickly, "slept like a log." She smiled slyly at Luke. They'd been at anchor off the new hotel site, having got the early evening views before dinner on board and then seen the sun flooding the beach as they'd had breakfast that morning — four happy-looking people. Alphonse assumed it would have no consequences for Luke or Sue, however wildly enthusiastic their activities had been. He and Bree had found themselves laughing as the crescendos came loud and distinct from the far corner of the boat.

Their own were quieter. "The other advantage of sixty-nine," she'd said as she'd gone down on him again.

They went to the back deck together to be confronted with another lavish but simple spread. The huge prawns were the principal feature, but there were cold meats and salads looked splendid around them.

"I'm not cooking," said Sue. "Nothing'll go cold if you wanna swim first."

Luke shrugged. "No cozzie."

"You're wearing one," Sue said, then stripped off completely and dived off the back steps.

Luke looked to Breeana with embarrassed hesitation.

"Booby," she said, then stripped off and dived after Sue.

The men soon followed.

***

Alphonse felt strangely elated on the long flight north, more at ease than he'd been for weeks; since the New York trip, he reflected. Yes, he needed some clarity with Mei — if there were an issue; and he found himself laughing at the unintended pun. He was calmer and more philosophical now, telling himself that life was a succession of accidents you had to cope with, all stemming from the first accident of acquiring parents.

Although, for Mei, this, if it were happening, seemed like something other than an accident. He thought for a moment about Mei's own birth and wondered how aware Shen Wengwei had been at the moment of conception — of Mei's mother's intentions, or even of his own subconscious ones. He decided against crediting Wengwei with too much sensitivity, but it was too easy to dismiss the workings of tyrants. The more successful ones he'd met, and Wengwei had certainly been one of those, nevertheless showed some sensitivity to the reactions of people around them — not sympathy, he told himself, the tyrant's will was paramount, but certainly awareness. So, where was Zhao Meitang on that scale? He been seeing more and more of her father in her as time passed.

But what of the greatest tyrant? Peter Dickinson? For the first time, he was seeing Peter differently — immensely sensitive but, with all that charm and subtlety, as tyrannically exploitive as anyone he could think of. And Mei? How would that now evolve? It struck him suddenly, very forcibly, that he should not be the passenger on the ship of his own life, however privileged that role had been. He needed to be its captain.

***

He missed no connections, but his flight was late arriving in Shanghai, and he was more than an hour late getting to Mei's apartment. The driver had waited while he dropped his bags off at the hotel and showered and changed. He gleaned nothing from the driver's face, but his speed through the traffic and his getaways from lights told him the man was under pressure to make up time.

He'd texted even before take-off of the expected delay, and dinner, he assumed, would anyway be prepared at home by her staff. The frosty reception was expected. "Why this week for Australia?" was her greeting.

He smiled, feeling less tense now things were clearer for him and, not inclined to have any gesture of welcome or remorse being rebuffed, he stood looking at her, making no motion to kiss or embrace. "I apologise for being late…"

"The driver could have brought you straight here from the airport." The man had obviously contacted the apartment.

She wasn't even irritating him. "And I would have arrived dirty and dishevelled…"

"And Alphonse wouldn't ever do that, would he?"

Sarcasm, for him, was always a blunt knife. "Unthinkable," he said, smiling slightly, "but here I am, and I'm very happy to be here."

"You'd have chosen different flights if it had been that important to you."

He laughed, and she looked furious. "Many things are important to me, one of which is a business which you happen to have a lot of money invested in, and it will now be expanding into Australia. Another important thing is my relationship with you. Relationships, maybe, we have a business relationship and a personal relationship, and I think I'd like to spend some time on that one this evening. That depends, of course, on whether we can get past this little tantrum first."

The one thing Mei would not do, he knew, was storm off. She would attack this one way or another. "That actually depends on whether I want to sustain it."

"OK, well, while you're making your mind up about that, perhaps we can eat and talk about the business relationship. I'm committed, though, by the way."

"To the business? Of course you are!"

"Of course I'm not, actually; I was talking about the personal relationship." This was bizarre, they were still standing in the spacious hallway, neither of them moving and he wasn't sure why he felt so relaxed. It was partly because he was making his own choices, he knew, but he had a growing certainty, even as he confronted a woman who was becoming ever more proud — arrogant, even — that she would want what he wanted, in large part because he wanted it.

"We'll talk about that later," she said eventually — he'd wondered if she'd crack first — "let's eat now." She turned and walked quickly to the dining area at the end of the huge drawing room, nodding to the senior staff woman, who'd stood waiting just inside the doorway from the hall.

Once they'd sat down and wine had been served, it was as if the earlier conversation hadn't taken place. Mei was animated and talked about business, particularly about the progress Lee was making with new opportunities, and she wanted to know more about the Australian resort project.

The meal, as always in her apartment, was a few small, simple courses, served in quick succession, and they were soon drinking tea. "Are you worried about next week?" she asked.

"Why should I be worried?"

For the first time during the evening, she smiled. "Why should you not be? What are you expecting?"

"I'm expecting Will to go through the options. I expect you know about them?"

The smile disappeared. "I expect you to say a little more about them. We have a business relationship, remember. What do you expect to happen to property?"

"And resorts."

"Yes, and resorts," she said coldly. "Alphonse, you're trying to play with me. I understood you had some issues with what was expected of you. Isn't there a misunderstanding about the offer Peter has made to you?"

"That's cleared up now. I understand the proposition."

"So, what will you be doing?"

"That depends, in part, on other people."

"Alphonse!" she shouted sharply.

That brought the head maid running in, but she retreated to the kitchen as soon as she saw that neither had moved. She may have noticed Alphonse's small smile. "I'm serious," he continued. "We're going to talk about our personal relationship later, and that plays a part."

"You said we should talk about our business relationship first. That's what we were trying to do, but you insist on being irritatingly enigmatic. What are you going to do?"

"I'll tell you what I want to do."

She sighed, and seemed to relax slightly. "That's what I would like to know."

"I would like to continue running the Dickinson property and resorts business…"

"Which you will partly own."

He nodded. He would assume she knew everything. If she made some false assertion, he wouldn't correct her, simply be aware that her knowledge was partial — but in all dealings so far, Peter seemed to have told her everything. "Yes, the biggest challenge there is selling at the right price when people know we're looking to offload. I'm hoping Peter won't want money out too quickly."

She was nodding, she understood the business. "My impression was that he would take his time. What about your role for Senlin?"

"You have Yang Li now. I was impressed." That was true, but he doubted whether she was competent to run everything without a few big mistakes being made.

"We've made the change, but I'd assumed you came with the Peter Dickinson package he arranged with my father. That has three years to run. He has committed to that."

"And you think I'm part of that deal. You see, we talked earlier on about how I can merely respond to the offers put to me. But I may choose not to stay involved."

"You're a gay, Alphonse, not a girl. What the fuck do you want to do? I can negotiate penalties with Dickinson if the conditions or key personnel change. What do you want?"

She could normally stay calmer than this, and he wasn't baiting her for fun, rather to find out what she wanted. It seemed obvious now, in business terms at least. "I want to stay on in the role I have for you. Yang Li works for you on your Senlin organisation chart, but she takes direction from me — and I do mean that I sign everything off, OK?"

He finally got another smile. "OK. Good, in fact."

"And whatever the Dickinson deal with your father was, I'll take five percent of that."

She seemed to ponder. "Maybe you should push for more."

Now he smiled, "Yes, I should. It'd be worth it to help him avoid your penalty clauses."

She smiled. "I'll make it clear to him how severe they'd be if he loses the main man. But what about buyers? How do you see that?"

"Well, I have to assume we keep a good relationship with the bank, and they won't start withdrawing because Peter's pulling out. I expect Will would know first if that were threatened, but I am picking up gossip that there's money looking for homes in the property business. Peter will tell me more about that."

She looked thoughtful. "I hear things too."

"Your bank?"

"No, my father's old friends. They say there is more traffic between here and Europe and the Middle East, you know, the people who move money are talking more. My idiot brother should know more. Well, he probably does, but he talks to me less and less. I want to fire him."

"Why don't you? Although I'm told he's quite good."

"If I fire him, I can't see him at all, I'd have zero control, and my father's friends tell me they couldn't see him so easily, either. They watch him for me; he knows that, and it makes him nervous. Anyway, the important thing for me is you stay."

"That's the business relationship."

"I was the one who wanted the personal relationship, and I still do. I asked you, remember?"

"I remember the conversation very well. You wanted someone you could trust to talk to."

"And someone I admire."

This had moved on, now. This was Mei moving towards being seductive — or as near as she could get to it.

"Yes, thank you, and I appreciate that. What I hadn't realised was that you apparently also wanted someone that you desire."

"But we had… already… we talked about that," she looked a little uncertain now. "I like your body, it's a lovely body. It's the only male one I want."

He smiled. It was hard not to laugh, but he should stay engaged and not provoke her, he would find out nothing otherwise. "And I like your body. It's a very sweet body, but it's obviously a little strange for each of us. Do you still see Lily?"

"Of course. She comes here sometimes." She was a little prickly now, "do you still see… oh, let me see," and she put her finger theatrically to her chin, "where do I start? Very attractive man, I must take my place in the queue."

"I think ordering me here every month isn't exactly taking your place in the queue."

"You don't want to come? You have business here anyway."

"No, of course I want to come." he smiled. "I've flown all the way from Australia to have dinner with you."

"And you turn up fucking late!" She exploded with laughter, and he joined her. "Come on, my lovely man, it's bedtime. I expect you stay busy in your social life, but you're my special monthly treat."

Couplings with Mei were unlike any others he experienced. There was little spontaneity, he had to take some blame for that, but it was almost like 'sex by numbers,' at least until the important body-zones became excited and engaged — but that came only after a sequence of now well-practiced moves.

But one new step found her completely unprepared. "A condom!" she shrieked, as his last move after discarding his pants was to drop the pack on the bedside table. She'd seen it after casting her bra aside and her thumbs stayed in the thong's waistband.

He lay down on his side of the bed. "No point in not being careful."

She was sitting up on her knees on her side, "I told you, there's no danger for me." Then she managed to think wider — to think beyond herself. "Have you been somewhere?"

"You know I've been somewhere, but I don't think that's the question you meant to ask."

"Have you been with someone?"

"I have been, but is that a discussion we want to have? Don't we give each other space?"

She seemed to look puzzled and betrayed by turns. "Man or woman?"

"In this case a woman."

"And you wore a condom with her?"

"No, but…" He wasn't sure what he was going to say, but she leaned across him, picked it up, and threw it violently into the furthest corner.

"So, not with me then either." She was back, sitting on her knees glowering at him.

It was an odd phenomenon he'd noticed, even in himself, how the onset of jealousy is as likely to promote desire as to destroy it. But Mei had different motives anyway, if he listened to Daiyu and Isobel, and he wanted to know more about that himself. For that plan to work, however, his body had to respond, and that wasn't always easy with Mei anyway, and his eyes followed hers down to the unusually shrivelled object lying where he would normally hope to find the root of a proud staff.

"Well," she said, "you didn't do much with that, did you?"

"Shouldn't we just talk a while?"

"Talk? You're here to fuck me!"

He looked calmly at her. "That's what we should talk about."

"What? That you have other people to fuck, is that it? That's what we talk about?"

"No, we should talk about why we fuck, as you put it."

"Don't! This is too stupid. Nobody asks about why they fuck. Just do it!"

He looked down pointedly at the unwilling member. She looked briefly too, then attempted to take it in her hands, but he wriggled away, took her wrist and pulled her towards him. She reacted fiercely and brought her free fist down hard on his chest. "No, no cuddles, no shit like that. You want me to suck your cock, is that what she does?"

"We're not talking about that." Her eyes were still angry. He stayed calm. "I like you sucking my cock, as it happens."

"And you like my arse. Am I a boy for you?"

"Mei, that's…" he stopped himself saying 'stupid', he was on the edge of losing control. His grip moved from her wrist, he held her hand. "We're here because we mean a lot to each other and, however odd it is, we like fucking each other."

"But not with condoms."

"Why not with condoms?"

"They're horrible things. I hate them."

"You'd rather take risks?"

"Yes, I'd rather take risks." And, finally she lay beside him and wrapped her arms around him.

Too quickly, it seemed to him. For her to get over all that so quickly did seem to confirm that she had a different motive.

But so did he, now.

It still took time for her to get his cock to rise, but her mouth had been getting better, and it helped him now when she took her thong off and sat down gently on his face. It was a sweet, neat pussy, and his tongue made her easily wet — something that merely sucking his cock had been unable to do — he'd guessed that her enthusiasm there was mostly faked — but she still had a nice mouth, and he'd become decently stiff. And she was soon decently wet and, as soon as that happened, as he'd expected, she spun round and straddled him. "Time for you to fuck me."

He looked up into her eyes and smiled. "What are we going to call her?"

She looked completely serious. "Just fuck me. We'll talk about that later."

So he did, and it was easy now. He was very stiff, and she was sweet and small and gripped him up in her stomach. Her hands stayed on his shoulders, her arms straight, a smile slowly spreading on her lips. There was no need to go slow, he could let go as freely and as quickly as ever and she seemed to scream even louder and she was coming so naturally with him with just gasps of "Oh, yes, oh, yes, oh, yes."

As their breathing slowed and she settled beside him, looking into his eyes, he smiled and asked, "No 'fuck my cunt' tonight?"

She smiled back. "You didn't seem to need it."

"I don't know that I needed it the other times."

"I couldn't take a chance. I had to talk dirty to be sure to make you come." He looked sceptical, but got a cheeky smile in return, "Anyway, it worked."

There was something in her smile. "What do you mean, it worked?"

"It worked. You came." But the smile stayed.

"But tonight?"

"It was nice to know you didn't need it. I liked it, I like it better without the dirty talk. I like it when you just come like that. Will you do it again?"

"I'm happy doing it again."

"In spite of the risks?"

"What risks, my sweet?" He was still smiling at her, but suspiciously, and she was plainly enjoying his doubts.

"Maybe no risks, maybe the risky thing has happened, maybe it's too late."

"So, was tonight about pleasure, or insurance?"

She squealed and hugged him. "You'd guessed, you knew, am I right?" He smiled and nodded as she looked into his eyes. She hugged him tighter. "And you still…" She kissed his chest; she kissed his lips. "you wanted…"

"I wanted…" She sat up on her knees again, her eyes interrogating him. "Well, how else would we, you and I, I mean, if not with each other, but," he said emphatically, "my darling Meitang, this is something we will talk about."

She snuggled in again. "In the morning though."

"Yes, in the morning."

"After you fuck me again."

"After I fuck you again, yes, but Meitang…"

"Yes?"

"For fun, not insurance."

"For fun, of course, now go to sleep, you talk too much."

33

'We can do it by video,' Peter had said, but Will wanted to be sure Peter and Claudia were aware of all the problems that would confront them next week. It would be easier also to assess what outcomes they would tolerate if he were face to face with them. Two B was important for him, but how important was it for them?

"Well then, you must stay with us. Will you be bringing Martha?"

"Oh, no, not for a weekend." The secret was holding, apart from with Tania, who was very pointedly asking no questions — just wanting to know how he was doing a little too often, and hinting at 'interested buyers for the IPO, but I'm not allowed to talk about those without the CFO's permission' but even she'd got the sense that this was no teasing topic anymore. One sour look had seen her retreating: 'Not one more word, I promise, just saying you should talk to Al Frederick.'

"No, I suppose not," Peter had said, "the poor woman's got Atlanta with all of us the following weekend, hasn't she?"

Maybe Will was being oversensitive, but something in the way Peter asked the question made him wonder if their secret was quite as secure as he thought. Claudia could have squeezed something out of Tania, maybe a suspicion, if not information; they read each other very well, he knew. "She's not sure she can get away. Bank commitments."

"Oh, the Gunters are going to be very disappointed. Still, it can't be helped — and here I am offering to play host to you and I'm off myself on Saturday."

That surprised Will. "Going to New York early?"

"Yes, but via China."

"Problems?"

"No, just conversations."

It was unlike Peter to be so glibly dismissive, but Will's own movements would be furtive. He'd booked the Lanesborough for Friday and Saturday, and found Peter's impending trip a good reason to decline the invitation to stay in Barnes overnight.

"Very well, then, my boy, but you can use one of the rooms as a day room to shower and change."

Will was relieved to have escaped the obligation, but Peter lapsing into his 'my boy' habit made him wonder how much confidence was being placed in him. Did you hand over control of your multi-billion-dollar business to a man you still referred to as 'my boy'?

But Claudia's welcome was warm and effusive when Andreas dropped him at the door. "Thank you so much for making the trip." She hugged him and kissed his cheek. "I know he thinks video would be OK, but I think things are too critical for that, aren't they?"

He felt guarded. "I wouldn't want to spread alarm."

"Oh, Will." She hugged him again. "We know who we're dealing with; these are not small egos."

"Who has small egos?" Peter had come out on to the step and was beaming. "No place for them here. Come in, anyway." He wrapped his arm around Will's shoulder, then turned to Andreas. "Could you put his things in the main guest room? We may persuade him to stay."

"I really have made other commitments, I'm afraid."

There was a glint of suspicion in Claudia's look, but maybe he was being, once again, too sensitive. That's what a conscience did for you, he told himself.

"Too bad, too bad, but I suppose we'll have enough of each other over the next ten days. You haven't been here before, have you? Well, it wouldn't matter if you had, I barely recognise it myself after Isobel's transformation. Anyway, just follow Andreas up, we'll be in the garden room through there," he pointed to large open doors at the rear of the vast reception area, "just drinking coffee. Take your time."

"I'll just be a minute. I showered and changed at the airport."

"Of course you did, my boy." He stopped and sniffed. "Fragrant as a peach. I wish I looked like you after a night flight."

When he came down, Peter seemed relaxed, but was the first to stand when Will suggested they start the meeting, and led them into the library. "Claudia's had it fitted to do presentations," said Peter, eyeing Will's laptop and raising his eyebrows at Claudia's.

"No need," said Will, "just some paper for you, but the range of answers I have ready in my head doesn't match the range of questions you're likely to ask. The laptop's my back-up." He turned to Claudia. "I do mean both of you," he said, and she smiled.

Will went through his four options. Little had changed in the principles of each, but some of the numbers had moved significantly and the questions were detailed and well-informed, particularly from Claudia. When he'd concluded the review, he said, "I think next week's debate will hinge on the attitudes of the other directors, and here I have to admit that I've not had particularly fruitful conversations, and I haven't been able to talk at all to Tony."

"Which tells us something, doesn't it?" said Peter.

"You haven't spoken to him, have you?" Will asked.

He got only a cool stare from Peter. "And what would that tell me, do you think?" he asked. Claudia looked uncomfortable.

This is not a time to shrug, thought Will. "I'm having to conjecture."

"Oh, dear, no facts and numbers?" Challenging was common, sarcastic was not.

"Henry is already uncomfortable. He sees the fund shrinking, driven by your withdrawals, which he feels will bring collateral fallout, and he sees himself unable to move out because of his contract conditions."

"They could start again. They're clever men." He seemed to think a moment, but that was probably more for drama, thought Will. "Although their systems belong to the business, as well as the client base."

"I'm not seeing winners in that fight; not Henry, not us, not the clients, and, ultimately, not the Foundation."

"Well, let's hope you have a more persuasive argument by next Thursday if you're going to keep this thing together. I assume Two B is still your preferred option."

"I'm still convinced it would be the best way of freeing you two to focus on the Foundation, and of sustaining Dickinson as one entity capable of providing you with the most reliable sources of funding for the future."

"I note the use of the subjunctive, young William. I was looking for will from Will, not would."

It was unusual to find him so hostile, and he could sense Claudia's discomfort.

"I appreciate that. If I can't make Two B workable, that tells you something about my fitness to run this for you, and if your key players won't work in that configuration…"

"They should be changed," Peter said sharply.

"I don't believe wholesale changes are in your or Claudia's best interests."

Peter shuffled in his chair. "You know where your failure leaves me?"

"It would — no apologies for subjunctives — leave you in the uncomfortable position of being dragged into the other areas too often because you don't trust Henry and Tony, and you haven't ever let Alphonse grow up."

Claudia breathed in sharply, then looked embarrassed. Peter looked at her with narrowed eyes, then turned slowly back to Will. "And your solution, O wise one?"

"You make Henry head of funds and fire Tony…"

"Harsh penalty for not returning a call."

"Calls, not call, and he hasn't called you either. In your words, that tells us something."

"Lou?"

"We keep Lou, but make him a clear and independent number two to Henry."

"But he likes working with Tony."

"There, meister, you have work to do, with him and the sister. That's something I have to delegate."

"Upwards?" But Peter was smiling now. Looking proud of his boy, thought Will, it hadn't hurt to make decisive proposals.

"Put the effort in now, you'll save time later. Can you fit it in on your way?"

"What do you mean, on his way?" Claudia looked more shocked than surprised.

"Yes, my darling, I meant to tell you, I'm going via China, off tomorrow afternoon. Sorry, I should have said. I'll be in New York by Wednesday."

"What's your sched... oh, never mind." It was said with resignation, rather than annoyance. "What about..." she stopped, as if reluctant to pursue the thought.

"Alphonse?" offered Peter, his eyes narrowing, then he turned to Will. "My other boy?" And the warmth had left him again.

"Every decision goes through you, gets worked out with you," said Will. "I see that because he keeps me well informed from the early stages of anything big, but very little changes with any project from the time I first hear about it. I'm not saying you two shouldn't discuss overall goals and areas of interest, but that's once or twice a year. He shouldn't be feeling that every step needs approval. You could appoint him chairman, as well as CEO, make yourself just a director, but leave the control to me."

"But you'd be his number two, then."

"I wouldn't get hung up on that. The three of us should meet twice a year; you set the direction, I work out the financial framework, but the business is his to run and mine to control."

Peter looked pensive. "You think I interfere too much?" He looked at the two of them in turn. Claudia seemed committed to silence.

"I think he invites it, to some extent. I'd ban you from talking outside of our two meetings a year." Peter's eyebrows rose. "Well, I mean I'd ban you from discussing property. You'd need to be very disciplined." He turned to Claudia. "You'd have to help them." She looked very uncomfortable again.

Peter waved an arm. "Oh, we both do exactly what she tells us." He was looking hard at Claudia. That wasn't a throwaway aside, thought Will, but Peter was looking at him now. "And we do what you say, apparently. You're his number two, but he could only do what you let him."

"It can work," said Will. "The big question for us is whether you sell properties off or invite new investors in."

"And?"

"You've more flexibility and scale if you do the latter. It keeps the Dickinson name, and it keeps the main man — except he really becomes the main man now, not your boy."

"My other boy."

"Peter!" said Claudia sharply.

Will was untroubled; he smiled at Peter. "I think you owe me about seven dollars for breaches this morning but don't worry, it will all go to charity."

"Ha!" Peter exploded. "I wondered if you'd react. I haven't treated you like a boy since…"

"Since we agreed on the resort projects and the Senlin tie-up three years ago."

Peter seemed to think. "I hope it was before then, I think it was."

"What are you going to do about Henry, then?" asked Claudia. Then she looked to Peter. "Would you really fire Tony?"

"No," said Peter, then, without looking away from her, added, "he would." Will couldn't conceal his surprise, but knew there must be more to come. He waited for Peter's dramatic pause to run its course. "That establishes the new relationships with everyone. They'll all see you're the boss. Now you can answer her first question."

"The situation's different from properties. Henry and Tony do rely a lot on each other, rather than you, although they do enjoy your money and your name. They'll miss you as the glamour investor."

"See, darling," he was looking at Claudia again, "I'm glamour."

"Of course you are, my love," was not said warmly.

This wasn't a time to pause, thought Will. "I would like to persuade Henry to get Rachel back in the picture."

"I've been trying to do that for years."

"The children are older now and Henry would need help." Peter was nodding slowly.

"That's a very good idea," came enthusiastically from Claudia.

"How do I feel comfortable about my money?"

"By checking it every day, just as you do now." Will was smiling at him, he knew Peter's 'little weakness,' as he called it.

"You check every day?" Claudia was surprised.

"No, I don't," huffed Peter, but he'd been caught.

"I noticed it early on," said Will. "I have a large finance department, and I have my spies in GKD, GKS, sorry, and yet he insists on checking all his own funds every day, and their overall performance too. My selling point to Henry is that I stop you doing that. You'll get your comfort and control through me. I'll play a similar role as I will for Alphonse. But you have to commit, or I can't sell the idea to Henry. He takes you too seriously. He doesn't have Tony's facility of being able to tell you to fuck off."

"He doesn't tell me to fuck off." Peter was indignant.

Will gave an open palmed shrug and tried his best Australian. "Mate, how the fuck do I know?"

Peter snorted. "Not bad."

"But firing him?"

"Two things," said Will, "he's not really funny, and, for every client that finds his approach refreshing, there's another who finds it inappropriate."

"Martha? Is that where this is coming from?" asked Peter pointedly.

"I have my own sources," said Will, but he knew he was sounding defensive, "but Martha talks to me too about what she picks up."

Peter nodded slowly. It would be too easy, thought Will, to read too much into that. But then Peter continued with, "You seem to have given yourself two dogsbody jobs. What about your day job?"

"For all the complexities of the IPO and the Giddings tie-in, I think it's the area that, in the mid-term, needs least attention. It's hard to overstate how good she is." He looked to Claudia.

"Oh, I agree," she said. "I've never felt left out of an important discussion, and I've never felt dragged into a trivial one, and she rates you very highly, Will. I think that's something I'd trust you to work out'

They both looked to Peter. "I must say I agree. But I think we're looking a little different from how I expected the situation to look. I don't think I can call it Two B anymore. But let's have lunch and come back to it."

"You know that trick, Will, don't you?" Claudia asked with a sly smile.

"Of inserting a gap to allow thoughts to solidify; yes, he uses it too often."

"Am I being ganged up on? In my own house?" He was smiling, and stood to leave, but stopped. "I still, to some extent, am keeping an open mind. I still want dialogue next week. We may end up with a better solution with seven minds around the table."

"Seven?" Will was glad Claudia had asked the question.

"Tania must be there. I happen to agree with you both, it would be silly to leave the best mind outside the room."

"And Tony?"

"Will can decide after the meeting when to fire him."

"When? Or whether?" Claudia asked.

Peter looked to Will.

"When," he said.

"Come on," said Peter, "lunch." He put his arm around Claudia's shoulder to guide her from the room and whispered theatrically, "It's still a harsh punishment for not returning a call."

Claudia turned her head to Will, but found him smiling.

***

As he'd expected, the afternoon made few changes to the thoughts of the morning and soon after four, Andreas was driving him along the Cromwell Road. He'd resisted the sudden urge to ask him to turn off at Hammersmith and take him to Fulham. Any conversation with Henry, who would almost certainly be at home now, would need careful preparation — and he wondered how he could broach the Tony topic anyway. But calling tomorrow was a possibility. That would add an additional justification for this trip.

Tonight's plan was no justification, and he didn't even know if she would be coming. Well, he reminded himself, if he were to stick to his theoretical commitment to be very clear with Merle about their future, inevitably distant, relationship, it would be a trip worthwhile. But he knew how he would feel when he saw her.

In the early evening the text had come from an unknown number, but the source was obvious:

I just can't make it, my dearest love, I am so, so sorry M

followed by a long string of sad emojis and four huge hearts.

He stored the new number under Merle 2, then let his fingers hover over 't' — but could she even commit to tomorrow? And in the emotional turmoil, there were elements of relief. Perhaps one massive complication might recede. He knew now that it would never disappear, but it had lived eight years without becoming threatening — until four weeks ago.

He spent the evening with a room service dinner and reformulated the four options, preparing for next Thursday. Property looked like status quo, possibly disrupted by new investors. That would leave Peter potentially talking to Alphonse even more about how to manage new people with powerful interests, and his own position impotent and frustrating, with Alphonse unwilling to discuss anything with him. Funds? How would Henry react to a forced divorce? How would key clients react? Tony, he knew, had a particular entertaining style, which Lou had willingly emulated, and some major clients enjoyed. That had caused tensions when Will was new in his job and he'd discovered how his department had to manage the accounts for those expenditures. 'I don't have a line in the budget for hookers, Tony,' wasn't a little speech he was proud of, and he'd deserved the rejoinder: 'Grow up, little boy, how the fuck do you think business gets done out there?'

He'd not found similar accounts in Henry's areas and had once asked him, 'Are you just cleverer? I can't find out where you hide what Tony does.' He'd got one of Henry's sly smiles. 'Clever enough to have grown out of old-fashioned business practices, you mean?' Will had stayed humble. 'I don't know what I mean, Henry. I've looked, and asked questions, and I can't find anything similar.' In those distant days, with Will new in the job and less obviously Peter's main man, Henry had stayed helpful:

'I'm not being moral, Will, but it's less useful these days in my geography, so I've been able to do without it. It helps that I've no desire to participate myself.'

Relations with Henry were different now, but there was still a core of friendship, Will hoped. So, he sent the text:

In town tomorrow, can we meet? Will

The reply was not long in coming, but surprised him:
We're both here between four and six. H
Thank you. See you both then. W

He wondered why Rachel was being involved, had something been said? But, given the morning's discussion, it could be very useful.

He smiled when another text came fifteen minutes later:

Delighted you're coming to see us. I'm going to be a bit distracted — lovely people coming later — could you stay and have dinner? R xxx

His Merle plans now in tatters, and he was sensing relief amidst the regret, this was now a chance, perhaps, to re-establish the bond, and have Henry looking at the new options more favourably.

That would be wonderful, I should like that very much W xxx PS I am on my own.

The PS was practical, he thought. It told them he remained part of a couple normally. But why would anyone have doubted that? he thought. And he found himself with an empty Friday evening, wondering what Martha was doing. For all the enjoyment and satisfaction work brought him, for all the colourful people he met — even in finance, he smiled to himself — Friday evenings had become the highlight of his weeks, especially if either, or both of them, had been travelling. Seven pm was an absolute commitment to be either at home, or in the Blue Orchid. Except for those evenings when she would arrive ten minutes late, and grinning, and he found himself smiling at the memories of what would happen then, and thinking about when they would be past this — what was it? Hiatus, difficulty, readjustment? — and how they would build Noah's opportunities into their activities. He did feel those little stabs of betrayal and jealousy, but they didn't match his awareness of his curiosity, his weird excitement, whose source he was never able to trace. Yet his morning reveries found his cock rising to the thoughts of how an evening with Martha and others might be even more exciting than their previous Friday nights. But now he was worrying about Merle; he was now desperate to see her.

Hope things are OK. Missed you. Wxxx

That was surely innocent enough, but the wooziness induced by the two large whiskies after the half bottle of wine reproached him that it might not be.

He woke to a lovely summer morning with a chance to walk in Hyde Park and let the new thoughts settle themselves. He crossed to there before ten and met the expected jostle of runners, but a surprising number of people just walking in the shade of the luscious, full-leafed trees, but not enough to disturb his aimless progress. He was letting the ideas settle, wondering how naïve he was being. Offering himself, effectively, as a number two to both Alphonse and Henry may have been more sensible than wise. It recognised that he had run Dickinson as the number two for a few years now, but that had been possible because the number one was the undisputed owner and had all the confidence necessary to allow Will to function that way. It would be different working for smaller people — he shocked himself with the thought but, talented and admirable as they both undoubtedly were, Alphonse and Henry didn't have the scale of Peter Dickinson. But as he walked on, he thought glumly 'neither does William Uprichard.'

How would Peter deal with the text that suddenly appeared?

Could we meet for coffee in the Carlton Tower, just like the first time? M XXX

The memory was so vivid, although eight years old now, being caught by her in the Agent Provocateur shop and invited for coffee to the nearby hotel; how dream-like that had seemed, how trance-like those few months before everything imploded and he found himself in the rubble of his life with her gone. Now, having wrestled with how to make new arrangements work and how to grow into a different form of Peter Dickinson, how to move on from past complications, how to embrace a newly reconstructed life with Martha, he was now trembling and fumbling, pressing the screen to write:

Yes. That would be lovely. 11.30 W X

He'd at least retained enough awareness to remember to keep the tone dominant but, by the time he'd walked to the hotel, forcing himself to be five minutes late, he knew his self-control was threatening to abandon him, and it disappeared when he saw her, the chestnut hair falling in waves, the beautiful print dress under the pale linen jacket.

She was poised to see him come in but had been distracted by the waiter, so he had those few seconds of grace to try to compose himself again. He forced himself to stand still and merely look, she was so beautiful in profile… stupid, he thought, beautiful from every angle, especially sleeping, and he thought back to writing out 'Lullaby' for her and the line 'human on my faithless arm' was in his mind when she turned and caught sight of him, smiled, but then looked anxiously around the room as he strode towards her.

She stood up, but didn't seem to welcome the embrace he was ready to give. He took her hands, kissed her cheek lightly, and took the chair beside her once she'd sat down. He let a raised eyebrow ask the question. "I'll just get coffee ordered for you," she said nervously, "or is tea better? I'm having tea. I don't suppose you want camomile, do you? Coffee? You're a coffee man, William."

He tried to take her hand to calm her, she pulled it away. "You mustn't."

"Now I really do have to ask."

She looked around again, then leaned towards him and said softly, "I was being followed last time."

Somehow that seemed to fit. He found himself less surprised than he would have expected. "And you haven't been followed here?" He looked around, with not the remotest idea, he admitted to himself, of what he was looking for.

"Could you get us a room?"

"I have…" No, Will, he thought, there are reasons for this, more than just about the organisation of a clandestine tryst. "Don't worry about coffee for me. I'll text you from the room."

For the first time, she seemed to relax a little. He'd plainly understood her predicament.

"We do have a suite that's available now, sir," said the receptionist, and he'd smiled and nodded and found himself saying, "That will be perfect, thank you," in absolute defiance of his instinct for frugality, which three years with Martha, and eight with Peter, had not yet extinguished. But even Will recognised that there are moments when costs couldn't be counted.

He texted Merle from the elevator, his accompanying porter remaining discreet and concealing his surprise at having no luggage to deal with, although he did seem perturbed by Will's curt, 'Is there anything that isn't obvious?' when he tried to begin his description of the rooms' features. 'No, sir,' he'd replied, and left, twenty pounds richer but apparently puzzled.

Moments later Merle was falling into his arms. "I'm sorry, I'm sorry, I'm sorry." She was hugging him almost violently. "I am so sorry."

He held her and could feel her body shaking and tears dropping on to his shirt. He wouldn't move or speak until she wanted to. This was no time for roles. She'd been followed last time. The emotions now didn't let that seem like a fanciful suspicion, but that story would be told when she was ready.

It seemed to be taking too long, however. She might need encouragement to speak — that was the way with embarrassing topics sometimes. It had been with them in the past. It had been like that with Martha more recently, apparently, and he'd been surprised. But Merle avoiding difficult topics was not new.

"Do you want me to organise camomile tea?"

At least she chuckled. "I think I should get down to business, shouldn't I?"

He led her to the sofa, resisting the desire to kiss her, sensing he should let her tell her story as quickly as possible. "He didn't tell me for three weeks. He knew I'd been with you two nights. I've been frightened since."

"You do mean Gerry, not Michael."

"Yes, I mean Gerry, although Michael was in on it. I hate them both. How could I have been so stupid? But I'm worried now, worried for me, worried for you."

"Why are you worried?"

"What are you trying to do at Dickinson? Why would it interest Gerry? Would it interest Gerry?"

"I don't see why it would."

She stopped wringing her own fingers and reached for his hand. "Is that a necessary lie?"

He smiled. "No, it's not a necessary lie," although it was, of course, he thought, but he had to say something. "I really don't see why it would, but I could think about why it might. How much do you want to tell me?"

"I'd rather tell you nothing, I'm ashamed and embarrassed, but I'd made such a fuss about wanting to see you again, and I really did want to see you again, so crying off last night was painful, but I didn't want to be followed again, not caught again."

"Is the new number part of this?"

"Of course it is. Only you have it, though."

This was worrying now. He was worried for her, knowing what Gerry could do, but he was worrying also about what plots might be being constructed against Dickinson. There was too much he didn't know.

"How are you with Gerry?"

"Oh, I've told him I'll never speak to him again, but he laughed of course; he won't take it seriously, it's happened before." Now she seemed to calm down, "The thing is, I mean it this time. That goes for Michael, too. He might believe it, he may even care, but he'll still just go on, taking his lead from Gerry."

"What will you do?"

"Oh, I'm independent now, financially. Just a bit scared."

Now he took both of her hands and tried to stay as calm as possible, but he was worrying too, "Merle, I really don't know what's happening, but I do need to find out — and I will be doing more looking. But my biggest priority now is to be sure you're safe. We do think Gerry is dangerous, in a number of ways. Do you understand that?"

She looked uncomfortable. "I've always tried to tell myself he just gets out of hand sometimes."

He needed to be patient; it wasn't hard for him. "Are you seeing it differently now?"

She shrugged. "It doesn't matter. I just don't want anything to do with him anymore. I'll have to let Sadie know. I don't think she'll care, she hates him, and I do now, although I've no idea what he's up to."

"You hate him because he had you followed?"

She pulled her hands back and began rubbing them together, looking away from him. "Oh, that and other things." She looked at him again and reached for his hand, "It's not because of you and me four weeks ago. I'm not trying to steal you from your new life, you must believe me, and I know that two Lanesborough nights with an old flame doesn't mean your marriage isn't wonderful," she gushed, but then paused and, for the first time that day, let a small smile play on her lips, "but I'd still like the odd London visit." He started to try to tell her he couldn't, but her hand came to his mouth. "Hush, we'll see what we want. But one thing I want is for you to stay happy with Martha. That is her name, isn't it? Sadie swoons about her, and she's older than me, how could you?" It was a tease, but it didn't work for him.

"You left me, Merle," he said gently.

She looked away. "Sadie says it wouldn't have worked."

Somehow, he relaxed. "She says that about almost all relationships and, since most of them, statistically, end, she can pride herself on being right most of the time."

She laughed. He was puzzled. "Oh, William, only you would discuss relationships statistically. But she says you and Martha are wonderful together."

"We are," he said, but it jarred to be dishonest, "but we have problems like any couple."

"And I don't want to make them worse."

"You don't, Merle, I do that, but it is partly because of you."

"Does that mean you won't see me again?"

But, looking into those brilliant, sad green eyes, it was impossible to say 'no.' He was shaking his head slowly, involuntarily. "One thing I have to do is make sure you're safe." She frowned. "I need to explain your situation to a man I trust." This must surely be a situation for Henderson, he thought, and he would be aware of the background.

"You think it's that bad?"

"You're scared already. This man will know what to do, and he knows how Gerry operates." Now she looked puzzled. "You'll hear from him soon. I'll give him the new number, his name's Henderson, Rod Henderson."

"That means you'll have to explain everything."

"Yes, it does."

"Even about you? About us?"

He smiled. "If I don't tell him, he'll just guess and, the way he works, there is absolutely nothing that will surprise him."

She was silent, pensive, and still worried.

"What's concerning you most?"

She shook her head. "I'm being silly, really. I won't have to meet the man, will I?"

"I don't imagine so. He moves in the shadows anyway." Will was aware of how little he knew about Henderson and how he worked, beyond the fact that his invoices could be very large, and it struck him that, with any business option they decided upon next for Dickinson, he'd have to get closer to Henderson's operations.

Now she slid along and nestled into him. It felt safe to put his arm around her shoulder.

"I don't know how much I'll have to say about Gerry."

"I think the more open you can be, the easier it will be for him to help." That was an assumption Will was making, but it felt very plausible.

"I can't tell him what I won't tell you, but I'm too embarrassed to tell you."

She wasn't looking up at him. He kissed the top of her head. "We've had our own embarrassing confessions from many years ago, remember? Does this have anything to do with your little kink?"

He waited. "Yes, it does," she murmured, and then sat up. "Is that how you truly see it? Just a little kink?"

"Of course, that's how I see it. It's something we share, remember."

"But it seems to get me into trouble. Thing is, I still have it. I don't seem to have anything normal, and you know that it's an enthusiasm of Gerry's." He nodded, but now she looked thoughtful again. "I have to admit we still did play a little, and he'd find one or two nice men to join us." She huddled in again. "I'm really embarrassed by this, but I have to tell you now. You know what I liked, don't you?"

He had to say, he thought, to make it easier for her. "You liked boys to come over you after you'd been spanked. And if that embarrasses you, then I can tell you how much it embarrasses me to tell you how exciting I found the idea."

She looked up, kissed his cheek quickly and snuggled in tighter. "Thank you. The next bit's horrible, but it's easier to tell you now. I got to his place last weekend and I was expecting a normal evening, well, a normal naughty evening, and I can't honestly deny that I used to get a little bit excited by the prospect. It's weird, I can't even explain it to myself. It's not really sex, although I suppose it is, but I only want normal sex with you. I just like showing myself off, I suppose, and watching them get excited. The spanking nearly gets me there, but I touch myself and think of you inside me when I want to come afterwards. It's crazy, I like to think of you coming over my bottom, but coming inside me at the same time."

He could feel his cock stiffening, but knew how wrong that was.

"But this was different. The men looked rougher. I think they were just three of Gerry's heavies. I said, 'I don't want this tonight, Gerry,' and he just nodded to them and they grabbed me and stripped me and held me down over that couch of his. I couldn't move, but I knew what was coming. It was like Wiltshire all those years ago but much worse. 'I know you don't want it tonight, you just want to sneak off and fuck your old boyfriend in the Lanesborough. Well, this is what happens to naughty girls'." She was shaking now.

"It's all right," he said. "You've said enough." He wanted Henderson to find a way of hurting the man, but something in the back of his mind told him that he needed to find out more about Gerry Calvert and his strange plans.

She was sniffing. "I haven't said enough yet. You see, I was so thrilled when I got your message. I did so much want to make love to you again."

"But you were worried about being followed."

"It's partly that…"

He had to wait.

"Will, I was very badly marked. I am very badly marked. There are so many reasons why you can't want me."

But there were so many reasons why he did, but he was disturbed to find both how much he loved her, and by the weird excitement he felt.

"I'm afraid I still do." Their mouths were on each other's instantly, they moved to lie on the couch in each other's arms, and she was grinding her pelvis against the rising stiffness of his cock.

"Come to bed. Just let me sit on you. Just don't touch me, just come inside me, please, give me everything."

They were quickly in the bedroom. He was almost naked, she seemed to be hesitating, still looking worried. "Please Will, lie down for me. Let me get on top of you." She looked at his crotch, his cock straining to escape. "Do it for me, please."

He slid the pants down and kicked them away. Now she smiled and looked a little more relaxed. "I would kneel down and suck you to death if my," she hesitated and her smile broadened, "if my cunt weren't so desperate for you. Lie down."

He lay back, holding his cock more for comfort than support; it was pole-stiff.

She undressed carefully, slowly, letting the dress slip off her shoulders, kicking it insouciantly away. The bra came off with a flourish and was flung across the room. The shoes were kicked away, their eyes staring into each other's all the time — until her pants were slid down and he couldn't resist looking at the gorgeous, neat copper tuft, which rapidly straddled him and took him into itself as she sighed loudly and he felt all his senses overwhelmed. This was the time to just let go, with only a moment's hesitation at her "No!" when his hands began to slide down from her hips, followed by "Please, just come, I want all that filthy, mucky stuff inside me," she laughed and, without him even touching her, ground down onto his pelvis to make herself come, and take him so deep that he easily followed.

She slumped on him as they slowed, but lay there only a moment before she slid off and lay beside him, kissing him, letting her hand encircle his softening cock. She smiled. "How long do we have the room?"

"I had to book for the whole night."

She had a look of mock regret. "All that money wasted. Could we make use of it?"

He smiled. "I've said I'll have dinner with people tonight."

"You said you wanted to see me!"

"Merle, sweetheart, you became mysteriously unavailable, and this might be important, it's with Henry."

"Oh, Henry." But she still looked miffed.

"But it won't be late."

"All right, but when are you going out?" Her hand squeezed his recovering cock.

He smiled. "I need to be in Fulham by four, that's the work part, so you've plenty time to deal with him however you choose later, but first, without infringing your new-found coyness about the world's most beautiful bottom, I'm going to eat…" He smiled and kissed her, his hand sliding down her belly. His fingers moved slowly through the tuft and on to the waiting wet clitoris.

She smiled back. "You're going to eat my cunt, aren't you?"

"I am, my darling, and you may not even stop after two. You used to be very greedy when I ate you." She smiled and nodded. He slid down and wrapped his arms around her thighs to pull her wide open and let his mouth cover her completely. It was such a voluptuous, gorgeous feeling, a distant hint of her perfume but, more powerful, the sweet musky smell of her natural self that he had so come to love. He licked and teased, and plunged his tongue into her. She rose quickly to meet him. He loved licking her and eating her, loved nibbling her gently with his lips, with his teeth, but she was writhing more and more wildly; he'd no need to be patient, he could enjoy her even more after her climax, when she would calm down and still want him. He spread his tongue flat on her clitoris, heard her moaning more loudly, felt her hands on his head, pushing his mouth on to her, heard her begin to scream and scream as she came, heard her exhale. "Wonderful, wonderful, wonderful, oh, nothing's like that, my beautiful man. Come up here and kiss me," He slid up to kiss her smiling face, and felt her hand wrap his cock again.

"That is lovely," he said, "but the only reason I let you come so quickly is that I adore kissing your cunt, and I can enjoy it even more when you're half-relaxed." He slid his fingers into the tuft again. "I will be there again soon, whatever plans you have for him." He kissed her lips lightly. "He's there however you want him."

She pulled him onto her, not releasing his cock. "I think she'd like a little of him now, but I'm very happy with your plan A." He moved on to his elbows as she manoeuvred his cock into her and they lay, rocking gently, looking into each other's eyes and smiling. She raised her knees to take him deeper.

He shook his head. "You can't do that. It ruins plan A."

She laughed and smiled. "Very well, master, I suppose I shall have to let you eat my cunt again soon."

"Yes, but I could look at your face for hours," he chuckled, "but not with him up in your tummy." He slid down and began eating her again. He remembered the hours they would spend, and how slowly they could extend the second and third climaxes, how they could linger on the edge of that welcoming abyss before taking the blissful plunge again. She seemed to rise soon to the edge again, moaning and writhing, but more gently now, whispering 'wonderful' more softly, as if from some distant bliss. He loved her cunt, its sweet lips, its easy wet hole, the nerves everywhere that seemed to respond to every tongue touch, the opening that would always welcome. She lifted her knees and spread them wider, moaning louder now as his tongue flattened on her clit again, "Soon, soon, soon," she was murmuring. He slid his hands beneath her to lift her higher, more open — and felt the ridges across her arse! He stifled his shock, pushed his tongue deeper as she hovered on the edge, and he ate more greedily, strangely fascinated by this novel feeling, the bands of bruised textures across those perfect mounds, and was amazed to feel how stiff he had become, how excited, relieved that she had become so oblivious. He carefully slid his hands out from beneath her as her screams began to soften and slid up to hold her in his arms as she sank into him.

They were silent a long time before she said sleepily, "I can stay here this afternoon, can't I? Did you mean it, you won't be late?"

"I meant it anyway. I mean it even more now."

"And I meant it about having him. I just haven't decided how." She reached for his shaft. "Gosh, that's going to be easy. I'll have to be very careful. Shall I sit on you again? Or suck you?"

"You can suck me a little first, but you're right, you'll have to be very careful."

She smiled. "I'll try. No, I'll try very hard, I want your cock deep in my belly again."

His hand rose to her face and he kissed her. "You know how he's deepest."

"No, you can't, you can't see me there."

"I've felt you there, Merle. I know what you're hiding. I don't want you to hide."

"But I'm so ashamed."

"Of what?"

"Letting myself get caught like that. Ashamed and stupid, and I don't want you to see. You shouldn't have touched me."

Now he chuckled, which had always irritated her when she was flouncing, but it never lasted. "I wanted to eat you more deeply and it just happened. I am very sorry that happened to you, I just want you to know it makes no difference to me. What I also want you to know is how thrilled I'll be to come in your cunt again when you're sitting on me."

She smiled slowly, and tightened her grip on him. "But I can suck your cock first?"

He smiled. "Oh, you have to suck my cock first." He watched her slide down, carefully covering herself with the duvet to hide her stripes from him. What he hadn't been able to say, because it shocked even him, was how thrilling he'd found the feel of the stripes, and the thought of how they'd been inflicted — and now how hard it was not to explode quickly into her mouth. "Please come up and sit on me," he was gasping soon, and was pouring himself into her before she was even fully on him.

***

As he climbed into the cab to Fulham, he felt relaxed and euphoric, but by the King's Road his mood had changed to one of apprehension; where was the Merle relationship going, and how far should he go with Henry — and Rachel — this afternoon? But Rachel had invited him to dinner; that consoled him. They can't have been expecting strife.

But Henry was cool, and uncommunicative.

But he had said they would both be available.

But Will had neither sent flowers, nor bought gifts for the children.

"Our weekend times are more rigidly planned," said Henry as he opened the door. "They're both out at parties. Come through. What brings you to London? Plotting next week in your usual fashion?"

Relief came seeping in for Will. Henry had made a number of things easier. "Exactly right, although it was rather spur of the moment…"

Rachel had appeared with her usual smile to contrast with Henry's studied coolness. "I expect he's grilling about why you're here, but I'm just thrilled to see you." She hugged him.

"But equally curious," said Henry drily.

"Stop it!"

"Deny it!"

"Fuck off!" she said, and laughed.

"You see," said Henry, smiling now. "Study or garden room?" He looked to Will.

"Garden room, if you want me," said Rachel. "I can multi-task, but it's helpful if I'm in one room."

"Suits me," said Will, and they moved to the dining table. Rachel fetched water and glasses. Will waited for her.

"Start," she called from the kitchen area.

"We're still looking at four options, although they have materially changed. I wanted to put Peter and Claudia in the picture, but get a sense also of which outcomes meet their needs best, or are most palatable to them."

"He's still committed to the Foundation, then?"

"He does stay committed to things."

"Marriages?" asked Henry acidly.

"Different thing," said Rachel. "He stays committed to his business ideas."

"Two have failed," said Henry. There was tension between them.

"Before my time," said Will, "but I looked at the history, and he supported them for too long."

"So, are you going to tell us the status of your options, or tell us what Peter will accept?"

"His last point yesterday was that he wanted a full discussion next week."

"Are we ready for that?"

"That's hard to say. I've sent Tony a presentation pack, but he's still not responded to a call."

Will studied Henry hard, but Henry, as ever, stayed coolly neutral. Rachel's eyes twitched slightly, but Will told himself to read nothing into that. Rachel had been the perfect hostess when he'd been a guest here with Tony, but he felt sure there was hidden antipathy.

"Anyway," Will continued, "I'm hoping Funds will be our least urgent issue."

Rachel at least looked interested. Henry moved his head slightly from side to side and said, "Go on."

"We think the IPO of the Group will bring the first cash injection, but I'm hearing that we may have some big buyers in the pipeline anyway."

"Big enough to want overall control? What does Peter end up with if you put Giddings into the pot?"

"Ten percent, is the plan, but he and Arthur Gunter would be twenty together."

"They're not married," said Henry. "I wouldn't put Fund money into that enterprise."

"That's an easy point to make. You shouldn't invest in Dickinson businesses anyway, it's in your charter."

"My point is that, with only ten percent, it's barely a Dickinson business. Go on, what about property? What's Alphonse doing? Still want to take off with his little five percent and play by himself?"

"I think we'll find next week that they've got past that, but we'll see. The bigger issue there is whether the market's right to get any big players buying in."

"The bigger issue is whether the bank wants to stay with you. What does Martha say?"

"We don't talk about that. She stays very professional." And she did, but that wasn't why they weren't talking.

"Prospects?"

"It's a very attractive portfolio. Alphonse has done a superb job and there's money around looking to buy into property."

"Are you sure it's the sort of money you want?"

Will drew a deep breath. "No. That's probably the hardest part of it. But you're confronted with that all the time."

"And we manage it very carefully."

"Some more carefully than others," said Rachel, and provoked a sharp look from Henry. "You can look at me like that, darling, but this glorious growth in the Asia region is a disease that might spread."

"We worry about new sources of money," said Will.

"We?" asked Henry, still rattled by Rachel's intervention.

"Peter and I, Martha and I. And Alphonse would have to worry, he's had only Peter and the bank to be concerned about until now." He turned to Rachel. "Can you say what's worrying you?"

"Tony, mostly, and if I knew his sidekick, Lou, isn't it?" Will nodded. "I'd probably worry about him too."

Henry put on a look of exaggerated patience, and looked at Will. "This is not a new discussion in this house. I'm just looking for demonstrable legal ownership when I'm looking at new money. My wife has higher standards."

"Don't you, Will?"

"I'm not sure even Martha does," he said, wanting to support her but not, objectively, able to do so. "Once it's legal, we regard it as clean, but it's not that simple."

"Pray enlighten us," came from Henry with an edge of sarcasm.

"You know why. If any of it comes under suspicion, then you come under suspicion and your clients withdraw. No one really wants their money mingling with Russian money."

"It doesn't mingle, that's the point. And we've not had an investigation of any account yet."

"Henry, look, it's up to you, ultimately. It's your business, you have to put the safeguards in place."

"It's Peter Dickinson's business — and your department double-checks the safeguards."

"But it won't be Peter Dickinson's business anymore. That's the point."

"It'll be yours then, if he appoints you to run everything, your Two B option."

"I wouldn't say that was the most likely course now. It seems a more sellable proposition to run as three independent businesses."

"And you?"

"I'd probably chair the Group, although…"

"Although Tania Gunter's the one you'd most trust to run a business."

"Look, I see myself, for the foreseeable future, making sure that we generate funds for the Foundation. We'll find a way of doing that from the Group, from Properties — and from Funds, but let me ask you a question…" He had their full attention. "Would you be happy running the funds business?"

"Tony and I?" but Henry had looked surprised.

Will left a pause. "No, just you, Henry Gideon." He left Henry to think and turned to Rachel. "And could we get you back in? It's not like you don't do it every day."

"If you're talking about Henry as head, on his own, and you're talking about more secure sourcing standards, yes, I'd consider it."

Henry was shaking his head. "You people! Most money has dirty sources, there are ways of cleaning it up." He looked at Will. "You know that."

Will nodded. "I'm only taking a pragmatic view."

"And your pragmatic view is to stab my friend in the back because he won't answer your phone calls." That was unusually petulant from Henry.

"He can be as rude to me as he likes, Henry, but he can't hide from me."

Henry didn't leap to his partner's defence, and Rachel looked smugly content, but was wise enough to steer the conversation away into Will's processes for ensuring money was clean. He had the sense that she was becoming enthusiastic about a full-time return — and that he might leave it to her to do more work on Henry before the board meeting. Henry stayed pensive and quiet in the rest of the discussion, but Will felt that trying to push harder now would be counterproductive.

"So, what does this leave you doing, Will?" Henry asked eventually, when Rachel's interrogation had run its course. "It looks like bits and pieces, if you don't sell the Two B idea."

"Two B was just one way of providing for the Foundation. Like I said before, I'm seeing that as my main task. We'll just organise ourselves as best we can to do that. Oh, Peter's asking Tania to join us next week."

Henry looked surprised. Rachel said, "Brilliant!" The men looked at her. "I don't know her, but everything

Claudia tells me is outstanding, and I'd even put our own money in that group."

"That's how I see it," said Will.

"So, you're not even needed in that business," said Henry.

"Henry, don't…" but Rachel stopped there when she saw Will smiling.

"Think of me as your navigator, Henry, and don't think of trying to get to where you want to go without me."

Henry was nodding, and a smile spread slowly on his face, "Well said," he paused, "my boy!" and they both laughed, with Rachel just shaking her head.

"It's time you went for Miranda," she said to Henry, then turned to Will. "Archie will be back on his own later, but he'll probably just go and play games. You can chat to me in the kitchen."

***

Dinner was, as Rachel had predicted, lovely and informal with couples Rachel had met via school connections, which made it an evening free of business talk. It hadn't felt too rude to leave at ten. He found Merle dozing on the sofa with the television on and kissed her gently awake. He got that magical smile. "What time is it?"

"Not half ten."

"How long have I got you?"

"I'll be leaving at lunchtime."

"See, that's all I want."

"You'll also get Henderson's services."

"Must I?"

But she looked happy when he insisted. Happy, maybe, that he cared that much. He had a sense of danger about the situation, and knew he had to act. But he did care, too.

"Do I have to tell him everything?"

"It's best if you do."

"Also, about us?"

"He'll ask me anyway. The first thing he'll look for is discrepancies in our stories. Tell him everything, he'll understand. You don't have to show him anything."

"I didn't show you anything. You cheated."

"I didn't. I was pleasuring you. But when you're pleasuring me later, I will be having everything, and seeing everything."

"No, Will, I'm…"

"Going to do as you're told."

She pushed her face into his neck, "Going to do exactly as I'm told."

34

I'm fairly sure it wasn't the most surprising phone call of my life, but I couldn't actually think of one to top it. These things don't fluster me normally but, 'Isobel, it's Peter Dickinson, do you have a few minutes to chat?' certainly did.

Now I'm at the airport, waiting for him. He told me not to be but, as I'd said, we wouldn't have that much time with the schedule he was planning, we should make the best use of it. He didn't protest. Once the car was pulling away, I didn't wait. "I'm going to confess, Mr D, that I wasn't at my most coherent during your call. I remember thinking you were making perfect sense, but I've retained almost nothing of it."

I got that adorable, booming laugh. "I seldom achieve perfect sense, my darling Sadie, but I will thank you for the undeserved compliment — and now I shall attempt to genuinely earn one."

I'm not really comfortable about Sadie in the circumstances. Fuck it, I shouldn't leave it. "Sadie?"

"We're controllers, you and I. We play. But we play for other people. I just happen not to have a play name. I like yours. I've even heard the story about how you came by it."

"You've been doing your research, Mr D."

"I also seem to have acquired a play name of my own inadvertently."

I smiled at him. An idea struck me. "Mr Dominator. It's not bad."

It was just a chuckle this time, but it was so warm. "I'll take Mr D, if I may. I think Dominator goes beyond what I like to do."

I looked into those gorgeous blue eyes. "Yes, I'm being unfair, but what Sadie suggests also isn't accurate."

"I accept that, except for that one poor wretch..."

"He definitely deserved it, but I wasn't proud." I wasn't, you know that, I'm there for the bottom's pleasure. Like Mr D, I presume.

"You know about next week, I assume."

"I've heard a number of different versions, all similar though. You want to set up a Foundation. I think it's a wonderful idea."

He looked thoughtful. "Thank you, but the key there is you've heard several different versions, and the point I was trying to get across in the phone call, and the reason why I wanted to see you, is that you know more, and understand more, about the people involved than anyone, myself included. I don't wish you to break any confidences, but anything you are prepared to tell me about the individuals involved, I would be happy to hear."

He's a large man, and he radiates, does Mr D, but he's always listening, you can tell from his eyes. And you can tell that he cares.

"You're asking a lot, you know." I have very deep feelings for Will, and for Alphonse — and he surely can't

expect me to discuss Claudia with him. "I barely know Tony and I've never even met Henry."

"I'm sure you know Lou better than I do, but I do take your point. If I could tell you a little more about what I'm striving for, I might get you comfortable with the thought that I'm also trying to do the best for Will and Alphonse; also for Henry, although you don't know him. And you should feel free to ask any questions you like."

I smile at him. "I was hoping you'd say that — well, it's a condition of my speaking openly, frankly — but the reason for trying to maximise our time, I'm going to confess, is that you intrigue me."

He doesn't try any silly modesty; he just smiles. "I will just assure you that I wasn't digging for information on you when I spoke to Conrad earlier in the week."

"You spoke to Conrad?" No reason why he shouldn't, of course.

"I assumed..."

"No, the bastard hasn't told me." He looks hesitant now, but I laugh. "He tells me we're a couple, but then does exactly what he wants — and doesn't bother to tell me. What's your opinion of him anyhow?"

He laughs again. It's not obvious why. I wait. "I have rather invited the open question, haven't I?"

I'm feeling smug now. This could be informative, helpful even. I give him a look. "I think I can probably help you, Mr D. So, are we trading?"

"We are trading, Sadie, but if we come through this experience with a bond of friendship established, I shall feel that my life is richer."

I smile to match his. "You can even have the first confidence from me. Claudia says you are the grandmaster of bullshit, and I'm now seeing that — but I love it." He laughs again. I do like this man. Trust him? That's funny, isn't it? I do, but I know I have to be careful. I really believe he's thinking about everybody he cares about, but there are few straightforward paths, and there are always conflicting interests. "Anyway, Conrad, what do you think of him?"

"I admire him. I don't understand his business very well, but I would be surprised if anyone did. He's very adept at steering you away from conversations about sensitive areas." He's looking at me now, trying to gauge my response — he is a listener, Mr D, a watcher, too. "I have the feeling that it's genuinely being done for the listener's protection; in this case mine, but from the little he told me, also yours." I do nod here; he deserves active feedback. "It was easier once we got on to property. I hadn't realised he had quite so much. On funds he seems to be planning to do more, but he's moving more carefully, and I think wisely. So, my impression was of a very astute and well-connected man who's trying to move his businesses into safer areas. A man, incidentally, who's very fond of you," he smiles, "but probably hasn't told you." We both laugh.

He's made me a little pensive, though. "I think I'm fond of him, but I probably haven't told him." We don't laugh this time. I'm getting a look from him; it's kindly. But it tells me I should think more about that. Damn you, Peter Dickinson!

"He did say he hoped you were getting more comfortable with the couple idea." But there's something on his mind that the thought has provoked. He's looking out of the car now. We're on the bridge, the views are amazing, but that's not what he's thinking about. He turns back to me, "We didn't discuss it much but, of course, he and I have a similar problem." I frown. "We both adore one woman," he's speaking quite matter-of-factly, "who is unavoidably emotionally engaged with other people." He leaves me time to ask a question if I want to.

"I'm thinking about your word 'unavoidably'," and he's leaving me time to think about it. "I quite like it." I should go for it now, if this is going to be a worthwhile experience. "Does that describe Claudia and Alphonse?"

It's still a kindly look, but he shrugs. "I wish I could get them to be more open about it, for each other, as much as anything."

"They worry about you too much, don't they?"

It's a soft laugh I get. "Well, Sadie, I was prepared for an open conversation, but I didn't expect to get here quite so quickly. How are your feelings for Alphonse?"

"Woah, Mr D. I am going to tell you about that, but we shouldn't leave broken toys by the wayside. You and I, we fix things, don't we?"

"Yes, we do." He's looking out of the window now, quite moved, I think.

"Give them permission, man, don't make them come looking for forgiveness."

"I've tried." He's looking back to me now. He seems almost to be welling up.

"Try harder!"

He laughs so loud that the car twitches as the driver is caught by the blast. He recovers some composure, but the question has an edge. "Do you really think it's that simple?"

"I know they both love you and admire you. Maybe I've put those words the wrong way round, and maybe that's your problem."

He's a little puzzled, but not very; this is a sensitive man. "Admire first, you mean?"

I nod. "I don't even know you that well, but it's very, very easy to do that." *I have him thinking, now it's time to lighten up.* "I mean, I could fall in love with you as well, but the queue's a little long — and we two are not quite suited for that." *I have him smiling again.*

"Is that what keeps you and Will safe?"

This man's too sharp. I like it. "Of course, and that helps me through the times when I feel I let him go. But he's happier with Martha, I know that."

"What's happening there?"

I'm shocked by that, and I hesitate. "They're fine."

Now the smile has gone a little sly. "I think you've just hinted that they're not. You've more to tell me."

"I haven't. Well, very little, and we've left a broken toy back there. What are you going to do about Claudia?"

"Love her forever, of course."

"And that helps you precisely how? You want to live happy lives, all three of you and, my God, Alphonse has some issues to sort out to do that." *Now he's the one looking puzzled, of course.* "Yes, I will have more to say about that later, and it should help your situation but, good Lord, man, you all three have to be open that you love each *other and that you share each other's lives. It's very manageable. Well, I'm not sure about Alphonse's. We'll come on to that when you tell me you'll take the initiative with Claudia."*

"I've..." but he stops and laughs at himself. "I must try harder. Not Alphonse?"

"That's easier, and anyway both I, and his new circumstances, will help you on that."

The conversation becomes simpler, although he's a little shocked by Mei's plan. I get the impression there'll be a strict 'fatherly' conversation when he gets to Shanghai — but he knows he'll get no more than an agreement to manage it tactfully. We're neither of us aware of how the scandal will play out anyway, and we agree to invite Daiyu to dinner for the Chinese perspective. She's on standby, of course, desperately keen, I know, that I find a reason to invite her.

He has no more than a suspicion about Will and Martha, but I see no reason to be discreet about his meeting Merle last month. No one comes through those events unscathed, and Martha will have picked up something. We agree we want them staying together, for their own sakes. "But I suppose you also have things to say about them opening up their relationship?"

"I think they're both big enough to do it." I hesitate a minute, then smile at him. "And I do intend to be a beneficiary of that occasionally."

He laughs. "And is Conrad prepared for that?"

I tell him about Conrad's favourite pastime, although I have to admit to enjoying the presence of the third party.

He's smiling, plainly amused and, of course, broad-minded. "I think you'd have enjoyed my old parties."

"I'm very sure I would have done. Your wives seemed to, from all I hear."

He's nodding, but the smile has left him.

"Tell me about Ellen."

Now he looks shocked. "How?"

"Does it matter?"

He thinks a while, then says slowly, "It might do. I don't know." *Now I get the blue eyes again, not unfriendly.* "We've gone a little past being coy, haven't we?"

It made us a little late meeting Daiyu, my fault entirely. We were talking in his suite and I hadn't told him what time we'd be meeting her, but I had to listen to the story about Anne and his best friend just before their wedding, which he'd called off — we agreed on the nonsense of regrets — 'but it was a terrible mistake.' He'd committed himself to open relationships after that, Ellen — Ellie, as everyone knew her then, he said — being the first he'd married. They'd got bored with each other and moved on — 'Well, that's too simple, but you understand,' and I'd nodded — she made a success of being single but then got entangled with Gerry, who'd also enjoyed her enthusiasms initially — 'but she could be an awful cow, especially when she'd had too much' — but she'd kept in touch. Apparently, she was missing him and, against his advice and wishes, began making comparisons of him and Gerry — 'I wasn't surprised when they diverged,' he said. I found it a funny term. 'Well, Gerry seemed to find her exploits entertaining for a while — and she organised an enjoyable life for him without ever, was the impression I got, missing a chance to compare him unfavourably to me.'

That was what kept us. He was a little distraught at that point. It's what made us late. I was worried about how he'd seem to Daiyu. When I told him she was waiting, I offered to cancel dinner but he wouldn't hear of it — and he was, strangely, I thought, quite his normal self by the time we met her. Normal self? He was enchanting her, and I got a withering look when I told her he'd had a long flight and would need to go to bed early.

I'd taken that opportunity while he'd gone for a break. I got a withering, 'And not alone, I suppose,' from her. I told her that was unworthy, but I don't think I convinced her.

The reason I stayed with him was that we still had ground to cover, and I didn't know when he'd sleep. He thought that was very sweet and I got the most chaste of kisses — but he did need to crash.

There was a day bed in the suite: that was enough for me. I had to be very sharp with him when he wanted to take it. 'I have time to recover, you don't! And we need all the time we've got to talk.' He'd nodded, and was asleep within moments.

I slept a few hours, I think, but I woke to the sound of him stirring. I got up and made coffee for me and I called to him. He came through in blue pyjamas and a too-small robe — even in a suite of a global hotel, the Asians can't believe how big our men are. He opened his arms in a gesture of helplessness, but was smiling and looked reasonably awake.

"We'll come back to Ellen later," I said. "I don't think we can leave it."

He looked a little glum. "I fear you're right. Conrad knows, doesn't he?"

"It's how I knew."

That seemed to cheer him up. "Good. It's gone no further, has it? Only there may be some connections somewhere. The whole thing's bothering me. But you're happy waiting until later."

"Your flight's this afternoon, we have time, and I think it's time I told you more about William and Alphonse."

I don't think I surprised him much. I'd already confronted him with the complexities of Alphonse's life, and he was aware of how much the two men respected each other, but seemed pleased to have it confirmed.

"But how does it settle down? A child with Mei, a relationship with Daiyu, does he still see Lee?"

"They see each other. I think Lee's got over it."

"Does Alphonse..."

I smile. "Mr D! A man of your perception!" He looks a little shame-faced. "I don't know, and I don't ask, but I assume not. I also, by the way, never ask him about Claudia, but I do wish the two of them would stop being so silly and faux-noble." I have his attention. I give him his coffee mug. "Let's sit down."

He sits and looks out of the big window. "I don't think I'd ever tire of the view."

"I don't," I say, "although mine's even better than this, for which I thank you."

He looks puzzled for a moment. "Oh, of course, we helped you set up." *Then I get a cheeky smile from him.* "Will tells me we're very successful."

"We are, but I also have an interest in who my new benefactor will be. Your financial interest will become smaller. I obviously would like William to head everything up, but I sometimes worry he puts your interests far in front of his own..."

"Without realising how much they should coincide."

"How much are you testing him with this process?" *He seems reluctant to speak.* "It's a lot, isn't it? Don't worry, I shan't say anything to him, he's assumed that anyway."

"Well, that's a relief. I just need to see a little more ego, although maybe he's more sophisticated than me. Maybe he can be a master by being a servant." *I'm puzzled. It shows.* "He thinks he can let Alphonse and Henry run autonomous organisations with himself in each as a controller."

"You're not convinced."

"Two problems. I get drawn in too much — and he has a bigger worldview than Alphonse or Henry."

"And you've not mentioned Tony. You worry about him, and about Lou, don't you?" *He nods.* "You're right to. I hear stories about Tony. I know more about Lou, but that's where your Shen family role needs addressing. He is quite good, though, isn't he?"

"Well, Tony says he is, but that's also my impression. But if we can't repair the family bridge, it's doomed."

"Next stop, Shanghai!" I get a smile for that. "Back to Alphonse, but I think we know where we want to be on that." I freeze for a moment.

"What's up?"

"Well, we have a number of people being fucked up by trying to be too goody-goody monogamous when a little bit more openness could help them. It's a shame that wisdom requires you to be old." We laugh again. But that thought is nonsense, of course. I think Will's quite close to being wise — unless he gets sucked in by Merle again. "I'm talking rubbish. I think Claudia's old enough to know better. I think the two of you would have more fun if you send her off on the odd holiday with Alphonse."

He laughs, but then looks thoughtful. "Is that our recommendation?"

I realise this is important for him, no time for glibness. "It's about you being happy too, you know."

I look at him looking thoughtfully out of the window. "I think I would be, if they managed that. And I think they would be."

"You know you'll never lose her, don't you?"

He looks almost shocked. "But she won't marry me."

"That's what tells me. She doesn't need that. She loves you and admires you." I let that sink in. "She may not desire you as much as you'd like her to."

He's nodding silently.

"But guilt's a big inhibitor for some people. Anyway, you have enough to think about there and, like you said, we have a plan."

"We have a plan." He looks a little cheered. "And it sounds like you think Alphonse will stay in the business."

"He loves it, and he has too many people to care for to abandon it, and I think he'd work it out with Will."

"So do I, but William has to show me he can sell that to Alphonse."

"I think he could, but I don't know Henry. I know he rescued Will initially and got him into your organisation, so he's probably always thought of himself as senior."

"It's tricky. But Funds is so complicated, and the new money is so dangerous, that I want Will close to it. Henry's ethical, but I think he lacks a bit of human nous. His wife's better for that. I'd love her back in that business."

"That's for our boy to work out, isn't it?"

He smiles as he turns to me. "Is this you closing that off and bringing the conversation back to Ellen, Sadie?"

"This is me bringing the conversation precisely back there, Mr D."

34

"You're in early," Will said, as Tania appeared in his doorway.

"Need to make the most of my day with the big people," she said, but it was said as a careless aside. She closed the door behind her — unique, he thought — and sat down with a grim expression on her face. "Why the fuck didn't you tell me?"

"Tell you what?"

"That I was being invited to join you."

"Because that's the chairman's job. I must assume that he's only just asked you."

"Late last night, with a careless 'Oh, hasn't Will told you?' It's obviously not the best way of getting prepared for me but…" she paused, as if trying to make her mind up about saying something. "Will, it's not really my place…"

She looked unusually troubled, so he smiled and said, "Which has stopped you precisely how many times before?"

She didn't relax. "Will, are you sure you're taking hold of this the way he wants you to, or the way you should?"

"Well, thank you, Ms Gunter, that about sets me up perfectly for my big day." But he wasn't being flippant; she saw that.

"I am actually here to help, you know that."

Of course she was, he'd never have doubted that. "I know, but I don't know what you can do. You won't even be able to cast a vote because Peter hasn't asked the board to confirm your appointment."

She looked surprised. "Am I being appointed?"

"That was my assumption."

Now she looked irritated. "Will, I don't want to waste your time here — and I'd rather get prepared myself, quite apart from having to go cancel some video meetings that I'd told people were important — but you're illustrating exactly the vacuum you've allowed to emerge."

"That Peter Dickinson has allowed to emerge." But he knew he was making excuses.

As did she, she was shaking her head. "I think you're misreading what's required of you, and you're missing an opportunity."

"Which opportunity? I'm trying to give the best possible start to their Foundation, and then make sure it has sustainable support."

She was shaking her head slowly, a look of incredulity on her face. "It's not my place to comment, although I do believe your motives are noble — but I had two other things I needed to tell you."

"Other things?"

She waved an arm. "You've had your bollocking about not letting me know about today."

He had to smile. He usually did with her. "Two things?"

"I had a call from Al Frederick yesterday, and yes, I am fully aware that he calls me because he thinks I'm a softer target than you are, and I'll take my bollocking for that later when you've heard my second point…"

"Your second point, or your third? The first was my bollocking."

"Still the second, then." He was getting intense Tania now; he had to let her speak. "They have high interest in the IPO from a European Group. They're big in logistics, so there's a direct Giddings tie-in, and they're in other sectors that would fit."

"Has he said how much money?"

"They're talking up to three; that's almost thirty percent of what we're looking for."

"It would make them bigger than Peter or your father. Are you comfortable with that?"

"I would be, personally, because I'm kinda the guarantor of the Dickinson Gunter tie-up. I speak for the most shares, so I'm not worried, but I need to talk about my other point. I had a phone call yesterday."

She was hesitating again. "Go on," he said, "we don't have secrets, do we?"

"Well, I wouldn't have expected you to tell me about your London girlfriend, it's not my business normally, and you're tactful about my life…"

"Why is this…"

"Because Martha called me yesterday, and I made her tell me more than she wanted to. She rang about today, of course, but the way you've been, I wasn't letting her get away with just that. I wanted more background."

"What did she want?"

"She wanted me to tell you that organisations need a head, that you shouldn't overintellectualise — she said it's one of your biggest faults — but I'd already made her tell me about your biggest one."

Whether it was criticism, or supportive teasing, he didn't care. He wasn't in a mood to accept it, and he was sure it showed.

"Don't give me that look. I'll talk more after the meeting about that, just you and me; Martha going awol isn't something you want me tittle-tattling about."

He felt almost angry, "You unscrupulous bitch!"

She forced a smile. "I'm going to take that as a compliment, Master William, and finish what I came in here to say…"

"Which is relevant to today?"

"Which is relevant to today. She'd also spoken to Al Frederick, and she's telling him, and me, to be careful about who we get into bed with and I've just realised that that's an entirely inappropriate metaphor in the current circumstances and I apologise." But her smile had almost toppled into a laugh by now, and he had to join her. "Is she very beautiful, your London woman?"

"Out!" he almost shouted, but her smile made him laugh again. He'd have to check on potential buyers, but someone taking a big stake early would make the whole package an easier sell. That could wait. He had to think about how to approach today.

***

"So, William, the agenda for today?" began Peter at precisely ten o'clock, before anyone else was seated. The others shuffled to their usual places, Claudia making sure that Tania sat beside her.

Will stayed standing until all were in place, then sat himself opposite Peter at the head of the table. "The agenda is exactly as published yesterday, but would you mind if I introduced Tania first?"

"Of course not. That's exactly what you should do."

Well, it's what you should do, thought Will, but maybe Peter was making his first point. "Ladies and gentlemen, I'm delighted to welcome Tania Gunter into our meeting today…"

"Point of order, Mr Chairman," said Tony, sitting further down the table than was necessary, having arrived late enough to preclude any discussion with Will, "are we to understand this as a permanent addition to the board, with full voting rights?"

"Of course," said Peter, smiling at Tania, "and we're very fortunate to be gaining someone of such talent and energy."

"I entirely agree, Mr Chairman, but our articles require us to vote on any new addition to board membership…"

"I'm very happy to allow a vote. Tania, would you…"

Tania began to stand to leave.

"Having been given one week's notice, Mr Chairman." He turned to Tania, "Nobody doubts your talent and suitability, toots, but we're allowed a week to check and reflect."

Will could see the anger on Tania's face — but he trusted her self-control. "We also have a point in our articles, Tony, that we treat each other at all times with respect." Will hadn't planned to use Tania's new position to create a majority, but he had seen that possibility as a useful safety net. Tony had now ensured it couldn't apply.

"That doesn't mean that we have to be at all times stuffy, mate, does it? Besides, we haven't elected her a director yet. She ain't one of us, your stiffy rule doesn't apply." He turned to Tania again and winked brazenly. "Sorry, again, toots, but I'm sure it will do soon."

"We have two items on the agenda," Will went on quickly. "Claudia will talk first about the Dickinson Foundation and our first steps to establishing that. The second point is to discuss the organisation of the whole group and its three divisions. We think those items will take us a full day. I am prepared to give a financial review, if required, but the full position was attached to your email. I'm hoping that we'll simply spend time on any issues that you see arising."

"Well, if the whole thing's going down the toilet anyway, there's not much point in discussing a look-back," said Tony, "I'll be more interested in how you think you'll make money going forward, enough to feed the greedy wastrels of so-called charitable institutions."

Peter, normally so calm and cheery, seemed ready to explode.

"Let me take that," said Claudia coolly, "because there's a very important point at the heart of it. I'm not going to say I can put Tony's mind at rest, but I'd like him to feel that we at least have recognised the problem."

Will wondered, as he watched Tony moving uneasily in his seat, whether he'd been making a genuine point or was merely trying to disrupt.

"I'd be grateful if you would," said Tony, without much grace.

"Your other point, Tony," said Will, "about the future financial shape of the business, will be covered for each of the options later. Should we let Claudia talk about the plans now?"

"Yes, please," said Peter. Will watched Tony merely nodding.

Claudia ran the presentation from her laptop but, as she usually did, drew people's attention to her, rather than any words or charts on the big screen, and Will felt slowly proud of what she and Peter were striving for. The focus had been on finding how to impact child health and child nutrition and she covered Tony's point very frankly. They would want to work through existing organisations and structures but were aware of, and very sensitive to, the amount of money that was directed at overheads and advertising. 'Don't forget corruption in that,' Tony had interjected. 'I hadn't intended to,' Claudia had said. They would build their network gradually, ramping up over three to five years and assessing where they could have most impact. 'That means where the maximum benefit will accrue to the children. We don't underestimate the challenge of creating an effective delivery system.'

Will was impressed, as was, he could tell, Tania on the other side of Claudia. Alphonse was slightly obscured by her; he asked no questions. Henry stayed engaged, without looking enthusiastic, but asked several questions about the organisations Claudia had spoken to, and how effective they were being. 'I'll be frank, Henry, many have disappointed us, but there are several where we see good prospects of doing something worthwhile.'

"Worthwhile is getting less than twenty percent of the money, best case, to the point of benefit. Worst case, they actually deliver nothing. I was reading the other day…"

"Not listening to what a mate told you, Tony," said Peter acidly. "That's your most common source."

"Go on, please, Tony," said Claudia calmly. "It is a major concern. We've even briefed Henderson to help us look into it. Sadly, your number is accurate in many instances, and it's something we'd be determined to do better than."

"Everybody's determined to do that. And you're right, Peter old chap, I do listen to my mates on this and every single one of them thinks he's wasting his fucking money."

"Are they setting it up properly, or just pissing it away to make themselves feel better?" That was Tania, and it brought a sudden silence. "I can tell you from closer to home. My family pisses a lot away. It annoys the fuck out of my dad, but he'd rather not fight with my mother over it, but neither they, nor, I suspect, your mates, are approaching it with the idea of making sure they deliver the maximum to the point of benefit." She'd stayed entirely calm, which made the profanities even more telling. "Are your mates any different from my family, do they go to big events and get fleeced?"

"Some of them do more than that. A lot of them, in fact." But Tony was hesitant in his delivery now.

Claudia continued, "I appreciate I haven't given a complete picture, but we're not expecting a major cash injection until the IPO. So, we probably have a year to sort that out and get systems and organisation in place."

"Not necessarily," said Will. All eyes turned to him. "Yes, we get a major tranche then, probably three billion if you stick to your share objective." He looked to Peter.

"Have I said I'm changing it? What's your point?"

"Well, an injection now would help you get started, and be more effective when the big money comes in next year. It would obviously be hard to move quickly on property, but fund money is flexible and quickly available. You could set up a headquarters and seed the more promising organisations with some cash and a challenge to show how effective they can be."

"And we could announce to all our major clients that GKS is now in the business of pissing money away, if I may borrow Tania's elegant expression, and we no longer have any interest in remaining in the top ten. Perhaps some of them will catch charity diarrhoea and want to join you." Tony was getting agitated.

"Interesting mix of toilet metaphors, Tony, are you sitting or standing?" Tania's question made even Henry smile. Peter laughed very loud.

"I'd be doing nothing. I just look at how those things work and think it's all waste — minimum eighty-percent waste, as Claudia's admitted. I have to wreck my business for that? I'm not even being offered five percent to buy my silence."

"It's a totally different business, Tony," said Will, seeing Peter get agitated again and keen to head him off.

But Peter, in spite of himself, seemed keen to be conciliatory. "But there are things we could discuss. Will's right, of course, but if you thought some asset participation would help, we could discuss it. But Alphonse has worked for a package over the years which in no way equates to the bonuses you two have earned, but he's created at least as much value for Dickinson."

Will wondered if it was the right moment to try to drag Henry into the argument.

But Tony went on, "It's too late anyway, mate, we're going independent."

Henry looked a little annoyed. "I'd rather hear the whole argument first before we go nuclear."

Peter now looked icy. "Are you going to share your deterrent's capabilities? Isn't it a threat better used as a negotiating tactic? What's independent anyway? You can't take clients. You can't take systems. You have nothing without Dickinson."

"We can in Asia, mate, we changed the terms when we tied in with Senlin."

"Who changed the terms?"

"It was agreed, when we became GKS, no new business was subject to a no client poaching arrangement. Smart boy, Lou, it was the only way he'd sign, not sure the translation's perfect."

Will was stunned. "It's the English language version that has precedence."

"Not sure that argument works too well in Shanghai these days, mate. Anyway, there's plenty new money looking to come in with us."

Peter seemed to take that more calmly than Will expected him to. "All of our systems, all your methods, all your software, are company property. You can't use them."

Tony looked to Henry. "Better tell him, mate."

Henry looked uncomfortable, "That's true, Peter, but you must be aware that Rachel runs different systems."

Colour seemed to be draining from Peter. "That produce better results, you say, I acknowledge that. But I thought you also said…"

"She can run everything better without client interference, that's true, but it only helps a bit. What's been surprising us, though, admittedly not on such a large scale — she can allow herself to be very choosy — is that her systems do significantly better than our current ones. We could make it a big selling point."

"But so many clients would just go elsewhere. They couldn't come to you. Not in the West, anyhow."

"That's why it's a nuclear option," said Tony. "Yeah, we'd get hit by the fallout. That's why the best deal is you leave Funds out of your charity adventure, make us equal partners with share value and not just bonuses, and let us expand the business even quicker. Our new money safeguards are hopelessly outdated."

"They're only outdated," said Will, "in that they're not robust enough to deal with where new money is coming from. Are you comfortable in Fulham, Henry?" It was a gamble, but Henry had seemed troubled, and Will doubted whether Rachel would be keen to align herself with Tony.

"As you and I discussed, Will, this is all about risk management."

"So, you're both comfortable."

"Which 'both' are you talking to, Will?" asked Tony pointedly. "Both the Fund directors are here."

"You're quite right, Tony," said Peter, "both of the Fund directors are here."

"Well, I meant three, obviously you're a director."

"Exactly, so both of us are here." He turned to Henry, at his side, but avoiding Peter's stare. "Or am I alone, Henry?"

"Wait a fucking minute," said Tony.

"I'm going to move that we remove you, Tony," said Will. "I wish to put that motion to the board. May I ask you to leave the room while the point is discussed."

Tony seemed to embed himself in his seat. "You don't get me out like that. That needs a week's notice."

"You're quite right, but I can give notice of a resolution that can be discussed here for implementation in one week, just as we could discuss Tania's nomination for a vote in one week. What we can also implement today is an instant dismissal for gross misconduct for the way you tampered with the group's legal arrangements in Asia. You may be right, of course, legally you may get away with going for our client base, but if we're firing you at a time when the funds are performing well, you're not a very attractive fund manager, are you?"

Will was sweating but felt strangely calm. Henry might follow Tony, or threaten to. Will would then have to resign, rather than doing that much damage to Dickinson and the prospects of the Foundation.

"I think we're all getting more heated than we need to be," said Henry. "We have, at least, outlined some extreme positions, but we've tended to do very well in the past by being innovative and radical, rather than extreme."

"Mate, that is just one hundred percent pure distilled bullshit. We don't need this Foundation crap for the greater glory of Saint Peter here."

"I hear your arguments, but I'm not ready to be so dismissive," said Henry. He turned to Will, unsmiling, and said, "and I don't like the way you tried to pull Rachel into the argument, but I will admit that Fulham is not ready to be so dismissive of setting up the Foundation." He turned to Tony. "I think we should listen to how the options look and see if we can minimise the damage to Funds." Now he turned to Peter, "I would like to work something out, but you should be aware that we do have alternative systems and, even without the Asian manoeuvre, which I wasn't aware of at the time, we can, with the business in Rachel's name, talk to our existing client base."

"You can't. We'd establish the link," said Peter coldly.

"We could, you'd have a tough time making it stick, but it's nuclear. That's why I'm suggesting we talk this through and find a balanced solution. I like what you're trying to do in principle, Claudia, but a lot of well-earned water could just seep into sand."

"It's a good time to take a break," said Alphonse firmly. "I agree with Henry. I believe we should look at all the options, and I don't have a problem with the three divisions contributing in different ways at different levels. Let's see how the total picture looks, but let's take half an hour to calm down."

That was a surprisingly assertive, thought Will, not like Alphonse's usual, more measured style.

"You go on, mate, let's keep your Claudia's pet project alive," said Tony, standing and leaving with at least four pairs of eyes following him, hating him. Will included himself in that group.

Henry followed Tony quickly, intent, Will hoped, on pulling him to a sensible position to negotiate from.

Alphonse put his hand on Will's arm. "May we?" and they headed for Will's office. Will turned to Peter, who nodded and moved, Will assumed, to talk to Claudia.

When they'd sat in Will's office, door closed, Will asked, "Were you expecting that? You handled it very well, by the way, thank you."

Alphonse gave a wry shrug. "I wasn't expecting quite that, no, but I know he's been getting himself stirred up about it. There's a lot going on in the background, isn't there?"

"Alphonse!" Will exploded, but managed a smile. "A lot of the complexities revolve around you, my man. I've tried to be even-handed with everyone, but I've found it impossible to get Tony, so today wasn't a complete surprise to me, but I had no idea he'd gone that far towards independence, and you have to admit, you haven't been giving me clear guidance while you make up your mind about whatever you want to do."

Alphonse smiled — enigmatically, thought Will, and smiled himself — "I don't think Henry's comfortable."

"With staying or going?"

Alphonse laughed. "Just uncomfortable. He's like you in some ways. You can come into a day like today genuinely interested in having a discussion to get best solutions. Peter pretends to, but he has a decided preference. Usually, it's whatever you're guiding him towards, so you can always look like you're neutral." His smile was warmer now, with a hint of admiration.

"We could stop speculating about others. Let's make this simpler. I have no idea where you are in this. Are you staying?"

"I'm staying, running Dickinson properties and staying as senior advisor on Senlin, at least until we see out the remaining three years of Peter's commitment."

"Am I allowed to tell you how desperately relieved I am to hear that, for a number of reasons?"

Alphonse sat calmly, unemotionally. "And you?"

"I'll make anything work."

"From what position?"

"I don't care. I just want to get the Foundation up and running for them. I feel at least that you and I can get on to planning your area, and the group IPO should be straightforward. We could leave Funds entirely alone."

"You've two problems with that, haven't you?"

"Do you mind saying what you see? I probably see the problems differently, but Tony is at least one big one."

"I'm seeing him as one problem, yes, but it's also a problem that they're so ready and prepared to leave. Had you expected that?"

"No. I hadn't. I'd tried to make Henry feel comfortable with the future, but I couldn't get to Tony; it's obvious he's been too busy getting his alternative set up. Even if he's got new arrangements he can defend, they've got a vast amount of work converting clients to match the scale they operate on."

"Doesn't that tell you they're confident of new funding?"

Will thought about the meetings Henry had been invited to, "I'm already worrying about that. That's why I made the point, I don't want them going after funny money."

Alphonse sat very still and looked straight at him. "I'm getting offers to look at big tranches of property. Well, not to take property off us, but to buy in big shares."

"Offers?"

"Yes, two different companies, all of a sudden, when no one should know we're in the market for that."

"What are you doing?"

"Saying I'll talk."

"How much are we talking about?"

"It would make you happy for the Foundation."

"Bigger than Peter's?"

"No, that's the interesting thing. We want to keep him as the major shareholder. I've got one talking about just less than him, and one talking about a billion for starters, with possible increases."

"You know these people?"

"I know the businesses, but I can't find out who's behind them. It's often the way."

"Henderson could."

"Which is what he's working on now, but even he might be stretched to unravel some of this."

"Does it worry you?"

"Two things worry me. I really will want to know who I'm working with and for, especially the one company that's come in with a proposal that would make them close to Peter's size."

"Go on." Will was missing something.

"They could buy out some of the bank's share, then become the loudest voice. We'd lose control."

Alphonse was waiting for Will to make a connection, but it seemed so improbable to Will, until, suddenly. "Maybe I'm joining your dots."

"I don't know that I'm joining them yet. I don't have a full picture, but there's something there… where are you going?"

"Time to talk to Mr D."

"Do you want me with you?"

"Yes," said Will, then paused. "Hmm, maybe not. I'd have to invite Claudia if I invite you, and I need Peter to be frank with me… look, I'm sorry about that jibe of Tony's."

"Go and see Peter." But Alphonse was smiling.

Peter was in Tania's office with the ladies. "Peter, could I have a word?"

"Of course. Should I come to your…" but Claudia and Tania were leaving.

"You have fifteen minutes, I think," said Claudia with a small smile. Tania closed the door behind her.

"Were you aware…" Peter began.

"I'm going to say no, whatever you're going to ask," and Will sat down in the big chair opposite him. "How much does Gerry Calvert hate you?"

"More than I thought, apparently. Are you seeing a pattern in some of this?"

"It looks like you're starting to."

"What do we know?"

"I don't know why he hates you."

"It's so implausible. Can we come back to that? It doesn't help us at the moment. What are you picking up?"

"Alphonse has mystery companies looking to buy into property, there's someone sniffing around the IPO already — a European company with logistics interests, which points a finger for me — and Henry was invited to dinner with Gerry and Michael McKenzie, which is a name which will..."

"Your former boss."

"Yes, I'm surprised..."

"And the husband of your lover."

It was not an easy stare to confront. "As you say, can we come back to that?"

Peter relaxed and began smiling as he shook his head. "So, your plan now?"

"I still aim to get the Foundation set up for you, but I'm not going to jeopardise our control of the Dickinson businesses."

"Our control?"

"I'm finally getting a point, I think."

"Good, because I really can't make it work unless you run it all. Let's see how we get on."

"Wait, we still have a few minutes. How safe are we from the China threat?"

"My last meeting in Shanghai was with Lou. I'd agreed with his sister that she should let Lee and Lou progress towards their ten percent ownership of the corporation over three years and not ten. I told her it's what her father wanted..." Will raised one eyebrow at him. "Well, he would have done, had we discussed it."

Will laughed. "OK, and what do you know about Alphonse's property suitors?"

"I know about one of them."

"Do you want to tell me more?"

"I don't need to. You know the man quite well. He's an admirer of yours."

"Conrad Kitter?"

"Yes, and the thing that will appeal to you about that is that he's sucking in money from China that Gerry put him in touch with."

"But we don't want that money." Will was worrying again about sources.

"We don't touch it. I don't know how Conrad does it, but he's letting them buy into his Middle East properties where he's, shall we say, less squeamish than we are, and that frees up funds for him to buy into us. So, he makes his own money safer — and no doubt makes several percent on the transactions."

"And you're not worrying about him gradually taking control of properties."

Peter's laugh boomed around the room. "Oh, William, I do love you. If I could just persuade you to stop underestimating yourself quite so much. No, he won't, he wants in because he admires Alphonse, he sees the portfolio the man's put together; he admires you, so he wants you involved; and he, along with you and I, would be terrified of ever upsetting you-know-who by screwing anything up."

"Isobel?"

He laughed again. "If I'd had to spell that out, I can't tell you how disappointed I'd have been."

35

I was expecting messages, and the ones from Peter and Will said pretty much the same thing. They were both obviously pleased and would call next week when they'd got back from Atlanta. 'Martha's here!' had been part of Will's message.

That hadn't surprised me, not after she and I had spoken.

The surprise was hearing from Claudia. She called from Atlanta. Couldn't sleep, she was in the garden early in the morning. I made her tell me about it, slowly. She had too much on her mind. She needed to slow down. She was grateful, I think. She'd hardly had a chance to talk to Peter but he seemed very intent that they acknowledge her feelings for Alphonse, and his for her. I told her about my conversation with him and I said, 'I can't think of any people I'd trust more to work that out.' She seemed only partly reassured. I guessed why. She asked me what the men weren't telling her. I knew they wouldn't but, of course, she instantly spotted that I knew something. I was nervous about that, but I couldn't hide it, not from her. But she got there anyway, you know: 'You're saying he sees Mei, I knew that, no wait... you're not saying she's... my God, you are, oh, that's wonderful!'

You see, sometimes these things are much easier than you expect them to be. Honesty, I tell you, it's underrated!

Although, as you've gathered, I really just let her walk down the path of her own intuition.

We didn't have to talk about the meeting much, but I wanted to know how Will had done. She was lovely, she wanted to talk about Martha first, even though she has history with Martha, but they've become close through that — you do, if you handle these things properly, that's what I kept reassuring her about Alphonse. As long as you keep the central relationship solid, these other things sort themselves out — we're humans, we enjoy each other, and enjoy other people occasionally. But that got her on to Ellen — and I wanted to hear more about Will, but I could see why Ellen was so important to her — and I did know them both. 'But I never knew she was Peter's first. I do know she was a bitch to Gerry. I think that's part of what's made him what he is. I think once the first few months had passed, she kept belittling him as being a much lesser man than the one she'd let go.'

"Enough to have her killed? Enough to pursue Peter?"

"I know we all have suspicions, and we're probably right, but we know what she was like, Peter and I, and it was a very plausible accident. That's what he told the police, isn't it?"

"Yes, he says, although he's only just told me. I feel bad that we don't feel bad, if you see what I mean."

"Oh, completely, but you're more worried now about what Gerry does next, aren't you?"

"I seem to be worried about what everybody does next — but that is a major concern, I admit."

"Peter won't like it, I know, but I think he and Conrad will work something out with him."

"I haven't met Conrad."

"Oh, believe me. You're better off with the two you've got."

"Isobel!" But we were laughing about that.

"He's lovely, but fortunately not your type, but we should get together when we're in London next."

"That would be wonderful."

"I agree, the beauty of it is, we can expect to be ignored, the two of them find each other so fascinating. So, we'll have plenty time to chat, but I can't let you go without hearing about my Will. How did he do?"

"Your Will?"

"Oh, come on, Mrs Brodie, you're not a stupid woman. I love him, but we're too alike to be suited."

She laughed again. "I'm sorry, it's very rude of me. I know you're close, but I just don't see you as being alike. Oh, you mean that way..." And she got sweetly embarrassed.

"Yes, Mrs Brodie, I don't want to overcomplicate your life, but you could enjoy an evening with young William."

"I think Mr Dickinson and your bedroom chaise will do me nicely if I'm feeling naughty, thank you, and now I'm embarrassed enough to move on to what you wanted to hear about. Will was masterful. The big thing was, he got Alphonse and Henry wanting to work with him as head of Dickinson. I think they can both see that they'll get more help from his guidance than from my beloved's more mercurial interventions. Also, because of the way Conrad's played it with property, we're in no rush to move money out of Funds, which are all under Henry now, and he can move at a sensible pace. Well, Henry, Lou and Rachel, I

should say. It sounds like she'd be happy to come back in with no Tony and with Will at the head. And Peter's satisfied himself that Will can take command."

"Oh, he can that, Mrs Brodie, you're missing a treat."

"I've treats enough, thank you, and I've you to thank for helping the three of us."

"Oh, you're very welcome, but you realise it makes Mr Dickinson available."

There was a silence. That had made her think.

"Do you mind if I say I'd rather he weren't, even for you?"

I laughed then. I told her, that's how she should feel — and he'll be glad she does, even with Alphonse in their lives. Every relationship is different, work it out for yourselves.